The Other Half

Dana Edw

D1581535

The Other Half

Dana Edwards

Published by Accent Press Ltd 2014

ISBN 9781783751334

For Richard

Acknowledgements

With sincere thanks to:

Catriona Robb, my editor at Accent, for her expert guidance, thoroughness, endless patience, and general good humour.

Richard Edwards, my ever-supportive husband, and Siân Matthews, my lifelong friend, for their helpful comments and encouragement on this, my first novel.

Jane Belli and the members of the Carmarthen creative writing course, without whom I would never have begun what has been a fascinating journey.

Prologue

Catrin loved winter afternoons like this, when the east wind forced the leaves to dance around the back garden and the rain lashed against the windows. And she liked them best of all when she was inside, snuggled up against the Aga in the kitchen, and the rest of her family were home too, doing their own thing maybe but there all the same. This morning she'd managed to complete all her homework and had done some sketches of her father, frowning as he read an article on diabetes in one of the GP magazines piled high on the kitchen table. Now she could look forward to a couple of free hours, before supper and Sunday night television, to look at the university prospectuses she'd kept to one side until she could give them her undivided attention.

She could hear groans and the occasional 'Yesssss' as her father and brother practised their putting on the living room carpet and her mother's 'Oh yes,' and 'Oh no,' as she sat on the stairs, cordless phone in hand, responding to a long account of *her* mother's week. Catrin's mother, Jane, spoke to Granny Olwen most days but this long Sunday evening chat was a ritual. Catrin's other grandmother, Granny Lewis, lived with them. Catrin wondered why she'd been brought up to call her paternal grandmother by her surname and her maternal grandmother by her Christian name. She smiled to herself. No, really it was obvious. Granny Lewis was always kind but formal, distant, 'stand-offish' some might say, while Granny Olwen was warm and cuddly, full of hugs and laughter. A low rumble of thunder erupted somewhere in the distance. Catrin looked down as Lucky, Granny Lewis's little spaniel, moved

1

swiftly from his basket and tucked himself between her and the Aga.

Durham. She'd start with Durham. This very traditional university seemed to do well in all the league tables. Catrin picked up the prospectus from the pile on the floor beside her and gazed at the gowned young people smiling on the cover. They all looked so happy, so confident, so convinced they were about to embark on glittering careers. Could that really be her in four years time? Another thunderclap, much closer this time, and the little dog's body shook uncontrollably against her leg.

'Dad, can you put some Mozart on please?'

'Get in the hole!' Tom, Catrin's brother, roared.

Catrin, realising she had no chance of being heard, dumped the prospectus on the floor and wandered through to the living room, closely followed by Lucky.

'Dad – thunder. Lucky needs his music.'

Lining up his putt her father did not look up. 'OK, love, symphony or piano concerto?'

Catrin shrugged. 'Whatever Dad; who's winning?'

Her father said nothing until the ball made a pleasing clink, indicating that he'd hit the target. 'I am now,' he laughed, 'so that means Tom's making us all a cup of tea.'

Catrin and the shaking Lucky retreated to the kitchen and settled once more by the Aga as the strains of Mozart's 'Piano Concerto No. 21' filled the air. Lucky relaxed a little but still hugged Catrin's leg as she again opened the prospectus.

'Oh my God, it smells foul in here – leftovers of Sunday lunch with base notes of scared dog,' Tom commented as he and their father joined Catrin in the kitchen. 'Cup of tea, Catz?'

'Please, Tom.'

As Tom organised the tea, while surreptitiously scoffing a large piece of cherry cake, Catrin's father, Ben, settled beside her on the big leather sofa. He pulled the Welsh tapestry blanket, that her mother had artfully thrown over it, around

2

their legs and grabbed the pile of prospectuses. He chose the one for Bangor University.

'This would be a great place to go Catrin, between the Menai Straits and Snowdon – ideal I'd say.'

'Ideal for you, Dad, maybe not so great for Catrin.'

Her father ignored Tom. 'North Wales – you can't get more Welsh than that.'

Catrin continued flicking through the Durham prospectus.

'Dad, you seem to think North Wales is more authentic than the rest of Wales; what's that about then?' Tom rolled his eyes as he put their mugs of tea on the Aga.

'Well they speak the lingo there, don't they? And that makes them very Welsh.'

'Oh, Dad, people who speak that guttural gobbledegook aren't any more Welsh than you – you were born in Cardiff, brought up in the city, you've lived here all your life; you can't get more Welsh than that.'

Their father frowned. 'Sadly you're wrong there, son. If your Granny Lewis had encouraged me to learn Welsh, as she did with you and Catrin, I reckon I'd feel more of a Welshman.'

Tom laughed. 'Oh don't be ridiculous Dad; we're all Welsh, end of. Anyway, now we've got our own government everyone who lives in Wales, whatever their ethnic origin, thinks of themselves as Welsh. Fact.'

Her dad shrugged. 'So how about Bangor, Catz?'

'No, it's a definite no, Dad; they don't do a Fine Art degree – well, not a full-time one anyway.'

'I thought all arts degrees were part-time by definition,' Tom said, picking up the Bristol prospectus from the pile on the floor.

'Oh very funny, Tom, and your Sports Science course involved a forty-hour week? I don't think so somehow, or how could you play football every afternoon?'

'OK you two, enough. Can we help you plough through these then Catrin?'

3

'If you want, Dad,' Catrin replied selecting another prospectus. Really she would far rather go through them on her own but she didn't want to hurt her father's feelings.

Their conversation was interrupted by determined banging from the bedroom above.

'The walking stick calleth, Catrin, I'm sure it's your turn,' Tom said.

'Definitely yours, Tom, and anyway you're already on your feet.'

'And on your way take your mum a mug of tea will you, Tom? It sounds as if your other gran is telling her everything that's happened in Treorchy, no, correction, the whole of the Rhondda Valley, for the past week.'

Tom nodded, his mouth once more full of cherry cake.

'Is there any cake left, Tom?'

There was no answer for a few seconds as Tom gulped down his mouthful. 'No, sorry Dad, all gone.'

Their father sighed.

'Really, Dad,' Catrin said without looking up from the prospectus, 'you should know by now that's the price you pay for having Tom make you a cuppa; he always hoovers up the treats before they make it on to any plate.'

'And they make me the sweet person I am,' Tom said cheerfully as he headed off to deliver their mother's cup of tea and to check on Granny Lewis.

'I like the sound of Manchester, Dad,' Catrin said hesitantly, 'looks like it's a very studenty kind of place.'

Before he could respond her mother came into the kitchen clutching her Valleys Girl mug.

'That was a quickie, love, a mere forty-five minutes,' her father said, clearing some newspapers away to make room for her to sit.

Her mum laughed as she settled herself in the armchair on the other side of the Aga and took a long sip of tea. 'Thirsty work, your Granny Olwen. Oh and she says hello and sends you her love. And yes she wanted to tell me all about Mavis,

4

next door's new kitten, and how she's been chasing grey squirrels away from the bird feeders ...'

'I'm surprised they let the kitten out so soon; don't they have to have their jabs first?'

'No, Ben, it's not the kitten that's chasing the squirrels, it's Granny O.'

Catrin smiled in sympathy. She was well used to the bemused look her mother gave her father to indicate that, brilliant as he may be, he sometimes did not understand the most basic of things.

Her mother looked at the pile of prospectuses, took another gulp of tea and added casually, 'Mrs Tanner from down the road says her granddaughter is really enjoying the Fine Art course here in Cardiff; she says the staff at UWIC are very friendly and the campus is brilliant, lots of night life too – you know Catz, it's just off Newport Road.'

'Gran's fine; she just wanted her shawl,' Tom reported as he rejoined the family in the kitchen. 'You must get out of Cardiff, Catz. However good UWIC is you need to get out of Cardiff, get out of Wales; now's your chance to escape.'

'Why would Catrin want to escape? Cardiff's a brilliant city, Tom,' their mother said indignantly, putting the UWIC prospectus on the sofa next to Catrin. 'And anyway you can't hate Cardiff that much; you were quick enough to hurry home last June, two whole days after your final exams if I recall correctly and, hey ho, eighteen months later you're still here.'

'Needs must, Mum – no job, no dosh,' Tom replied, picking up a banana as he passed the fruit bowl.

'And you're eating us out of house and home, Tom,' his father teased.

'Growing lad, Dad.' Tom went back for an orange.

'Actually, not, Tom; the average male stops growing at twenty-one.'

'And since when have I been average at anything, Dad?' Tom laughed, 'Twenty-four and still growing, I tell you.'

'Yeah, time you grew up,' Catrin said, throwing a

prospectus in his direction.

Tom neatly dodged the missile and turned towards their mother. 'So, let's get this right; you want Catz to go to university in Splott. Hardly Cardiff's most leafy suburb is it? And can I remind you that 'Splott' not only rhymes with 'blot' but means the same?'

'It's to be known as *Sp-lo* now that it's becoming all gentrified,' Catrin said.

'And of course Cardiff's got a very distinguished list of alumni,' their father remarked.

'Oh, yes, Dad; anyone in particular come to mind?' Tom enquired with a laugh.

'Look no further, son, look no further. I was one of the distinguished class of '89 I'll have you know. And one of our set, Arthur Pennant Jones, is now a medical advisor to the British Olympic team.'

'Reflected glory, Dad!' Tom scoffed.

Catrin picked up the prospectuses and headed for the hall. 'Well, thanks for your ideas, guys, but I like the look of Manchester, Durham, and Aberystwyth. I'm going to browse their websites to find out a bit more'.

'You could do it down here Catz, on the laptop,' her father suggested.

But before he had finished his sentence she was already halfway up the stairs.

Chapter One

'Catrin, I ...'

Catrin leaned over Granny Lewis, who looked so small in the big white bed. Turned on her side and curled up like a little animal, her breathing was so soft that Catrin several times during the morning had put her hand on her gran's back to check she was still breathing. Now, hearing the soft, raspy voice momentarily startled her.

'Yes Granny, what can I get you? Will you take a little sip of water?' No answer. Her gran had again slipped back into the deep sleep that had enveloped her for most of the past week. Minutes passed and Catrin was once more engrossed in the chaotic world of Katie Price's autobiography when another whisper shook her. She leaned in close and gently stroked her grandmother's thin hand.

'Ben? Is Ben home?'

'No, Gran, Dad's still in Pontypridd at the surgery. Mum's here, shall I get her?'

The old lady's eyes opened just a little but did not seem to focus on Catrin. 'Your dad works too hard – good doctor.' The watery eyes closed but the thin lips opened as if Granny Lewis was struggling to say something else.

'Would you like a drink, Granny?' Catrin got up to reach for the water on the other side of the bed but her grandmother placed her hand on Catrin's arm and indicated she wanted her to sit down. Catrin sat and waited.

The old woman's eyes flickered slightly. 'You're a good girl and, and ...' Catrin held her breath as her grandmother fought to form the words, 'so like me – as if – you were –my own blood.' Her gran's eyes closed again. Catrin sat completely still, staring at her grandmother's pale, expressionless face, waiting for her to say more. Nothing came and the slight gurgle in the back of her grandmother's throat indicated she was once more asleep.

Catrin was stunned. 'So like me,' that part made sense. Catrin was blonde and her grandmother always claimed that she had been a strawberry blonde; at one metre seventy, or five feet seven inches, they were both tall for Welsh women; and, just like her father and brother, she had inherited Granny Lewis's long nose, the feature Catrin disliked most about her own appearance. But why would her gran say 'as if you were my own blood?' Catrin felt panic rise inside her, as if a trapdoor had suddenly been opened and she was falling, falling out of control. Willing herself to think straight she struggled to make sense of her grandmother's strange words. She pulled the blankets gently over the old woman's cold hands and got up.

She stood at the window looking out at the front garden clothed in November grey. A blackbird scuttled up and down the flower bed, scattering the fallen leaves in every direction as it foraged for the last of the windfalls from the big apple tree. Concentrate, she told herself, work it out; there has to be a perfectly obvious explanation. But her mind felt foggy, heavy. She silently repeated the words. 'As if you were my own blood.' She put emphasis on different words to see if it changed the meaning. It didn't.

Catrin could hear her heart beating loudly in the silence. She breathed deeply, willing herself to keep calm, and waited, desperate for her grandmother to say something else, something that would explain what she meant. Yes, that's what Catrin would do. She'd concentrate on her breathing until her gran woke up again and could explain what she had said. In: one, two, three, out: one, two, three. In: one, two ...
She heard the big grandfather clock in the hall strike eleven. In the darkened room, its heavy curtains stealing the paltry November light, Catrin felt time was at a standstill. Outside cars passed with monotonous regularity, the whooshing of

tyres on the wet road reminding her that city life was carrying on as normal. For a moment she was taken aback by the realisation. And then she thought of all the days that she'd gone about her business – walking to school, exercising the dog, doing the shopping – and on every one of those days there would have been someone looking out of the window, feeling as she felt now, their world turned upside down by some personal crisis. And she'd walked by totally unaware.

She sat down at her grandmother's bedside and picked up the book she had abandoned on the floor. Distraction, that's what she needed, she thought, as she felt another wave of panic threaten to overwhelm her. Katie Price's words now swam meaninglessly in front of her eyes, making her feel sick. She put the book down on the dark oak bedside cabinet, the cabinet which, along with the rest of the furniture in the room, her grandmother had insisted on bringing with her when she'd moved in with them some three years previously, following a stroke that had left her unable to care for herself. Despite Catrin's father's gloomy predictions Granny Lewis had made a good recovery and within months was again able to walk Lucky, the last in a long line of spaniels on which she doted, and irritate Catrin's mother. Her gran was quite capable of recovering this time too, Catrin consoled herself. A lorry thundered by and the bay window shuddered. The clock struck half eleven. Catrin coughed, hoping this would be enough to wake her gran and prompt her to say more. No reaction. She got up and straightened the bedclothes, mopped her gran's brow, put a little water on her parched lips. Eventually her grandmother moved very slightly.

'Cariad.'

Catrin leaned in close, her face almost touching her grandmother's, eager to hear every word as clearly as possible. She felt the warmth of her grandmother's shallow breath brush her cheek.

'I'd like – to see – Lucky.'

'Of course, Granny, I'll get him.'

9

Catrin rushed downstairs and into the kitchen where her mother was cleaning the cooker. 'Granny wants to see Lucky,' she blurted out as she picked up the old King Charles spaniel from his basket.by the Aga. Stroking him, she put him down and he trotted after her. Her mother wiped her hands on her apron and quickly followed them upstairs. The dog whimpered as he saw his mistress and tried in vain to climb on to the old metal bed. Catrin lifted him up and instinctively her gran held her hand out. Lucky licked it and then settled, without any fuss, tucking himself into the old woman's side, laying his head gently on her arm. And then she slipped away.

There was a knock on Catrin's bedroom door and the handle turned. Instinctively Catrin held her breath.

'Catrin? Catrin? I know you're upset love but please unlock the door.' Her mother sounded anxious. There was a pause and her mother said more quietly, 'It's natural to be upset about Gran love, we're all upset, please just open the door.'

Catrin did not reply and after a few seconds she heard her mother's steps retreat along the landing. She was lying on her bed looking up at the aurora borealis she had painted on the ceiling – or her 'psychedelic nightmare' as her brother called it. Sometimes its deep blue base with bursts of emerald green, yellow, and red energised her; sometimes it made her feel relaxed. But now she wasn't sure how she felt. On second thoughts she knew she felt angry. Angry with Granny Lewis for not explaining what she meant, angry with her for leaving it so late to say something so astounding. And guilty … Guilty for being angry with someone who had just died. Guilty too, because what was filling her head right now was how to make sense of her gran's words, rather than sadness at her passing. Gran must have known what she was saying; she certainly wasn't suffering from dementia. It was the cancer that had taken her and up until last week she had been herself, effectively ruling the roost from her bed. Catrin loved her, of course she did, she was her gran. But Granny Lewis hadn't been the type to have long intimate conversations with, or big hugs, as she was accustomed to with her other granny; Granny Lewis was a doer rather than a talker. 'Brisk and brusque' was the way her father described his mother.

Catrin cuddled the two teddies she'd had since she was a little girl and who still shared her bed. Absent-mindedly she stroked Little Ted's bald head. Downstairs the front doorbell sounded a few times and the telephone seemed to be ringing continuously. Earlier she'd gone to the bathroom and had lingered for a while on the landing, wanting company, not wanting to be upstairs with Granny Lewis's body in the next room, but yet not wanting to face her family. She'd heard snippets of a one- sided conversation – her dad saying, 'yes, yes, very quickly in the end ... we knew she was ill but ... yes, just this last week really; thank you ... so kind ... I'll let you know ... yes, she was a character.' And she'd heard his big voice threaten to crack and felt a surge of love for him.

Catrin wasn't sure how long she'd lain there but now the light was fading so it must be about 4.30 p.m. She'd repeated Gran's words over and over in her head – she had literally thought of nothing else for hours. In an attempt to stop her mind going round and round in circles, she took a clean sheet of A4 and her favourite pen from her desk, writing the title in large capital letters, convinced that would bring clarity to the process.

'NOT BLOOD' – POSSIBLE EXPLANATIONS:

1 Granny was confused?
    No. I don't think so. Everything else she said made sense.
2 I misheard what Gran said?
    No. She said it slowly, clearly. The room was quiet. I could not have misheard.
3 I was asleep and dreaming?
    No. I remember reading about Katie Price's horse

immediately before Gran said those words

Catrin sat staring at the number four. If none of the above was likely what other explanation could there be? 'Not blood.' She turned the words slowly around in her mind. She tried to distance herself from the meaning. She considered what she would have understood from the words if she'd heard them in a television soap. Not related, surely that was the meaning. 'So like me … as if … you were my own blood.' How could she not be related to her grandmother? The white page challenged her to plaster it with explanation but her pen now rested on it forlornly, mocking the over-confident heading.

As she began writing again she knew the explanation she was about to offer would have to be dismissed but for completeness she wrote it anyway.

4 *'Not blood' because I am adopted?*

No, I've seen photos of mum pregnant with me and Mum, Dad and Tom holding me in hospital.

So, there had to be a number five. She struggled to concentrate. Why was it so difficult? Hadn't her teachers always said how logical her arguments were, how clear her reasoning? And now those skills were so needed, they seemed to have deserted her. Perhaps a diagram would help.

5 *Granny L > Dad > Me*

She felt the bile rise in her throat. She scribbled furiously as if getting it all down quickly would lessen its significance.

Dad is not my father?

She crossed it out. Just seeing the suggestion in black and white made it seem more real. Her mind was racing. If Ben was not her father then who was? In soapland an illicit fling would be the obvious explanation.

Mum had an affair? were the next words she wrote.'Impossible' was Catrin's first reaction. Her mum and dad really loved each other. For goodness sake, they embarrassingly still held hands when they walked down the street, hardly ever rowed and still laughed at each other's jokes.

Perhaps, of course, their relationship hadn't been as perfect eighteen years ago. Tom would have been five years old and she knew her father had worked very long hours as the junior partner in the surgery; perhaps her mother had been lonely and ... She let the thought go, did not want to visualise any likely scenarios. Instead she concentrated on the abstract. If that was the explanation and her mother had had an affair perhaps it had made their marriage stronger. Catrin had never actually believed that any affair made relationships stronger as so many erring celebrities claimed, but perhaps this really was true of her parents. Perhaps they had really worked at their marriage. Certainly she could never remember any serious problems between them but, perhaps, by the time she was old enough to be aware of any tensions they were back on an even keel.

So instead of *'Impossible'*, she wrote *'Possible'*.

Catrin looked again at the list. If what her grandmother had said was true she could think of no other explanation. And if it was true, did her father know she was not his? Or had Gran found out somehow and kept it from him? Surely he didn't know. He looked so happy in those photographs taken with her as a newborn, holding her safely in his arms. She felt sick.

'Catz, I've brought you a sandwich – open the door, Catrin love, please?' Her dad sounded exhausted.

Catrin got up slowly and turned the key. Her father was standing there in his old Aran cardigan holding a tray with a mug of tea and a round of sandwiches. He took one look at her, placed the tray on the floor and put his big arms around her. She smelled pipe smoke and felt herself smiling into his

13

cardigan. At the first sign of trouble or stress he took himself off to his shed where, although he had officially given up smoking many years ago, he kept his emergency pipe and a packet of Golden Virginia tobacco hidden in an old cracked plant pot on the top shelf. Hiding it was unnecessary as his little smoking habit was well known to all the family but for some reason they all maintained the pretence that he had given up.

'The doctor's been love and the undertaker's here now – he's taking Gran to the chapel of rest. Why don't you come down and have your sandwich with Tom in the kitchen?' Catrin relaxed, reassured by the familiar embrace, and nodded into the scratchy Aran. She gently pulled away, picked up the tray and followed him downstairs. He joined her mother who was talking in hushed tones to two black-suited men in the living room.

Tom was sitting at the table with a large plate of sandwiches and the newspaper open in front of him as Catrin came into the kitchen. He looked up and said gently, 'You OK, sis?'

'Mm,' Catrin mumbled, taking a sip from her mug of tea. 'Oh, yuck, sugar.'

'Good for shock,' Tom said through a mouthful of something with mayonnaise, his gaze already back on the sandwich.

Catrin stared at him. Stocky and auburn-haired, everyone said he took after their father, and he did, but he had their mother's bright blue eyes. Catrin had those eyes too and people said she looked like her mum, although taller and blonde to Jane's dark. Come to think of it, had anyone, ever, said she resembled her dad in any way?

Aware that she was studying him intently Tom mistook her interest for criticism. 'Don't look like that, sis, you know food is my way of coping with stress.'

Catrin sighed dramatically. 'Tom, food is your way of coping with everything.'

'Good point well made, sis,' Tom licked his forefinger and made an air-sign to indicate she had indeed scored a point.

They sat in companionable silence, Catrin taking a few surreptitious glances at her brother as he studied the sports pages. Confident, secure Tom, who knew exactly who he was. She caught sight of her reflection in the back door. The bevelled glass had distorted her face. How appropriate she thought bitterly; she wasn't what she seemed to be. The front doorbell rang and, seeing that Tom had just crammed another sandwich into his mouth, Catrin got up to answer it. On the doorstep stood a young man hidden behind a bouquet of white roses.

'Looks like you've got an admirer – either that or someone has done something mega-bad and has to apologise big-time like,' he quipped.

'Thanks.' She took the roses and closed the door sharply but not before she registered the startled look on the deliverer's face. Dumping the flowers on the kitchen worktop she went back to her tea.

'Yuck, this is gross,' Catrin made a face and got up again to make a fresh brew.

'Pretty flowers, who are they from?' Tom asked.

Catrin shrugged and passed the little white card to her brother.

'"From Vera and Bertie Jones, No. 42, with deepest sympathy". Wow, they were quick off the mark; must have got straight on to Interflora as soon as they heard the news. Impressive.'

She sat down again and sipped at the scalding tea. Somehow it didn't feel right to turn on the radio or to read the newspaper or a magazine or really to chat about everyday things. She thought they should talk about Granny but the only thing she could think to say was, 'I don't think Granny likes white roses'.

'Liked,' Tom corrected.

He turned another page but Catrin could see he wasn't

really reading.

'She had very definite ideas about what she liked and didn't like,' Tom said after a while.

Catrin nodded. 'She really liked you,' Tom added. 'You were definitely her favourite.'

Catrin did not argue and said instead. 'And I really liked her.' Her chin began to wobble, a sure sign that she was close to tears. Tom went back to his newspaper.

Eventually there was movement in the hall, followed by subdued conversation and then silence as the voices disappeared up the stairs. Minutes passed and Catrin could hear her heart pounding loudly; she wondered if Tom could hear it too. And then there were feet on the stairs again, heavier this time and slower. She heard the agonising squeak of a trolley and instinctively both she and Tom looked towards the hall. Tom got up and hovered and Catrin picked up Lucky from his basket and went to sit with him in the armchair by the Aga, burying her head in his thick coat. She felt the draught as the front door was opened and then listened to the sound of the trolley being forced along the gravel path. Granny Lewis being difficult right to the end, Catrin thought grimly.

After a few minutes Jane and Ben came into the kitchen.

'Lovely flowers.' Her mum held the bouquet to her nose.

'From the Joneses, number 42,' Tom replied.

'I'll put them in water in a minute; they'll look nice in that Portmeirion vase I've got. We won't have enough vases though I'm sure; so many people send flowers now don't they? Perhaps we can borrow some; what do you think, Ben?'

'I'll make us all a fresh pot of tea and then we'll need to talk about what kind of funeral Granny would have liked,' her dad said firmly.' Catrin pushed back her chair and made for the door.

'Catrin, we really need your help with this.'

'Whatever Dad, I don't care, you choose; it'll make no difference.' She let the kitchen door slam carelessly behind her.

16

Jane opened and closed three kitchen cupboard doors before she managed to find the vase she was looking for. She filled it from the cold water tap and trimmed the stems as her mother-in-law had taught her to do, so that the roses could drink thirstily. Handling the prickly roses was a damn sight easier than handling a teenage daughter she thought. No, she was being unfair. Catrin was normally so easy-going and she and Ben had not had to put up with any serious teenage angst from her.

'Catrin's taken it really hard – I feel guilty now that I let her be there at the end. I should have seen it coming, Gran asking to see Lucky, she knew ...' Jane trailed off.

'Come on love, don't start blaming yourself; Catrin's eighteen now, she's an adult, you can't protect her from life – or death – for ever,' Ben said, putting the teapot on the table.

'I can understand upset but she seems more angry somehow,' Jane replied, feeling totally drained.

'You know I've lost count of how many people I've had to break bad news to over the years and you never know how someone's going to react – those you least expect to hold it together are usually the strong ones. Initially anyway.' Ben gave Jane's shoulder a gentle squeeze.

'Oh Dad, I wouldn't do your job for all the world – ill people, dead people, upset people. Hardly a bundle of laughs is it?'

'It's not all doom and gloom Tom; we see the other end too. Births are great – I just wish we were still called to attend home deliveries. When I started in practice I'd get to see half a dozen births a year – now it's all done by the midwives.'

'More blood and gore and screaming if the ones on the telly are anything to go by.' Tom screwed up his nose. 'And anyway Catrin's just angry at Gran – it's abandonment issues and stuff.'

'Oh Tom, I think you read too many of Catrin's magazines.'

'And watch too much morning television,' Ben added

17

jokingly. Jane snatched away the salt her husband was about to add to the milk in his mug. As he started to pour the tea the doorbell rang again and the first of the visitors arrived. Ben was to make five pots of tea that evening as a succession of neighbours came to pay their respects.

Chapter Two

More sympathisers arrived to offer their condolences at 9.10 the following morning. Seven more called during the day and there were four deliveries of flowers, three pies, one casserole, and five cakes. The family quickly fell into their respective roles – Jane sat in the living room and spoke to the visitors, Tom made the sandwiches (and consumed a good many of them), Catrin busied herself with making tea and washing up endless cups, and Ben disappeared for long periods to his garden shed.

'Family conference,' Jane called up the stairs when the last of the day's callers had left and they were settling down to a warmed casserole at 10 p.m. Catrin slid into the kitchen and sat opposite Ben. Momentarily Jane wondered why Catrin had not sat opposite her as she usually did, but seeing the look on her daughter's face decided not to comment.

'Dad and I think that Saturday would be the best day for the funeral – so people don't have to take a day off work – you both OK with that?'

'Let's just check we're not in for a tornado that day,' Tom said, tapping the keys on his phone to Google a weather site.

'Tom – we're not organising a picnic; it's Gran's funeral,' Jane said, her voice rising in exasperation.

'OK – Saturday it is, assuming that's OK with the undertaker and everyone else involved,' Ben said quietly, reaching out to rest his hand on Jane's arm. 'Now we've got to decide whether it should be a burial or cremation – Gran didn't tell either of you what she wanted by any chance?'

Catrin and Tom both shook their heads.

'Well I think burial,' Tom volunteered. 'After all, she always buried her beloved dogs so that's a good clue I think.

Mind, I don't know if it's possible to cremate dogs, is it?'

'I think burial too,' said his father, 'in Llangrannog – with Dad. And I think the service should be in the chapel in Llangrannog too; that's where Mum was baptised and married.'

The other three nodded.

'The good news is BBC Weather says no tornadoes are forecast for Saturday; the bad news is there's 90 per cent chance of rain,' Tom said frowning.

'I wish she'd said what she wanted though … I wish I'd asked her,' Ben said quietly.

'People don't, do they. I mean, say what kind of funeral they want. Not unless they feel very strongly about it. I guess she just assumed she would have the same kind of funeral as your father,' Jane said putting her arm around him.

'I thought she might have put something in her will so I phoned the solicitors – the ones she used when she sold her house,' Ben stalled.

'And?' Jane prompted.

'She hasn't made a will with them.' Ben said flatly. 'And I can't imagine she'd have gone to any other firm; she was so full of praise for Thomas and Sons, and she knows – knew – a couple of the partners through chapel. "Trustworthy," I remember, that's how she described them.'

'Oh that's just typical; she never did go out of her way to make things easy did she? Jane blurted out and then stopped suddenly. 'Oh Ben, I'm so sorry, I didn't mean –'

Ben smiled at her. 'I know love, I know exactly what you mean, but the solicitor says it will be straightforward; everything will automatically come to me. To us.'

Nobody said anything for a while. Lucky snored gently in his basket.

'Well I think it's a jolly good thing she didn't plan her funeral,' Tom ventured eventually, 'you know what she was like, all practical, no-nonsense – she'd have us singing "Pack up your troubles in your old kit bag" or something like that.'

Ben smiled and nodded.

Catrin had been silent throughout supper, pushing the casserole around her plate. Ben now turned to her, 'Catrin, you read beautifully; would you read in the service? It would mean so much to her and to me ... read something in Welsh, love, Gran would like that.' Tom rolled his eyes dramatically and Jane kicked him gently under the table. She noticed that her husband's big brown eyes were filled with tears and she smiled gratefully at Catrin as she leaned over to kiss her father's damp cheek.

The day of the funeral was dank and grey. Ben drove his family westwards along the M4, very aware of the subdued silence. Such restraint was not normal for them but of course today was not a normal day. Now they were skirting Port Talbot, the rain lashing mercilessly against the car's windows, the windscreen wipers struggling to cope with the downpour. Cardiff was half an hour behind them and Llangrannog still two hours away.

'Dad, can you open the window a bit? I'm feeling sick.'

'Catz, it's pouring – we'll get soaked.' Ben opened his window anyway and the sulphur-like smell belching from the steelworks filled the car.

'It would have helped if you'd eaten some breakfast, Catrin,' Jane remarked.

'Close the window, Dad, that foul smell is enough to make everyone sick,' Tom moaned.

'Why on earth do people have to live in such conditions in the 21st century? It can't be good for their mental or emotional health,' Ben muttered as he closed the window and shut out the stench.

He was thinking how this journey had changed over the years. He'd been born and brought up in Cardiff where both his parents were teachers. But they were from Cardiganshire, or Ceredigion as it was now, and Ben had travelled this route with them every summer to spend the holidays at his grandparents' home in Llangrannog. He'd loved those long summer holidays: six weeks of what had seemed like endless sun-filled days spent on the beach, messing about in the rock pools and racing the waves. He remembered the excitement of arriving home from school on the last day of the summer term and jumping into the car which his mother had loaded the previous night. His father had checked the oil and the windscreen wash and then driven to the local garage to check the tyre pressure and fill up with petrol. The car of course had changed over the years: the Hillman Imp became a Ford Cortina and ultimately a Ford Capri, but the ritual was always the same. Every year they stopped at Cross Hands for fish and chips and for Ben that really marked the start of the holiday. He remembered just how good those chips would taste on the way westwards. On the way back no one ever had an appetite.

And for those six weeks his parents were very different from the way they were at home in Cardiff. They laughed more, they played with him, and they spoke to each other in Welsh. Everyone around them spoke Welsh too, the family and the neighbours, and by the end of the holiday Ben himself could understand quite a lot. But back in Cardiff he heard the language only in chapel on a Sunday and although he could still sing hymns in Welsh he'd never been able to hold a conversation in the language. Wryly he smiled to himself. As a grown-up a lot of things had irritated him about his mother but the main thing was her insistence he be brought up to speak English only. He remembered once, as an adult, asking her why she had chosen not to share her first language with him. She'd shrugged and said dismissively, 'English is the language you need to get on in the world.' He'd tried to argue that learning Welsh would not have harmed his English. He'd enjoyed telling her there was proof she was wrong, that scientific research had shown that people who were fluent in two languages had a higher IQ. But in her customary manner she had pursed her lips, the familiar closed look had come over her face and he'd known there was no point pursuing the

22

matter. She had, however, eventually realised that he was right, though naturally she'd never admitted this; but she had encouraged both Tom and Catrin to learn Welsh and had even helped with their Welsh homework. She'd had to, he thought resentfully, as she was the only one in the family who could. Realising he was thinking such negative things about his mother, and this on the day of her funeral, he blushed, shifted in his seat and determined to think only good things of her for the rest of the day.

'Dad, don't you know it's against the law to drive at under 30 mph?' Tom quipped from the back seat. Ben realising he'd been sitting behind a slow-moving lorry for quite a while, moved down a gear, checked his mirror and indicated.

Catrin too was thinking of the times she'd made this journey with her grandmother. For a week every August, until she was eleven, grandmother and granddaughter would have what they called their 'girls week' in Llangrannog, staying at the same little bed and breakfast on the quay every year. Her grandmother still had several cousins living in the area and would always visit them during the week, taking tea with one and supper with another almost every day. But Catrin knew it suited Granny Lewis to be independent, although she herself claimed she stayed at the boarding house to save her cousins from 'going to any trouble'. The preparation for the trip would start on the first day of the school holidays in mid-July. There would be the outing to Howells' department store to buy a new bathing costume for Catrin followed by a scone tea in the second-floor restaurant. Then they would head to the higgledy-piggledy, dusty bookshop in the Hayes, crammed with all kinds of treasures, the highlight of their afternoon. Her grandmother's taste in books never changed and she'd choose a crime novel by P. D. James or Colin Dexter. But of course Catrin's preferences had altered over the years and Granny Lewis had encouraged her to try different authors and different types of books. She remembered how her gran would often

23

rummage about in her large handbag to find a crumpled review she'd cut out from a newspaper of some book she thought Catrin might enjoy. And then the day before they set off for Llangrannog there would be another trip, to Woolworths on Cowbridge Road, to stock up on sweets for the journey – 'pick and mix' for her and humbugs for Granny. Catrin had continued buying them both sweets from Woolworths until it had closed four years ago. That was the end of an era too.

How they enjoyed their week by the seaside in Llangrannog. Whatever the weather. Actually Catrin had probably enjoyed it more when the weather was wet and the two of them would sit in the B and B looking out on to the beach and draw, play games and, of course, read their novels. Granny never let her win any game on purpose and so, when Catrin did win, the victory was very sweet indeed.

In Llangrannog Granny spoke to her in Welsh, telling her it was good practice and would help with her schoolwork. Why that didn't apply when they were at home in Cardiff Catrin never understood. At home her grandmother, glancing through the Situations Vacant section of the *Western Mail*, would often tut and comment how times had changed, how English used to be what was needed to get on in the world, but now, in 21st century Wales, Welsh seemed to be the passport to success. And getting on in the world was very important to Granny Lewis.

Their week in Llangrannog always involved a visit to Catrin's grandfather's grave. Granny Lewis never seemed sad on these occasions, unlike Granny Olwen who always seemed wistful when she visited her husband's grave. Familiar with Granny Olwen's custom of never visiting the cemetery in Treorchy without being laden with flowers Catrin had once suggested they take flowers to put on the Llangrannog grave but her other grandmother had shaken her head, saying flowers were wasted on the dead. Catrin had been eight or nine at the time and shocked at the offhand response; now she knew her

24

grandmother had not been uncaring; she was simply of a generation and personality not given to displays of sentimentality.

Catrin wished she'd carried on going on these holidays with her grandmother for longer but, once she'd gone to senior school, sport camps and sleepovers and hanging out with her new friends had seemed more attractive.

Ben turned the Volvo's nose on to a single-track road. The signpost indicated there were three more miles to Llangrannog. Those three miles took them nine minutes as Ben was forced to reverse twice and perilously hug the hedge to allow a pick-up carrying several straggly, bleating sheep to pass. Now driving through Llangrannog village he could see Bethania chapel, the box-like grey stone building stark against the mountainside high above the village. A long row of cars was parked on the single-track road, clinging to the high hedge that separated it from the cemetery, which climbed the steep hill behind the chapel. He slowed down as he approached and parked in front of the undertaker's gleaming black hearse. Despite its shine everything about the car was gloomy and Ben was glad he had chosen not to follow it in convoy along the motorway from Cardiff that morning. Immediately the undertaker, clad in black with a bright white shirt, opened the car door and busied them into the chapel porch. Ben checked his watch, quarter to two. There was a full fifteen minutes to go before the service started and he wondered what the rush was. But deciding that the undertaker would not take kindly to his authority being questioned, and anyway relieved that someone else was in control, he simply did as he was told and followed him into the chapel.

Ben walked along the narrow aisle his eyes fixed on the slate flagstones a few feet in front of him, grateful to feel Jane warm and solid at his side. He could sense, without looking around, that the little chapel was full. The four of them squeezed into the front pew and sat, still and upright. The air was heavy with silence and the cloying sweetness of lilies. Ben could feel the back of his neck burning between his hairline and the stiff white collar of his new shirt, as if the eyes of everyone in the silent congregation were focused on that one spot. He put a forefinger inside the collar and gave it a little tug, easing it gently back and forth to see if he could loosen it. Eventually the minister coughed and got slowly to his feet. Ben pondered the full chapel, glad to have something to think about rather than the coffin filling the 'sedd fawr,' the large seat directly below the pulpit, usually occupied by the deacons. His mother had left the village some sixty years previously and, although he had a few distant cousins living in the area with whom he had virtually lost touch, he didn't understand why all these people had come. But somehow, just by being there to share his grief, they made him feel better, stronger. And when they sang the first hymn, 'Calon Lân', the richness of their voices seemed to soar high above the small, stark chapel. Being a confirmed atheist he was surprised to find himself imagining their voices were accompanying his mother's soul on the next part of the journey. What a fanciful thought he mused; what a strange effect death has on totally rational people.

He tried to remember his father's funeral here thirty-five years previously. The little chapel had been full on that occasion as well. But for Ben it was very different from today. Then he'd been in such shock, his father's heart attack having been so unexpected, he'd been isolated in his grief and unable to take comfort from the support of the community. He remembered crying as he sat in this same front pew with his mother; she'd leaned over, ashen-faced, and told him to pull himself together. That night they'd driven back to Cardiff and, at supper time, she'd made him sit in his father's chair at the table and told him firmly he was now head of the household. How bitter he'd been at her seemingly easy acceptance of their dreadful new situation, her determination to erase his father from their lives. It appalled him how within days she'd

26

bundled his father's clothes into plastic bags and dumped them at the local Salvation Army. The fact she'd crammed them into plastic bags – his father's tweed jackets, thick corduroy trousers, checked shirts and woollen ties – had seemed to him disrespectful. Had she folded them neatly and put them in a suitcase for delivery to the Sally Army that he could have forgiven.

Ben felt Jane nudge him as Catrin squeezed past. He watched his daughter read and did not attempt to understand but focused instead on willing her to be able to get through the piece. He saw her bite her lip and the minister put a reassuring hand on her shoulder as her voice quivered and she fought for control. And then with relief he realised she had finished and was walking back to the pew. As she passed him he caught her eye and touched her arm. She smiled back and he felt her strength radiate through his body. He got to his feet for the final hymn. The organist pedalled furiously and the little organ begrudgingly emitted the first tinny notes of 'Cwm Rhondda'. For a moment it seemed to him wrong, the rousing chorus 'Bread of Heaven,' so beloved of the Welsh rugby crowd, replaced by less familiar Welsh words. Then he decided it was totally right. This was where the hymn belonged. In the pews behind him members of the local male voice choir were singing their hearts out. He wanted to join in but such rich voices singing in unison always moved him and today of all days he couldn't be sure whether a sob or a song would come out. Jane nudged him again as the singing finished, and he saw the undertaker had opened the little door that penned them into their pew. He felt Jane's hand, low now on his back, encouraging him to follow his mother's coffin out of the chapel.

The drains outside were blocked and the water was running like a river down the narrow road when they emerged at the end of the hour-long service to find the rain now coming down in sheets. In hushed tones the undertaker suggested to Ben they forgo the traditional reception line and head straight to

27

the cemetery. Ben nodded and was glad only a few people chose to join them. The rest of the congregation dashed straight into the vestry for tea. The coffin was lowered and the minister said a few words of committal. Then Ben, flanked by Jane holding his hand on one side and a tearful Catrin clinging to his arm on the other, threw his mother's favourite flowers – some sweet smelling freesias – into the grave and said a silent goodbye.

'Let's go, Dad; Granny would tell us all off for getting wet,' Tom said.

Approaching the vestry Catrin could hear laughter, which struck her as being entirely inappropriate. As the family entered there was a sudden hush and a few embarrassed coughs. Her mum and dad were immediately waylaid by a middle-aged man who Catrin presumed was a relative since he had auburn hair and that familiar family nose. He put his hand firmly on her father's arm, ensuring her dad was rooted to the spot until the man had had his say. The noise level increased steadily again. Tom grabbed Catrin's hand and bagged the two last seats at the end of the long trestle table, covered with all kinds of sandwiches and cakes. It was laid with white china embossed with a blue stamp indicating it belonged to Bethania Chapel. They both accepted the cup of tea offered by a smiling, rosy-cheeked woman, and Tom leaned across to fill his plate while Catrin ventured a look around.

She was struck by the blackness. Everyone seemed to be dressed in black apart from her. She felt herself blush furiously. It was her parents' fault – they should have known but the only guidance she'd got from them was 'nothing too bright.' Catrin knew her gran would have added 'nothing too short or too tight'. In the end she'd chosen a dark green jumper over grey trousers, topped with her dark grey leather jacket. How wrong she looked, dressed almost casually compared to the locals and her parents. Even Tom had found his old black school trousers, a white shirt, grey pullover, and dark navy

28

coat. Sitting there she felt she was somehow a second-rate mourner and had she heard someone in the chapel earlier whisper about 'lack of respect'? Were they referring to her and what she now felt to be her garish clothes? A second flush washed over her.

She listened to several conversations going on around her, glad Tom was concentrating on eating cake and not trying to talk to her. The locals were discussing the weather, what was happening in the local school, somebody's engagement, the price animals were fetching at market and how the politicians were getting everything wrong.

She kicked Tom under the table to divert his attention from the large piece of Victoria sponge at its far end. 'I think it's a disgrace; people are just talking about everyday things; nobody is thinking of Granny,' she whispered.

'They probably didn't know her, Catz; I expect most of Granny's friends are dead or have moved away.'

'Then why are all these people here?' Catrin persisted.

'Perhaps they're like me; they go anywhere there's free food,' said Tom 'Or perhaps funerals are their only opportunity to get together, to socialize; there's nothing else here is there?' He grimaced.

Catrin cast what she hoped looked like a casual glance at her neighbours to check they weren't being overheard. But the fat man in his too tight suit and the ruddy-faced man sitting opposite him were loudly lamenting the unfair prices being paid by supermarkets for milk.

'Oh don't be ridiculous Tom; just because they don't have cinemas and bowling alleys – the buildings that say something is happening.'

'Well I'm really glad I haven't got to hang around to join some crochet class, that's for sure. It would be my worst nightmare, man, stuck in somewhere like this and to cap it all they all speak Welsh.'

'Tom, you're such a townie, and anyway you speak Welsh.'

29

'Not any more Catz; the day I left school was the day I left all that behind me too.'

Catrin gratefully accepted a second cup of tea and spent the rest of the afternoon making small talk with distant relatives who were at pains to clarify exactly how they were related, which generally involved complicated explanations revolving around the phrase 'twice removed.' Her father's family were all either dark-haired or auburn and generally like her father in build, short and stocky. She desperately wanted to find a tall blond among them. There was none.

Chapter Three

As she awoke on the Sunday morning Catrin knew her life was about to change. She didn't want it to and yet she knew she couldn't just ignore what her grandmother had said. In the lead-up to the funeral she had decided not to think about it and she had managed to keep to that resolve. Instead she'd focused on finding something suitable to read at the service and in the end had settled for a Welsh translation of a Kahlil Gibran poem. Then there had been the task of deciding what to wear – which she'd obviously got so wrong. Now as she lay in bed she allowed her grandmother's words to fill her mind – 'So like me, as if you were my own blood.' Catrin lay there for a while in the darkness, the grey November light failing to make any impact through the heavy, lined floor-length curtains. She let the thought that Ben was not her father consume her for some minutes and then consciously tried to grasp how this knowledge would actually change her life. Well, Ben would always be Dad; that was clear. But who was her real father? And could she find out? Catrin decided that although all this was awful, far more awful was her mother's possible betrayal of Ben. How could she? And then how could she go on playing happy families after doing such a thing? Most of all Catrin felt deceived; she'd always thought their relationship as a family was built on truth. Hadn't her parents always said to Tom and her there was nothing they could not ask them, nothing they could not discuss? Obviously truth was a one-way process in the Lewis household.

Catrin reached for the bedside lamp. She needed to contact people, needed to talk. At least that was clear to her. For the past week she'd lived in a bubble, the strangeness of the pre-funeral period with its endless round of visitors and tea and cake somehow making it inappropriate to hang out with friends, to text, to Facebook, to chat on the phone. She realised she'd had no contact, apart from a few brief text messages, with anyone outside her family for almost a week and suddenly she felt almost caged. To be fair no one had actually said she shouldn't meet up with her friends; it just somehow had seemed right to stay at home. But now she was desperate to talk to anyone who wasn't family

She got up and turned on her laptop to see who was online. An icon indicated Siân was up for a chat. Catrin was delighted her best friend was at her computer and did not bother to look at who else was currently logged on.

OMG Siân, Thanx for your txt, but I really need to talk, babe.

Catrin hit the keys with practised speed.

Hi Catz, soooooooooooooo sorry bout your gran – your txt didn't say much, you gutted? came Siân's immediate response.

Yeah, but there's something else, really need to see you.

You worried about your lead role in "The Wizard of Oz"? Oops I mean "Dewin Oz" – no, sorry I'm sticking to "The Wizard of Oz," sounds too strange in Welsh – well no need to worry; nobody's stolen your part and the chorus is still a shambles!

No, it's not that, I'll explain all later.

No worries but going to have tattoo this morning, cute swallow, back of neck – guess with your needle phobia you don't wanna come with me?

No way babe, meet you after?

Cool, I'll text you when I'm done, meet 4 hot choc in TG's?

Wicked x.

Catrin pulled on her skinny black jeans, comfy Uggs, and favourite Jack Wills red hoodie and fleetingly considered whether she should tell Siân of her suspicions after all. Siân did spend a lot of time at her house and would find it virtually impossible to pretend to Catrin's mother that she did not know or to hide her disdain. Catrin shrugged. Why should she worry about her mum? Hadn't she cheated on her father? He may

32

have been able to forgive but she couldn't. Really her mother deserved any fallout that came her way.

As she came downstairs she was aware the house was quiet. Lucky's basket in the kitchen was empty; she guessed her parents had taken him out for a walk. Tom always played football on a Sunday morning, football being the one thing he took very seriously indeed. Losing a match really upset him – be it with his own local five-a-side team or when his beloved Cardiff City played. When they were younger Catrin had teased him endlessly that 'it was just a game' but by now she realised it was far more. She even felt it herself when Wales won or lost. A win meant a great night out was guaranteed and the nation's collective good mood usually lasted at least a couple of days.

She felt a bit spooked at being in the house on her own so she grabbed her coat from the understairs cwtch, checked she had her phone, key and purse, left a message to say where she'd gone posted on the fridge and pulled the door tightly behind her. She stood outside her home on Pencisely Crescent trying to decide which way she'd walk into town. Assuming Siân wouldn't be done at the tattooist for at least a couple of hours she plumped for a longer route than necessary, turned right and headed for Victoria Park.

The park was almost empty. A few Sunday fathers loitered by the swings, pushing their offspring half-heartedly, keeping one hand in their pockets. She turned left as she left the park and walked quickly to generate some heat. At the junction with Cowbridge Road, a house – every inch of which seemed to be decorated with flashing Christmas lights – demanded she stop. Flashing fairies, gnomes in Santa hats fishing for presents, a Santa hung precariously from the roof, and another Santa twinkling and waving at her from his present-laden sledge, vied for attention. A red neon banner instructed her to 'Have Happy Holidays.' It struck Catrin how different Christmas would be this year, so very different from last year when everything had been fine, uncomplicated – before her

33

grandmother had been diagnosed with cancer and before the phrase 'not blood' had become so much part of her psyche. She hurried on, leaving the plastic Christmas trees and red and gold tinsel of the Cowbridge Road shops behind her, and turned into King's Road in affluent Pontcanna where the boutiques were decorated in restrained shades of white.

Crossing Cathedral Road she decided to walk along the river into town. The Sunday morning joggers breezed past her in their skimpy running vests; next she saw a couple of mothers multitasking – running with their buggies – while a third outdid them all as she had a buggy and a large, thin greyhound in tow. But Catrin paid them little attention as she tried to find the words to explain to Siân not only what her grandmother had told her but how she felt about it. She'd stick to the facts she decided; she needed to hear herself explain the situation, and then, maybe, how she felt about it would become clear to her.

Catrin and Siân had known each other since the day they had both started nursery school and had been best friends ever since. Certainly they were very different; Catrin was tall and blonde, Siân, short and dark. Catrin was the thoughtful one, Siân the gregarious half of the pair. They had other friends, of course, but over the years those friends had come and gone depending on which class they were in at school or what hobbies they were involved in. But the friendship between the two of them never waned, even when one of them had a boyfriend. In fact, Jonathan, Siân's current love, would often joke that he knew he came second to Catrin. He wasn't really joking.

There was no shelter along the river today as the wind blew bitterly through the skeletal trees. By the time she crossed the Taff Catrin felt almost anaesthetised. Her phone rang deep in her coat pocket and she struggled with numb hands to fish it out.

'Hi, Catz, spring has arrived,' a loud, cheery voice declared.

34

'Hi Siân, what are you talking about?'

'Doh! The Swallow, silly, it's done.'

'Ah, good, I think, where are you?'

'In TG's – how long will you be?'

'With you in five and I need a large double choc with cream and marshmallows.'

'Want or need?'

'Need.'

Catrin walked quickly past the castle and along the Hayes towards the glass-fronted St David's II shopping centre. She took the escalator up to the first floor to the accompaniment of a cacophony of 'White Christmas', 'Rudolph the Red-Nosed Reindeer', and 'Jingle Bells' escaping from the stores which opened onto the central hall. Catrin barely registered this, her head filled with what she had to tell her friend. Siân spotted her immediately and waved enthusiastically from the corner table of the busy cafe where she had just settled with two very large hot chocolates. Catrin could not help but smile. Siân's exuberance was always catching and now her petite friend engulfed her in a big hug then promptly pushed her away so Catrin was at the optimum distance to view the new tattoo.

'Oh, that looks painful.'

'No pain, no gain my friend; isn't she beautiful?'

'Mm,' Catrin mumbled non-committedly, sitting down and taking off her coat. She grabbed the hot chocolate in front of her, closing her eyes as its sweetness hit the back of her throat.

Her friend nudged her. 'Sooooooo, what's your big news?'

'You need to pinkie-promise first that you won't tell anyone else.'

Siân held out her hand and the two solemnly entwined their little fingers.

Catrin leaned towards her. 'Well, it's something my gran said; just before she died.'

'Whatever she said, Catz, I'm sure she wasn't trying to upset you. You know what your Gran was like; she didn't always have the edit switch on between her brain and her mouth.' Siân put her arm around Catrin and gave her shoulder a little squeeze. 'Remember the time when I spent all my birthday money on those black Goth clothes, had my hair spiked and everything, and she said I looked like Cruella de Vil?'

Catrin smiled. 'That was so typical of Gran. But this is different Siân.' Catrin paused and needlessly lowered her voice so it was almost a whisper. 'She said I was "not blood".'

For a second Siân was quiet amidst the cafe's late Sunday morning chaos of lively toddlers, stressed parents, and giggling teenage girls. 'Are you sure that's what she said? Did anyone else hear her?'

They huddled together as Catrin explained the scenario and her theory that it could only mean her mother had had an affair. Siân took a long sip of her hot chocolate and then gave it a vigorous stir to re-mix the milk and the chocolate which had begun to congeal at the bottom of the glass tumbler.

'Your mum and dad are the most together oldies I know Catz; I can't believe that's the explanation.'

They both sipped some more. Catrin could see Siân was thinking things through and suddenly she looked as she did in their maths class when she actually understood something that had long been a mystery to her. Her 'light-bulb moment' as she liked to describe it.

'There is another explanation.' Siân beamed.

Catrin looked at her incredulously. 'Which is?'

'Far more likely your dad was adopted; that would explain what your gran said.'

Catrin took a deep breath, paused for a second to check Siân's explanation was plausible and then enveloped her friend in a hug which developed into a sitting dance. She then burst into tears. Siân's shoulders absorbed most of the loud sobs but the clutch of girls at the next table stopped giggling for just long enough to glean they would not be finding out any time soon what had caused the outburst and then went back to their business. It was the toddler from two tables away tugging at Catrin's sweatshirt who eventually stopped her sobbing. Catrin looked down at his concerned face as he held out a brightly coloured sweet to her. 'Thank you,' she said, taking it and smiling at him as he hurried back to the safety of his mother's legs. Catrin briefly closed her eyes to shut out the audience that had just witnessed her little performance. When she opened them again Siân was the only one paying her any attention.

'You OK?'

'Totally, thank you so much; I'm so sorry, I don't know what came over me.'

Siân passed her a tissue from the pile at the bottom of her bag.

'Oh Catz, don't be so silly; you've had so much to deal with, what with your gran and then this stuff.'

'Siân, you are brilliant, thanks soooooooooooo much,' Catrin said, taking another mouthful of hot chocolate. 'It makes so much sense too. That explains why Dad's an only child.'

Siân sat back and smiled.

'I wonder why Dad never told us he was adopted?' Before Siân had a chance to respond, she went on, 'Oh my God, perhaps he doesn't know! Or maybe he does and he didn't want Gran to be embarrassed – she was like that wasn't she, didn't want to show any weaknesses. He would probably have told us eventually, now that Gran's gone.'

Catrin got up, finished her drink and, as she grabbed her coat, said quickly, 'I've got to go home now, I've been really mean to Mum, ignoring her and being so quick to think the worst of her. I'll make Sunday tea for everyone, flapjacks – Mum's favourites. You want to come?'

Siân wiped away the chocolate marks around Catrin's mouth and replied, 'Tempting, but I've promised to meet Jonathan in the Apple store to do some serious drooling and to show off my new swallow. I'll call you later.'

As soon as they parted outside the cafe Catrin began to run.

Suddenly she felt lighter as if she wanted to skip down the street. She couldn't wait to get home.

Jane sat on her mother-in-law's high metal bed and looked around the room. Lucky lay beside her, having wandered upstairs to investigate what she was doing. Jane knew the little spaniel sneaked in here whenever the door was left ajar. She stroked him gently. 'I know, Lucky, you really miss her, don't you?' The little dog licked her hand in response.

Well, Lucky might love this room, but to Jane it seemed not to belong to the rest of the house: its heavy oak chest of drawers, dressing table, and wardrobe, in contrast with the pale wooden furniture that was Jane's choice for the other rooms, made it feel small and dark. And it smelled different – of lavender and talcum powder and boiled sweets. Now she could get rid of all that. Jane had secretly fantasised about this moment for much of the last three years – ever since her mother-in-law's stroke had changed her household overnight.

The old woman had won then. She'd shamelessly played the emotional card and that could not be trumped. Pleading not to be sent into a nursing home, reminding Ben of how she'd virtually raised him as a single parent and of the generous gift she'd given them towards the deposit on this house. And Ben had folded, assuring Jane it would only be for a few months, until his mother was well enough to cope on her own again. But Granny Lewis had insisted that she be allowed to move Lucky, her bedroom furniture, and her grandfather clock in immediately and Jane had known that was it. And it had been. Until now.

So why was she not silently pleased? How Granny Lewis had irritated her in those first few months and Jane had struggled with yet another role – that of carer and caretaker of her mother-in-law's empty home, added to being a wife, mother, shop-worker, housekeeper and cook. She had been overwhelmed, both by the thought and by the reality. Ben had promised he would do the bulk of the caring, but his long

38

hours at the surgery inevitably meant that Jane was lumbered with seeing to his mother's practical needs – the feeding, the bed-baths, taking her to the toilet.

As her mobility and speech recovered Jane had fleetingly felt hopeful Granny Lewis might be persuaded to return to her own home. But she had pleaded to stay and Jane had succumbed, knowing she would have had no qualms about letting her own mother move in. Granny Lewis had quickly put her house on the market and the sale had gone through infuriatingly smoothly and quickly. Jane had believed things would get easier when Granny Lewis's health improved; in fact they had got worse. Despite it being her own wish Ben's mother was clearly frustrated about her loss of independence and sought to make sure everyone in her new household did things her way. Jane had found more and more reasons to stay out of her own home, until one night she found herself sitting on a park bench in the rain, waiting until either Catrin would be back from her drama class or the six o' clock news would be on to distract her mother-in-law. That was the night when all her pent-up venom had been released and Ben, shocked at her distress, and equally shocked that he had been oblivious to it, had taken her in his arms and assured her that she would always come first; that he would always take her side. Immediately she had felt better. She had started standing up to Granny Lewis, encouraging her once again to visit her chapel friends and attend the Sunday services and the concerts she so enjoyed, giving Jane some much-needed time alone in the house or with her family. She'd also suggested her mother-in-law might like to help with the ironing and the cleaning. The 'helping' had turned into more than that and Jane had felt grateful to her mother-in-law for taking charge of two chores she detested. Granny Lewis had continued to tackle both until the cancer had weakened her barely three months ago.

But still, sometimes, she'd resented having to share her home with her mother-in-law. How pathetic, how childish, she thought, as she started folding the clothes she had emptied from the wardrobe into a large suitcase. Jane had never expected to feel guilt or regret when it came to Ben's mother. Hadn't she given her a home, nursed her, attended to her physical needs? But, of course, she now recognised she could have done more, or at least done what she had done with more grace. Jane rubbed her eyes determinedly; she would not cry, that would be too self-indulgent. She would be crying for her own shortcomings rather than for Granny Lewis.

A few moments later Jane heard the front door open and her daughter's footsteps on the stairs. She called out. 'In here love, I'm sorting Granny's things.' She blew her nose and tucked the tissue up her sleeve. Catrin entered the room and hugged her so unexpectedly and so hard Jane was taken aback. When she was allowed up for air she said, 'What was that for?'

'For being the best mum in the world.'

Jane smiled at her.

'Oh Mum, you OK? Your eyes are red.'

Jane sniffed. 'I'm fine love; better now that you're here though.'

Catrin nodded and stroked Lucky who was fast asleep on his old mistress' bed.

'Your outing has done you good; Siân OK?'

'Siân is brilliant, Mum.' Catrin tugged open one of the dressing table's heavy drawers. 'Right, let me give you a hand.'

'Thank you Catz, that would make it much easier. I thought I'd do it while your dad's out. He went to watch Tom play football this morning and then they were both going to the Cardiff City game. And if I sort Granny's clothes out today I can take some with me to the shop tomorrow; I'm on the afternoon shift.'

'Are you sure Oxfam will want this?' Catrin laughed as she held up a flesh-coloured corset with stocking garters attached.

Jane smiled, glad to have her daughter's company and grateful Catrin seemed more herself than she had for days. She was also grateful for a little injection of humour into what she was finding to be an unexpectedly grim task.

'Well, someone wanting to dress up as Madonna might buy it; we always have people coming into the shop wanting all kinds of strange things for fancy dress.'

'It's more Nora Batty than Madonna,' Catrin said.

They spent the next hour going through drawers of carefully folded clothes smelling of mothballs and lavender as Lucky snored gently on the bed.

'Mum, do you think it would be OK if I kept this?' Catrin held up a black and beige dress circa 1970 – the label stating proudly that it was from Marks and Spencer and 100 per cent polyester.

'That's from when Marks and Spencer was just that; not your trendy M&S,' Jane said.

'Mum, I can hardly believe you put M&S and trendy in the same sentence.'

Jane laughed at her daughter's exaggerated grimace and told her to keep anything she wanted.

By the end of the afternoon Catrin had put aside the dress, a pussy-bow blouse, a Chanel-type jacket, a lavender-coloured wool cardigan that her grandmother had often worn, and a brooch shaped like a horseshoe made up of eight tiny creamy pearls.

'You know vintage is really in,' Catrin said from beneath a 1950s floral dress she was trying to pull over her head. 'Granny must have been tiny then; this is about a size eight.'

'I think people were smaller when your gran was your age; what with the war and rationing, and washing and cleaning everything by hand, I don't think there were many overweight people around. Even I would have been thin if I'd been born earlier!'

'Oh Mum, you're not fat; you're just cuddly.'

'Oh, my goodness, look at this. This is what your gran wore to our wedding. Look at the size of the shoulder pads. Do you remember those videos of *Dallas* I used to have? Well,

Granny Lewis looked like Sue Ellen and Granny Olwen – well she looked like Miss Ellie, all homely in a summer frock she'd bought in Ponty market. I tried to get them both to compromise but they were as stubborn as each other. Shoot me, please, if I behave like that when you get married!'

'Mum, I think talk of my wedding is a bit premature; I've got to find a boyfriend first.'

'And you will, love; all good things come to those who wait. And Catrin, love, I've waited a long time for a cup of tea.'

Catrin went downstairs to make them both a drink as her mum settled to empty yet another drawer of unopened handkerchief boxes. The relief she felt at getting back to normal with her mother was immense. She wanted to tell her mum about her grandmother's revelation that she was 'not blood'. Now was a good time, she reasoned, with her father and Tom out of the way. But she was reluctant to bring up the subject for fear of spoiling the atmosphere. As she stirred two sweeteners into her mother's tea she decided to broach the subject. Tomorrow her mother would be back at work, she would be in school, and communication would revert to a series of notes on the fridge saying where they had gone, what time supper might be, requests to get milk, or to feed or walk Lucky.

Too late. She heard her dad and Tom at the front door. Tom was laughing; the Bluebirds had obviously won. They came into the kitchen.

'Hi Catz, oh brilliant timing, you just making tea? Usual for me please.'

Catrin threw two more teabags into the pot and topped up with water. Tom put a couple of overfilled shopping bags on the counter as their father cleared the piled up Sunday papers from the table to make room for their mugs.

'Really, Tom, do we need to have three different Sunday papers delivered? That's a couple of trees we don't read every week.'

42

Tom shrugged and shouted up the stairs. 'Mum, tea's ready. Are you coming down? It will be worth your while; Dad's bought a very expensive cake.'

'Oh, I was going to make flapjacks, but I can do them next Sunday,' Catrin said, unwrapping the black forest gateau from its fancy box.

Their dad turned towards Tom. 'What happens on tour, stays on tour.'

'No chance, Dad,' Tom scoffed, cutting the cake and picking up a piece in his hand.

Jane appeared with Lucky at her heels and gratefully took her mug of tea from Catrin.

'What's this about cake? You know you're not allowed any, Ben. One word, Big Ben Lewis – cholesterol.'

'Oh, come on Jane, a little bit won't hurt, and anyway we're celebrating the Bluebirds return to form, four-nil, back of the net!'

Jane cut herself a slice of cake and placed it carefully on a plate. 'Great, well done the boys,' she said and closed her eyes as she took a bite of the gateau. 'Mmm, this is seriously good cake and I deserve a treat.'

'But why did you say very expensive cake, Tom?' Catrin asked.

'Oh you know what Dad's like. We got to the till – can you believe it they had about twenty tills open and we still had to queue for ten minutes; you'd think people had better things to do on a Sunday afternoon. Anyway, at the till the cashier said the total was £11.23. And Dad, having done his usual thing of calculating how much the bill was going to come to unbelievably said, "I don't think that's right, it should be £21.98." So embarrassing. If Dad had just paid up and shut up we'd now be eating free food.'

'But that would be stealing, Tom,' their father chipped in, cutting himself a very generous piece.

'But it was their mistake, and anyway they're a huge company; your £10 is nothing to them – it's not like they are a small corner shop or anything.'

'The principle is still the same, Tom, stealing is stealing whoever you do it from.'

'And there's no such thing as a free lunch, Tom,' their mother added. 'It would cost you – it would be on your conscience for evermore.'

'Well I'll have another piece anyway, seeing as it's all free for me – whether it's Dad or the supermarket paying for it!' Tom grinned, cherry jam oozing out from the corner of his mouth.

'Maybe, Jane, it's time we changed the locks,' their dad suggested, giving Tom a nudge.

Chapter Four

Returning to school the next day was harder than Catrin could have imagined. Seeing friends and teachers for the first time since her grandmother's death was upsetting and she found her eyes welling up several times as people commiserated with her. And the nicer people were, the more she cried. Her tearful reaction took her aback as the previous day she had felt life was getting back to normal.

Between catching up with the notes she had missed and rehearsals for the end-of-term musical, the rest of the week was hectic. As they walked home on the Friday afternoon Catrin took Siân's arm and told her she felt she'd turned a corner and things were on the up once more. She was also excited because her mother had found out the previous day there was an Open Day at Aberystwyth University that weekend and was going to take her there to have a look around. It was one of the universities Catrin was considering for next year. The friends parted at the entrance to Victoria Park and Catrin walked home through the park thinking about what she would wear the next day. She thought maybe her red skinny jeans and her new Topshop block-coloured tunic would look good but then she realised she'd probably have to meet some of the lecturers too and perhaps something less bright might be better, as being invisible was preferable to having to make conversation with some well-meaning tutor. But she did want to look cool; after all some of her fellow visitors might well turn out to be her coursemates come September and first impressions were important. By the time she reached home and had been through several virtual costume changes she'd decided on her favourite black skinny jeans, biker boots, and her long grey snakeskin-patterned jumper with her camel duffel coat. She felt pleased she'd sorted that out so she could spend the rest of the evening giving herself a manicure, painting her nails and watching her favourite soaps.

The house was quiet. Lucky leapt up to greet her, wagging his tail with such enthusiasm she knew he hadn't seen anyone else for hours. She turned expectantly to the fridge to find three notes: one in big block capitals from Tom saying – 'GONE OUT,' one from her mum saying 'Gone to Zumba, extra class!!! back 6ish. 1st in pl put pots in oven x.' and one in her dad's untidy scrawl saying 'No pots for me. Curry with the boys!!!!'

Catrin explained to the little dog still scuttling around her legs that she needed to get the jacket potatoes going before she took him for a nice short walk, clarifying the need for a brief outing by listing all the beautifying procedures that had to be achieved ahead of tomorrow's visit to Aberystwyth. Lucky, his head cocked to one side as if listening intently, wagged his tail enthusiastically and circled around her feet until she grabbed his lead. They did a short circuit of the surrounding streets and returned to the house. Catrin wiped Lucky down, gave him a fresh drink of water and a treat and rushed upstairs; she'd start with a mud face mask while she had the house to herself and did not risk frightening anyone. By 6.30 p.m., when she heard her mum crunch up the path, the trays were laid and the smell of cooking potatoes filled the kitchen.

'Hi love, I'm home. A bit late. I did some shopping on the way back from class.' Her mum struggled through the door carrying two large bags of groceries and two dry-cleaning hangers from which hung a couple of Ben's sports jackets. She looked flushed, her short dark hair, still damp from the exertions of the class, clinging to her round face.

'*Emmerdale*'s on in twenty minutes Mum, I thought we'd have supper on trays; we can watch it in peace for once, as the boys aren't here to mock us.'

'Where are they then?' her mother asked.

Catrin pointed with her newly polished blue nails towards

the fridge.

'I'm guessing they're not in the fridge, Catz!'

'You're in a good mood Mum but alas it won't last. Dad's gone on the razzle and I don't know where Tom is; out with his mates I guess.'

Her mother looked at the notes and sighed. 'Oh, well, the potatoes smell good, you happy with ham and cheese filling and some salad to go with it?' She donned an apron.

'Perfect Mum, thanks. I'd help but I've just done my nails. How was Zumba?'

'Hell, horrible, hot.' She added brightly, 'but it means I've earned a piece of cheesecake for afters.'

Catrin continued to admire her nails. 'Oh Mum, you know you hate exercise. Wouldn't it be easier to give up both – puds and Zumba? They just cancel each other out.'

'You know me and my sweet tooth Catz, so hell and heaven it is – and tonight my particular bit of heaven comes with a scrummy strawberry topping.'

Catrin awoke before dawn on the Saturday morning. She lay there for a while, enjoying the warmth of her bed as she cuddled Big and Little Ted, trying to organise in her head the things she wanted to get out of this trip to Aberystwyth. She wanted to see the department and where she would have her lectures. She wanted to check out the choice of accommodation and she wanted to look around the library, Students Union and the town itself – to see where the students shopped and where they partied. And she really did want to speak to some of the students. She'd looked at the website and prospectus of course, and it all seemed great, but she knew that these were written by slick marketing experts and she wanted the students' own viewpoints.

The house was still quiet but there was no way she could go back to sleep. She got up and showered, dried and plaited her long blonde hair and pulled on the outfit she had carefully set out the night before. She sat at her desk to put on a coat of

47

mascara and a slash of red lipstick, tilting the mirror towards the light. Out of the corner of her eye she saw her gran watching her. Granny Lewis –the only stern-faced one in the photograph of the family taken at Tom's graduation. Catrin picked up her gran's pearl horseshoe brooch and pinned it to the collar of her coat. She got up to survey the finished look in her long bedroom mirror, wiped off some of the lipstick and, satisfied, smiled at her reflection. Then she took off her boots and coat and wandered downstairs.

As soon as she came into the kitchen Catrin knew there was something wrong. The room was still dark with the curtains drawn but the air was distinctly cold and she could hear something banging against a hard surface. Her heart beating loudly she felt for the light switch.

'Oh,' her father groaned, as the light hit his eyes. He was slumped at the kitchen table, nursing his head in his hands, the back door open behind him

'You OK, Dad?'

'Mmmm, I over did it,' he mumbled.

'It's freezing in here.'

'Sorry love, I had to let Lucky out – and I thought if I left the door open he'd be able to wander back in.'

'Poor you, Dad. Cup of tea?'

'Coffee, black please, and a couple of paracetamol too; need to get better before your mum comes down.'

'Too late, Big Ben, I've clocked you,' her mum said from the doorway

He groaned again, slowly lifted his head and propped his elbows on the table. He rested his head on his upturned palms. 'Morning, Jane, my love – too much Brains.'

'Not enough brains and too much Brains beer, I'd say, Ben. This little outing won't help your cholesterol test on Monday. So until then, Ben Lewis, it's water and salad for you – and no dressing.'

Her father winced as her mother flung back the curtains, the metal rings grating on the pole, and banged the back door shut.

'Honestly Jane, it will make no difference; little binges have no effect,' he said wearily.

Catrin handed him a mug of black coffee, a pint of water and the paracetamol as Tom came into the kitchen in his football kit.

'Big night, Dad – you shot away?'

'And he's got his cholesterol test coming up on Monday,' their mother muttered.

'Shouldn't Catz have that test too now? I had it at eighteen and of course it proved that I'm perfect.'

Their mother glanced at Catrin. 'Stop stirring, Tom,' she said sharply.

'I'm not having it,' Catrin said, glaring at her brother, 'I've told you before no one is sticking needles into me.'

'Well sis, look at it like this, a needle's not going to kill you but sky-high cholesterol could.'

Catrin was suddenly conscious of the throbbing pulse in her neck. She would never admit it to Tom but she often worried about the possibility she had inherited their father's health problems. She knew her father's father had died of a heart attack when his son was quite young, she knew her father had high cholesterol, and sometimes she lay awake worrying that she would just drop dead from this undiagnosed problem. She was morbidly drawn to reading magazine articles about young people who died unexpectedly and she sometimes even imagined her own death and the thousands who would leave comments on her Facebook page mourning her tragic loss. The throbbing eased slightly as it dawned on her that, if her dad was adopted, the fact her grandfather had died of a heart attack would have no direct impact on her health, and having one relative prone to high cholesterol was surely not as significant as having two.

'OK, love. I'll just have a quick coffee and then we'll go,' her mother said as she took the car keys from the pottery bowl on the windowsill. 'Are you almost ready?'

Catrin nodded. Really she needed time to think this through; there were just so many implications if her father was adopted. Tomorrow, she promised herself, she would try to get her head around it.

'I'm going in the Volvo, Ben, just in case we have snow, you never know. You'll have to use my car today.'

'I'm sorry I can't come with you,' he said, now gingerly holding his head up but still cradling his pint of water. 'I'm on call tonight and I don't think we'd get back from Aberystwyth in time for the start of my shift. I'm afraid I couldn't get any of the other GPs to swop with me – they're all on Christmas shopping duty this weekend.'

'Don't worry Dad, I'll tell you all about it when I come back.'

'I won't pretend I'm sorry I can't come,' Tom laughed, cramming two bananas, a family-size Galaxy bar and a bottle of Lucozade into his sports bag.

'Have you got the satnav, Jane?' her dad asked.

'Yes thanks, and sandwiches, a thermos, torch and flare,' she replied.

'Mmm, very funny, but you know what you're like; anywhere north of Merthyr is North Wales to you.'

'Thank you for that Captain Cook.' She dropped a kiss on his lips.

'Uh, guys, very very gross,' Tom commented, grabbing his football and making for the door with his fingers in his mouth and making loud vomiting noises.

Catrin went back upstairs thinking how strange it was her gran would not be there to hear the news when they got back. Of everyone in her family Granny Lewis was the one who had valued education the most. Catrin put on her boots and coat, touched the little brooch, and fixed a smile on her face. She really didn't want to allow herself to become upset now or she'd have to re-do her makeup. But she would make a point of phoning Granny Olwen tomorrow to tell her all about it, even though she knew Granny O would far rather she go to secretarial college or do a beautician or hairdressing course – nice 'ladylike jobs' as she would say. Catrin bristled – really she could think of nothing worse. She could see these jobs would appeal to lots of girls but not to her.

The journey over the Beacons that Saturday morning was glorious. It never ceased to amaze Catrin that the Brecon Beacons National Park was so close to the industrial town of Merthyr Tydfil. Just a couple of miles north of Merthyr the landscape changed dramatically, everything was green and lush, beautiful and natural. It was, of course, people who had spoilt the Valleys. Without the infrastructure of so-called civilization – the mean little houses, the utilitarian factories and, latterly, the American-style out-of-town shopping centres with their dreary architecture, Merthyr would be beautiful too.

Today, the view from Storey Arms was breathtaking. It had been a frosty night and the silvery-white roadside verges glistened in the weak winter sun. The patchwork of fields spread for miles in front of them, the valley floor a rich green, with hues of lighter green, topped by a faint dusting of snow, on the surrounding hillside. Jane pulled into a lay-by. They were not alone. Tens of motorbike riders in their black leathers huddled around a van serving tea and burgers, some gazing at the far-reaching view, some admiring each other's bikes, but all exhaling little bursts of white breath, hands cupped around their warming mugs.

'Shall we have a coffee? And a burger? I'm starving – no breakfast and I didn't see you eat anything either.'

'Do we have enough time, Mum? The campus tour starts at two o'clock.'

'The satnav says it will take us another hour and a half. Factor in another hour to get lost and to find a parking space, so we've plenty of time.'

'How about we share a burger, Mum?'

'Very sensible, Catrin; that will only be 200 calories each!'

They set off again, Catrin feeling a little sick. Her mother was quiet, obviously concentrating on the road. She rarely drove, choosing to walk to work, take the train up to Treorchy, and let Catrin's dad drive when they were going out together. Leaving Merthyr and the dual carriageway her mum turned the radio off; 'too distracting' she explained. Catrin too was happy to travel in silence. She looked out of the window as they climbed over the Pumlumon range, revelling in the barren beauty and wilderness. A couple of kites soared overhead, swirling to reveal flashes of white wing and russet body. Huge, but graceful and elegant, Catrin was mesmerised as more and more of the birds circled high above the road; she tried to log every detail; tomorrow she'd have a go at drawing them. The sign told them they were ten miles from Aberystwyth and Catrin's stomach gave a little lurch. And then they turned the corner and had their first glimpse of the town in the distance, nestling in a deep valley, surrounded by mountains and edged by the sea.

'Wow, what a beautiful approach.' Catrin glanced at her mother who was frowning at the road ahead.

'It's very twisty, all these bends. I hope it's not like this all the way down.'

It was. Well for at least six of the ten miles until they reached the valley floor where the forested slopes gave way to rich green pasture. For the last couple of miles they were accompanied by a slow-moving river, it too sensing its journey was almost done. Catrin opened the window a little so she could smell the sea. It made her think happy thoughts, of holidays and Granny Lewis. She smiled and felt better, less nervous.

A banner proclaiming: 'Aberystwyth: Probably the Best Place in the World to be a Student' was draped across a roundabout as they entered the town. A big boast for a small place, she thought.

By the end of the afternoon she was convinced the banner was right. She'd enjoyed the visit to the Art Department which was housed in a fine Edwardian building. The lecturers had been cool, probably selected because they were so, and none had asked her embarrassing questions. She'd talked to current students who raved about the friendliness of the place; she'd walked with her mother around town and got a feel for just how visible the student population was among the locals and she'd fallen in love with the Pantycelyn Hall of Residence. She hadn't expected to. It had no en-suite rooms and the kitchens only had two cooking rings but it had a canteen and a student lounge and it was just so 'old school,' as she explained to her mother, it was perfect. Her mum suggested it was a little bit Hogwarts.

Driving out of Aberystwyth that evening Catrin smiled as she mentally ticked university choice off her list of things to do. Now feeling sleepy and warm with the Volvo's heater set to maximum, she allowed her thoughts to drift back to her grandmother's claim she was not a blood relative. She was well aware she had used her gran's funeral as a reason for not doing anything with the information. And for the past week she'd decided to ignore it until she'd made the biggest decision of her life so far – where she wanted to spend the next three years. Now it was time to ask her mum what she knew about her father's adoption. She glanced at her. Her mother's profile was lit up now and again by the passing orange street lights. She turned, aware that Catrin was looking at her.

'It's been a lovely day, Catz.'

'Mmm, Aberystwyth is definitely where I want to come. I'll have to work really hard though to get the grades. Mum?'

'Yes, love?'

'Thanks for taking me today.' Catrin suddenly felt too tired to broach the subject. She'd ask her mother another time.

By the time they got to Ponterwyd Catrin was fast asleep.

Jane concentrated on the road ahead. By now they were again in open country, climbing steadily towards the lonely hills of Pumlumon, which in the dark felt very eerie indeed. She could sense the hills closing in on her and the thought that, if the car

53

broke down, there would probably be no mobile phone signal caused her to press even harder on the accelerator. She wasn't used to driving without any street lights to help her but was glad Catrin could not see her face. She was already thinking ahead to September and how she would feel when Catrin left home. She'd missed Tom of course, when he went to Bristol University, but somehow that wasn't the same. Tom spent most of his time playing sport with either his friends or with Ben; it was Catrin who came shopping with her, Catrin who enjoyed sharing nights in with a DVD or watching the soaps. And Aberystwyth seemed so far and so foreign. She knew if she said this out loud she would sound ridiculous even to herself. But then she had always lived within twenty miles of where she'd been born. Brought up in Treorchy, in the Rhondda Valley, she remembered the fuss her mother had made when she'd said she was moving to Cardiff. Even now, a quarter of a century later, her mother very rarely came to the city except to spend a few days with them over Christmas and for birthday parties. Jane would instead go up to Treorchy or they would meet halfway, in Pontypridd, on a Saturday morning – her mother travelling down the valley by train. Pontypridd was where Olwen's valley ended and, like her mother before her, she felt little desire to wander beyond it. The ritual was always the same. They would browse around the market, Olwen would buy some home-cooked ham and faggots and then they'd have a beef dinner in Giovanni's. The menu never changed.

Catrin felt a huge relief at finally having decided she wanted to study Fine Art at Aberystwyth. Over the last few weeks she had toyed with applying to several universities and had gradually whittled them down. Firstly she'd determined this was a good opportunity to sample life in a more rural area. After considering a few universities in England she'd decided such a move was too scary and that had eliminated several others. Now, with the UCAS form in front of her, she resolutely entered Aberystwyth as her first choice. She'd finally settled on the Mid-Wales town for two main reasons. The first was she knew no one else going there, so she would be able to reinvent herself as anything she pleased, and secondly Aberystwyth was a Welsh-speaking area and she was curious to live life in Welsh Wales – really live it, not just visit for a fortnight's holiday. Up until now Welsh had primarily been her language of education and, although she and her friends spoke it together in class, once the teachers were out of earshot they all reverted to English. She felt excited at the prospect but apprehensive too. During the morning she had wobbled. Should she stick to what she knew? Siân was going to Swansea to study languages. Swansea had a good Art department; would she be better off going there? At least she'd be guaranteed one friend and it would be far easier to come home for the weekend.

Both Siân and Tom had questioned her reasons for choosing Aberystwyth – Siân asking with a laugh why on earth she would want to reinvent herself – and as what exactly? – to which of course she did not have an answer. Tom had asked why she wanted to 'fuss with that stupid, outdated language, anyway?' and had said language was just a means of communication and that, as everyone understood English, there was no reason to bother with Welsh. She had tried to argue that language was more than that. That it allowed the speaker a different perspective on the world and access to another precious stack of literature. And that Welsh was an ancient, beautiful, and rich language.

His response had been typical Tom. 'Look, it's a useless language but let's just see how wonderfully rich it is, shall we? So, what's the Welsh for caravan? – oh yes, it's 'carafan'; what's the Welsh for bus? – mmm, 'bws'; what's the Welsh for radio? – well, surprise, surprise, it's 'radio'. Point proven.'

But she had stuck to her guns. As she popped her application to UCAS in the postbox on this cold Sunday in December she felt relieved she had completed the application and could forget about it until next summer. Now it was time to concentrate on other things and in particular what Granny Lewis's statement that she was not blood actually meant.

Chapter Five

The school week had been a busy one with endless rehearsals for *The Wizard of Oz*. There were to be three performances and, with just days to go before opening, Catrin had spent most of her time in the school's music room. Not that she minded, in fact she loved every minute of it. This would be her eighth musical and she never tired of the rehearsals, the costume fittings or the make-up sessions. As for the performances themselves, they always left her on an exhausted high. There had been stiff competition for all the lead roles this time and she was delighted to have been cast as Dorothy. But today she'd woken up with a sore throat. This was the last thing she needed; there was no way she was going to let Loud Louise, her understudy, steal her role now. Thank goodness it was Sunday and she could rest for a while and 'dose herself up' as Granny Olwen would say. She'd do some drawing and finally ask her mum 'the question'.

As she lay there looking up at her colourful ceiling she could hear her family downstairs in the kitchen. What were the implications if Ben wasn't a Lewis by birth after all? Catrin pulled the duvet up to her chin as an unwelcome shiver shot through her body. She had never thought about it before but she now realised she liked knowing her grandparents had been born in Llangrannog, that both her great-grandfathers on the Lewis side had been ship captains. Her grandmother had told her stories of their perilous journeys from the little West Wales village to romantic sounding ports such as Valparaiso and Rio, their sloops laden with herring on the way out and lime for the local farmers on the homeward journey. If her dad had no blood connection to these grandfathers, whom he had never actually known, then really there was no link between them and her. The thought saddened her. The stories she so treasured might not be her family's stories after all; they didn't belong to her. She felt strangely bereft, robbed.

Really she did not want to ask 'the question' at all. Her stomach did a little flip just at the thought. But she knew she could not forget what her grandmother had said and it would go round and round in her head until she knew the truth. Nor could she stay in bed all morning. She threw back the duvet, tugged on her jeans, a grey T-shirt and her gran's lavender cardigan. As she pulled it on she smelled *Tweed* perfume, her gran's favourite. She looked at herself in the mirror and, despite her anxiety, smiled as she felt the cosy cardi give her a big hug. She remembered the last time she'd seen Gran in it. It must have been late summer before she had fallen ill with cancer. Catrin could picture her throwing a ball to Lucky in their back garden and leaning down to pat him as he brought it back, dripping. Catrin felt a huge sense of relief she could remember her gran like that; not tiny and lifeless as she had been in those last few days.

Her timing was perfect, she thought with satisfaction, as she came into the kitchen and saw her mother tackling a pile of washing up at the sink and her father and Tom about to leave: her dad to play golf and Tom to play football. The feeling of satisfaction quickly turned to trepidation as she realised she would have no excuse not to ask 'the question'.

Her dad smiled at her. 'You look nice, love, not usually a colour you wear, purple. Suits you.'

'Thanks, Dad, but it's lavender; it's Gran's,' Catrin said.

'Uh, spooky, wearing a dead person's clothes.' Tom made a face.

'Don't be silly Tom, lots of the clothes we sell in the shop are given to us because someone's died,' their mother said sharply.

'Well I hope you've at least washed it, sis.'

'No and I'm not going to; it smells of Granny; it's nice.' Catrin felt her chin tremble as she struggled to control a sudden sob that came from nowhere.

'You are seriously weird,' Tom said, circling his finger in the air to emphasise the point.

'Weird and very wonderful,' she replied, smiling determinedly. And you'll get to see just how wonderful on Thursday night.'

'What's happening Thursday?' he asked.

'Opening night of the school musical starring the one and only Catrin Lewis!' She did a little twirl and bowed. 'So shall I get you three tickets?'

'Oh, of course, how could I forget? Your "Over the Rainbow" – or whatever it's called in Welsh –sounds great in the shower but count me out, thanks; I'll be washing my hair,' her brother said, pulling his fingers through his very short crop.'

'Well nothing will keep me away,' their father said.

'Me neither,' their mother agreed.

'You two sure? It's all in Welsh as usual, don't know how much of it you'll understand,' Catrin said, knowing full well they had come to every show in which she'd ever performed, however minor her part, and usually to more than one performance.

'Wouldn't miss it for the world,' her mother said.

'Can't wait.' Her father nodded.

'OK Dad, you ready? Tom asked, 'could you drop me off at the AstroTurf?'

'No problem son. OK see you two later. Bye.' He and Tom went out the back door

Her mother piled the last saucepan on top of the dishes on the already overfull draining board, wiped her hands on her apron and settled down with a large mug of tea, spreading the Sunday papers out in front of her. 'Ah, I've missed this, you know Catrin, my Sunday morning routine, with all that's happened in the last few weeks.' She sighed with contentment. 'But I still feel guilty – even though your gran's not here any more to tell me off. Do you remember, Catz, how she'd walk in, tutting, and ask pointedly if there was anything she could do to get the Sunday lunch underway?'

Catrin nodded as she dawdled at the sink, stirring the honey into her hot lemon drink until every last bit had dissolved. She looked out at the garden and said, 'Mum?'

'Yes love?'

'Gran said something very strange just before she died. She said I was like her, but ...' Catrin took a deep breath. 'Well, what she actually said was, "so like me, as if you were my own blood". What did she mean?'

Her mother slowly put her glasses down. She closed the paper and tidied the different supplements into a neat pile, placing them carefully at the corner of the table. Catrin could tell she was stalling for time and a deep dread washed over her. Instinctively she knew the explanation was not going to be as simple as Siân had suggested.

'Catrin love, come and sit down'

One look at her mother's crumpled face confirmed Catrin was not going to like what she was about to hear. For a brief moment she wished she could rewind time. Her mum shuffled up on the bench to make room for her but Catrin opted to sit in her usual place on the other side. She felt her face flush as she looked at her mother, whose pale complexion was now ashen.

'I'm so sorry, Dad and I – we should have told you before. We always meant to tell you, but ...' her mother trailed off.

'Tell me what, Mum?'

'Technically your gran was right; your dad is not your biological father.'

Catrin felt as if she'd just crashed into a wall. Her first response to her grandmother's words had been right after all. She felt another deep flush creep up from her chest. 'You had an affair?' Her voice seemed to have deserted her and she hardly heard the question herself.

Her mum gulped. 'No, no, of course not. I could never –'

Catrin's mobile rang in her pocket, the tune of 'Somewhere over the Rainbow' sounding loud and shrill. Her hands were trembling, useless, unable to hit the right icon. She eventually managed to silence the phone; she did not recognise the number. At that moment Siân walked through the back door. 'Hi, you two, it's very calm in here, no boys?'

'Golf. Football.' Her mother jumped to her feet. 'Cuppa?'

'No thanks, Jane,' Sian replied, 'I just need Catz here to tell me everything she knows about the Impressionist painters – preferably in words of one syllable.' She added, 'dreaded essay' by way of explanation.

'You could have just phoned me,' Catrin frowned at her.

Siân laughed nervously and took a step backwards, feeling for the door handle behind her. 'I've obviously called at a bad time. No probs, I'll call you later, Catrin. I'm seeing Jonathan at seven so I'll ring you before then.'

But before Siân could make her escape Catrin's mother had grabbed her arm. 'Don't be silly, Siân, you're here now, and you know you're always welcome. Coffee? I've made some biscuits, chocolate chip or lemon, which would you prefer? Tom says they're both good but as you know he's not that choosy – tell you what, I'll put both out and you can decide. Or there's some fruit cake if you prefer, not fresh today mind, but it gets better, more moist, after a few days anyway.'

'No, no really, Jane, I'm fine.'

Catrin considered insisting her mum continue with the explanation Siân had unwittingly interrupted, but, close as she was to Siân, Catrin knew she wanted to digest the news herself first, to sort out how she felt about it before letting someone else's response influence hers. So instead she glared at her mother, pulled Siân free from her grip and led her out of the room and up the stairs.

'There was a very strange atmosphere in the kitchen just now. What's wrong, Catrin?' Siân asked as soon as Catrin closed the bedroom door behind them.

Catrin sighed. 'Something I will tell you about, but not now,' she replied firmly. 'So Impressionists.'

'Look, Catz, if you've got a book I can borrow I'll just get out of your way.'

'No, really, Siân, I'd be glad of the distraction; I need a bit of time away from Mum to get my head around something.'

Catrin settled at her desk and switched her laptop on. As it was coming to life she pulled a chair up for Siân and her friend sat down. 'I'm sure there will be lots of useful info on here about the Impressionists and far easier than ploughing through books. We'll be able to download some images too, really impress Mr Jenkins.'

Catrin pushed the laptop closer to Siân and let her friend do the work of trawling through the various websites as she sat back and tried to take in the information her mother had already given her.

As soon as the girls disappeared upstairs Jane slumped at the table. She had occasionally imagined this moment but it was never like this; it was always Ben and her sitting Catrin down and talking to her at a time of their choosing. She'd had years to prepare so how come she was still at a loss what to say when Catrin asked her to explain Granny Lewis's words? She would just have to tell Catrin the whole story and hope she would understand.

Tom had been two and a half years old when she and Ben had decided they wanted to have another baby. She'd fallen very quickly with Tom and assumed it would be the same the second time round. After six months she'd found herself becoming more and more obsessed with becoming pregnant and decided Mother Nature needed some help. Every morning she'd taken her temperature, religiously plotting changes on a chart and insisting their lovemaking coincided with the significant dip. Then she'd changed their diet, having read somewhere that pumpkin seeds and oysters were good for fertility, replaced their orange juice at breakfast with pomegranate juice which they both hated and made Ben wear loose pants. She'd constantly looked at other people's babies and trailed around Mothercare planning what she would buy when she did became pregnant. She'd sobbed when friends announced excitedly they were expecting. She remembered confiding in her mother-in-law who had called one day to find her cuddling Tom, tears streaming down her face. Granny Lewis had promptly told her to concentrate on the little boy she had rather than on the child she didn't. Ben had tried to reassure her, saying he saw lots of patients in the practice who had trouble conceiving and that most had fallen pregnant in the end. After a year she'd begun nagging him to arrange some tests for them. He'd protested, saying they'd had Tom without any help and it was only a matter of time and relaxing into it; they should just enjoy practising a lot. But eventually he'd agreed, telling her he did not really expect the tests to show up any problems and he hoped hearing everything was well would make her relax and give up the regimentation that was threatening to take over their lives.

The day Ben had come home with the letter stating his sperm count was very low marked a shift in their relationship. Although she'd felt devastated at the results, she'd felt relieved to know what the problem was and probably, if she was totally honest, relieved the problem wasn't hers. Ben had just felt devastated. She remembered trying to hurry Tom into his bed that night, eager to talk to Ben about what they should do and her disappointment when Ben was reluctant to talk and even more reluctant to make any plans. He took the stance he probably had always had a low count but Tom's very existence proved that having a child was not impossible and they could get lucky a second time. It had taken another year of zinc overload, lovemaking timetables, and a very broody Jane to persuade Ben there had to be an alternative.

When Siân left about an hour later Jane was still sitting at the kitchen table. She heard the front door shut and moments later Catrin came into the kitchen and set about making herself another hot lemon drink, the first one having gone cold undrunk.

'I'd like a fresh one please, Catrin,' Jane said, not really wanting a drink but wanting to say something normal, something ordinary, that would reassure Catrin, and herself, that fundamentally nothing had changed. Something to convey to her daughter that everyday life would carry on as ever, despite everything.

She waited until Catrin had placed two fresh mugs in front of them and was again sitting at the table and then said gently, 'You know your father loves you hugely but it turns out he was infertile and we needed a little help to have you so you were conceived with donor sperm.'

Catrin said nothing for what seemed to Jane a very long time, her gaze fixed on the newspaper in front of her. Then she lifted her head and said very quietly, 'And Tom too?'

Jane knew her answer would be another blow.

'No love, Tom arrived before we were aware there was a problem; maybe something happened after Tom was conceived or maybe Dad's always had the problem and we were just lucky with Tom.'

Another silence.

'So do you know who the donor was?'

Jane moved to sit beside her daughter, putting an arm around her. She felt the thin shoulders tense under her touch. 'No, all I know is he was a very kind man who allowed us to have the most wonderful daughter.'

Catrin sipped her drink. Then very slowly she said, 'This is such a big thing to get my head around; suddenly my dad's not my dad and Tom's my half-brother.'

Jane's reaction came out in a rush, as if the sentence had been scripted, well-rehearsed. Subconsciously she realised it probably had. 'Family is more than just genes, love. Nothing has really changed.'

'They have, Mum; they have for me.' Catrin got up abruptly, grabbed Lucky's lead and the little dog shuffled out of his basket and followed her out of the door.

It was raining hard and getting dark when Ben and Tom

arrived home to find Jane standing anxiously by the kitchen window. Beside her was Lucky. Ben took one look at his wife's pale face and felt the colour drain from his own as Jane explained what had happened and that Lucky had returned home without his lead and without Catrin.

'Where on earth can she be?' he said for what seemed to be the hundredth time. 'Tom, you try her from your mobile; see if she'll answer you.'

'I'm sorry; the person you called is unavailable. Please try later.' Tom held out the phone so his parents could hear the message. 'I'll text her, Dad.'

'Thanks Tom,' Ben replied, already dialling Siân's phone number. It was Siân's father who answered.

'Oh, hi, it's Ben Lewis here, Catrin's father. Look I'm sorry to be ringing you on a Sunday evening but Catrin doesn't happen to be there with Siân, does she?'

'Sorry Ben, haven't seen sight nor sound of them. I think our Siân's over at Jonathan's; don't expect she'll be in much before midnight.'

'Ah, ah I see ... sorry, what time did you say you expected Siân back from her boyfriend's house?'

'Well, her mum and I say she should come in by ten, she says two, so usually it's a compromise, somewhere around twelve. Mind you, I think that's far too late, especially when there's school the next day. But Siân tells me they all stay out late so what can you do? Now when I was that age I was on the six o' clock shift, and my dad ...'

'Yes, well, if Catrin happens to turn up at yours perhaps you'd ask her to give us a ring?'

'Will do, mate.'

'Thank you, and sorry again to have disturbed you. Goodnight.'

Ben replaced the receiver and turned towards Jane and Tom to explain Catrin was not at Sian's. But one look at their concerned faces told him they knew already.

He could remember feeling like this once before. Catrin

had been about two and a half and, because of her protests at the unfairness of being confined to her buggy while her brother walked free, he'd let her out in Marks and Spencer after she had solemnly promised not to wander off. He'd turned for a moment to look at the coat Jane was holding up against Tom and in that moment Catrin had disappeared. He remembered his panic as he scanned the shop for his little girl, desperately aiming for every small person dressed in pink. In the end she'd been found hiding under a rack of clothes and, as he scooped her up, he'd sworn he would never let her out of his sight again. But of course he had had to and as she grew up he'd had to step back, forcing himself to allow her increasing independence. He smiled wryly as he remembered the first day she had been allowed to walk to school on her own and how he'd followed her to make sure she arrived safely, hiding behind pillars and posts so she would not notice the surveillance.

Now he found himself making silent pacts – if she comes back safe I'll never tease her about her soap opera habit; I'll never make fun of her insistence her two teddies still sleep in her bed.

He remembered with incredulity his fear he would not be able to love this second child as he loved Tom. He could still feel the shock of finding out it was unlikely he would be able to father another child. His medical training told him this was so but he had held out hope, unbeknown to Jane, repeating the sperm test four times over the following months in case there had been some mistake in the lab readings or that somehow all the zinc Jane was feeding him had worked miracles. But, just as Jane was left disappointed as the telltale stomach cramps gripped her month after month, each lab report left him feeling increasingly despondent.

When Jane had become pregnant Ben had struggled to imagine this second child. With Tom he had pictured a 'mini me.' The child, whether boy or girl, would have the Lewis family trademark auburn hair and Jane's blue eyes. But this new baby could have none of his features. He also uncharacteristically began to worry what people would say when they found out this child was not his. In the end he and Jane had agreed that only their two surviving parents would be told. He frowned now at his mother's response, remembering her cutting: 'So you think it's OK to play God now, do you?' Jane's mother had been understanding, dismissing his fears with a hug and reassurance that a child was far more than an amalgamation of its parents' genes. In the months leading up to the birth he had chosen to read every report possible that came down on the side of nurture versus nature.

He needn't have worried. The moment he had held the screaming bundle in his arms he was once again head over heels in love. And that love was as unconditional tonight as it had been in that moment. The irony that before her birth he had feared he would reject this new baby and that, ever since her birth, he'd feared she would reject him was never as real as it was tonight.

Catrin had left the house and turned towards the vast expanse of Pontcanna playing fields. Lucky's enthusiasm had quickly waned when it had started to rain and, having let him off the lead as they reached the fields, he had given her one apologetic look, turned on his heels and headed straight home. Alone now Catrin found tears of frustration streaming down her face. She walked aimlessly on, coming out on Cathedral Road. The street lamps made her realise just how dark it had been on the fields and she shuddered at her stupidity in taking such a potentially dangerous route. She carried on through Plasturton Gardens with no thought of where she was actually going. As she walked she glimpsed a snapshot of other peoples' lives through their open-curtained windows. One family was sitting down to supper, the dimmed lighting in their dining room giving off a cosy glow. Catrin realised she hadn't eaten all day but she wasn't hungry. The couple four doors down were watching television, the flickering lights of the box making it possible to see them sitting huddled up on the sofa; next door two little children were helping their father put up a Christmas tree.

She walked on, her wet jeans clinging uncomfortably to her legs, remembering how she and Tom had so looked forward every year to putting up their tree. After the excitement of Guy Fawkes that would be the next big event and on November 6th they would start asking when they could buy it. Their parents usually managed to hold out until December 1st with Tom reasoning that the advent calendar started on that day so it meant Christmas really had arrived. And so one of their family traditions had been established. On the Saturday after December 1st their dad would make them all a pancake breakfast – she would have hers with strawberry jam, Tom would choose maple syrup, their mum would have banana with hers and their dad would put peanut butter on his. Then her mum would spread a big blue plastic sheet in the boot of whichever Volvo estate they had at the time and they would all pile in and head for Pontypridd market to choose the tree. There was always a discussion about which kind would smell best (important to their dad), which would make the least mess (important to their mum), and which was the tallest (important to her and Tom). When they got the tree home their mother would heat up some soup and then came their dad's pilgrimage to the attic to retrieve the box of Christmas decorations. As the years went by the box grew ever fuller as their parents kept all the decorations she and Tom had made in school and they were carefully hung on the tree, together with some glass decorations that their dad had had since he was a little boy and the purple and silver ones that their mum had optimistically bought one Christmas, envisaging a colour-themed tree just like the designer ones in *Homes and Gardens*. But their dad had insisted that taste and Christmas simply did not go together and Christmas had won. Then there were the lights which somehow always got tangled up, even though their dad swore he'd put them away without a single knot the previous January. Then came the moment when they all gathered round the tree and their dad ceremoniously switched on the lights. Catrin would often sit for a long time on the stairs in the dark admiring the twinkling tree in their big hall.

The pedestrian lights in front of her were flashing and the waiting driver angrily sounded his horn. She raised her hand in apology, her heart racing as she reached the other side of the road. She stopped at the nearest bus stop, realising she had to concentrate and decide what she was going to do. Siân was with Jonathan so there was no point in going to Siân's. She didn't want to see any of her other friends but didn't feel ready to go home either. The number 25 bus drew up and the door opened. Inside the light was bright and inviting and it was dry. The bus driver looked at her and mumbled something, As Catrin fumbled in her pocket for her bus pass he shrugged his shoulders, the doors slammed shut and the bus pulled away with a puff of indignation. Darkness and loneliness once again engulfed her and she bit her lip.

'Hey, fancy a swig?'

Catrin jumped as the man appeared at her side. He was standing too close and his odour of alcohol and stale sweat made her feel nauseous. She moved a fraction to her right, slowly, so he would not feel her recoil and be offended. When she did not answer he thrust the bottle at her, 'Seventy per cent proof – wicked, man.'

'No thank you,' Catrin replied. To her own ears she sounded prim, stuck-up even.

She looked down the street, away from him, desperately hoping to see the welcome orange light of another bus approaching. She was aware the man was tall and, although she had not looked at him directly, she knew he had a long, thin face, as it was briefly reflected in the bus-shelter glass by the passing cars. She'd always been surprised at how people in threatening circumstances were afterwards able to remember enough detail for the police to create photofits. Now she knew she could too. She had a very real sense of what this man looked like.

Relief flooded over her as a bus turned the corner. She stepped forward and thrust her arm out. It stopped and the doors opened to welcome her inside. Catrin showed her pass and sat down, only then allowing herself a brief glance at the man still standing at the bus stop. As the bus pulled away she became aware she had been breathing far too quickly. She closed her eyes, took a deep breath and breathed out to the count of five. Again, she told herself firmly: one, two, three, four, five. At the bus station the driver shouted loudly 'all change'. Realising she was the 'all' referred to she got up reluctantly and shuffled past the impatient driver, catching his eye in a token challenge. She stepped out and into the multi-cinema complex. Relieved to find the emergency £10 note she kept with her bus pass was untouched, she bought a ticket for *Great Expectations*; she really admired Helena Bonham Carter.

Catrin did not try to follow the story. She knew it anyway. She liked sitting there in this safe darkness. After a few moments she tried to focus on her mother's confession. Yes, that's exactly what it was: a confession. And a confession was always associated with something bad. So the next thing to work out was what was bad about it. Everything, Catrin thought hopelessly. She was aware that her cheeks were wet. How could they have lied to her for so long, kept something from her that she, more than anyone else, had a right to know?

And she'd been conceived in a clinic. She knew the thought was repulsive and tried to understand what she found so sickening. Come on, be rational she challenged herself. It was professional after all, scientific, proper. Yes, that was it, scientific. Conceiving a baby shouldn't be like that; it should be passionate and loving and all those things. But her conception had been so cold, so calculated. Her mind whirled. Would she have felt less upset if she'd been conceived as a result of a one-night stand? That would no doubt have involved some passion, but of the cheap and sordid kind. So

70

wasn't it better to be conceived as a result of a deliberate plan, a deliberate choice by her parents to have a child? She couldn't decide; she was confused. But one thing she was very clear about – it was her parents' fault she now felt so wretched. Catrin felt suddenly cold and, as she struggled to get a tissue out of her jeans' pocket, she was aware her hands were trembling. Shock. She must be in shock. Well little wonder: she had just found out her whole life was based on a lie.

Ben felt relief wash over him when he heard the front door open then immediately braced himself as he knew from the way Catrin slammed it shut she was furious. He got up and hovered by the kitchen door watching her take her coat off and fling it on the stairs.

'Catz, I'm so glad you're home safe love. It's after midnight. Where have you been? You're soaking.'

Catrin pushed past him to the sink and turned the tap fully open. Half the water found its way into the glass she was holding, the other half landed in glistening droplets around the sink and on the work surface.

'How could you not tell me?' she said turning to face him.

'I've … we've been meaning to. I'm sorry Catrin, don't blame your mum; it was me. I was the one who kept putting it off. I was afraid, afraid it would change things,' he said quietly.

'But you let me worry; worry I might have your cholesterol problems; worry I would have to have the test; worry I would die …'

He held out his arms but she ignored the gesture and he let them drop limply at his side. 'Oh, love, I'm sorry, I had no idea you were bothered about that.'

She glared at him and shouted, 'How could you not know? You obviously don't know me at all. And I don't think I know you either.'

With that she stormed out of the kitchen and ran upstairs. Ben heard her slam her bedroom door behind her.

He felt wretched. Catrin had never spoken to him like that before. But he couldn't blame her; he knew they'd been wrong to keep the information from her. He corrected himself; he'd been wrong. As Catrin was growing up Jane had several times tried to persuade him that they should tell her. Why hadn't he listened to her? Why hadn't he listened to himself? Deep down he'd known Catrin had a right to be told and that he was being dishonest in hiding the truth from her. But somehow there had never been the right time.

The first time Jane had suggested they tell her she'd been about three years old and Ben had argued that she was too young to understand, her world then revolving around her dolls and teddy bears. And then she was in primary school and Ben had feared telling her because she was of an age where there were no secrets, where she shared everything with her friends and teachers and he was worried that later in life she would regret revealing such intimate information.

And how to tell her? He'd spent hours in his shed considering how he could broach the subject. He'd bought a book, *We chose you specially*, and considered leaving it somewhere she would find it, hoping this would lead on to the conversation he needed to have with her. The book was mouldy now, hidden on the top shelf alongside his tobacco. He'd considered letting Jane explain to Catrin about her biological father when she was explaining the facts of life to their daughter but he'd decided that would be too much information for the eleven-year-old Catrin to cope with all at once. And then suddenly she was a teenager and so keen to be like every other teenage girl he'd felt the revelation would be too distressing for her, making her feel different. He knew how important it was for her to fit in, to be part of the crowd. Then before he knew it she had turned eighteen and he'd never got around to telling her. But his mother had.

If he was completely honest Ben knew that it wasn't when or how to tell her that had prevented him from doing so. It was fear. Fear that it would change their relationship; fear that she

72

would somehow reject him. Fear that she would not love him, not respect him any more.

How ironic that despite keeping the secret from her for all these years his worries could still be realised. And of course the way Catrin had found out made those fears all the more likely to be realised. Damn his mother. No, damn himself.

When Jane came down at 2 a.m. he was still sitting at the kitchen table, clutching his World's Greatest Dad mug. The coffee in it was cold.

Chapter Six

Catrin awoke early. She knew it was early without looking at her bedside clock as the house and street were quiet. For a few seconds everything appeared normal and she struggled to work out what had woken her then she remembered. She also remembered how angry she'd felt. The anger had vanished overnight but the adrenalin that had been coursing through her veins had left her feeling weak and exhausted. She blushed as she remembered what she'd said to her father. How odd, she thought, that she'd focused her anger on her fear of having inherited his high-cholesterol problems. Yes, it had worried her, but really that wasn't why she was angry about her parents' failure to tell her her dad was not her real father. She was angry with them for not trusting her enough to know she'd cope with the revelation. And she was angry that Granny Lewis, and presumably Granny Olwen, had known something so fundamental about her that she herself was unaware of for eighteen years. Who else knew? Catrin felt sick at the thought.

Eventually she heard her parents getting up and going about their normal workday routine. Still she squatted beneath her pink duvet. Shortly after 8 a.m. there was a gentle knock on the bedroom door.

'Catrin love, Dad and I are off to work now; are you awake?'

Catrin did not reply but lay there, rigid.

She heard her mother try the handle. The relief as she realised she had locked her door was immense.

'You OK, Catrin?'

Again she did not reply; in fact she did not breathe until she heard her mother's footsteps retreat down the stairs.

Then she heard them leave the house and she padded to the

window, still wrapped in the duvet, to watch her dad throw his work bag, his sandwich box, and last night's paperwork on to the back seat. Her mum opened the passenger door and, as she turned to get into the car, looked up at Catrin's window. She waved as Catrin ducked back behind the curtains.

Catrin dressed then stuffed a pair of jeans, a sweater, underwear, pyjamas, and toiletries into a bag and headed downstairs. She really didn't feel like going to school but she couldn't miss another rehearsal with only three days to the opening performance. From the hall she could see Tom sitting at the kitchen table, dictionary to his right and his laptop open. She hesitated for a second. Did Tom know? She decided he probably did as he had been at home with her parents the previous evening and had left a couple of messages on her mobile asking where she was. But she wasn't angry with him, she reasoned; it was her parents who were in the wrong. Of course what she now knew changed things between Tom and her too. He lifted his head, sensing her presence.

'Hi, sis, you OK?

He sounded normal, if a little more attentive than usual, she thought with relief. 'Morning, Tom, unlike you to be up at the crack of dawn and on a Monday!' Catrin passed behind his chair and took a swipe at his head.

'Got a deadline to meet – job application,' he said, spraying a mouthful of toast crumbs in her direction.

'Oh, gross Tom; not the job; you talking with your mouth full.'

'Your fault, you asked me a question.'

Catrin smiled, reassured by the familiar sparring.

'So what's the job then?' she asked over her shoulder as she filled the kettle.

'Something Mum saw in the paper; she thinks it's mine already because they say they need someone who can speak Welsh.'

'Ah, that explains the dictionary.'

'Mm, this is the first time I've written anything in Welsh

since I left school so I was wondering, as you're such an expert, if you'd have a quick look at it for me?'

'No problem. Pass it here then.'

Catrin read the laptop screen for a minute and then burst out laughing. 'Tom, I hardly recognise you in this: 'hard-working, enthusiastic and committed to the Welsh language!'

'It's called being creative, sis.'

'Sounds good, bro. Pity it bears very little resemblance to reality though,' she said as she made her tea.'

'Well I've tried being me and it's no good. I've been me in the last twenty-three applications I've made and how many interviews have I had? A big fat zero. None, zilch, not a sausage. So this is the new me. And if I get it, then I'll turn into that person. No problemo, sister.'

'It'll need a miracle, not a makeover.'

Tom stuck his tongue out at her.

'Harsh but true, big brother.'

'Thank you, Catrin; now just cut the comments and look at the spelling.'

Catrin suggested a few corrections, gulped down her tea and then grabbed her overnight bag and her school bag. She pinned a note to the fridge: 'Staying over at Siân's,' and took another swipe at her brother's head as he bent forward to make the corrections on his application form.

'Bye Tom, see you.'

As she reached the back door he shouted after her: 'Catz, it makes no difference to me; you're still my irritating little sis.'

She said nothing but smiled as she closed the door.

Catrin always confided in Siân but now for the first time she wasn't sure she could tell her best friend, or anyone for that matter, what she had found out. As she walked to school she tried to work out why this was. In part, she decided, she blamed Siân for convincing her the explanation for her grandmother's words was that her father had been adopted. And now that explanation had been proven false she felt let

77

down. How she wished Siân had been right. How simple that would have been in comparison. How silly of her to have imagined that her father being adopted would have caused her any real distress. That upset would have been insignificant compared to the anguish that the truth was causing her. But Siân had only been doing her best to help, Catrin reasoned and really how could Siân have been expected to come up with the actual explanation? It was just too strange.

No the real reason for not telling Siân was that she felt ashamed. Why did she feel shame? she reflected, as she kicked a loose stone along the pavement. Two Year Eight boys loitering outside the corner shop giggled as she passed them, one pushing the other towards her. 'Dylan really thinks you're hot,' the pusher shouted after her. 'Really fit,' he added for good measure. She could hear their good-natured scuffling as she strode on. A secret. That was the problem. The fact that her parents had kept it from her. And people kept things secret when they were ashamed or embarrassed. There were few happy secrets. Now she was lumbered with their secret too. And if she shared it with Siân she would be betraying them. By the time she got to the school gates she had decided she would tell no one.

The first person she saw as she crossed the schoolyard was Siân.

Her best friend sprinted across to her. 'Hi, Catz. Oh you look awful.'

Catrin smiled. 'Thank you for that, makes me feel a whole lot better!'

'Sarcasm, my dear Catrin, is the lowest form of wit.'

'And the highest form of entertainment,' Catrin finished for her.

Siân linked arms with her. 'You running away from home?' she joked, pointing at the bag Catrin was carrying.

Catrin said nothing but picked up the pace, forcing Siân to break into a trot to keep up with her.

'Throat still giving you grief, Catz?'

'No, it's much better thanks; I think I will be able to be Dorothy after all.'

'Good, that yellow brick road was made for you!' They walked a few strides in silence.

'So, Catz, tell all – what was that about yesterday; your mum behaving so strangely and then your dad phoning my house looking for you last night?'

Catrin pretended to be interested in the football game going on at the far end of the playground.

'Come on Catrin, you know how boring my life is, give me drama, pleeeeeeeeease.' Siân pleaded.

Five minutes later they were sitting in the school canteen. Siân listened to the whole story and did not interrupt as Catrin haltingly described what had happened the previous night.

'Oh, Catz, that's awful.'

'I can't describe how awful, Siân; I just feel so betrayed by them, so angry.'

Siân nodded. 'Is there anything I can do to help?'

Catrin lifted her overnight bag off the floor and held it up.

'Yes of course you can stay, no problem at all. You know how much my mum and dad like having you around; they'd swop me for you any day given the chance!'

Catrin gave Siân a grateful hug.

Over the next couple of days Catrin returned home to collect her schoolbooks and changes of clothing at times when she knew her parents would be at work. Tom, not having any work to go to, was more unpredictable but, as she didn't mind seeing her brother, that was not a problem. She did leave notes on the fridge. On Tuesday she wrote 'Siân's again tonight.'

By Wednesday evening Siân's mother, aware there had been a row, but not knowing the exact circumstances, suggested Catrin should at least go home and speak to her parents and then come back to stay if she wanted. Catrin chose to interpret the suggestion as a sign she was not wanted at Siân's and the fifteen-minute walk to Pencisely Crescent did nothing to improve her mood. She let herself in and decided she would go straight to her room, leaving the door slightly ajar and the lights on so her parents would know she was there. That way they would have to speak to her first; they could hardly come to her room and say nothing could they?

But as she made her way quietly up the stairs she could see her father in Gran's room. He had his back to her and was saying, 'Well, I suppose if you dislike them so much, we could take them to that charity shop on City Road – the big one on the corner; I'm sure they take furniture.'

Then she heard her mother's determined voice, 'They're really ugly and old-fashioned, Ben, and if we get rid of them we could turn this whole room into a walk-in wardrobe. I could always use more hanging space and Catrin could use it too as you've never got round to putting up those shelves in her wardrobe she wants.'

'That will give you licence to buy even more clothes.' He laughed.

'I need room for fat and thin clothes, Ben, you know that.'

Catrin had heard enough. 'I can't believe you're getting rid of Gran's furniture', she said, her voice full of indignation.

Her dad turned around sharply. 'Oh, hi, Catrin.'

She stood on the stairs, glaring at him. 'You can't, Dad; Gran loved that furniture, she'd had it for ever.'

'Well, it's too dark,' her mother said. 'Too heavy. It's just wrong for this house.'

'Well maybe I'd like it for my house,' Catrin came back at her like a shot. Lucky appeared behind her mum, wagging his tail and rushing towards Catrin.

'But love, that's years away,' her father said rationally.

Catrin bent down to acknowledge Lucky but held her dad's gaze.

'Not if I move out now it isn't,' she responded.

Her mother came to stand in front of him. 'Oh don't be ridiculous, Catrin, you're going to university; it will be years before you can afford a house.'

Catrin pushed her chin out. 'Maybe I won't go to university after all. Maybe I'll just get a job.'

'You'd throw away everything if you did that,' her mother retorted.

'It's you who's throwing things away, Granny's things, Granny's memories.' Catrin noticed how distressed her father looked, knew how much he hated arguments. But still she was determined to stand her ground. 'And anyway, it should be Dad's decision, not yours,' she added.

Her father gave her mother an apologetic shrug. 'I do think Catrin has a point love. How about we give the wardrobe and bed away and keep the dressing table,' he suggested calmly, 'I spent hours sitting at it when I was a little boy watching Mum getting ready to go to chapel or to one of her concerts. Happy memories that will stay with me for ever.'

'Well,' her mother started but he ignored her, turned Catrin around and followed her downstairs.

'I think we need a cuppa,' he said cheerfully.

'Not for me, Dad, I'm going back to Siân's.' Before her mother could arrive down in the kitchen Catrin left, closing the back door behind her.

Catrin walked quickly back towards Siân's. She was glad to feel her heart pumping and a rasp in her throat from the exertion, a physical pain to momentarily override the emotional pain. As she strode along she could feel the anger slowly seeping out of her body. It was an unfamiliar feeling, this anger, a feeling she did not like at all. And such exhaustion afterwards. Now she tried to work out why she felt more anger towards her mother than towards her dad. It was he, after all, by his own admission, who had insisted she wasn't told she'd been conceived by donor sperm. Catrin felt revulsion at the term. By the time she got to the church on Grand Avenue Catrin had begrudgingly conceded she could understand why he hadn't wanted her to know. She'd read enough articles in *Cosmopolitan* about male virility to know that for some men it defined who they were. She would never have thought her father to be one of those men though. How little we know the people we live with, and love, and trust, she thought bitterly. And why hadn't her mother insisted she be told? She had nothing to lose, did she? Catrin was aware she expected more from her mother. They had always had a special bond, always been close. It was a sisterhood thing, a girl thing. And Catrin felt even more betrayed because of it.

'Hi Catz, you're back soon.' Siân said as she answered the front door.

'Too soon you mean?'

'Oh Catz, don't be silly; we're besties aren't we? I'm always glad to hang out with you.' Siân reached out a hand and pulled her into the warmth of the house.

Catrin smiled. 'Sorry, Siân, I'm just being too sensitive.'

'Things didn't go well then? No, you don't need to answer that; I can see from your face that they didn't. Tell you what I'll fix us a hot choc with marshmallows and you can tell me all about it.'

On Thursday Catrin popped home at lunchtime. Her father had left her a fridge-note saying, 'Hope you OK. Good luck 2night, break a leg! Love u lodz, Mum and Dad.' She attached her parents' tickets to the fridge with a reply note that read 'thanx.' Before leaving the house she picked up the horseshoe brooch from her room and pinned it to her bra. Feeling it cold against her skin was reassuring, as if a little part of her gran was with her. She smiled to herself. Granny Lewis wasn't your archetypal guardian angel – she wasn't soft and sweet and fluffy. But perhaps she was just the kind of angel Catrin needed right now – a strong, determined, get-on-with-it-you-only-have-one-life kind of angel.

Jane found the tickets when she got home from work and was relieved. Part of her had wondered if Catrin would want them at the performance at all. She'd decided to make an effort with her outfit anyway and was hopping from one leg to another when Ben arrived home from his evening surgery. She'd guessed he would be delayed – Thursday surgeries were always heavy as two of his partners took their half-days – but really she could do with him being later still tonight. She was not dressed yet and she liked to have the bedroom to herself when she was getting ready to go out. As he came into the room she tried to crouch down on their bed, hoping he hadn't noticed the few extra rolls of fat fighting for room around her waist.

'What on earth are you doing?' he said, obviously trying to stifle a laugh.

'Magic Knickers bodysuit thing' she replied with a groan.

'Mmm, very sexy.'

'Oh shut up, Ben, or better still go away.'

Jane pulled and tugged and had all but managed to get the all-in-one bodysuit on when one of the bra straps came loose. She shuffled into the en suite, away from Ben's amused gaze, and tried to re-attach it in the mirror. But her glasses were downstairs and try as she might she could not get the hook into the required loop. Faced with having to take it all off again or asking Ben to help, she decided facing Ben's mirth was the lesser of the two evils.

'Ben, you're going to have to help me.'

'OK love, coming,' he said, opening the en suite door. He muttered something about gravity as he tugged at the strap.

'Ah, your hands are cold.'

Ben blew on them and tried again. Eventually, with Jane hoisting up her breasts and him tugging on the strap, the task was accomplished.

'You're obviously not planning on breathing, Jane.'

'Ben, tonight I can do without your Smart Alec comments. Please pass me the dress that's hanging on the wardrobe door.'

'Is this new, Jane?' he asked as he handed it to her.

'No, I've had it for ages,' she replied as she struggled to pull on a pair of sheer black tights. Really 'ages' was open to interpretation, she reasoned.

The dress had actually been hers for forty-eight hours and

83

had been bought after Jane had seen Kate Winslet wearing something similar to a film award ceremony. The papers had raved about the slimming effect of the dress with its pale front panels and darker sides. Unfortunately it seemed to be made of pure elastic and it took her a good ten minutes to struggle into it, having by now firmly closed the en suite door on Ben.

'Love, what do you think, brown or black cords?' he called through the door.

'Whatever,' Jane muttered under her breath.

'Brown or black cords, Jane?'

Jane emerged from the en suite and shuffled into the bedroom 'Brown, black, Ben – whichever you prefer.'

Bending to retrieve her shoes she cursed herself for not positioning them in front of the long mirror so she could just step into them. Ben had opted for brown cords and was now pulling on his Aran sweater.

'Could you pass me my black patent shoes, Ben, please?'

He peered into the wardrobe. 'Imelda Marcos has nothing on you Jane.' He laughed as he handed her a pair of navy shoes.

Jane tutted impatiently. 'No, not those, Ben, the high ones, right at the back.'

The shoes Jane pointed to were covered in dust.

'Well, these are obviously not new,' he teased, as he wiped them clean with a discarded sock he found on the floor.

'They're not the most comfy,' Jane admitted, holding on to the mirror as she gingerly put them on.

'OK, we have to go, love; you ready?'

As Jane slowly negotiated the stairs Tom came into the hall from the kitchen. Unusually for him he was not in sports kit but had on a clean pair of jeans, a pale blue shirt, and his old school tie. As usual though he had something to eat in his hands – tonight it was a banana and a flapjack.

'Why on earth have you got that tie on, Tom? You didn't even wear it when you were in school.'

'Thought I'd come with you Mum, give my sister a bit of

support, and as I don't have a ticket, the tie will prove I'm an old boy and they'll let me in.'

'I'm sure the teachers will remember you, Tom; probably not in a good way though.' Ben laughed.

'Anyway, Mum, talk about what I'm wearing; what about what you've got on? You've really gone to town. Does look a bit like a skeleton fancy dress outfit though.'

Jane smiled as she gave herself a last glance in the hall mirror. 'Skeletal is good, Tom; it must mean I look thin.'

'We'll all be skeletons by the end if this performance lasts as long as usual,' Ben murmured.

'You don't look very comfy Mum,' Tom added.

'No pain, no gain, boys, and I don't want to look fat. I don't want to be an embarrassment to Catrin. '

'And you don't think passing out is going to embarrass her, Mum?'

'OK, let's go. With you only able to take baby steps, Jane, we should have left an hour ago,' Ben ushered her and Tom out of the house, locked the front door and strode towards the Volvo. Jane tottered behind him. Perhaps this wasn't the best choice of outfit after all, she thought; ah well, too late to change now.

Catrin sat at a big mirror putting on her stage make-up and gazed at her features. She could account for her eyes – her mother's. Her long, straight nose she'd assumed had come from Granny Lewis. Obviously not. Her blonde hair and the dimple in her chin had always been a mystery. And still were. As she studied her face closely she seemed to be growing increasingly unfamiliar. The Catrin she had thought herself to be had changed. Who was she really? Would she ever be able to find out?

The room was noisy with lots of the younger pupils running about laughing excitedly and telling each other how great they looked in their costumes. Catrin felt somehow removed from it all, just as if she was looking at a television documentary. She hadn't been able to eat properly since Sunday and she felt hollow and a little sick; the smell of the make-up aggravated her nausea. Someone passed and said, 'Cheer up, it may never happen.' Catrin took a red lipstick, painted a smile on her face and pulled on her gingham costume. She looked at her reflection and seeing her smiling lips actually made her feel better. Slowly a genuine smile spread across her face.

'Five minutes to curtain up; this is your five minute call,' someone called out in an officious voice.

She took a few deep breaths to try to settle the butterflies flitting about in her stomach, pressed her grandmother's little brooch to her chest and made her way to the wings. She was aware this was not how she usually felt on the opening night of a show. Of course there were always butterflies but usually the overwhelming feeling was one of excitement. Tonight she just felt unsure. Unsure she could perform well; unsure she knew the part well enough, she'd been so distracted all week. Unsure she even wanted to go on stage.

From the wings she could glimpse the hall quickly filling with parents and friends. Now she was acutely aware how alone she had felt over the last few days. Siân and her parents had been lovely to her but it wasn't the same as being with her own family. She felt so confused and worst of all she couldn't envisage a time when she wouldn't feel this way – bewildered and upset.

She wondered whether her parents had arrived yet or if they would even come? Yes, they would come, she felt pretty sure of that, and no, they probably weren't here yet. Her dad always walked in just as things were starting, claiming he would save a whole month during his lifetime if he did not turn up the accepted ten minutes early. 'Dad.' Should she still call him Dad or was Ben now more appropriate? The thought darted through her mind; promptly she pushed it away. No he was still Dad; for now anyway. She glanced at the backstage clock: two minutes to curtain up.

Her mother was convinced his tardiness was a way of staging a little rebellion against Granny Lewis's insistence they turn up early to everything. She probably had a point. Certainly he'd often told them how endless the thirty minutes between 10 a.m. and 10.30 a.m. on a Sunday morning had felt to him as a child, sitting on the hard pew, waiting for the chapel service to begin, forbidden to talk or to look around. The only saving grace had been the old woman in the pew in front who kept passing him Jelly Babies. But he had had mixed feelings about her. On the one hand she provided a welcome source of sweets but the fact she wore a fox-fur collar from October to May really troubled him. As she leant back to pass him a sweet the fox's head, dangling over the back of her pew and encroaching into his own, would come ever nearer, its two shiny eyes staring at him accusingly. As a child he'd told them he'd often wake up screaming as the fox pursued him relentlessly in his dreams. Catrin felt a surge of love for him; childhood under Granny Lewis had probably not been easy. Her mind raced on as a snapshot of her own happy childhood flashed before her – her dad teaching her to ride her first bike; Tom pushing her on a swing their father had hung under the big apple tree; her mother and her sitting at the kitchen table, creating something they'd seen being made on *Blue Peter*.

Just as the band was striking the first chord and the lights were being dimmed, she saw her parents, followed, to her surprise, by Tom, making their way into the hall and causing a small commotion as they edged along a row to sit half way in and about three quarters of the way back. As Catrin joined the rest of the cast on stage for the opening chorus she felt her eyes involuntarily drift away from the director's baton, trying to locate her family in the now darkened hall. She thought she saw them; it must be them, a shortish woman, a bulky man and a taller, slimmer form. She had a sudden impulse to wave. Fleetingly she remembered stern Miss Hughes, the tutor at the Little Angels School of Musical Theatre, instructing her pupils not to acknowledge their parents in this way and how she had disobeyed her every time. She hadn't done so for years, of course, but now she felt the same need to connect as she had as a six-year-old. One of the Year Seven pupils moving the wrong way at the beginning of the dance sequence, causing a ripple of shoves from adjacent cast members and a ripple of laughter from the audience, brought her back to reality. Concentrate, she admonished herself sternly, or you'll be a laughing stock too.

Ben sat in the audience with tears in his eyes, focusing only on Catrin. Since his daughter had started performing, and even more so since she had been cast in some of the main roles, he loved seeing her on stage. But he also felt extremely nervous. Nervous she would forget her lines; nervous she would trip over or would not get the applause she deserved. Not once in the last ten years or so had his fears been realised and every year on his way to see a performance he reminded himself of this. But try as he might he was unable to control his feelings and the immense relief he felt as the final chorus was performed and the audience burst into enthusiastic applause was as real tonight as ever.

As the applause died down and the lights came up, Ben relaxed back into his seat. All around him people were gathering their possessions, telling each other what a wonderful performance it had been and making their way to the exits. Someone from behind patted him a little too heartily on the back and boomed, 'Congratulations.' He turned around to thank him but the man had already shuffled further along and was now engaged in a conversation with a woman three rows back.

'She was good, wasn't she?' Ben whispered to Jane.

'She was; they all were,' Jane patted his hand.

'But she stood out,' Ben added.

'Come on Dad, let's go.' Tom was on his feet looking down at them. He gave Ben's shoulder a gentle shove to try to galvanise him into moving.

'What's the rush, Tom?'

'This place is bringing back bad memories of never-ending morning assemblies and tadpole pudding.'

'I've heard of snail porridge – what that Blooming Hestington feeds to people – but tadpole pud?'

'It's Heston Blumenthal,' Jane corrected, standing, 'and tapioca.'

Ben was still in his seat; the rest of the row had cleared. 'We'll have to wait for Catrin to get changed anyway.'

'Do you think that's a good idea, Ben? Perhaps we should just go home and let her come at her own pace. She might not want to come home; she might be staying over with Siân again.'

'We always wait for her at the end of the show; she always comes out to the foyer to meet us.' Ben knew he sounded pathetic and he waited for Tom to comment. Tom for once did not do so and instead turned away and joined the crowd making their way out of the hall.

'What if she just ignores us Ben? It will be embarrassing for everyone.'

Ben said nothing but grimaced, stood and took his wife's hand. By the time they got to the school entrance hall, having stopped several times as they walked along the corridor to chat to other parents they knew, Catrin had had time to change and hastily remove her makeup. She was standing chatting excitedly with a small group of sixth-formers. As soon as she saw her family she said her goodbyes and hurried towards them smiling. Ben felt they had turned a corner.

'You were absolutely brilliant, love,' he said loudly, not caring who overheard him.

'Thanks, Dad.' Catrin beamed.

'Yes, you were,' Jane confirmed, 'we're really proud of you, Catrin.'

'Yeah, respect sis,' Tom said, punching her arm lightly.

'High praise indeed, Tom!' Catrin laughed. 'How much did

89

you understand, Mum?' She put her arm around Jane's shoulder.

'Oh most of it, Catz,' Jane replied, as they moved away from the mingling cast. 'It did help that I knew the basic story but the new bits your producer had added were a bit tricky. Did I understand right that the wicked witch was a city trader?'

Catrin laughed. 'Genius, Mum – you I mean, not Mr Isaac's weird ideas.'

She linked arms with both her parents as they crossed the car park. Tom criss-crossed in front of them.

'Oh for goodness sake Tom,' Ben said, 'just because you're back at school doesn't mean you have to act like a schoolboy.'

Tom laughed and aimed an imaginary catapult at him.

Chapter Seven

Catrin sat at the kitchen table, her books, files and laptop open. Now that term was over, and the excitement of playing Dorothy in *The Wizard of Oz* was but a memory, she needed to focus on her coursework to be sure of getting the grades she needed for Aberystwyth. But she was finding it hard to focus when the implications of learning she was 'not blood' were still sinking in. During the past few days she'd been aware of something changing and now she felt able for the first time to give it a name, a description, something that made her feelings concrete. Grief. That's what she felt. Grief at not knowing her donor and his family.

Slowly the donor was taking on a form, as yet not identifiable by the colour of his eyes, his facial expressions or his mannerisms, but he was there, in the shadows, waiting. She wondered if he felt the same, in some kind of limbo, waiting for her to find him. She was curious, of course she was, wanted to see if she looked like him, whether she'd inherited some of his personality traits, his interests, his skills. But she also felt a certain relief, despite all the uncertainty that faced her. Thinking of the donor as a person somehow made it all less threatening, humanised it all. Yes, that was it; she'd felt de-humanised. Donor-conceived, how she hated the term: so cold, so clinical, so mechanical. But the donor wasn't just that at all: he was flesh and blood, her flesh and blood. And if she could meet him then she would know exactly who he was and who she was.

She watched her mum fold up the paper and open the bulging kitchen cupboard where she kept the tea towels and aprons. Her mother never did any housework without putting on a pinny; she said it just didn't feel right. As a result her family and friends inevitably bought her aprons as presents and she had a huge collection. Today she selected one of the French ones that almost wrapped around her entire body. She got out a big yellow stoneware bowl and lined up flour, mixed fruit, figs, and brandy on the worktop.

'Making something nice, Mum?'

'Well I hope so. I've left making the Christmas pud so late this year but I've found this new recipe in a magazine and it's supposed to be ready to eat in a fortnight so it will be just in time. Besides, it'll stop me worrying about how your brother's job interview is going.'

'Is there anything I can do to help?'

'No need, Catrin, I don't want to drag you away from your work.'

'No, really, Mum, I'm due for a break, so what can I do?'

'How about peeling some apples then; I need 300 grams please.'

'No prob; anything's got to be better than doing this history coursework. Before I start though I'll put on the Christmas CD to get us in the mood.'

To the strains of 'White Christmas', to which Catrin sang along and Jane hummed, they began to peel and chop. Jane measured flour and mixed fruit into the stoneware bowl.

'Why do you always use this bowl at Christmas time, Mum?'

'Because this is the Christmas pudding bowl. I used it to make the pudding with my mum when I lived at home and she used to use it to make the family Christmas pudding with *her* mother.'

'My great-granny?'

Jane nodded. 'Not that she would have approved of chopped apple and grated carrot in a traditional Christmas pudding.'

Catrin thought her mum sounded nostalgic for the grandmother she had never known. It must be comforting to know you were carrying on a family tradition. She wondered what kind of Christmas traditions her donor father kept and whether she would ever get to know. Perhaps his family was doing the exact same thing at this moment, making their Christmas pudding.

'Time to stir and wish, Catz.'

Her mother gave the pudding a good stir, closed her eyes and made her wish. Then she handed the spoon to Catrin.

'How many wishes do I get Mum?'

'As usual Catz, just one, so make it a good one.'

Catrin began stirring. She knew what she wanted to wish for – to find her donor – but she didn't want to upset her dad. She quickly dismissed the thought. He would understand; she'd make him see she was just being curious, that no one would or could replace him. She'd win him over; she always did. And if not – well, he hadn't been that careful of her feelings in all of this, he would just have to cope with it. Catrin suddenly felt so grown-up. Here she was making decisions without first talking them through with her family. This, she knew, without discussing it with anyone, was the right course of action.

'You stirring, or beating that mixture to death, Catz?' Her mum laughed as she laid a restraining hand on her arm. 'You must have made your wish by now. It's nearly ready – we just need to add the brandy – but we'll have to wait for the boys to get back to add their wishes before we put it in the basin to cook.'

'Can't we just cook it, Mum, and let them make a wish afterwards?'

'No, Catz, we can't. That won't work.'

'And it will work if we stick to the rules?' Catrin said, laughing.

'Guaranteed, it always has for me.'

'Come on then, Mum, give me some examples.'

'Don't know if I can tell you my wishes – they're supposed to be secret.'

'Not after they come true, Mum, so come on, share.'

93

Catrin added a slurp of brandy to the mixture and carried on idly stirring. Jane stood beside her, dabbing with her forefinger at bits of Christmas pudding mix that had splattered onto the work surface.

'Well, one year I wished for a baby sister and, right enough, by the time we were making the Christmas pudding the following year your Auntie Gwen had been born.'

'I don't think that was the fairies' doing, Mum!'

Her mother smiled.

'Did you wish for the other three as well?'

'I can tell you I wished several times for those boys to be taken away. Luckily those wishes never came true, but they weren't Christmas pud wishes – that's obviously why! I wish now they were all living nearer; I'd never have believed when we were growing up that I'd be the only one to stay in Wales; never thought we'd even leave the Rhondda. Our world was so small then.'

'Can you think of anything you wished for that was unlikely to come true but did?' Catrin persisted.

Her mother pondered as Catrin stirred and sang. The CD was now blasting out one of her mum's favourites – David Essex singing 'Blue, Blue Christmas'. Catrin stopped stirring and gave the old pudding basin a good lick of butter.

'One time I did wish for a car,' her mum said thoughtfully. 'Mr Prydderch, who owned the ice cream factory in Treorchy, was the only one in our street who had a car back then. We kids would often pile into the back and he took us all the way to Barry Island for a trip one summer. And I so wanted our family to be able to go on trips like that, I wished for a car.'

'And Father Christmas brought one?' Catrin asked incredulously.

'No but in the spring, oh I must have been about thirteen then, Dad bought one – the Rolls.'

'Your dad bought a Rolls-Royce?' Catrin was surprised. She knew both her grandparents had worked in the Polikoff factory and were hardly wealthy.

94

'Not exactly.' Her mum chuckled. 'It was an old Ford Anglia – a white one; its full name was 'RollsbutHardlygetsup' – as it rolled down the hills but could hardly get up the other side.'

Catrin laughed. She had never known her grandfather as he had passed away when her mother was seventeen, but she cherished the snippets she heard about him. She loved little tales like this, which highlighted his sense of humour, and how the storyteller inevitably finished by affirming that he was 'such a case'. Of course he had been dead for a long time and when her mum or Granny Olwen talked about him they did not do so in the hushed tones they used when they were talking about her recently buried grandmother. She was able to enjoy him in a way that, at the moment, she was unable to enjoy the memory of Granny Lewis. And now, of course, her mother's side of the family were more important to her than ever.

'We had the Rolls for years. Dad would turn off the engine when going downhill, to save petrol, but in the Valleys you always have to get up the other side!'

The pudding basin was now thoroughly greased. Catrin looked at her mum. 'Are you sure we can't we just wish for Dad and Tom? I bet I know what Tom would wish for.'

'Yes, no brainer – to be offered that job.' Her mother looked at the clock. 'His interview is probably over by now; your dad's picking him up on his way home from the surgery so hopefully they'll be here soon. No doubt Dad's insisted they stop in the little Co-op on Cowbridge Road to buy a bottle and some chocolates – either in celebration or commiseration.'

Catrin nodded. Her dad was so kind and thoughtful. 'What do you think Dad would wish for?'

'Probably for us all to be happy, Catz, but anyway we've got to leave the wishing to them. Let's have a cup of tea while we wait. Shall we tackle the crossword? Quick or cryptic?'

'Tea – good; crossword – not so.'

Her mother put the kettle on and Catrin opened the

cupboard where the cake box was safely stashed away. She laughed out loud. On the cake tin, in A4 size, was stuck a far from flattering picture of her mother.

'Mum, have you seen what Tom's done to the cake tin?'

'Raided it?'

'No, for once he hasn't, but he's put a photo of you on it.'

'That wasn't Tom, that was me.'

'Why, Mum? Your itsy bitsy bikini – not your best look.'

Her mother sighed dramatically. 'I know, but I read in a magazine that it's the best way of making sure you stick to a diet. And with Christmas coming up I need all the help I can get.'

'Ah so you don't want a piece of chocolate cake then?'

'Get behind me, Satan.'

Catrin cut herself a large piece of cake and bent down to replace the cake tin. Perhaps now would be a good time to ask about her biological father? Without getting up she said, 'Mum, what could I find out about the donor?'

Her mum had just finished making the tea. She looked slightly shocked and probably was; there was no way she could have known what Catrin was thinking. Catrin stood and waited for her answer.

After a pause her mum said, 'I'm not really sure what you can find out. I think the law was changed recently.'

Catrin frowned. What did that mean? Her mum crossed the kitchen and put her arms around her. 'Look, I'll do all I can to help you find out everything possible. I guess contacting the fertility people would be a good place to start.'

Catrin gave her mother a big hug, unhooked her arms and fished out her laptop from under the pile of papers on the table.

'Let's start now Mum, I'll Google them; what was the name again?'

Her mum hesitated. 'I think it's HFEA – stands for Human Fertilisation and embryos, or something like that.'

Catrin typed in the details. 'Here it is Mum, Human

Fertilisation and Embryology Authority,'

She read the web page intently, twirling a strand of her long blonde hair round and round her index finger in the way she always did when concentrating. Her mum reached for her glasses and sat down beside her. Catrin scrolled down the page, anxious to read more and found the form that needed to be filled in so that details of her donor could be sent to her. She downloaded it, barely glancing at the section alongside that warned of the possible emotional impact and suggested she might like to consider counselling.

'How about just finding out what's possible, for now, Catz? No need to rush to get that form filled; it looks long and complicated to me.'

'Oh, Mum, it's simple and shorter than an application for a library card.' Catrin showed her mother the screen.

'Still, better if you just sleep on it; send it off tomorrow.'

'What's the point of delaying?'

'Well, what if you're disappointed; what if they don't have the information you want or you don't have the right information to complete the form?'

'I just need to give them my name at birth, date of birth, your name and dad's, and identification. That's about it. Oh and it asks whether I want to know "identifying information" about the donor, if they have it.'

'I guess that means name and contact details?' Her mum sounded dubious.

'Mm. You were right – it looks as if the law was changed in 2005; after that date the donor had to give his details but before that he didn't.'

'So, for someone like you, born in 1994, they don't have the names?'

'No, they don't by law, but they might. It says here that after the 2005 law was passed they invited donors who donated before then to come forward and re-register. Yes, that's what it says but it looks like most haven't …'

'I don't know, Catz; it's a big decision. Sleep on it love.'

'No Mum, I'm going to say "Yes" and see what happens.'

Catrin read on hungrily. 'It also asks if I want information about any siblings ... Oh my God, I didn't even think about the possibility of more brothers and sisters.' She smiled broadly, 'But, hey, yes, I'd definitely be up for that.'

'Careful, Catrin, you have been known to complain about the one brother you already have.'

'I've always wanted a sister, though, and now I might have one or two or lots.'

Catrin pressed the send button and, flushed with excitement, turned and looked at her mother. She was sheet-white. Momentarily Catrin felt guilty, felt sorry for her mum. But such empathy was quickly overcome by the feeling of indignation that had been steadily building as she'd identified several occasions when she'd inadvertently given her parents the chance to tell her Ben was not her biological father. And still they'd failed her. There was the obvious time – she must have been twelve or thirteen – and the topic of the science lesson at school that day had been red hair. Mr Giles, the science teacher, was always good at that – finding an interesting hook on which to hang complicated ideas. Genes, and how particular characteristics were passed from one generation to the next, had been under discussion and Mr Giles had informed them that eventually there would be no red-headed people in the world as the gene that controlled red hair was recessive. She'd been particularly interested because from the photographs she had seen almost all of her father's side of the family had auburn hair. She remembered coming home from school and telling her mum. She remembered remarking that she, with her blonde hair, was an example of Mr Giles's theory in action. It would have been so easy for her mother to have told her then.

And there had been an earlier opportunity too. In Year Four when Georgia had joined her class. Beautiful, exotic Georgia, who had declared on her first day in class that she was adopted. It had all sounded so exciting: her parents' journey to

China, picking her from all the little girls in the orphanage, the long overland journey in an unreliable car and her arrival in London where her new grandparents had arranged a lavish party and everything was pink. Georgia, of course, did not actually remember any of this but had been told the story over and over by her parents and took every opportunity to retell and embellish it herself. Catrin, thrilled with the story, had rushed home and asked her mother if she too was adopted. Jane had laughed and told her that she certainly wasn't and then had probably just got on with making the tea. Another gifted opportunity rejected.

Her mum stood, poured the now stewed tea away and put the kettle on again. As she did Catrin heard the throaty roar of the Volvo sweeping up the gravel drive past the front door and around to the side of the house. The car was turned with a flourish and she knew, without looking, that little stones would have been sent dancing in every direction. That one movement told her her father was in a very good mood. Loud voices approaching confirmed this and the back door was thrown open with such enthusiasm that Lucky, woken by the commotion, leapt out of his basket, tail wagging to greet the returning men.

'You are now in the presence of the Cardiff Schools Community Sports Facilitator.' Tom bowed with an exaggerated flourish.

'Oh well done, Tom; I knew you'd get it.'

'Mm, just as you knew I'd get the other twenty-three jobs that I applied for Mum?'

'Well, yes; well no, this one felt right.' Their mother smiled and gave him a big hug.

'Congratulations, bro, or should I say Llongyfarchiadau, as it's Welsh all the way now,' said Catrin, standing.

'I knew sending you to that school would be good for you,' her dad added, lugging two heavy shopping bags on to the kitchen work surface.

'Thank you Dad, even an "I told you so" isn't going to

99

irritate me today,' Tom said, laughing. 'And now I'm going to relax by watching telly.' Catrin followed him into the lounge.

Jane watched Ben unload his bags full of celebratory food. He put a bottle of champagne on ice and donned one of her aprons which posed the question "Do my buns look big in this?" She could hear Tom and Catrin arguing about whether to watch a repeat of *I'm a Celebrity Get Me Out of Here* (his choice) or *Friends* (her choice), while Ben poured two large gin and tonics and set about forking the potatoes which Jane had earlier put out on the work surface.

'I think I'll coat these in a splash of olive oil and rock salt – I saw Jamie do it on telly the other night; it crisps up the jacket.'

'And adds 150 calories.'

'Oh, what does it matter, Jane? We're celebrating.'

Jane said nothing but sat flicking through the newspapers stacked on the table. She looked at the photographs but the print blurred into a monochrome pattern and she couldn't seem to make out any of the words.

'I've bought us steaks and some nibbles too – try this,' Ben said, passing her some pancetta.

Jane shook her head.

'Some olives then? These ones filled with feta are delicious,' he said popping one in his mouth.

'Not just now thanks, Ben.'

He sloshed some olive oil into a dish, added garlic and herbs and then put the steaks in to marinate. 'How far have you got with the crossword today? Want me to finish it off for you?' he joshed

'I haven't started it,' Jane replied

'OK, let's do it together; you read, I cook.'

'Sorry, Ben, I don't feel like it.'

He came over, put his hand on her forehead and examined her closely. 'You do look paler than usual. You must be going down with something. I think a little brandy, hot water and honey and an early night is what's needed – you'll be right as rain in the morning.'

Jane shook her head. 'I'm not ill. Ben, Catrin has sent off for information about her donor.'

Ben sat down heavily and downed his gin and tonic. His face was flushed, a sure sign he was agitated. For a second he didn't say anything. In the background she could hear the screams as some celebrity or other encountered his or her jungle demons.

'How did she know how to go about it?'

'I suggested she look at the HFEA site.'

'I can't believe you encouraged her.' Although his voice was even, Jane knew he intended this as a criticism and felt indignant.

She sighed. 'I didn't encourage her, she was determined; we've got to support her in this Ben.'

'It's OK for you, you've nothing to lose; you're always going to be her mother.'

'And you her father, Ben.'

'Not if she finds her biological father – I won't be; she won't be my little girl any more.' He sounded desolate.

Jane softened her own voice. 'She's not anyone's little girl Ben; she's eighteen, an adult; it's her decision.' She tried to put her arm around his shoulder but he pushed her away, stood up and went out to his shed.

Jane knew better than to follow him, knew that he needed to be on his own. The Aga had gone out and she pulled the tapestry blanket from the back of the sofa and wrapped it around herself. Its roughness scratched her skin. She'd try to relight the Aga in a minute. Bloody Ben – she couldn't win. All these years she'd kept the secret, protecting Ben from the stigma of being infertile, protecting him from acknowledging he wasn't Catrin's biological father. And now he was blaming everyone else for the fall out, a fall out that could have been completely averted. If they had told Catrin as a little child, as she, Jane, had wanted to, this wouldn't be happening. Being

101

donor-conceived would always have been part of Catrin's history, part of who she was. But Ben had insisted they wait and Jane had given in. She'd known it was wrong, known they were all living a lie. And there had been the fear. Fear that somehow, maybe after too much wine, she'd let something slip. Well, she needn't fear that now. But a new fear had come to replace it, she thought bitterly, a fear that her relationship with Catrin would never be so close again. And it was Ben's fault.

Chapter Eight

For the last seven days Catrin had rushed downstairs to pick up the post – quickly casting the daily pile of Christmas cards aside. But still nothing had come from the HFEA. Now it was Christmas Eve and there would be no more post for several days. Catrin decided she was too distracted to start on the pile of coursework she had to tackle during the holidays, pulled on her green parka and Ugg boots and took Lucky's lead from its hook. Immediately the little dog was by her side, wagging his tail in anticipation.

Catrin's feet crunched on the frozen ground as she made her way across Victoria Park. She let Lucky off the lead and drifted towards the bandstand, where a group of boys were kicking a can of Coke to each other, their hands firmly in their low-slung pockets. She sensed their half-heartedness. Catrin paid them little attention because she had lapsed once more into the daydream that seemed to be filling almost all her waking moments.

The daydream had been fixed for days now. Originally she'd fantasised that the donor was someone really rich and on meeting him she'd be whisked into a world of fabulous yachts, holidays in the Maldives and Michelin-starred restaurants. But, after a few days of failing to develop this scenario any further, she had settled for a biological father who was a talented artist living in a converted barn in France. She would holiday with him and they would inspire each other's art. There would be a joint exhibition and their work would be acclaimed and sold to prominent collectors. Now she concentrated on creating a backdrop to this father's life. She decided he would have no children, making him extremely happy he now had her, and he would be in-between partners, so there would be no competition for his attention, apart from his dog – a chocolate Labrador puppy who would be welcoming and friendly.

'Grrrr.'

'Shoo, shoo – hey, this dog is dangerous; should be on a lead.'

Catrin looked up to find a very cross man being accosted by Lucky some fifty metres in front of her. Lucky looked even crosser. Catrin ran towards them, calling out Lucky's name but he took no notice. Reaching them she bent down and slipped on Lucky's lead, dragging him away from the clearly furious man.

'I'm so sorry; he's not usually like this. I'm afraid it's your wellies,' Catrin struggled to explain over the dog's incessant growling.

'My wellies?' The man looked down at his green Hunter boots, clearly failing to see how they could offend a dog.

'Lucky's a rescue dog,' Catrin explained. 'We think he must have been mistreated by someone who wore Wellingtons.'

'Well, it certainly wasn't me,' the man replied indignantly as he turned and marched off, obviously keen to get away from a still growling Lucky.

'Oh Lucky, come on, calm down; there's a good boy, good boy, yes, you are,' Catrin whispered to the shaking dog, kneeling beside him and patting his silky brown coat reassuringly.

'Let's go home, Lucky; treat for you, hot chocolate for me.' The little dog wagged his tail and walked obediently by her side. Turning into the biting east wind Catrin pulled up her faux-fur hood. Lucky looked as if he was smiling as the wind blew his fur coat away from his face.

Jane laughed as Sue ushered the customer out with a cheery, 'And a very Merry Christmas to you.'

'Wahey, success. The chocolates for the sale of the day are mine,' Jane shouted as she twirled around the shop, between the rails of assorted skirts and dresses, jackets and trousers, racks of wide 80s ties, forlorn handbags and slightly scuffed shoes. They had tried, at various times, to organise the merchandise according to size, according to colour, even according to the decade in which it was made, but the very nature of a charity shop meant that no system worked for more than a couple of days as stock was sold and replaced by something totally different. Now, with the remaining Christmas decorations, party frocks and fancy-dress outfits given a prominent position, it looked even more shambolic than usual. But experience told them that rifling through the items and coming across something totally unexpected was what appealed to many of their customers; carefully arranged, organised displays took away much of the fun. And for Jane the shop now looked and felt its best; it seemed to be comfortable with what it really was, not trying to be anything else.

'You really could sell sand to the Arabs, Jane. So let's see now: the challenges chart. Mmm, that's seven sales to you, four to Barbara, and mmmm to me.'

'Sorry, Sue, I didn't quite hear that; how many to you?'

'Two,' Sue said sheepishly, adding, 'I'd better watch out or you'll be promoted and I'll be demoted, Jane.'

Jane laughed. 'So you're telling me that Barbara, who volunteers two mornings a week, has sold 50 per cent more than you – our esteemed manager, who is full-time and paid!'

Sue laughed. 'You selling that plastic duck in just five hours must be a record.'

'I think it does help that it's Christmas,' Jane replied, 'people seem to lose all sense of judgment at this time of year.'

'Suggesting the duck might just scare away those grey squirrels was a stroke of genius. Glad you didn't offer a money-back guarantee though. Anyway well done, Jane, and now you get to pick the next challenge. What's it to be?'

Jane walked around the shop. She was constantly

astounded at what people dumped in their charity shop bags – often surprised why anyone would want to give away their fabulous designer clothes but flabbergasted why others would think someone would want to buy a top hat (minus its top), a pair of false teeth, one shoe, or unwashed underwear. She had learned by now to wear plastic gloves before delving into any bag and she teased Ben that the internal investigations she performed were just as personal as the ones he undertook in the surgery. She grimaced. There had been very little laughter at home recently and Ben seemed to have lost his sense of humour completely. Last night she had teased him about a tear in his underpants, knowing that usually he would have enjoyed the opportunity to indulge in some lavatorial humour. But he'd simply shrugged and dumped them in the bin. Jane knew something distressing had happened at work and that, coupled with the turmoil at home, was clearly getting to him.

She picked up a pair of plastic reindeer antlers. 'Here we are – our next challenge. These have a shelf life of one hour; if we don't sell them before we close today I don't think there will be much demand for them after Christmas.'

'OK, game on,' Sue agreed enthusiastically. Jane smiled at her. Sue was certainly not the best salesperson ever but she knew exactly how to motivate the others. She really was a good manager of people.

That afternoon their customers were different from usual. Hardly anyone looked at the ordinary clothes and all requests were for help with fancy-dress outfits and last minute presents. By 3 p.m. the street outside was quiet and Sue suggested they shut up shop. As she tilled up Jane tidied the shoe rack, once again trying to pair up lonely shoes abandoned here and there.

'You go now, Jane; I'll lock up.'

'Oh, I'm in no hurry; Ben's at home today so he'll hopefully have done the shopping and chopping.'

The shop door was pushed open and two young girls came in bringing a blast of cold air with them. They wandered aimlessly around picking things up and putting them down again. They reached the books and magazines stand and started flicking through the pages of *Hello!* Sue firmly closed the till and turned off the window light.

'Are you looking for anything in particular, girls?' Jane asked.

'We need a present for our friend – she's ten,' said the taller of the two girls.

'But we're on a budget,' said her companion.

'Times are hard,' agreed the other.

Jane nodded sagely and smiled at them. These two sounded just like their grandparents. 'Well, how about a book? They're 50p each,' she suggested.

'No, reading's for school innit?' came the immediate reply from the shorter of the two.

Jane tried again. 'A mug then? I've got a cool Kylie one here – that's 50p too.'

'Oh, not Kylie, she's ancient; my mum likes her.'

The taller girl nodded.

'What about these antlers then? She could wear them for a joke on Christmas Day and then use them upside down to hold her beads and bangles. So two presents in one.'

The taller girl waited for the smaller friend to react and then nodded her agreement. 'Cool, yeah, cos they're always getting tangled. How much are they?'

'Seventy-five pence,' Jane replied hopefully.

'I'll give you fifty,' the smaller of the two replied firmly, nudging her friend. 'Deal or no deal?'

'Deal. Done, thank you and Merry Christmas,' Jane replied, handing over the antlers, accepting the 50p piece offered and popping it under the till. Sue opened the door for the girls and closed it behind them with a flourish.

'Eight–two to you,' Sue laughed, 'and as we've already tilled up that can count as your first sale after Christmas – when you'll be in sole charge, Jane. Come on then, let's get out of here; let Christmas really begin.' Sue passed Jane her coat, put on her own, switched off the lights and locked the shop behind them. 'Have a lovely Christmas, Jane.'

'You too Sue, enjoy your holiday – lucky you going to the sun, I'm so envious. Anyway, have a great time and see you next year.'

'Yes, see you next year.'

Catrin awoke to the smell of turkey. Of course, it was Christmas Day. Her mother had stuffed the bird the previous evening while her father had driven up to Treorchy to collect her grandmother. The turkey had been placed in the Aga just before they'd all gone to bed and now the aroma had spread throughout the house. Catrin thought she probably liked the smell more than the taste of the meat itself. She was too excited to lie there looking at her ceiling so she flung back the quilt, slung her long fluffy dressing gown over her pyjamas and went to the bathroom. In fifteen minutes she was showered, dressed and heading downstairs.

'Happy Christmas everyone,' she said cheerily as she came into the kitchen, kissed her grandmother and sat beside her at the table.

'Happy Christmas Catrin,' her father, mother and Granny Olwen choroused.

'Mmm, pancakes,' Catrin said appreciatively. She helped herself from the plate as her mother put a fresh pot of tea in the middle of the table. Catrin smiled at her. 'Oh Mum, you've got your holly and ivy tea set out. It's lovely. We should have Christmas more often!'

'And I'm wearing my special Santa apron.' Her mum smiled.

'You're brother's still not up,' Granny Olwen commented, looking at her watch. 'And it's twenty past eight.'

Ben laughed. 'It's early rather than late, Olwen.'

Granny Olwen gave her daughter one of her looks.

'OK, OK, Mum,' she said, 'I'll go and call him now.'

'Good,' Granny Olwen said, sounding satisfied, 'don't want him to miss Christmas completely do we.'

Her mother went out and Catrin heard her call up the stairs from the hall. There was no reply. Then Catrin heard her go upstairs, knock, say something and come down again.

'Well, I think the word pancake seems to have done the trick,' her mum said as she came back into the kitchen.

They were on their second cup of tea by the time Tom joined them.

'Happy Christmas everyone,' he said. Catrin thought he didn't sound very happy himself.

Granny Olwen got up to hug him. 'Early to bed, early to rise, makes a man healthy, wealthy and wise,' she said cheerfully.

'Doesn't apply to Christmas Day, Gran,' Tom moaned as he unwrapped himself from her embrace and sat down at the table, grabbing a pancake and pouring syrup all over it. 'Why are we all up so early anyway?'

'I thought we'd go to the chapel service this morning; it's at 9:30,' Ben replied.

Tom rolled his eyes. 'What on earth for? We never go to chapel', he said through a mouthful of pancake.

'Well,' their dad said quietly, 'Granny Lewis always went on Christmas morning and I thought it would be nice for us as a family to keep up the tradition.'

Tom looked at their mother who was now making cranberry sauce on the hob.

'I think it's a good idea,' she said with a note of warning in her voice.

'So do I, Granny Lewis would be pleased,' Catrin added, clearing some of the dirty dishes from the table and putting them in the sink.

'But why do I have to go?' Tom grumbled, as he held on to his plate and reached for another pancake.

'Because it's Christmas and we do things as a family at Christmas,' their mother replied sharply.

'I'll stay and finish off the vegetables,' Granny Olwen volunteered. Catrin saw the alarm on her mother's face and stifled a laugh.

'If you really don't want to come you don't have to, but you don't need to do anything with the food, honestly, promise?' her mother said forcefully.

'Really, Jane, I was cooking Christmas lunch before you were born,' Granny Olwen said indignantly.

'Yes, and very badly too, no doubt,' Tom said under his breath.

Actually it hadn't been a good idea to go to the chapel service, Catrin thought afterwards. Her mother hadn't understood much, Tom had all but fallen asleep several times and she'd had to nudge him, her father had become emotional and she too had felt a lump in her throat as she'd tried to sing the familiar carols. She so wished she'd come to this service with Granny Lewis last year – now that would have pleased her. At the end, when everyone had emerged wishing one another "Nadolig Llawen; Happy Christmas," and was catching up with each other's news, she had felt they did not belong. The minister was kind and shook their hands, saying it must be a difficult time for them with their loss being so recent but everyone wanted a piece of him on this special day and he'd moved them gently on. One or two of the other chapel goers had put a hand on her father's arm, a silent acknowledgment of the family's loss, but as they drifted back to the car she'd felt somehow cheated.

The lump in Catrin's throat seemed to be there at lunch too. They ate in the dining room infrequently and Catrin couldn't remember eating here since last Christmas when all six of them had been together. As usual her mother's food was delicious but Catrin couldn't help but notice the empty place at one end of the table. It wasn't completely empty of course. A big white candle flickered in the spot where Granny Lewis used to sit. Catrin wondered if her dad, who had laid the table, had put it there on purpose but she couldn't ask. She gulped down a mouthful of turkey, scolding herself for being morose.

Really what was so different today? But Christmas of course was a marker, made comparisons with other Christmases unavoidable.

'Who is that from, Jane?' Granny Olwen asked breaking the silence and pointing to a card showing a couple and two children, all with alarmingly white teeth, in front of a roaring fire.

Catrin saw her mother smile gratefully. 'That's the American branch of the Lewis family – Ben's second cousin in Ohio.'

'They're the ones who win the prize for the most boastful Round Robin every year – and that's quite something because the general standard of boastfulness is very high,' Tom said, laughing. 'Why anyone thinks we'd be interested that a seven-year-old we've never met has passed Grade Three violin with distinction escapes me.'

'Oh, don't be so grumpy, Tom,' their mother chided, 'I'd much rather people send those kinds of letters than say nothing. What really bugs me is those Christmas cards you get from people you haven't seen for a long time that just say "from Fred and June" and nothing else. So disappointing.'

'More turkey or veg anyone?' their dad asked.

Everyone, except Tom, shook his or her head.

'I'll help you out since you seem to have cooked enough to feed the five thousand,' he said, piling a second portion of everything on to his plate. 'What is it that makes people go shopping crazy at Christmas? The shops are only closed for one day, for goodness sake.'

'Siege mentality,' their father said. 'It's like you, Olwen, stockpiling tins.'

Catrin laughed, picturing Granny Olwen's little pantry piled high with tins of luncheon meat, pink salmon and diced mixed vegetables.

'Ah, you may laugh, Catrin, but if you'd lived through the war …'

'Did I tell you we're hoping to get a new partner at the

111

surgery?' her father said, directing his question at Granny Olwen.

'Lucky escape there,' Tom muttered under his breath.

Lucky, hearing his name, got up from under the table, wagged his tail against Catrin's leg and wolfed down the piece of turkey she fed him.

'Do you need more help in the surgery then, Ben?'

'Certainly do. It will be wonderful to have another pair of hands, if we can attract any applicants. Nobody wants to work in General Practice these days – too much paperwork, that's the problem.'

Silence descended again. The rest of the family sipped their white wine while Tom ate enthusiastically.

'Shall we have the pudding later? Best give the first course a chance to settle,' her mum suggested.

'Good idea,' Granny Olwen agreed, 'and then we can open our presents before the Queen's speech.'

Tom groaned.

'If you'd lived through the war and seen how brave the young Princess Elizabeth was you wouldn't groan, Tom. She could repair an engine and everything – quite the mechanic she was,' Granny Olwen said with feeling.

'Right, Tom, have you finished?' Catrin said quickly, keen to deflect her grandmother from the endless World War Two stories she tended to recycle on a regular basis.

As they got up from the table her dad assured them he and Tom would do all the clearing up later, which gave Tom another excuse to roll his eyes dramatically. Their dad gave him a shove and they all headed into the living room where Catrin began sorting the presents into little piles.

'Here are yours,' she said to her grandmother, putting a handful of presents beside Granny Olwen's chair.

'What if we all open one present now – it's ten to three – and then we'll switch on the telly for Her Majesty,' her dad said, giving a little bow in Granny Olwen's direction.

Her grandmother chose to open a gift from Catrin and was

clearly delighted with the colourful button-and-lace brooch her granddaughter had made for her. Granny Olwen immediately pinned it to her cardigan. Her dad unwrapped his gift from her mum – a reindeer-covered Christmas jumper which he also immediately put on, stating it was important to get as much wear as possible out of 'seasonal pieces' and that it was probably cold enough for him to sleep in it too. Her mum chose to open a present from Tom – an apron sporting the bold slogan 'Who needs three wise men when you have one wise woman?' She declared it was 'what she had always wanted,' adding that Tom could borrow it anytime. Tom tore at the wrapping of his present from work colleagues to reveal a bottle of pink bubble bath. As the family laughed he explained that pink-coloured gifts were de rigueur this year – and really he was lucky not to have been given pink pants. Catrin chose to open her parents's gift.

'Oh, Mum, Dad, this is beautiful,' she said, hugging both of them in turn. She held up the teardrop-shaped pendant to show Granny Olwen and its iridescent blues and greens danced in the light.

'We've had it made from one of Granny Lewis's brooches, Catrin,' her dad said gently.

'The stone is opal, Catz, your birthstone, so Dad and I thought it was only right you should have it. And we're really pleased with the way it's turned out,' her mother said, helping Catrin fasten it around her neck.'

'And Granny Lewis would have been pleased for you to have it,' her dad added.

Catrin nodded. She could not trust herself to speak. The lump was back.

The turkey leftovers had been eaten, the naked tree now lay forlornly alongside the bin in the back garden, waiting for someone to take it to the recycling point, and Jane was tired. Tired of the forced jollity and deeply upset that for the first time ever she felt her family seemed all out of kilter.

Christmas lunch had gone well enough – everyone had been on his or her best behaviour – but for much of the rest of the holiday things had been fraught. There had been some highs of course: Catrin had loved her pendant, and having her mother to stay until Boxing Day had been comforting, but there had been more lows. The chapel service had not been great – they clearly did not belong there and whatever solace Ben had hoped for clearly had not come about. But worst of all she'd caught herself saying things just to fill awkward gaps, trying desperately to think of possible topics of conversation before they sat down to a meal.

How different it had been a year ago when invariably they'd talked across each other, interrupting one another and sometimes shouting to be heard, with Granny Lewis interjecting her usual 'elbows off the table', or 'it's a fork, Tom, not a shovel'. Jane wryly acknowledged that she missed her mother-in-law; she'd found herself laboriously cutting little crosses in the top of each Brussels sprout, despite having argued with Granny Lewis for years that this made no difference to the taste. Ben had been particularly quiet and withdrawn, blaming his bleak mood on it being the first Christmas without his mother. Jane knew he missed her but she also knew his mood had much to do with what lay ahead. Over the holiday he had finally told her what had been troubling him for weeks; the death of a six-year-old in his care could not but affect him deeply. And of course Catrin being upset and now trying to find her donor was distressing too.

Now it was New Year's Eve. Usually she would have been delighted to hear that neither Catrin nor Tom intended to go out. This evening she felt differently. She looked at her watch – 5 p.m. Two hours until the tagine was ready. She picked up the half-full bottle of Merlot sitting on the kitchen table since last night, poured herself a large glass, and reached for the tin of cashew nuts, ignoring the bright orange post-it note on its lid on which she'd written with a green marker pen 'NOTHING TASTES BETTER THAN THIN FEELS'. Jane tipped half a dozen nuts into her palm, cupped her hand and poured them into her mouth. She munched, looking out vacantly through the patio doors into the darkened back garden, and took a generous sip of wine. After a few minutes she topped up her drink, found her glasses and her mobile and settled in the armchair beside the Aga.

Getting my happy new yrs in early before network overload. So HNY Mum, c u Wed, Station Caf, 11?x

She took another sip of wine, rested her feet against the warm Aga door and closed her eyes, waiting for her mother's reply. Olwen always had her mobile by her side and Jane could see her now hunting for her reading glasses, making a cup of tea, and then settling down to respond. Jane smiled, thinking how the generation gap between herself and her mother was continuously shrinking.

Predictably, in ten minutes, the little mobile shook and Jane forced her eyes open. Olwen's messages always extended to at least two screenfuls and arrived in instalments.

Yes, look forward to seeing you. The weather forecast is good. Christine called today with Callum and Amy to show me their Christmas presents. They liked the game you gave them – do you remember the fun we had with ...

Jane waited for the next ping.

Snakes and Ladders. I hope you've thought of your New Year's Resolution. Mine will be the same as usual!!! Look forward to seeing you on Wednesday then love. Happy New Year to you and love to Ben, Tom, and Catrin. Mumx

Jane had explained repeatedly that Olwen didn't need to sign her name as the sender's name appeared automatically. But her mum continued doing so, just as she persisted in using correct syntax and avoiding abbreviations. Jane was however impressed her mother could text at all. It would have been far easier for her to pick up the phone. But she persisted with texting and Skyping, possibly in an attempt to impress on them just how 'with it' she was for seventy-five, but more probably, Jane thought, just to please herself. How lucky her mother was to have only herself to please, Jane reflected, as she hauled herself out of the deep leather armchair to check the tagine.

Ben's day had not gone well. It had started much as usual: his list was full, there was a mountain of paperwork to be done as well as a memo from Stella, the practice manager, asking how he was getting on with his audit. He'd unceremoniously tossed the memo to one side. How on earth was he supposed to have time to do an audit, and anyway what was the point? Well, he knew the point, to keep the government happy, but he'd be damned if he spent his precious time doing that rather than treating his patients. Herbert Jones had been his first appointment, arriving with a written list of ailments. Ben didn't have the heart to tell him practice rules now dictated he could only deal with one illness per visit as he knew old Herbert, like all the other patients that morning, had waited over three weeks to see him. And so, after the first case of the day, he was already running ten minutes late. A message in red on his screen alerted him to the fact Stella was also aware of this. By eleven o'clock there was another message asking him to come up to her office as soon as he had finished his surgery.

At 12.30 p.m. Ben knocked on Stella's door, blushing furiously and feeling as if he was 12 years old again, summoned to see the headmaster regarding some misdemeanour.

'Come in,' she shouted.

He opened the door and stood leaning diffidently against it. 'I know what you're going to say, Stella, but how can I be expected to be on time if every patient is only allowed ten minutes? For old boys like Herbert it takes at least two minutes to wheeze their way to my room.'

'Dr Smart seems to manage it,' Stella said without looking away from the online spreadsheet she was working on.

'You know full well that my patients are different from Dr Smart's – I get all the chronic ones.'

'It's because you're too soft with them Ben; you're a

doctor, not a social worker.'

'Oh come on, Stella, we all know illness is far more than a list of symptoms; sometimes knowing the background can really help. Anyway I've got six house calls to do in an hour, which as you know is impossible, so if you've finished giving me a telling off I'll be on my way in the hope I'll only be an hour late starting afternoon surgery.'

'Please sit down Ben. I need to talk to you about something else. Anyway you've only got a couple of appointments booked this afternoon; early finish as it's New Year's Eve.'

Stella took off her glasses and carefully placed them on the tidy stack of papers on her desk. She took a letter from the top of her in tray and handed it to Ben who still stood leaning against the open door, anxious to get away.

'It's from the Local Health Board. Charlene Evans's parents have put in a formal complaint against you. I'm afraid it's going to tribunal, Ben,' Stella said quietly.

Ben felt all his strength drain away. He reached for the chair and sat heavily. Stella got up and closed the door. Ben had feared the arrival of such a letter of course but, as six weeks had passed since Charlene's death, he had hoped her parents had decided he'd done his best and that everyone was capable of making mistakes. Evidently not.

He'd spent sleepless nights trying to persuade himself he was not to blame. He'd seen Charlene in the surgery. She'd come in with her mother and said she had a bad headache. He'd examined her, noted her high temperature and concluded it was probably flu, advising her to take paracetamol and plenty of fluids. The following day her symptoms had worsened and she'd been rushed into hospital. Meningitis. Logically Ben knew that meningitis frequently presented with the same symptoms as flu and that most doctors would have come to the same conclusion he had. But he also knew that grieving families often needed someone to blame.

'They're probably just after the money, Ben, and who can blame them with these wretched solicitors urging people to

117

claim for everything.'

Ben shook his head. 'I feel so sorry for them but I don't know what more I could have done – she had no rash, she had no neck stiffness; this illness, it just takes over so quickly.'

Stella put on her glasses, her attention once again on the spreadsheet in front of her. She made one more effort to look at Ben and said briskly, 'Well, you'll just have to tell the tribunal that. If someone makes a formal complaint they have to look into it. You know that; don't worry.'

How could he not worry? But being forced to think again of the tragedy of six-year-old Charlene's death put his own family's turmoil into sharp perspective. He knew that he had been a bit grumpy recently, no, more than a bit grumpy, and he resolved to snap out of it.

And so Ben had arrived home from work and headed straight out to his shed. He'd put on his old gardening coat, a British Railway standard-issue long gabardine one that Jane had brought home from the charity shop a couple of years ago. When he had first had the coat it had been so stiff it could almost stand up by itself but by now it had moulded to his ample girth and covered him from neck to ankle. Although he officially called it his 'gardening coat' it was in fact his smoking jacket. It protected his clothes and when he knew he needed a serious smoking session he would don it. He was convinced it absorbed all the luscious smells that would otherwise give away his little secret. He'd now been sitting in his deckchair wearing it for about forty-five minutes, letting the fug of Golden Virginia ease his pain.

Tom stopped in Tesco's on the way home, happily tired from having run around the AstroTurf pitch for a couple of hours. He'd then gone for a quick drink with the boys and was now absolutely starving. As it was 5 p.m., and there were just two more hours before the special New Year's Eve supper his mother had promised, he decided that a pasty and a Mars bar would be enough to fill the gap. He wandered down the bakery aisle and the smell of fresh bread forced him to pick up a French stick – just in case his mum had any idea of making them all give up white bread again; something she did almost every January. He also picked up a 'just in case' lemon meringue pie and a bottle of what claimed to be half-price Moët et Chandon. Feeling pleased at saving money and pleased with life in general he made for the till. He refused the offer of a 5p bag, gathered up his purchases, ignored the *Big Issue* seller sheltering in the doorway and got into his mother's car. He bit into the pasty, sending flakes of pastry flying in every direction, and turned on the ignition. The car's petrol fuel gauge flashed a warning and bleeped irritatingly. He chose to ignore this too.

It was only a short drive to Pencisely Crescent. The scent of home greeted him as he opened the front door and headed for the kitchen. 'Hi Mum, where's everyone? Something smells good; I'm starving.'

'Dad's in the shed and Catrin's at Siân's – back by seven' His mother looked at him. 'I'm struggling to decide whether I can be bothered to ask you to lay the table, Tom, but yes, I think I will.'

Tom groaned loudly but said. 'OK, I'll do that for you, Mum.'

'Oh, not just a place for me, Tom, for the four of us.'

Tom thought it was obvious he needed to set four places. He turned towards his mum, holding up his hands to indicate he didn't understand the point she was trying to make.

'You're not doing it *for me* Tom. As far as I'm aware laying the table for every meal – and cooking it – and clearing up afterwards isn't in any job description that I signed up to.'

Tom shrugged, quickly laid the table and, deciding his mother was in a strange mood, disappeared upstairs.

Her mother-in-law's big clock in the hall struck nine but Jane did not feel inclined to make a start on the clearing up. She felt happy now, no doubt helped by the half bottle of Merlot she'd

119

drunk, but she was sure there had been a subtle change tonight, that they were all once again more or less in tune with each other. Now satiated, she relaxed and listened to her family light-heartedly teasing each other as they sat around the kitchen table.

'So, come on, Tom, you've got to think of a new New Year's Resolution this year now that you've finally got a proper job.'

'People who are perfect don't need them, sis, and so my New Year's Resolution is not to make one.'

'Perfect? You? Let's consider the evidence shall we? Mum, Dad, help me out here please – Dad, you first.'

Ben beamed and asked: 'How long have you got?'

Tom groaned.

Ben took a long sip of his wine, suggesting he needed to fortify himself before answering. 'Well, first off, you put empty milk bottles back in the fridge. So, Tom, I think you should resolve to get off your lazy backside and walk to the corner shop so the rest of us can enjoy the luxury of milk in our tea.'

While Tom was considering his comeback, Jane jumped in. 'I think resolving to fill the tank with petrol when you borrow my car would be a good one.' She added, quickly, 'and what about acknowledging the relationship between dirty clothes and the linen basket?'

Tom laughed. 'You'd have nothing to do, Mother, if I did all those things for you.'

'For me?' she said indignantly and turned to Ben.

'Time to change the locks?'

'Would I get the big bedroom then?' Catrin asked, making a mock-serious face. 'Anyway, case proven, bro.'

'OK, good points, well made, guilty as charged. So my New Year's Resolution is to be super house-trained.'

Jane raised her eyebrows. 'Catz, what's yours?'

'Simple – to actually get the grades to go to Aber.'

'Swot!' her brother said, as he gave her a shove.

'What about resolving to learn to drive before you go off to uni, Catrin? I'd be more than happy to take you out for a few goes before you book lessons with a driving instructor,' Ben suggested.

'No thanks, Dad; it's far greener to go by bus.'

'Greener still to walk,' Tom added.

'Mum, what about you, any resolutions?' Catrin asked.

'By this time next year I'm going to be svelte-like. If Nigella can do it, then so can I.' Jane topped up their wine glasses.

'Love, that's been your resolution for the last ten years and anyway I don't want you to change. I love you cuddly,' Ben said, reaching over to give her a hug.

'There's cuddly and there's obese, Big Ben,' Jane responded as she pushed him away. 'And what's more I think you could join me – let's resolve to lose weight together.'

'Jane, you are not obese. To qualify as obese you'd have to have a BMI of 30 or over and you definitely don't. But as for me, this year I've made a bucket list and losing weight is not in my top ten.'

'Oh, Dad, how morbid,' Catrin said, putting her hand over his.

Ben laughed. 'Not at all, it's a fun list – and number one is to learn to speak Welsh fluently.'

'How can that be fun, Dad?' Tom asked, rolling his eyes, 'and why would you want to do that? You've already got a job.'

'Look Tom I've been thinking a lot recently about connecting with my roots and I can't explain why but it's important I know exactly who I am.'

'Precisely,' Catrin said.

From the look on his face, Jane knew Ben understood exactly what Catrin meant – that her decision to find out about her donor and his wish to connect to his past had the same goal. But of course understanding and liking were two very different things.

Chapter Nine

January 1st was a beautiful day; the pale sunlight mellow and a light frost making the valley below seem clean and sparkly. Jane, Catrin, and Lucky, having had lunch with Olwen, were walking briskly on the hillside high above Treorchy trying to work off some of the corned-beef pie.

Jane thought how different the valley looked from when she played here as a little girl. What she remembered most of all was the smoke that would billow from every chimney pot. Now she spotted a few houses here and there with welcoming puffs reaching for the sky; all the others sprouted Sky dishes. How different the Rhondda had been when she was growing up, every door in the street open and people wandering in and out of each other's homes. That had changed with the closure of the mines. By the time she'd gone to the big school, in the seventies, there were no working mines in the area and people had to travel out of the valley to work or resign themselves to living off the social. Jane felt a deep longing for the way things had been, for the ease with which people had socialised, for the closeness of a community that had real roots, for the days when you shouted a greeting as you walked in through the neighbours' back door.

She loved this mountain. It had been such a part of her life at both happy and sad times. This is where she'd played with her friends during the long summer holidays. In those days trips out of the valley were rare, besides the annual Sunday School trip to Barry Island and the Social Club trip to Porthcawl. The rest of the time was spent playing in the park or here on the slag heaps on the mountainside. How could her parents not have realised the danger? But then everyone allowed their children to play on the slag heaps; it was their back yard. And then, when she'd started courting, this is where she had come with Rhys, and then with Johnny, and then with Morgan. Ah, Morgan. She hadn't thought about him for years. He could have been 'the one' Jane reflected, had they met when they were a little older. But maybe things had turned out for the best. Had Morgan not joined up, had the army not posted him to Northern Ireland for six long months, she would probably not have met Ben. Now of course the slag heaps had long gone, cleared as a result of the appalling Aberfan disaster, and nature had reclaimed the mountain and covered it in a blanket of green and purple. But it was still hers. Jane stopped to catch her breath.

'Penny for your thoughts, Mum?'

'Catrin, love, my thoughts are priceless and not to be shared with anyone, not even you.' Jane wheezed slightly.'

Catrin laughed. For a moment neither said anything as they gazed down at the valley below.

'I wonder how Cardiff City are doing? Dad and Tom will be in a good mood if they see them win today.'

'Well, the Bluebirds have had a good run recently, so the chances are they will, especially since they're playing at home,' Jane said, thankful she was able to breathe normally once more.

'OK, Mum, you ready to go on?'

Jane nodded.

They both fell silent again as they tackled a particularly steep stretch. Lucky had run ahead but now stopped and sniffed and marked his patch.

'When do you think I'll hear back from them, Mum?'

Jane knew immediately what her daughter was referring to. She'd been aware of Catrin's dash to the letterbox every morning and her escalating disappointment when the letter failed to arrive.

'It's holiday time, love. I'm sure you'll get a reply before the end of the month.'

'But the website said 20 working days, and that's up on the

14th.'

'Patience is a virtue, Catrin.'

'Oh, Mum, you and your old-fashioned sayings.'

'Old-fashioned but still true Catz. Shall we stop for a moment? Benches are few and far apart up here and I could do with another breather.'

They sat down and Jane looked out over Treorchy to the mountains beyond. She liked this big, wide airy landscape, so different from the narrow villages below which straddled the one road up the Valley. This was a good place to think, to get a proper perspective. She shifted as the coldness of something at her back penetrated the numerous layers she had on. Turning she saw a metal plate attached to the wooden bench. It read:

In memory of Trevor Pryce who loved the view from here

'Ah, I remember Trevor Pryce, old miner, always short of breath but he'd struggle up here with his greyhounds. He used to breed them to race. I remember he had a really fast one – Mustard he was called because he was keen as mustard. In one race–'

'Mum, what was it like going to that fertility clinic?'

Jane was momentarily taken aback. After her mother-in-law's revelation she'd decided she would be as honest as possible about the whole treatment with Catrin but she'd resolved not to broach the subject herself, knowing if Catrin wanted to know she would ask. And now she was.

'Well, it was very professional.' Jane struggled to find the words. What could she say that would satisfy her daughter? She chose to focus on the mechanics. 'I had to keep some temperature charts to try to work out when I was most fertile and then your Dad and I went to this clinic in Park Place and they injected the sperm through a syringe.'

Jane felt her daughter cringe or perhaps she was just cold. Jane put her arm around her anyway.

'Did you get to choose anything about the donor?' Catrin asked, still looking straight ahead.

Jane squeezed her daughter's shoulder gently. 'No, but I think they did try to match us up with someone who shared at least some of Dad's characteristics.'

'But you can't match up someone's personality, can you?' Catrin said flatly as she got up to retrieve a tissue from her pocket. Jane noticed she didn't use it and suspected the purpose of the movement had been to escape her arm. Catrin sat down again, a little further away and called to Lucky who had drifted off in pursuit of a rabbit.

Jane sensed there were more questions to come. She wanted to point out the old Parc and Dare colliery site where Catrin's great-grandfather had worked and died, wanted to change the topic of conversation, but decided that to keep quiet and wait was the kindest thing to do.

Lucky settled at their feet, panting, and Catrin leant down to remove a small twig from his coat. 'Were there lots of people who had this treatment when you did?'

'Well, I didn't know any, but your dad had patients who'd been treated there. I did meet someone at the clinic and we kept in touch for a while. She had a little girl at the same time I had you –and then she had another little girl the following year. I've got a photograph of them somewhere she sent when the girls were babies.'

'Could those girls have the same donor as me?'

The question surprised Jane. 'Well, I suppose so, Catz,' she said hesitantly.

'Do you know if they're still in Cardiff?'

Jane felt stunned at how quickly her daughter's mind worked. 'The last address I had for them was in North Devon somewhere – I think near Barnstaple. But that must be more than ten years ago. I haven't heard since.'

They watched as Lucky raced off to greet a beautiful golden retriever being walked by its equally beautiful owner.

'Hi, she do love it up 'ere,' the dog walker told them as she passed, and walked on.

Jane caught Catrin's eye and they both smiled.

'They say owners look like their dogs – well those two did – but I don't think a golden retriever sounds like that, do you?' Jane said when the blondes were out of earshot.

'Deffo not, Mum, a golden retriever would say 'Good afternoon, my owner loves it up here, don't you know?'

They laughed.

'Shall we go back to Granny's? Jane asked, 'I think we've had enough exercise for today.'

Catrin nodded and helped Jane to her feet. She called to Lucky and the three of them turned back down the hillside towards Treorchy.

Jane glanced at her beautiful daughter, feeling guilty now for being so ready to seize the opportunity to change the subject, anxious to give her more. 'The lady I met at the clinic had a very unusual surname.' She thought for a moment. 'Ramsbottom, that's it. Celia Ramsbottom. A bit unfortunate, a name like that.'

Catrin smiled warmly, linking arms with her. 'No, fortunate, Mum.'

'Well, I suppose you could say that; it's certainly memorable.'

'Fortunate because she should be easy to find; there can't be many Ramsbottoms in Devon or even in the UK.'

The path narrowed. They unlinked arms and Jane passed through the gap first, picking up her pace considerably as Catrin loitered trying to persuade Lucky to come to heel. Jane walked on, imagining the possible repercussions of Catrin making contact with her new family. She felt unable to grasp all the scenarios – her mind was too full – and, as she reached the valley floor, she decided to stop trying and let things take their course. She and Ben had attempted to control everything for too long and now they must let Catrin take the lead. By the time they reached Olwen's home in Prospect Street Jane had a blinding headache. A strong cup of tea and the run of Olwen's medicine drawer was very welcome indeed.

As soon as they got home to Cardiff Catrin picked up her

127

laptop and went to her bedroom, closing the door. Jane hoped this meant her daughter was keen to get on with some homework. She had begun to worry the search for her donor was distracting Catrin from her studies and jeopardising her chances of getting to university. Really all this couldn't have come at a worse time.

Jane put on an apron – choosing the one that said, 'Keep Calm and Carry On'. She'd just retuned the radio to the soothing tones of Classic FM and set about peeling onions and grating garlic to make spaghetti bolognese when she heard Catrin come bounding down the stairs. Her daughter began to speak before she swept into the kitchen and, although Jane could not make out what she was saying, she knew Catrin was excited about something.

'Wow, slow down, Catz, start again.'

Catrin paced up and down. 'Well, I went to 192.com but there was no Ramsbottom listed in Barnstaple. But then I did a search on Devon,' she rushed on breathlessly, 'and there are two listings – and the local electoral roll shows there was a Celia Ramsbottom in one of them in 2008. It's an Exeter address, mum.'

Jane carried on chopping, glad of something to focus on. She reminded herself she had decided to help Catrin in any way she could but still her stomach lurched at the uncertainty that lay ahead.

'Mum, can you find the photograph Celia sent you?'

'Yes love; I'll have a look for it when I get a chance.'

'I meant now, Mum. I'll get on with the supper so you can search.'

The earnest look on Catrin's face made Jane wash her hands and take off her apron without protest. 'I'm not sure how it's going to help you, Catrin.'

'Please Mum.'

Catrin's eyes filled with tears as she finished chopping the onions and she rubbed them with her sleeve. Jane went through the odds and sods drawer, depositing random items on the worktop until she found the crumpled photograph. She looked at the two little fair-haired girls and handed the picture to Catrin who took it to study under the pendant light over the kitchen table.

'The 192 listing has a phone number as well as an address. Can we phone them Mum?'

'But what would we say?' Jane said doubtfully.

'Well just that I've started looking for my donor and have they done so too?'

'Catz, I think getting that kind of phone call out of the blue would be a bit shocking for anyone. Did you say there was an address? How about we write to Celia instead?'

Jane put her apron back on and added mince to the frying onions. The apron came off again as Catrin handed her a pretty notelet and Ben's best fountain pen. Reluctantly Jane let Catrin take over the cooking and sat at the kitchen table, pen suspended over paper, aware her daughter was watching her.

'The meat will stick if you're not careful.'

Catrin turned back to the pan and stirred the mixture half-heartedly. She tipped in a tin of tomatoes and sprinkled on some oregano.

Jane decided to keep the letter brief. She explained Catrin was trying to find her donor and then asked how Celia's girls were getting on. Celia would understand what she meant without her probing in a forthright way her old friend might find threatening. She sealed the envelope, addressed it, and added a stamp she'd found in the odds and sods drawer. Licking it left a horrible aftertaste in her mouth.

'Are you done Mum?' Catrin asked, adding a splash of Worcester Sauce to the bolognese mix.

Jane got up and held out the envelope.

Catrin quickly washed and dried her hands, gave Jane a hug then grabbed the envelope with a 'Just going to post this, back in a minute' and ran out the back door. Wearily Jane put on her apron and turned back to the bolognese. Some of the mince had stuck to the bottom. She knew it would make the sauce taste a little bitter but she could not start again.

Later, when Jane popped her head around Catrin's bedroom door to say goodnight, she saw her daughter had got all the baby albums out. The photograph of Celia's two little girls was lying beside one of Catrin aged eighteen months.

Catrin woke up feeling as if she hadn't slept at all. She'd had a disturbed night, not helped by Tom rolling in singing 'Who Let the Dogs Out?' at two in the morning. She had heard her father traipse to the bathroom at least three times, recognising the distinctive clip-clop of his leather-bottomed slippers on the hard wooden floor and at 5 a.m. the hall light had been on indicating someone was downstairs. She must have finally dropped off then. Now it was 8.35 and the postman would have long been. Surely there would be something today; it was now almost a week since everyone had gone back to work after the New Year Holiday.

She got up, put her dressing gown on and went downstairs. In the kitchen her father was sitting drinking tea from his usual breakfast mug but he was wearing a dark suit and tie – not the cords, jacket and open-necked shirt he generally wore to work – and his face wasn't buried in the paper.

'You're late going in today, Dad. Was there post?'

'Good morning love,' he said, his eyes fixed on the garden.

Catrin glanced around but couldn't see any new pile of envelopes. There had to be post; there were always circulars. She tried again.

'Post, Dad?'

'Yes, there was I think. Tom picked it up; not sure where he put it though,' he said, devoid of the hectic energy that usually characterised his mornings.

Catrin shifted yesterday's papers and a pile of bills awaiting attention but could find no post. Her father did not budge.

'Has Tom gone?' she asked.

'No, I haven't heard the car start; probably still trying to

130

clear the windscreen – hard frost overnight.'

Catrin went out the back door, her bare feet stinging on the frozen gravel. Her brother was busy scraping ice off her mother's VW Beetle as her dad had suggested.

'Tom, where's the post?'

'Erm … oh, I think I left it in the toilet.'

'Of course, why wouldn't you?' she shouted at him.

'There wasn't anything for you, anyway,' Tom shouted back.

Catrin ran inside, hopping from one painful foot to the other, and past her still stationary father. Retrieving the post from the downstairs toilet she checked through it anyway. Tom was right, nothing for her. Her spirits plummeted. But there was a letter for her mother. A handwritten letter. With an Exeter postmark.

Back in the kitchen her dad stood by the sink rinsing his mug. Catrin reached in front of him to fill the kettle. He did not move aside.

'I'll take a cup of tea up for Mum. You got an interview Dad? You look really smart.'

'Mmm, something like that.' He put the mug down. OK, I'm off, see you later Catrin; love you.' He picked up his briefcase and went out the back door. A few moments later she heard the Volvo leave.

Catrin set a tray with two mugs of tea, made some toast, added her mother's favourite apricot jam, propped the letter against the mugs and carefully made her way upstairs. Her mum smiled as she came in to the bedroom and handed her the tray. And then she noticed the letter.

'Shall I open it, Mum?'

Her mother nodded, taking a long sip of tea and a bite of toast as Catrin tore at the envelope. A photograph dropped out along with a sheet of white embossed paper. The photograph showed two tall, pretty, brown-eyed girls with long blonde hair. It had been taken in Pisa and the girls were laughing as they posed, trying to prop up the tower. Her mum read the

131

letter and then handed it to Catrin. Catrin scanned the closely written page with its tidy blue handwriting. As she got near the end she read more slowly and her eyes filled with tears.

'But she doesn't say anything, Mum. It's just all about their lives now.' She picked up the photograph. 'I think they look like me, don't you?'

Her mother took the photo from her and held it at arms length. 'Well, they've blonde hair, Catz, but I'm not sure otherwise – it's always difficult to tell from a photo.'

'But they're tall and slim too, Mum.'

'As tall as the tower of Pisa from this photo, Catz; they say the camera never lies but it can.'

'Will you write to her again, Mum and ask her if she knows anything about their donor?'

'Oh, Catz, that's what I asked in my last letter.'

'But perhaps you didn't make it clear enough. I think we need to be specific now and ask if her girls know who their donor is.'

'But Catrin she obviously doesn't want to discuss it or she would have said something in this letter.'

'Please Mum … pleeeeease.'

'I'll do it on one condition.' Her mum paused. 'If you promise to get on with some of your coursework.'

Catrin nodded her agreement. 'I promise,' she said.

As Ben drove up the Rhondda Valley the clouds were gathering; by the time he arrived in Pontypridd it was pouring with rain and he had to turn on the car headlights. The daily stream of traffic was heading out of the Valleys towards the city and he was glad, as always, he was travelling in the opposite direction and not stuck in that jam. Beyond Pontypridd the valley started closing in on him. Usually he liked going beyond Ponty, into the Valleys proper – intrinsically Welsh, intrinsically working-class. But today everything was grey and heavy.

He was glad he'd opted to face the tribunal on his own,

declining the offer of moral support. Really he couldn't bear the thought of making small talk with anyone and he knew he would have felt obliged to do so. Now, as he pulled into the glass and red brick offices of the Local Health Authority, located in what looked like an out-of-town shopping complex, he grunted. This was such an anomaly: glossy and shiny and as far removed from ordinary Valleys people as possible.

The girl on reception was texting; clearly the office was not inundated with visitors.

'Bore da; Good morning', she said, without looking up.

Well at least he'd get to practise his Welsh on a real person. For the last week he'd been talking to a CD on his way home from work. 'Bore da, Ben Lewis ydw i ...'

'Sorry, don't speak Welsh.'

'Oh, I thought–'

'No, we've got to say good morning in Welsh; policy.'

'Ah. Well, I'm Ben Lewis and I've an appointment with the panel this morning.'

'Please take a seat. I'll let them know you're here,' she said, clearly uninterested but sticking to the agreed script. She went back to her texting before lifting the phone.

Ben sat staring at a photo of the Valleys. These valleys, and their friendly, say-it-as-it-is people, had been the backdrop to his whole working life. And now it could be over.

The phone buzzed and the receptionist said they were ready for him. As he walked along the plush carpeted and eerily quiet corridor he tried to remember whether she'd said room one on the second floor or room two on the first floor? He opted for the first floor and when no one answered his knock made his way up the stairs.

His heart sank when he saw the panel of three. It sank because of the woman sitting in the middle. He'd forgotten about her; hadn't seen her for years.

'Please sit down, Dr Lewis', she said in an accent that suggested she had been brought up in the Home Counties. Actually she had been born and raised a few miles up the

133

valley. Ben remembered meeting her for the first time and asking where she was from; the explanation for the accent was three years spent in 'Oxford as a student'. A colleague overhearing the conversation had later explained that Belinda Morris had spent three years training as a nurse in the John Radcliffe. What a silly woman, had been his immediate thought – he would have been far more impressed had she said she'd trained as a nurse rather than implying she'd attended Oxford University. A few months later she'd confirmed his suspicions that she was indeed a very silly woman.

By then she was the owner of a small, private nursing home just above Wattstown. Ben, on one of his on-call nights, had been summoned to the home at 2 a.m. and ushered into an upstairs room by Belinda Morris, her finger on her lips to indicate he should be silent. She'd then locked the door behind them and pointed to the bed. In it was a gentleman, clearly dead.

'We'll wrap him in the blanket and carry him down the fire escape to the car,' she'd whispered. Ben, taken aback, had protested.

'You've got to help me; I've got to get him out,' she'd insisted.

She'd then explained that she didn't want to leave it to the undertaker to collect the body in the morning as that would upset the other residents. Pointing out to her that a mysterious disappearance would be far more frightening to the others than a perfectly natural death, he'd unlocked the door and left her to it. A few days later she'd moved to another practice in Pontypridd.

'Do you know Reverend Dewi Phillips and Mr John Bowen?' she now asked.

He didn't. Ben acknowledged the two men.

'Now, Dr Lewis, as you know the family of Charlene Evans have made a formal complaint and our remit as a panel is to determine whether you are fit to continue practising as a GP.' She smiled, clearly enjoying her position of authority.

Ben nodded. For the next forty minutes the panel asked him about his experience as a family doctor, his experience of diagnosing meningitis and what had actually happened on the day he'd seen Charlene.

'So am I right in concluding that as Charlene did not have a rash you decided she had flu?' Belinda Morris asked.

'She did not have neck stiffness and neither was she vomiting at that stage,' Ben added.

'Mm', Belinda Morris looked down at her notes. 'And you did not arrange for her to come back to see you or to visit her at home?' she said, her voice indicating incredulity. She turned first to Reverend Phillips and then to John Bowen and gave them a knowing look.

'I did tell her mother to ring the surgery if she got worse,' Ben said, trying not to sound defensive.

'And, of course, by then it was too late,' Belinda Morris said in a matter-of-fact way.

The Reverend, his voice soft and expression sympathetic, was clearly taken aback by Belinda Morris's aggressive manner. He sounded apologetic as he asked if there had been other complaints about Ben's treatment of his patients during his nineteen years as a GP.

'No, none,' Ben replied. The preacher seemed satisfied.

'Of course, patients find the complaints procedure intimidating; they are really reluctant to complain unless they feel very strongly they have been let down,' Belinda said. Mr Bowen nodded and the Reverend shuffled his papers.

'And so your advice was for Charlene to take paracetamol and to drink plenty of water?' There was a note of disbelief in Belinda Morris's voice.

She did not need to try to make him feel wretched. He already did. Ben felt hot all over and knew his face was flushed. 'Look, if I sent everyone with a temperature into hospital the place would be even fuller – and even now there are people on trolleys. You can't send everyone in; you have to be selective. As GPs we're paid to take responsibility, make

135

decisions.'

'Clearly the wrong decision in this case.' Belinda Morris sighed as she piled up the papers in front of her, indicating he had taken up enough of their time. 'Thank you, Dr Lewis. The panel will now have to give serious consideration as to whether this is a case of medical negligence. We shall be writing to you, formally, in due course. Good day, Dr Lewis,' she concluded in clipped tones.

And that was it. Ben found himself back in his car and then sitting at his desk in the surgery. If anyone had asked him whether he'd come back on the dual carriageway or on the A4054, he wouldn't have known.

Jane looked at her watch then held it to her ear to check it was still going. It was. Would the tribunal be over by now or was Ben still before the panel? She could picture him, frowning as he concentrated, unconsciously wiping his sweaty palms against his jacket. He'd be flushed too, another sign that he was nervous. Ben blushed at the slightest bit of attention and the embarrassment that caused him made him blush even more. She remembered him telling her how he'd blush at school whenever the teachers asked him anything and how often that had made them presume he was up to no good. His mother had said he would grow out of it. He never had. Jane hoped the health authority administrator and the two lay members sitting in judgement today wouldn't be as hasty as his teachers and would see her husband for the caring, conscientious man that he was.

Catching herself checking her watch again she decided to wander down to the charity shop to see if she could be of use there. She put her mobile in her jacket pocket so she would be sure to hear it if Ben rang, closed the front door behind her and made her way down towards Cowbridge Road.

Arriving at the shop, Jane could see Sue inside taking clothes off hangers and putting them into a black bag being held by a well-dressed man. Strange, she thought to herself, that someone so smart would be bulk buying from a charity shop. She opened the door and went in.

'Oh hi, Jane, what are you doing here? You do realise it's Monday today?'

'Sue, I may be losing it, but yes, I do realise it's Monday. I was at a loose end and–'

'Well, good to see you anyway – you know there's always plenty to do here – but first help yourself to coffee. Bernard and I are just doing some salvaging. What about this one Bernard?'

'Well could be, I suppose,' said the well-dressed man.

'This is your size; it's an Austin Reed, what do you think?'

Bernard shrugged his shoulders and looked miserable.

'Oh, and a Jaeger coat; this came in this morning, possible?'

'I don't know; they all look the same to me,' he replied flatly.

Jane admired Sue's patience, left her to it and went down to the little sorting basement to make them both a coffee. When she returned the man had gone and Sue was sitting at the counter chuckling.

'What a miserable man,' Jane said, putting the cups down on the counter.

'You would be too. They're moving today and his wife sent him in with some black bags full of donations and – and – oh dear.' Sue gave way to the laughter that had been building since the start of the explanation. She tried again. 'And he brought in the wrong bags; they were full of his best clothes. I don't think I managed to retrieve them all; I'm afraid we'd sold some of his stuff already. Nice stuff. Oh, we're having quite a day of it today and it's not yet lunchtime.'

Jane laughed with her and felt her shoulders ache. Until now she'd been unaware they had been hunched up all morning. Possibly because it was cold but probably, she thought, because she was tense. The laughter made her relax and she smiled at Sue, again realising just how much she enjoyed this hopelessly low-paid job.

'He's the second today. The first left some bags, which were meant for us, and a very nice box of home-made fairy cakes, which were clearly not. He came back an hour later after his wife asked him whether the vicar was glad to have them for the church bazaar.'

Sue was off again and her infectious laughter made Jane feel much better. For a few hours, with the shop busy and Sue on top form, Jane was almost able to forget her troubles. She found excuse after excuse to stay on until Sue physically bundled her out at 5.30 p.m. As Jane walked home, she checked her mobile. Still no message from Ben.

When he eventually arrived home he explained, with a sarcastic laugh, that Belinda Morris had been the health authority administrator and intended keeping him in suspense for a few days as she and her committee considered his fate.

Three days later Jane received a mid-morning text saying: *'Holy trinity say fit to practise. Love you.x'*

Chapter Ten

'Bore da.'

Catrin and Tom looked up from eating their breakfast as their father came into the kitchen, beaming.

'Good morning, Dad,' Tom replied, smiling back at him.

'My, you're in a good mood this morning Tom.'

'Why wouldn't I be? It's Friday and tonight I get to jet off from this awful January weather – for three whole days.'

'Hardly think it's going to be balmy in Amsterdam,' Catrin quipped.

'Maybe not, sis, but I don't think rain falls as hard anywhere as it does in Wales – and whatever you say is not going to dampen my mood today.'

'The drizzle outside will do that bro.' Catrin laughed.

'Bwrw hen wragedd a ffyn,' their father said.

Tom arched his eyebrows.

'It's an idiom my Welsh teacher taught us this week – don't you know it, Tom? I like it – raining old women and sticks – makes much more sense than raining cats and dogs anyway.'

'Really? Does it though, Dad?' Tom scoffed, standing up and putting his empty cereal bowl in the sink. He grabbed his coat and travel bag and headed for the door. 'Bye, you two, see you Monday night.' The door slammed behind him in a sudden blast of wind.

'Another cup of tea, Catrin?' her father asked, moving to the sink to fill the kettle.

She didn't reply, distracted by a sound from the front of the house. By now she had trained her ears so that she heard the postman as soon as he closed next door's squeaky gate. She got up from the table and arrived at the front door just as the day's delivery dropped on the tiles. Before she leaned down she could make out a Lidl special offers pamphlet, a couple of brown envelopes and a white one. She could see that one of the brown envelopes was addressed to her and had UCAS firmly stamped in red on its front – she guessed it was the letter telling her which universities were offering her a place and what grades they required. The white envelope was addressed to her mother. Catrin checked the postmark, left the other envelopes on the floor and rushed upstairs.

'Mum, there's another letter from Celia, can I come in?'

'The door's open love.'

Her mother was standing in front of the full-length mirror wearing grey trousers and a long black tunic. On the bed beside her was a pile of discarded clothes.

She frowned at her reflection. 'Nothing fits today, I look like the Pilsbury dough boy in everything.'

'Mum, this letter; I think it's from Celia.'

Catrin waited impatiently as her mother pushed the clothes to one side to make room for the two of them to sit. She had thought of little else since seeing the photograph of Celia's two daughters. By now the fantasy she'd built around her artist donor with his chocolate Labrador puppy also involved weekend visits by her two sisters to the French barn. She had convinced herself Celia's daughters had to be her sisters – they just looked so much like her – and she couldn't wait to hear more about them, to find other similarities. Did they like art? Did they enjoy singing and performing? Did their voices sound like hers? Their Facebook profiles frustratingly revealed very little. When she was supposed to be doing her coursework she found herself daydreaming about meeting them for the first time: how they'd all get on so well; how she would, overnight, have two new sisters, two new best friends.

Her mum read the letter quickly. 'Oh love,' she said, patting Catrin's knee as she handed it to her.

Catrin scanned the letter then folded it carefully and lay back on her mother's clothes, closing her eyes. She felt the

140

tears well up and roll down her cheeks. Her mum tossed the remainder of her clothes and the decorative bed cushions on to the floor and lay down beside her.

'It's just so unfair,' Catrin mumbled.

'I know, love, but everyone's got to deal with it in their own way.' Her mother stroked Catrin's hair just as she had done when she was a little girl

'Girls, the letter has come,' her father shouted up the stairs, 'and you both need to hurry up or you'll be late.'

'The UCAS letter,' Catrin explained without enthusiasm.

'OK, Ben, we'll be down in a minute. Put the kettle on please,' her mother shouted in the general direction of downstairs.

'I thought you were on a detox from today? No tea or coffee,' said Catrin.

'I am, but it will divert your dad for a couple of minutes to let us get our act together. Anyway, perhaps today's not the best day to start a detox after all.'

They lay in silence for a short while before her mum got up. She took Catrin's hand and tugged gently. 'I think we'd better go down before your Dad comes looking for us,' she said quietly.'

Catrin nodded, stood and followed her mum downstairs.

As they came into the kitchen she could see her father was impatient. He was standing looking at the brown envelope propped up in front of the teapot, letter opener in hand. He handed the opener solemnly to Catrin and watched as she slit the envelope and slowly unfolded the letter inside.

'Aberystwyth, yes, 280 points and a satisfactory portfolio,' she said matter-of-factly, handing it to her father.

'Oh, Catz, that's great,' he said excitedly. 'What grades does 280 points equate to?'

'B, B, and C, Dad.'

'Cinch, you'll walk it, congratulations, llon – y – farch; llon – gy – far…' He gave up trying to say the Welsh version and enfolded her in a big bear hug.

141

'That's good news, Catz,' her mother said brightly.

'Thanks,' Catrin said, folding the letter back into the envelope. 'I'd better be off – French first lesson.'

Catrin placed the envelope on the kitchen table, picked up her school bag and put on her coat as she closed the front door.

Jane looked out of the kitchen window watching her daughter crunch slowly down the drive. She felt helpless, useless. If only she was still able to banish Catrin's troubles and make everything all right with soothing words and a cuddle. Those times seemed so long ago now.

Ben joined her and put his arm around her shoulder. 'She didn't seem very excited about the offer, Jane; is she having second thoughts do you think?'

Jane said nothing.

'Because if she is, it's not a problem; she could take a year out or go travelling or something until she decides what she wants to do' He moved to pour the tea. 'Maybe she'd like to spend some time out in New Zealand. I know my cousin Ann would be delighted to put her up. Or maybe she'd like to do a ski-season – I've always wanted to do something like that. There's just so much choice these days, not like in our day, eh Jane?'

'You make us sound like Neanderthals, Anyway, Ben, don't you have work to go to?'

'Administration duties this morning so no rush. Stella is making me look at our diabetic care plan,' he said picking up the newspaper. 'I'll drop you off on my way; otherwise you'll be late.'

'Thanks Ben, that will give me time for a coffee.'

She needed an espresso. She also needed the coffee machine's noise to make conversation between them difficult for a few minutes. She switched it on. By the time the coffee was made she'd gathered her thoughts. She stood against the Aga enjoying its warmth on her back, her hands wrapped comfortingly around her cup, and explained to Ben about the contact with Celia. 'And so she has no intention of ever telling her daughters they were conceived with donor sperm.'

'Perhaps we wouldn't have either had it not been for my mother's intervention,' he said quietly.

'Maybe not, Ben; she forced us into it but I'm glad she did.'

'You're probably right.' He didn't sound convinced.

The following morning Jane was in her Marigolds and her red 'Valleys Girl' apron having decided to take advantage of her son being away to get into his room to do some much needed cleaning. For months she'd been offering to do it but Tom always reassured her he would tackle it himself. He never had and now Jane was faced with green plates and coffee mugs that would need bicarbonate of soda and a good scrubbing. She stripped the bed and swept all the clothes from the floor into the big washing basket without bothering to find out whether they were dirty or not. Just then her mobile bleeped and she took it from her apron pocket. It was from Tom.

Boys having great time in Amsterdam – sampling local treats!!!

Jane smiled. Tom was possibly more lovable at a distance.

As she carried the overloaded basket downstairs she heard the thump of the post landing in the hall. She dumped the laundry and picked the mail up, only to let it fall back on to the red quarry tiles as if she was suddenly handling hot coals. There was the letter Catrin had been waiting for. Jane felt her legs weaken. Leaving the envelopes scattered on the floor she picked up the laundry basket and loaded the washing machine in the kitchen. Then she reached for the kettle. She wasn't sure why. She wasn't thirsty but she'd been brought up to believe that somehow a nice cup of tea made things better. It probably did she decided; having something to do with her hands always made her less anxious. She made a pot hoping Ben would soon be up.

But it was Catrin's light footsteps that she heard on the

143

stairs a few moments later. She heard her daughter stop by the front door and then run back upstairs. Then there was the firm click of Catrin's bedroom door closing. Finishing her tea Jane listened for any further movement. There was no sound. She climbed the stairs noisily hoping that would elicit a response from Catrin's room. Nothing. Jane went downstairs again, picking up the rest of the post and taking it with her into the kitchen. There didn't seem to be anything interesting and she added the brown envelopes and pizza flyers to the pile on the table. When the kitchen door opened she looked up expectantly.

'No need to look so disappointed, who were you expecting – George Clooney?' Ben teased. 'Is there any tea in the pot?'

She pushed it towards him. 'Yes, but it's probably stewed though.'

Ben poured the tea anyway, took a slurp and grimaced. He threw it away and made a fresh brew.

'The letter from HFEA has arrived.'

'Ah. Do you know what it says?'

'No she took it up to her room and she hasn't been down since.'

'Oh, you know what she's like; wants to sort things out in her own mind before talking about it. She's always been like that.

'Mm, I suppose so, Ben. I just want – well – to support her.'

Ben put his arm around her and gave her a little squeeze. 'Remember the time she misread your shopping list just before her seventh birthday party?'

Jane took up the story, 'and bought fifty packets of red jelly instead of five then went round the neighbours selling the spare packets before telling us of her mistake.'

'And old Mr Jones, who hated jelly, bought ten packets and sent jelly round here every Sunday for weeks. We haven't had red jelly since, have we?'

They both laughed, enjoying the shared memory.

'Ah Jane, it was all so simple then.'

She gave him a playful shove. 'It may have been for you but it certainly wasn't for me, I can assure you – endless laundry, chickenpox, the school run, homework, drama classes, karate club, junior football, endless birthday parties.'

'OK, OK point made,' Ben laughed, 'rose-tinted glasses and all that.'

'Mum, Dad, I've heard from the HFEA.'

Catrin stood in the kitchen doorway holding the white envelope aloft, her pale face flushed with excitement and her blue eyes sparkling.

'Good, love, so what does it say?' Jane heard the forced enthusiasm in her husband's voice.

Catrin read aloud from the letter. 'Occupation: Art student; Hair colour: Blond; Eyes: Brown, Interests: Painting/Architecture ...' She paused and looked at her parents.

'Oh, Catz, he sounds – nice' said Ben.

'I feel I'm beginning to create a picture of him in my mind,' said Jane. 'Are there any more details?'

Catrin smiled. 'Yes lots. Height: six feet two inches; Weight: eleven stone two pounds; born England, 1970, White. No children at this time.'

'That means you're half-English, Catz,' Ben said with a laugh. It didn't sound natural.

'Don't be ridiculous Dad. I was born in Cardiff.'

'Being born in a stable doesn't make you a donkey, Catrin.'

'Oh Ben, for goodness sake, can't you take anything seriously?' Jane said crossly. 'I did think, with Tom not here this weekend, we might all behave like grown-ups.'

Ben gave her a long look. 'Course I can; I am taking it seriously. But it's not life or death is it? There's no need to speak about it in hushed tones.' He turned towards Catrin and said brightly, 'It's good you've got the information, Catz; now we know why you're blonde and arty. Didn't get your looks or

145

talents from your mum, obviously.' Again Jane heard that strained laugh.

'Are you happier now, love, that you've got this information? she asked tentatively. 'It's obviously not enough to try to trace the man – and he's probably not still an art student eighteen years on.'

'Or still eleven stone two,' Ben quipped.

Catrin sat down by the Aga and looked at the letter again. 'Yes, I am happier and in a way I even think it's a bit of a relief he hasn't re-registered so the agency doesn't have his name and address.'

Ben nodded enthusiastically.

'Of course he may yet re-register,' Catrin went on. 'I guess as more and more people become aware the law has changed, and that all those who donated after 2005 are identifiable, earlier donors will see it is a good idea.'

Ben was no longer nodding.

'Have you no "gardening" to do?' Jane asked him pointedly. She knew him well enough to understand that, just like Catrin, he needed time on his own to mull over any new problem, to put things into perspective and see a way forward.

'You're right.' He picked up his mug of tea, collected the paper and all the supplements and headed out to his shed.

Tuesday mornings in the charity shop were usually quiet and, as they had been inundated with donations since Christmas, Sue and Jane were down in the cellar sorting through the bags. They always complained to the others that they hated the task but secretly they enjoyed the chance of a private chat and the inevitable hilarity that came with some of the donations.

Plastic gloves donned, the delving began. Jane's sack contained some lovely clothes – but all were covered in dog hair. Now as she pulled strip after strip of sellotape over them to remove the hair, Sue screamed and held a pair of false teeth in the air. 'Oh for goodness sake, who donated these?'

'They probably forgot they were in the pocket, Sue,' Jane

said, laughing at her manager's exaggerated disdain.

'How can you forget where you put your teeth? They're pretty vital aren't they; you'd notice you weren't wearing them – having to suck everything would give you a bit of clue you hadn't put them in.'

'I think you've found our selling challenge for this week, Sue.'

'If you sell these, I'll eat my hat. Come to think of it that's probably what happened to that top hat that came in without the top.'

'Well you know me, Sue, I'd eat anything but even I'd draw the line at felt,' Jane said, as she tried to find the end of the sellotape which had stuck itself down. 'Oh for goodness sake, this is driving me potty,' She tossed the roll towards Sue.

'Patience, Jane. You sometimes go like a bull at a gate, if you didn't you'd find life far less frustrating.' Sue found the end, peeled back the sellotape and handed the roll to Jane, who huffed loudly in response.

For a minute or two the only sound was the fierce ripping of sellotape against fabric.

'You're doing a good job there, Jane – honestly, the dog in that household must be bald,'

'Talking of food …'

'Were we?' Sue said

'Yes – you were eating your hat remember? Well anyway Tom arrived home last night and he's cooking supper this evening – treating us to some delicacies he sampled in Amsterdam, which means I don't have to cook after my Zumba class.'

'It's bound to involve cheese then.'

Jane agreed. She was partial to a bit of Edam and Gouda and her tummy rumbled in expectation.

When Jane opened the front door that evening the smell of onion and garlic wafted towards her. 'Something smells good Tom,' she called towards the kitchen.

'It does, Mother, but it's a surprise so you have to keep out of the kitchen. Dad and Catrin are in the living room watching telly.'

'Thanks, Tom; it's a real treat not having to cook for once and even more of a treat not having to think what to cook.' Jane struggled to balance her anorak on the overfull rack. Really, she must sort this heap out; some of these coats hadn't been worn for years. She noticed Granny Lewis's Sunday best among the pile. She'd take it with her to the shop tomorrow; another couple of weeks and no one would consider buying a winter coat.

'No problem, Mum. Oh, by the way, what diet are you on now?'

'The Dukan.'

'Du can, you can't, more like it, Mum.'

She popped her head around the kitchen door, savouring the aroma. She was very hungry. 'No really, this is one diet I can stick to.'

'So what are you allowed, Mum?'

'Well basically as much protein as I like – with a little bit of veg.'

'Good, then tonight's menu is going to be perfect for you.'

'Great. Have I got time for a quick shower?'

'Sure, Mum. I'll call you when it's ready.'

Tom completed his prep, laid the table, lit the candles, and opened the pricey bottle of Chateauneuf du Pape. 'OK, come and get it you lot.'

His mum came down the stairs, her hair still wet, and his dad and sister appeared from the living room, Catrin texting as she walked.

'Mm, smells delicious, son. I even gave up my teatime pasty to save myself for this.'

'Ben, you're not supposed to be eating pasties anyway,' his mother protested, pretending to slap his dad's head.

His father ducked, ignoring the comment. 'Shall I pour the

wine, Tom?'

'Thanks, Dad. I'll just plate up.'

Tom laid several small plates before them. 'It's like tapas, only Dutch, so the idea is to take a little of everything,' he explained.

His parents and sister looked at each other and then at what was in front of them.

'Come on, pitch in everyone,' Tom said, piling little bits of food on to his plate.

'After you, Dad,' Catrin smiled at their father.

'No, ladies first, I insist.'

Their mother dangled her fork nervously above one plate after another before slowly selecting a tiny brown morsel and depositing it on her white plate. She put her fork down and waited until both his dad and Catrin had chosen something.

'Bug appétit everyone,' Tom said raising his glass. The other three did not answer his toast but took slow sips of wine. 'Salt and pepper anyone?' he asked crunching his mouthful.

His dad poked at the little brown nugget on his plate.

'Tom, what exactly is all this?'

'Try it, Dad, and then guess.'

His father tentatively put the morsel in his mouth. 'Mm, tastes a bit nutty,' he said. Then his face revealed surprise. 'Now I'm getting, um, bacon; um, it's a bit …' He gulped and reached for his wine. 'The taste lingers a bit, Tom.'

'So Dad, any ideas?'

'No, son, how about you tell us what's in each dish?'

Tom crunched away as he pointed to the various dishes. 'These little delights are crickets fried in chilli and garlic otherwise known as Love Bug Salad; this is slug omelette; and these beauties are deep fried locusts.'

'Oh my god, Tom, you can't eat bugs,' screeched his sister, as if the insects were alive.

'Course you can; they have whole restaurants that specialise in this kind of nosh in Amsterdam – and in the Far East too. We went to one; it was dead good.'

'Oh, that's such a macho thing to do, Tom, it's disgusting.'
She looked at him with disdain.

'We'll all be eating bugs in a few years time; they'll be stocking crickets in the Co-op.'

'Well I for one won't be buying them,' Catrin said.

'Mm, yummy caterpillars: crunchy on the outside and then a lovely juicy ooze when you bite into them.' Tom took a bite from the bug on his fork and held its remains close to Catrin's face.

She screamed and pushed him away.

'For goodness sake Tom,' his mother said firmly. 'You're behaving just as you did when you were a seven-year-old terror.'

He laughed. 'Seriously mum, this is a responsible way of eating and these little beauties are full of iron and calcium; they're the next super food – you'll see. You're just prejudiced – you eat prawns and mussels; you eat little lambs; what's the difference?'

'People have always eaten those – that's the difference,' his sister insisted, her voice rising in indignation.

'And you've always eaten bugs.'

'Now let me think, when did I last order a bug spaghetti? No I can't remember and do you know why? It's because I've never, ever ordered a bug spaghetti.'

His dad put his hand on Catrin's to try to keep her at the table. 'Well, you've probably eaten bugs in salad and things,' he conceded, 'but setting out to purposely eat them seems a little odd.'

Tom refilled his plate while the other three refilled their wine glasses. His mother got up and fetched some bread and cheese which she placed in the middle of the table.

'Anyway, everyone eats eight spiders in their sleep during their lifetime. Actually it's probably more than that in an old house like this,' Tom said, laughing at his sister's obvious distress.

'Catrin, ignore him; that's a total myth – trust me, I'm a

150

doctor, I know these things.' Their dad gave Tom a kick under the table.

'Well, I think bugs are the future, they're cheap to produce and – delicious.' he said, licking his lips with bravado.

His father, tucking into bread and cheese, nodded. 'You're probably right Tom, with one in eight going hungry something's got to be done.'

'And we can't go on feeding the world with farting cows and burping sheep – it's bad for the ozone layer too.'

Well thank you for that, Tom,' Catrin said. 'Sometimes you can be so disgusting. You make me feel sick.' She pushed her plate of bread and cheese away. 'So selfish, so clever, so pretentious. I'm glad now that I've got another brother; he's got to be an improvement on you.'

For a moment no one said anything.

'What do you mean, Catrin?' their dad asked.

Catrin's face was flushed but her voice was calm. 'Well the letter that gave me the information about my donor also said I have six half-siblings and it turns out one of them is contactable. A boy, he's nineteen, and lives in Pontypridd. The other five, two boys and three girls, haven't agreed to be contacted – yet.'

'You didn't say anything about half-brothers or sisters when you read us the details,' their mother said sharply.

Catrin glared at her. 'And you've never kept anything from me?' she said sarcastically.

Their mother drew a sharp intake of breath, 'And you're going to contact the boy?'

'I already have.' Catrin stood and marched out of the room before any of them could respond.

152

Chapter Eleven

All week Catrin had been looking forward to Friday. For days she'd felt exactly as she had when she was a little girl waiting for Christmas. She'd counted the 'sleeps' and even dreamt of what might happen. On Tuesday she had chosen her outfit, deciding to dress down and not wear heels so she would blend in with the crowd. But would there be a crowd? Probably not, she thought; there couldn't be many eligible for this particular club. Melanie, her e-mail contact for the group, had sounded really friendly and welcoming and she was looking forward to the meeting although with some trepidation.

Now the big day had arrived. She hadn't been able to eat breakfast as the butterflies were already flapping in the pit of her stomach when she awoke, just as the milkman was rattling his way down the street. She'd skipped her French class to go into town to buy a new Mac lipstick in nude, avoided Siân at lunchtime in case her friend asked about her plans for the evening – which she was determined to share with no one – and now she was ready, forty-five minutes ahead of her meticulous schedule. Acknowledging it was too soon to leave home she nevertheless made her way to the bus stop. The orange bendy bus appeared around the corner a couple of minutes later so by the time she reached Central Station she was almost an hour early.

Catrin decided not to loiter but to make her way to the venue, just in case she met an acquaintance on the way and was delayed by having to stop and chat. She walked for ten minutes but saw no one she knew. Arriving at the community centre she pushed the heavy door just to check it was open and she was therefore probably in the right place and then quickly retreated.

At the shop on the corner she bought a magazine so she wouldn't look too conspicuous in the little cafe across the street from the centre. This wasn't the kind of cafe you could hide in. The chipped Formica tables – each with its bottle of tomato ketchup, sachets of salt, pepper, vinegar, and salad cream – were surrounded by four unwelcoming steel chairs. Oh for the slouchy sofas of the cafe-bars of Pontcanna. But this was Grangetown. The woman in the pink nylon pinny behind the counter looked up from the pages of the *Daily Mail* as Catrin approached. Catrin feared she was going to engage her in conversation. Looking around, she guessed the four other people were locals; the woman in pink probably didn't get many new customers and was likely to want to know exactly what she was doing there. Usually Catrin would have welcomed a chat – she liked the fact her fellow Cardiffians were a friendly lot – but today was different. She toyed with the idea of pretending she didn't speak much English but realised in time the magazine she was holding would make it pretty obvious that was not the case, so instead she stuck to mumbling and avoiding all eye contact. The strategy worked and the waitress handed her the tea with a curt '80p, love'. She sat at the Formica table facing the street, sipping the dark liquid, tasting nothing, turning the pages of her magazine.

Catrin looked at her watch. Ten minutes to go. Across the road people were drifting into the community centre in ones and twos. How strange she thought – what were these old people doing there? She made her way to the toilet and retouched her makeup, adding another layer of lipstick. She'd read somewhere that applying lippy made you feel and look more confident. She thought about taking the magazine with her but it didn't fit into her bag. She folded it and stuffed it in but it made the bag look misshapen. She put it in her coat pocket but it stuck out and looked ridiculous. In the end she left it in the Ladies, looked at her watch again – bang on 7 p.m., and walked across the road to the community centre.

On the reception desk there were signs pointing in every direction – Weight Watchers, Table Tennis club, Ballroom Dancing. Of course, she smiled to herself; she should have realised there were other groups meeting here too. Catrin spotted the DCSG sign, the abbreviation used probably to spare the attendees and everyone else's embarrassment. Donor Conception Support Group would look so odd among the other routine signs, the signs of normal life. She followed the arrow down the narrow corridor to room C67a. Although the door was closed she could see through its glass panel there were people inside sitting in a semi-circle. Catrin took a deep breath, knocked lightly, opened the door and walked in.

'Hi, I'm Melanie; are you Catrin?' Catrin nodded and smiled at the young woman who got up to greet her. 'Please sit anywhere; great timing, I'm just about to introduce our guest speaker. Oh, and this is the programme of events for the coming months,' she said handing Catrin a bright green sheet.

Without looking around Catrin settled in the nearest seat. It was unexpectedly warm in the room but she did not dare take off her coat. She was sure the telltale rash that appeared whenever she was really nervous would by now be rampant, spreading from her chest to her neck. Feeling her face flush, she fanned herself gently with the programme Melanie had just given her. As the guest speaker started to talk and all attention was fixed on him, Catrin relaxed enough to take a furtive glance at the others in the room. She was relieved. They all looked normal. She wasn't sure what she had expected – of course donor-conceived people looked like the rest of the population – and the ones in this room were all young like her. She flushed again; they must think her strange for keeping her coat on when it was so warm and everyone else was just in a jumper or cardi.

The speaker was now sharing his experiences of finding his donor father and Catrin focused on what the eloquent young man was saying. She couldn't remember being this interested in anything for ages and found herself clapping enthusiastically at the end of his talk. Then they were all milling around drinking juice and exchanging stories.

She walked back to the bus stop with Lisa. She'd got on well with everyone at the meeting but she had really made a connection with Lisa who was eighteen too, blonde, and exactly the type of girl Catrin was drawn to – gregarious, outgoing and fun. If she could choose a sister, it would be Lisa. As they swopped phone numbers and arranged to meet up for coffee in a couple of day's time, Catrin felt the evening could not have gone better. She couldn't remember the last time a couple of hours had made such a difference to her. Somewhere in the back of her mind there was an echo reminding her she felt like this at exam time, when dread turned to relief. But determinedly she pushed all thoughts of exams away. There were more pressing things to think of now; family was far more important.

That night she gazed up at her colourful ceiling for a long time, its vibrancy reflecting exactly how she felt. Eventually she pushed Little Ted and Big Ted to the far side of the bed, turned off the light and rolled over, feeling as if a whole new world was opening up for her.

The week since his daughter had taken herself off to the support group meeting had been a long one for Ben but finally it was over. He had always loved Fridays, the whole weekend stretching before him, yet today he felt wretched. He slept restlessly and, having heard the big grandfather clock in the hall strike the previous two hours, at 6 a.m. he got up. He stubbed his big toe on his mother's dressing table, which was currently on the landing while he worked out where he could keep it, swore silently, and went downstairs. He cursed himself as he walked across the cold hall floor for not finding his dressing gown and slippers in the dark, pulled the jumper he had discarded the previous night over his pyjamas and pushed his size ten feet into Jane's size five pink towelling mules.

Turning the light on he filled the kettle. He caught sight of his reflexion in the shiny aluminium cooker as he waited for it to boil. Why on earth did Jane have to keep the damn thing so clean? Suddenly he laughed out loud. He heard himself again in his head – really he was turning into a grumpy old man. And anyway he didn't look bad, he thought, as he turned sideways and automatically sucked in his stomach and tilted up his chin. Bloody miracle, he mused, with what seemed to him the daily increase in the demands of his job, that he hadn't lost all his hair. Or at least that it hadn't turned white. Perhaps he wasn't under as much stress as he thought. The rapid change in Blair and Brown's thatches once they became Prime Minister – that showed real stress. Maybe he was just overreacting. He considered this as he poured boiling water onto his industrial strength teabag.

As he sipped his tea he decided he really needed to keep this kind of perspective but, lying in bed in the dark and lonely small hours, that was so hard to do. He knew the letter from the health authority refusing him permission to prescribe Humira for Mrs Green, crippled at 31 with rheumatoid arthritis, was probably the cause of this latest bout of insomnia. But there was always some Mrs Green. He'd mentioned it to the practice's junior partner, who'd merely shrugged. He'd mentioned it to Jane who suggested he might take a few lessons in detachment from young Dr Jones but he knew he never could. He'd gone into general practice to look after patients to the best of his ability, not to compile statistics, hit targets, and deny patients treatment. Really, what was the point of the millions spent on research if the resulting new drugs could not be prescribed?

'Stop,' Ben said out loud. He turned on Radio 2 to Chris Evans's manic gabbling and set the table for four. He made pancake mix and let it settle on the Aga while he got the accompaniments from the pantry – banana for Jane, strawberry jam for Catrin, maple syrup for Tom, and peanut butter for himself. He put on the coffee machine so that the glorious smell of fresh coffee filled the kitchen, arranged some fresh fruit in a bowl and made the pancakes. He had just stored them in the Aga to keep warm when he heard footsteps on the stairs.

'Happy Birthday, love.' Jane's cheery voice called out as she stopped in the hall to pick up the paper. 'Mmmm, that coffee smells delicious, is there enough for me?' She came in and handed it to him. 'Oh, and you've set the table. I feel so guilty; I should be doing that for you today.'

Ben smiled, pleased at her pleasure. 'I was up and thought I'd make myself useful for once.'

'You, my lovely Ben, are always useful,' Jane said, putting her arms around his shoulders and kissing him on the forehead.

'Except when you ask him to make custard Mum; he's the worst custard maker in Cardiff,' Tom said as he burst into the kitchen. 'Penblwydd Hapus Dad.'

'Thank you Tom, forty-seven and still fit enough to be earning your inheritance, eh?'

'Much appreciated Dad – and do I smell pancakes? Wonderful.' Tom sat in his usual place at the table.

'Shall we wait for Catrin? I haven't heard her stir yet?'

'You won't Dad, unless you've got supersonic hearing in your old age; she stayed at Lisa's last night.'

'Really? She hardly knows the girl.' Ben poured all three of them coffees and sat down.

'They're obviously getting on very well.' Jane observed, taking the plate of pancakes out of the Aga and joining them. 'Lisa sounds nice.'

'What about inviting her over, Jane, so we can meet her?'

'I think Lisa's place has other attractions for our Catrin,' Tom said smiling and eating a pancake with his fingers.

'What have they got; a swimming pool or something?'

'Oh Dad, you're so naive. The big attraction is six foot two,' Tom said gulping down a mouthful of pancake and grabbing another two.

'Is that Lisa's brother?'

'Well done, Mum.'

'So what else has she told you about him?' Jane moved the pancake plate out of Tom's reach and offered one to Ben.

'She hasn't told me anything.'

'Well how do you know about the brother then?'

Tom gave her one of his superior looks.

'Ah, I see.' Jane nodded.

'Well, I don't.' Ben said, putting peanut butter on his pancake and looking from his son to his wife.

'Oh come on, Dad, keep up.'

'How does anyone know anything these days?' Jane asked as she passed a tissue to Tom who was about to wipe his hands on his trousers.

Ben felt as if he'd fallen asleep and woken up midway through a very tiresome sitcom.

'Facebook, Dad; heard of it?' Tom prompted.

'Well, actually I have, but if I recall you weren't exactly falling over yourself to let me see your page.'

'Pass me another pancake, Mum, please. Dad, these are delicious.'

'So what does it say on Facebook, Tom?' Jane asked, holding the pancake plate away from him.

'Oh come on, Mum; I need feeding up.'

'You've already had three Tom, if you want another you'll have to earn it so share what you know.'

'Well, I don't know anything, but there seem to be lots of photos of this Mark Sayers, most of them with Lisa Sayers, so I guess they must be bro and sis. And he's posted some stuff on Catrin's wall, teasing her like: a sure sign there's something either going on or about to go on.'

'I think that merits a pancake; you can earn another if you show us the photos.'

'Mm, tempting, Mother.' Tom munched while Ben and Jane gazed at him expectantly then licked his lips to savour the last drop of syrup. 'But no, thank you, I think I'm full.' And with that he grabbed his coat, his work and kit bags, grinned

159

and pulled the back door to behind him. Jane put the pancake on her plate instead. Ben stood and gathered the practice paperwork he'd left on the sofa the night before.

Jane sipped her coffee. 'Tell you what Ben, why don't we have a bit of a party, tomorrow night? It can be a late birthday party for you, and we could invite Lisa and Mark, get to know Catrin's new friends.'

Ben smiled. 'That's a great idea, Jane, we could all do with a bit of a boost and I really missed having a Christmas party this time.'

She nodded. 'Yes, everything was too raw then, with your mother and everything, but now I think it's just what we need. So I'll invite some of the neighbours, Mum, Sue, the kids and their friends. Do you want to ask some people from work?

'No thanks Jane, I spend enough time with them already; let's keep it small, shall we, so that we actually get to talk to Lisa and her brother. And don't go to too much bother; parties are supposed to be fun remember, not hard work.'

Jane grabbed a notebook and pen. 'I think I'll make a curry and some basmati rice and maybe a few side dishes. I'll ring round the neighbours later on.'

Ben kissed her on the cheek. 'I'd better get going: a quick shower and then away. If I set off in the next fifteen minutes the Gabalfa roundabout shouldn't be too bad. Do you mind if I leave the washing up to you, Jane?'

'The least I can do, Ben,' she said warmly.

In less than ten minutes Ben was showered and dressed. As he checked his appearance in the hall mirror he called to Jane in the kitchen.

'See you tonight, love, I should be home by seven; baby clinic this afternoon. Shall we go out or something to celebrate my grand old age?'

'What about I cook steak, chunky chips and salad?'

'Sounds perfect. Bye love' He struggled out of the door clutching his briefcase and with a pile of last night's paperwork tucked under his arm.

Jane made herself another coffee and sat in the comfy chair by the Aga. She loved having the kitchen to herself and, as she was not due at the charity shop until 1 p.m., she had plenty of time to clear up, do the food shopping and find Ben a birthday present. But first she'd get the party sorted. Fifteen minutes later she had six acceptances, one apology and had left two answerphone messages. Good, now she could concentrate on tonight. She grabbed her mobile, put on her glasses and sent Catrin a text:

Hi Catz. Party, ours, 2morrow night, invite Lisa and family, Siân and Jonathan. 6ish. Dad's birthday 2day! Steak 2night – 7 p.m. – cu. X.

She immediately received a comforting 'delivered' which she took to indicate Catrin was up and hopefully getting ready for school.

At 12 p.m., four fillet steaks and a mauve jumper bought, Jane stopped for another coffee. She chose a window seat in Howells' cafe and gazed out at the shoppers crossing the Hayes. This was one of her favourite places in the city, on the second floor of the department store; it was an oasis of calm, a world away from bustle of the street below. She held the jumper up in the natural light from the window and smiled to herself. She loved shopping for gifts, believing firmly the whole purpose was to give someone something they would not buy for themselves. Ben, partial to anything beige or tweed, would certainly not have chosen the colour himself. But he was malleable and, with enough encouragement from both Jane and Catrin, could usually be persuaded to wear anything. Yes, she was pleased with her purchase. She was less pleased there was still no little envelope sign on her mobile. She sipped her frothy coffee, held the phone at arm's length, squinted and jabbed in:

Catz, you ok for 7 p.m. supper 2night?

She took a bite of the biscuit, ruing the fact that coffee now came with these complementary little delicacies. She was relieved when the message sign flashed. It was from Catrin:

Not sure, Mum, think I'll hang out with Lisa.

Jane felt a sudden explosion of indignation. How could Catrin be so thoughtless; it really was out of character. She'd made it clear her friends were invited to tomorrow night's celebration – surely she could reserve one night for her family – but this donor-related stuff seemed to be all her daughter was interested in just now. She grabbed the phone and dialled Catrin's number, flinging her mobile back into her bag as it immediately went to answerphone. It was obvious Catrin was able to answer but was deliberately choosing not to. Jane fished for the phone in her bag again and sent Catrin another text:

Dad's spl day, please don't disappt him. C u home at 7.

No reply had come by the time Jane finished her coffee. She made her way up the street to the charity shop and was glad to find the place buzzing.

'Hi, Jane, so glad you're here.' Sue looked up from the pile of trousers she was refolding on the display shelves. 'We've had a complete house clearance in this morning; there are about fifty black bags awaiting you downstairs.'

'No problem, Sue, I'll just pop some things I've bought for tonight's supper in the fridge and then I'll make a start on them.'

'Thanks. I'll be down in a couple of minutes. Oh, and by the way, we need a new challenge.'

Jane laughed and said in a low voice, 'You never sold those false teeth?'

'Certainly did, at 4.20 yesterday afternoon.'

'Oh my goodness; did they fit?'

'Yuck, Jane! No, I'm glad to say they were bought as a prop by some drama students doing *Hamlet* on a budget.'

'Alas poor Yorick,'' said Jane with a smirk. 'By the way, Sue, we're having a get together tomorrow night, 6ish, can you come?'

'Love to, Jane; are you celebrating something?'

162

'Big Ben has struck 47 – well it's today actually but we're just having a family supper tonight.'

'Great, can't wait, and I've got the ideal present for him; it came in earlier.' Jane laughed again as Sue picked out an extra large T-shirt from the rail emblazoned with the words 'Trust Me I'm a Doctor,' under a cartoon of a man in a white coat with a stethoscope around his neck and a saw in his hand.

As Jane descended the steps to the basement sorting room she already felt better. She placed Ben's birthday food in the fridge, sat down, put on her gloves and began delving. The first bag was crammed full of cellophane-wrapped shirts – all a size 18 1/2 inch collar – some big man was going to be very lucky. When she was sorting bags on her own Jane loved to create stories for the characters who had donated the clothes. She imagined this man was very large and could only buy his clothes in a few specialist places so when he went shopping he bought in bulk. He'd obviously overbought in the shirts department. Today Jane decided to give his story a happy ending – he had lost a lot of weight on a miracle diet and no longer needed his supersized clothes.

She was soon joined by Sue and for the rest of the afternoon the two busily sorted through the sacks, deciding that a 1970s tome, *Introduction to Computers*, with a photograph on its hardback cover of an industrial-size machine, would be the next challenge. When Jane emerged from the shop at 5.30 p.m. she realised, with relief, that for the first time in weeks she'd gone several hours without thinking about Catrin. But she now looked at her mobile: no message.

Jane walked home and let herself in to the welcoming heat from the Aga and a friendly bark from Lucky. She knew from Lucky's enthusiasm that Catrin had not been home and the little dog certainly had not been out. She opened the back door for him, apologising that a walk was not possible tonight because she had to cook and, as she put on her apron, he barked his understanding and trotted out to the garden. Jane opened a bottle of St Emilion – Ben's favourite, marinated the

163

steaks in a little olive oil and garlic, and set about making chunky chips and a trifle for pudding.

At 6 p.m. the back door opened and Tom stumbled in bringing with him a blast of cold air.

'My turn to do the team kit wash, Mum,' he said cheerfully, letting the door close behind him and dumping two overflowing bags on the floor. He went and stood with his back to the Aga enjoying its penetrating warmth.

'That actually means my turn, Tom.'

'Well nice of you to offer, Mum, and they will be ready for tomorrow won't they?' He grinned.

Jane held her nose as she unpicked a tangle of shorts, shirts and socks. 'Where have these been till now?'

'Sorry, Mum, in the boot of your car. I forgot.'

Jane tutted as she loaded the washing machine and added a good dose of washing powder.

'Mmm, something smells good – when's supper?'

She pushed the 'on' button firmly and turned towards him. 'Well, I'm aiming for seven as your dad said he was able to get away earlier than usual tonight – something about doing a baby clinic instead of his usual surgery.'

'Cool, where's Catz?'

'Well my guess is with Lisa, but I'm hoping she'll be home by seven too. Oh, by the way we're having a party for Dad, here, tomorrow night, so hopefully we'll get to meet Lisa and her family then. If you want to invite some of the boys that would be nice.'

'Cool, I'll see who's around. OK, I'll just have a quick shower and then I'll lay the table for you.'

Jane groaned. 'Not for me, Tom, for us maybe?'

'Quite right, Mum, sorry,' Tom called out as he left the kitchen. She could hear him bounding up the stairs two at a time. Jane got out the candelabra inherited from her mother-in-law and found three new tapered white candles to replace the stumps that were lodged in the holders.

At 6.50 p.m. Ben struggled through the back door with a

large plastic bag.

'Been shopping love?' she asked, kissing him on the cheek.

'Yes, something for my bucket list; I'll show you later on – give you a little fashion show.'

Jane shook her head. 'Ben, please tell me you haven't been in one of those shops with opaque windows.'

'Why would I need to shop in a place like that?' He put his arms around her waist and pulled her to him.

'Oh, please you two, get a room,' Tom groaned as he came into the kitchen.

'Your dad's been shopping apparently; something to do with his mid-life bucket list.'

'As long as it's a red sports car with a spare set of keys I'm all for it,' he said, helping himself to a handful of olives from the fridge.

As the grandfather clock in the hall struck seven Catrin walked in. Jane felt her shoulders relax and turned from the grill to smile at her daughter.

'Medium-rare, Catz?'

'Yes please, Mum.'

'Good, perfect timing then, the steaks are all nearly ready. OK, you lot, come to the table. Tom, will you be the wine waiter?'

After they had enjoyed the steaks, the trifle and the wine, Catrin pulled a cake from her bag, arranged a rash of candles on top, and lit them.

'Come on, Dad, blow and make a wish.'

Ben blew as hard as he could while the other three enthusiastically sang 'Happy Birthday'.

'OK, now open your present, Ben, it's from all of us,' Jane said, handing over the package and planting a kiss on his cheek. Catrin cut up the cake and put the pieces on small plates.

As always Ben prodded the gift and made some wild guesses before giving in to pleas to 'just open it'.

'Oh, it's a jumper,' he said with mock surprise, pulling it

over his head.

'And a pink one,' Tom added.

'It's mauve, not pink,' Jane said firmly.

'Well, it really suits you, Dad,' Catrin confirmed, feeling the softness of the cashmere.

'Thank you, all of you, mmm, but the colour; won't people think that I'm, well, you know, if I wear mauve?'

'Oh for goodness sake, Dad, say gay; it's not a swear word, and no they won't,' Tom scoffed.

'Everyone wears mauves and pinks now. I saw Jeremy Clarkson in a pink shirt the other day,' Jane added.

'Oh, and he's a brilliant role model, is he?'

'Well, he's evidently not gay, Dad,' Tom confirmed, stuffing a piece of cake into his mouth.

'OK thank you. I'll wear it to the football on Saturday – if that's not test enough I don't know what is.' Ben laughed.

'This cake is delicious,' Tom said, enthusiastically helping himself to a second piece as the others nibbled theirs.

'Well, Ben, are you going to show us what you've bought for yourself?' Jane asked.

'I am but first it needs a little explanation. You may recall my bucket list – well, after learning Welsh, this is the next thing on it.'

'But you're not exactly fluent in the language of heaven yet are you, Dad?'

'No, son – it's work in progress. And I'm saving up my holiday so I can go on a language course for a whole month in Llangrannog over the summer.'

'And you are making good progress with your evening classes, Dad.' Catrin smiled at him.

'Thank you, Catrin.' He smiled back. 'Anyway the next self-improvement project is to get fit.'

'Dad, you say that every New Year,' Tom said dismissively.

'I know but now I'm really going to do it. I'm going to climb Kilimanjaro.'

Tom laughed. 'Dad, listen to me, I'm a pro. Getting people fit is what I do and I strongly advise you to set a more realistic target. Seriously'

'Look, if Cheryl Cole can do it, then so can I,' Ben said with conviction.

'Dad, it's not easy; remember last year some very fit rugby boys tried and failed.'

'I think Tom's right, Dad.' Catrin put her hand on his. 'You have to be lucky as well as fit to do something like that because lots of people get altitude sickness and however fit they are they just can't do it.'

Ben frowned. 'What's the matter with all of you? Is it too much to expect my family to support me? What's the problem – do you think I'm too old, that I'm past it?'

He added a little laugh but Jane knew he was being serious. 'What about doing something like the Cardiff 10K, Ben, just for starters, and then think about something a bit more adventurous after that maybe.' When he didn't immediately respond she decided to change the topic before Tom had a chance to answer in a characteristically undiplomatic way, 'Anyway what have you bought?'

Ben got up, grabbed his shopping bag and went into the little toilet beyond the kitchen. Jane, Catrin, and Tom exchanged amused and puzzled glances as they heard him bang various limbs against the door, sigh, huff and swear. Eventually he emerged clad in Lycra from head to toe.

Jane stifled a laugh and busied herself pouring another glass of wine.

'Dad, I think the style police need to be called,' said Catrin reaching for the wine as soon as her mother had finished with it.

'Nice kit, Dad, but maybe some loose rugby shorts over that Lycra would be even better,' Tom suggested.

Ben sat down very carefully and Tom laughed loudly. 'Was that a faint ripping sound I heard?'

'Oh shut up, Tom. I've paid a fortune for strength and

stretch so you really don't have to worry about my modesty being compromised.' Ben got up and squatted down. 'See,' he said, smiling.

Jane took a long sip of wine as Ben settled at the table once more. Leaning over she patted his leg and said, 'You do look a bit like a tadpole, love – but in a good way of course,' she added as he cast her a hurt look.

Catrin giggled then said seriously, 'Mum, you could join Dad for this year's 10K; if I remember rightly you've got some running kit somewhere.'

'Of course your mum has the kit,' Ben said, 'actually, she has the kit for every sport known to man including roller skating, lacrosse, tap-dancing, all the fencing paraphernalia – and all used, on average, once.'

Jane laughed. Her family often teased her about her fleeting enthusiasms and she readily agreed that she got far more of a kick out of shopping for a new sport than actually partaking in it. She really should sort that stuff out and take it to the charity shop; that way no one could bully her into donning any of it ever again.

'I'll let your dad do the 10K first and, if he survives, then maybe I'll give it a go.'

Ben put his arm around her. 'That's very considerate of you, love.'

'OK, Dad, I'll be your personal trainer,' said Tom. 'We need a plan of action. The 10K is always in September so we've got seven months to get you into shape – four sessions a week.' Tom smiled broadly, clearly enjoying the thought of bullying his father fit.

'Better make them morning sessions, Ben; you know how difficult it is to leave that surgery at a reasonable time in the evenings,' Jane added.

'Yes that's a good idea but I think you've got your work cut out, Tom; the last time I was in a race there was an egg and spoon involved.'

'Bet that was quite a scramble!' Tom teased.

Jane got up and started gathering the dirty crockery. 'OK, Ben, you get excused the washing up tonight; any volunteers?'

'Sorry, Mum; I've got a fitness plan to formulate.'

'And I've got to e-mail Steffan,' Catrin said quickly.

'Wwww, I thought Mark was flavour of the month; this Steff – another new boyfriend sis?'

'No, new brother.' With that Catrin left the table and went up to her room.

Jane sat down again and no one said anything until Tom spoke. 'Half-brother,' he said, 'he's only a half-brother.'

Jane heard the concern beneath his bravado. 'Yes he is love, and you and Catrin, well, you're a real brother and sister, brought up together.'

Tom seemed oblivious to her soothing words.

'And if any more of her brothers come out of the woodwork I'll be a quarter-brother, or maybe not even that.'

Jane, sensing that Tom would not be pacified, kicked Ben under the table and made eyes at him to suggest he did something. He got quickly to his feet. 'OK, Tom, shall we have a go at forming that fitness plan that's going to transform me?'

Tom nodded and they went off to the living room.

Jane stayed at the kitchen table for a long time, stunned at how what had been a convivial family meal had ended and mourning the fact she could no longer fix her children's problems. It seemed so long ago now, the time when she'd been able to banish their troubles with a plaster and a cuddle or a favourite treat. Jane wondered when that had actually happened and how she hadn't been aware of such a momentous change. She wished she hadn't been too busy to notice.

Eventually she got up to do the washing up, glad to tackle something she could actually sort out.

Chapter Twelve

Catrin and her father stood at the bottom of the garden looking back at the house. It was 5.30 p.m. and already dark, but the garden twinkled and the house was bathed in the soft glow of the table lamps Jane had switched on in every room. Catrin had spent the afternoon at the kitchen table glueing scraps of coloured tissue paper onto empty jam jars and wrapping wire around their necks to form handles. She hadn't had the craft box out for ages and its colourful scraps of fabric and paper transported her back to her childhood. As a little girl this had been one of the things she'd liked doing best of all, sitting at the kitchen table creating things with her mother. Today Jane had been preoccupied with making the curry and, although Catrin had enjoyed herself, she'd felt the finished lanterns looked like the work of a five-year-old. But now the flickering tea-lights she'd popped into each one illuminated the jewel-coloured jars creating a wonderful effect and turning the garden into a strange, magical place. She'd hung a couple of lanterns on the buddleia outside her father's shed and grouped them along the patio. And then she and Ben had draped fairy lights above the patio doors and down the ivy and honeysuckle plants that scrambled up the stone wall on the other side of the back door.

'Mm, perfect,' her dad said.

'Yes it is perfect,' Catrin agreed, shivering. 'Not sure who will actually come out to the garden to appreciate it but they'll get an impression from the kitchen.'

He laughed. 'You're right; not exactly balmy is it? Never mind, even if no one else notices, it's given us pleasure and that's enough for me.'

They stood there in silence for a few seconds then Catrin

took a step towards the house. As she did, her father put his hand lightly on her shoulder. She glanced at him but he was looking straight ahead.

'I never thought I'd be able to say this Catrin but I'm glad you know now; I've been so worried – worried the news about the donor would slip out and worried how you'd react.'

Catrin stood perfectly still, sensing he hadn't finished. How in tune I am with this man she thought, this man to whom I'm not related after all.

'And I'm so sorry,' he said. 'Sorry for the lies, the deceit. Even though the lies were to try to protect you.' He shook his head. 'No, that's not right, to protect me. I didn't want you to know because I thought you'd love me less.'

Catrin turned towards him. It was dark but she knew from his voice his brown eyes would be brimming with tears. She linked arms with him and pulled him gently up to the house.

'Right, better see what your mum has next on her list of things for me to do,' he said brightly as he led them in through the back door and a waft of fried onions, garlic and exotic spices greeted them. Catrin glanced at him and he winked at her.

'Fifteen minutes to countdown,' her mother said. 'I've all but finished cooking. Ben perhaps you could brush the floor – there are bits of onion all over the place – and, Catrin, if you could tackle the washing up, I'll go for a quick shower.

'Can't Tom do the washing up, Mum? And then I can get the music sorted.'

'Sorry, love,' her mum said, pushing a strand of hair back as she sliced cucumber for the raita. 'Tom's gone to pick up Granny Olwen from the station. I sent him down early to make sure he was there before the train arrived. Can you imagine Granny's panic if he wasn't there to meet her? She's been sending me texts from every station this side of Pontypridd just to let me know her progress.' Jane put the raita in the fridge and washed her hands. 'Tell you what; load what you can into the dishwasher and then your dad will finish off so you can choose the music. OK, that's me done,' She pulled off her apron and fled upstairs.

Catrin and her father worked in silence for a few minutes.

'Maybe start with some calming music, Dad, for when the guests arrive? What do you think?'

'Calming for us and for Lucky,' he said with a smile. Catrin finished loading the dishwasher and went into the living room, where Granny Lewis's CDs were still stacked underneath the coffee table. Catrin thought how the house even sounded different now her gran was no longer with them. She could count on one hand the number of times anyone had put on a CD since Granny Lewis had gone: her mother usually opting to listen to the radio, her father and Tom generally switching on the television as soon as they arrived home and she tending to listen to her iPod or to music on her computer. Their conversation had changed too: there was no talk now of Sunday services, whose obituary had appeared in the *Western Mail* or the merits of opera. Catrin realised how much she missed these conversations that she'd thought at the time were so boring.

As the first strains of Mozart's night music filled the air the doorbell rang. Catrin fiddled with the CDs listening to her father talking to the newly arrived guests in the hall. 'Oh, thank you, but really you shouldn't have.' The voices faded as he guided them into the kitchen to supply them with drinks and then rose again as her mother came downstairs and joined them.

The next to arrive were Granny Olwen and Tom, who was carrying his grandmother's surprisingly large for a two-night stay suitcase. Tom took it straight upstairs while Catrin greeted Granny Olwen in the hall. As she launched into a detailed description of her journey, the doorbell rang again. Then everyone seemed to arrive together. Catrin set about taking coats and serving drinks.

As the volume of chatter rose, masking the brilliance of Mozart, Catrin began to relax. She never usually felt like this

173

before one of her parents' parties but tonight was different. Tonight Lisa and Mark were coming and she so wanted them to like her parents and so wanted her parents to like them. Perhaps they wouldn't come after all and there was no need to feel nervous. As the possibility crossed her mind she felt acutely disappointed. No, she was being silly; they'd said they were going to come and there was no reason for them not to. Really, she thought, what do I want? A drink – that would help.

Catrin picked up a glass of white wine and then hovered in the hall talking to one of Tom's footballing friends. A loud burst of laughter from the kitchen briefly interrupted his story of the fantastic goal he'd scored that morning.

'Excuse me for a second, Greg; did I just hear the doorbell?'

'Don't think so.' He shrugged. Catrin opened the door to check anyway but there was no one there. Almost as soon as Greg resumed his story the doorbell did ring.

'Well aren't you going to answer it, Catrin?' he asked bemused.

Catrin nodded and opened the door with a wide smile. 'Oh, hi Siân, you're earlier than I thought.' She pulled her friend into the hall and gave her a hug.

'Yes luckily the restaurant was quiet tonight; only four tables booked so the manager didn't need me. Are they here yet?' Siân asked glancing into the kitchen.

Catrin shook her head. 'Where's Jonathan?'

'Big row; don't ask! Well actually …' The doorbell interrupted Siân's explanation. 'Ah, I think your special guests might be here.' She laughed. 'I'll tell you about juvenile Jono later.'

Catrin opened the front door and it was indeed Lisa and Mark standing there – Mark holding out a bottle of wine and Lisa a bunch of daffodils.

'Come in, come in.' Catrin accepted the gifts and put them on the hall table. 'Let me take your coats. Oh, Lisa, Mark, this

174

is Siân.'

Catrin left them introducing themselves and disappeared upstairs with the coats. She hung them carefully over the banisters and glanced at herself in the cheval mirror on the landing. She did up another button on her shirt, aware, without looking closely, that the telltale red rash had erupted on her chest then stayed absolutely still until she heard Siân and Lisa's laughing. Good, they had broken the ice.

When she came downstairs Tom had joined them in the hall. She smiled. Her brother was good at putting people at their ease. She heard him say, 'All I need to know about you two is that you are Cardiff City supporters.' Lisa and Mark laughed.

'Well, Mark certainly is, and I guess I am too – but not a practising fan as it were,' Lisa replied, grinning.

'That's good enough for me,' Tom said. 'So, Mark, what do you think of the new kit then?'

Mark paused before answering, 'Well, I guess it's a bit strange, the Bluebirds playing in red, but I want Cardiff City to survive and, if that's the price of survival, so be it.'

'Ah, a pragmatist.' Tom nodded. 'What about you, Lisa?' Someone had left a tray of drinks on the hall table and he picked it up and offered it around,

'Well to be honest I don't really know the ins and outs of it,' Lisa admitted, accepting a glass of red wine.

'Oh, Lisa, you'll be really sorry you said that,' Siân said. 'Tom here can bore for Wales on the subject of Cardiff City.'

Tom gave Siân a gentle shove. 'Impossible, Siân, my vertically challenged friend, the words boring and Cardiff City cannot by definition be uttered in the same sentence.' Having served everyone he put the tray down. 'Anyway, Lisa here needs some gaps filled in her basic knowledge so, in brief, Rich Malaysian buys excellent, but poor, club – aka The Bluebirds. Insists they play in lucky red instead of blue and have a big red dragon as well as a tiny bluebird on their badge. So now the Bluebirds play in red. Money talks. Loudly.'

'Ah.' Lisa nodded. 'And I gather you don't approve?'

'You gather correctly, my new friend. But needs must, as Mark says, and so far the new kit seems to be working; the boys are doing good. Not sure if it's the red that's bringing us luck or the dragon that's scaring the opposition.'

They all laughed.

'So, Mark, Catrin tells me you're a personal trainer? We're in the same line of business then – sport,' Tom said, manoeuvring Mark away from the girls.

'Come on Lisa, come into the kitchen and meet my mum and dad,' said Catrin. 'Siân, would you mind taking the drinks tray into the living room to see if people need topping up please?'

'Looks like I'm waitressing tonight after all,' she replied, picking up the tray. Catrin wondered if Siân was OK; she didn't seem her usual chirpy self. Perhaps the row with Jonathan had been worse than Siân had made out. Before she could ask her another roar of laughter erupted from the kitchen. When it subsided Siân had gone. Catrin turned back to Lisa, took her by the hand and led her towards the kitchen. The room was full and it took them a good few minutes to weave through the crowd, Catrin greeting everyone as they went. She saw her parents standing by the cooker and made her way over to them.

'Mum, Dad, this is Lisa.'

'Lovely to meet you Lisa,' her father said, offering her his hand. He could be so embarrassingly old-fashioned.

'Glad you could come,' her mother said warmly.

'My parents send their apologies. They couldn't be here tonight; they'd already arranged to go to a concert,' Lisa explained. 'But it was very nice of you to invite us all.'

'Catrin love, Greg and some of Tom's other friends are out on the patio; would you just go and check if they'd like more beers?' her mum said. 'And tell them we'll be serving the curry soon.' Catrin nodded, armed herself with beers from the fridge, and headed towards the patio doors.

Jane could see instantly why Catrin liked Lisa so much. She had one of those open faces and a ready smile.

'Catrin's really glad to have a friend who knows what she's going through. You've been a great support to her already. Thank you,' she said patting Lisa's arm.

'So you're on your final year in school? Ben asked.

'Yes I am, at Cardiff High.'

'A levels in a few months then, how's it going?'

'Oh, for goodness sake, Ben', Jane said, 'give the girl a break. How would you like it if people started asking you about your job on a Saturday night? No, on second thoughts don't answer that; you probably wouldn't mind at all.' She put her arm around Ben's waist and turned conspiratorially towards Lisa. 'You know, Lisa, Ben so enjoys his work he usually asks people how they are, even at parties. It's an occupational hazard.'

Lisa and Ben both laughed.

'True enough,' he admitted. 'You know, Lisa, the funniest answer I ever had to that question –"delicious". That stopped me asking for a while but old habits die hard.'

'OK, I think it's time to serve the curry,' Jane said, 'excuse me you two.'

She crossed the room to the Aga and bent down to open the warming oven.

'Do you need a hand?' asked a tall, lean young man. Gratefully she handed him the oven gloves and he took the stack of heavy plates out of the Aga and carried them to the worktop. He put them down and held out his hand.

'Hi, you must be Mrs Lewis? I'm Mark, a friend of Catrin's. It's very kind of you to invite Lisa and me to Dr Lewis's party.'

'I'm pleased to meet you, Mark,' Jane said, shaking his hand.

'Can I help dish up, Mrs Lewis?'

'Yes you can, Mark, but only if you call me Jane'.

He nodded. 'This smells delicious; chicken curry has got to

be my favourite.'

Jane smiled at him and heaped rice, curry, raita, and onion bhajees on to plates. He picked up several and set off to hand them out.

'OK, Mum, I'll take the next lot.' Catrin appeared just as he left. 'Sorry I've been so long. Granny Olwen caught me as I came in from the patio and launched into a long story. I couldn't get away until I promised to visit her for an overnight stay very soon.'

Jane nodded. 'You have my sympathy, Catz – I get my fair share of those; she usually saves them up for the Sunday night omnibus edition. Her weekend phone calls are free and she's determined to get her money's worth.' Jane laughed.

'Well, what do you think, Mum?' Catrin said quietly putting more loaded plates on a tray.

'I assume we're talking about Mark now?'

Catrin blushed.

'Good-looking, tall, blond, polite – what's not to like?'

Catrin giggled. 'And you like Lisa too, Mum?'

'Very much,' Jane assured her as Mark came back to collect more plates.

With his help the food was soon shared to all and the noise level dropped dramatically as everyone tucked in. Jane circled the room, topping up her guests' wine glasses and being complimented by all on her delicious curry. Finally she could relax – now that the food was a success and her guests were clearly enjoying each other's company. Contentment and tiredness washed over her and she felt suddenly emotional. There was nothing like having all the people she loved in one place. She looked around at them, one by one. Catrin had settled on the sofa with Mark and was feeding bits of chicken to Lucky; Ben, now sporting the 'Trust Me I'm a Doctor' T-shirt, was sitting at the table entertaining Sue, Lisa, and Granny Olwen with one of his stories; and Tom was at the cooker ladling out seconds and talking to Siân, Greg, and two elderly neighbours. She felt a warm glow, glad of what they were. Proud of them all.

Less than twenty-four hours later Catrin sat staring at her computer screen, consumed with disappointment. This was the third time. She couldn't understand it – he was always the one who made the suggestion and then, at the last minute, he'd cancel. The first time Steffan had offered to come to Cardiff they'd arranged to meet in TG's. All morning she'd been so excited, picturing exactly where Steffan was on his journey into the city from Pontypridd. Sitting on the bus into town she'd imagined him in the train passing Castell Coch, then he was getting off at Queen Street Station and making his way slowly down towards the St David's II Shopping Centre. At that point the text arrived telling her he was cancelling – no explanation – just an offhand 'something cropped up'. The following week he'd suggested they meet in the University of Glamorgan Students' Union at Treforest near Pontypridd. That had involved her taking the train up the valley on a recce – where she'd felt extremely conspicuous as she loitered around just to see what the students were wearing; she didn't want to risk turning up to meet her new half-brother looking like a schoolgirl. The Gap chinos and red Jack Wills' sweatshirt still hung unworn in her wardrobe. And now he'd cancelled again. Why? They seemed to get on so well in their online conversations and she really wanted to see him and to hear his voice – to make the relationship real.

Catrin decided enough was enough – she would seize the initiative. She quickly typed:

No prob, Steff but am in Ponty next Sat anyway; can we meet up? Costa @ 1ish good for u?

She pressed the send button before she could change her mind.

Immediately the answer appeared on her wall – *c.u.there!*

'Catrin? Siân's on the phone,' her mum called up the stairs.

'Tell her I'll call her back.'

It was Lisa she wanted to talk to now. Lisa who understood

179

why it was so important to make contact with her new family. As she was not online Catrin settled down to send her a long message.

Catrin had decided to tell no one except Lisa of her planned meeting with Steffan so when Siân asked her to go shopping on Saturday she'd mumbled something about a family commitment and when Jane suggested she go up to Treorchy with her to see her gran she'd replied that she and Siân were getting together to tackle some coursework. Catrin knew her mother would not try to persuade her away from her schoolwork.

And now she was sitting in Costa smiling her relief as Steffan walked towards her. She got up and, unable to decide whether to shake his hand or give him a hug did neither but raised her hand and said 'hi'.

He grinned back at her. 'What would you like to drink? I think I'll have an orange juice; I'm not that in to coffee really.'

'Orange juice would be lovely.' Her voice sounded strange, croaky.

Costa was quiet and he was soon back, placing the orange juices on the little table and sitting down on the chair opposite her. She took a sip of her juice. It was sharp and she struggled not to squirm.

'Thank goodness, you look just like you do on Facebook,' he said.

'Haven't quite reached the age where I need to use photos that are ten years out of date yet.' But she too was glad he looked just like his Facebook photo – tall, blond, and good-looking in a sort of not-trying-too-hard way.

Afterwards, reflecting on the afternoon, Catrin realised that first exchange had set the tone for their whole conversation. Thankfully Steffan too had been determined to keep it light, an extension of the online chats they had shared over the past couple of weeks. Neither mentioned their biological father, which Catrin later felt was strange – after all, that was their reason for meeting. She did, however, learn that Steffan had dropped out of his university Business Studies course but was still living in a student house. As he left her at the railway station entrance, he'd invited her to a house party the following Saturday. Catrin smiled – the invite confirmed Steffan also wanted some kind of relationship and that he did not think her too much of a schoolgirl for a student party. She had happily accepted.

'Come on, Dad, you're doing really well, but faster, shorter strides.'

Ben struggled to adjust his pace. He was already fighting for breath.

'And keep tall, Dad; you're bent forward as if someone has just punched you in the stomach.'

Ben was actually feeling as if he had already gone several rounds with Joe Calzaghe; everything hurt. What on earth were these 'runner highs' every fitness freak talked about? All he seemed to experience were the lows. He decided they were all crazy, including his son. How could anyone enjoy running?

This was Ben's fourth time out with Tom. His initial resolve to get up at 6 a.m. had lasted one morning. Since then they'd settled on late night sessions as by the time Ben arrived home from work at 8 p.m. he was famished and had to eat. Tom insisted on allowing a couple of hours for their meal to settle before their run and so Ben was now getting used to pounding the streets late at night. He thought how unfamiliar he was with Cardiff after dark. Really, he needed to 'get a life' as Tom would say, as now he did little except work, eat, and sleep. Even most weekends were taken up with never-ending surgery paperwork or dropping in to see how some of his patients were doing and today had been no exception. In his early years as a GP doctors were expected to visit and keep tabs on their patients. How things had changed and mostly not for the good in Ben's opinion. Now even those requesting home visits were strongly encouraged to make it down to the

181

surgery. He had once felt very much part of the community, part of people's lives – a friend. Now he was just another doctor who dished out antibiotics. But Ben, unbeknown to his five partners, continued to regularly call on a handful of his most vulnerable patients and got as much out of it as they did. In fact he often thought he benefitted more from these visits than them.

'OK, Dad, that's two miles; let's turn for home now.'

Ben grunted – halfway. That meant he had another two miles before home, shower and bed.

'Think how great you'll feel after you finish,' Tom shouted over his shoulder.

Ben could only grunt once more. He did not try to speak again until they arrived home.

Tom flung open the back door and kicked off his trainers. Ben followed him in, closed the door and leant against it trying to get his breath back. He felt his pulse and glanced at his watch. Worse than he thought – 120. Really he must get fitter, and quickly. Tom was at the sink, drinking a pint glass of water. He turned around laughing.

'Well, Dad's plan of killing two birds with one stone is not working,'

Ben hadn't even noticed Jane was sitting at the kitchen table. She looked at their son blankly.

'Getting fit and learning Welsh at the same time,' Tom explained, 'Dad's cunning plan was that he'd talk to me in Welsh when we were out running; problem is Dad doesn't have enough breath to speak at all.'

'Thanks, Tom. Give me a couple of weeks and it will be a different story,' Ben retorted before succumbing to a fit of coughing. He was still leaning against the door for support.

'Actually I don't think I ever agreed to be your Welsh tutor; being your fitness instructor is painful enough.'

'Well son, there is a small matter of that long-standing loan from your student days I might suddenly decide to call in if you don't do my bidding.' Ben wheezed, wondering if lying down would help him recover his breath more easily.

'Dirty tactics, Dad,' Tom groaned. 'Anyway, Mum, what are you doing up so late? You're losing out on your beauty sleep.'

'Catrin's not home yet,' Jane answered.

'Oh? Where was she going then?' Ben asked.

'I don't know; she'd gone by the time I got in from work – just left a note saying 'c u later – party!' And I've rung Siân's. She's at home but hasn't seen Catrin all day.'

'I dropped her off at Lisa's in Australia Road earlier; they were going on to some party but they're probably back by now,' Tom said, refilling the glass with water and handing it to Ben who was now lying flat on his back on the floor. Lucky came out of his basket to investigate and licked Ben's face.

He struggled to sit up, pushing the little dog away. 'Yes thank you, Lucky, but really no need for the kiss of life.'

'Looks to me as if full CPR might be needed.' Tom laughed as Ben gulped down the water.

'Where was the party, Tom?' Jane asked sharply.

'No idea, she didn't say. She was excited though – had enough clothes with her for a fortnight's holiday.'

'So she's probably stayed at Lisa's,' Ben said, wrestling off his sweaty trainers.

'But she's never stayed over anywhere before without telling one of us.'

'Well phone her then and see,' he replied, fatigue making irritable.

'Her mobile's off. I've left a voicemail and sent her a text but she's not answering. Something's happened to her, Ben.'

'Oh Jane, look it's only just gone midnight; she'll turn up any minute.' He got slowly to his feet.

'But she knows we expect her in by now; she's always phoned before, if she's going to be late. I want you to phone Lisa's house.'

He didn't answer. Jane raised her voice. 'Ben, did you hear me?'

'Mum, you're overreacting; she's probably at Lisa's fast asleep by now.' Tom turned towards his father, circling his finger in the air to indicate his mother was mad.

'Well, I won't sleep until I know she's OK, Ben. Call them, please.'

'But I don't know them and it's really late.'

Jane handed him the phone and flipped through the telephone directory. 'This must be them; they're the only Sayers in Australia Road.'

Ben took the phone with a shrug and punched in the numbers.

'Well, I'm off to bed. Happy sleuthing you two.' Tom said, closing the kitchen door behind him.

Jane wiped the clean kitchen worktop as Ben waited for what seemed to be an age before the phone was answered. 'Hello there, is that Mr Sayers? Lisa's dad?'

'Yes, who's this please?' The voice sounded hesitant, worried.

'Ben Lewis, Catrin's father, there's nothing to worry about; I was just wondering if Catrin was with you?'

'I thought the girls were with you.' Mr Sayers sounded more concerned now.

'Erm, I'm afraid not. They're probably with another friend –'

'Which other friend?' Mr Sayers asked dubiously.

'Erm, I don't know. But I'm sure they're fine. They must be together somewhere and that's some consolation,' Ben said, trying to soothe the obviously anxious man.

'Mark, Fiona – do you know where our Lisa is?' Ben heard him shout. He couldn't make out the replies but after a moment Mr Sayers came back on the line. 'My son and wife – they thought our Lisa was staying over at yours too. It's very late for two young girls to be out.'

'Well I'll ring you if they turn up here. Perhaps you could do likewise?'

Mr Sayers huffed. 'Yes. Will do. Kids these days, I don't

know.'

'Yes, thank you, sorry to have bothered you. Goodnight now.' Ben replaced the phone on its cradle.

Jane stopped wiping. 'Well?' she asked as she flung the cloth into the sink.

'She's not there. Neither is Lisa. They thought Lisa was here with us.'

Jane crumpled into the chair by the Aga. Ben sat on the sofa opposite her. 'Look, love, she's eighteen; there are probably boys involved.'

'Is Mark with them?'

'No. He's at home. But Catrin and Lisa are somewhere together – she's not on her own. They're both sensible girls; they'll be fine. Let's go to bed, love; there's no point sitting up.' He rose and took his wife's hand. She did not resist as he led her up the stairs.

Jane eventually dropped off to sleep but Ben lay listening for Catrin's key in the door. At 4 a.m. he got up and peered into Catrin's room, in the hope she'd come in without him hearing her. She hadn't. He went downstairs, grabbed his fleece from the coat rack and made for the back door. Lucky, hearing unexpected movement, raised his head, reluctantly left his warm basket and dutifully followed Ben out to the garden shed.

At its door Ben leaned down to stroke the little dog. 'I don't know if this is wise, old boy, you risk getting lung cancer; passive smoking, it's a big concern right now. But I would appreciate some company if you're willing to take the risk.'

The little spaniel looked at him, his big brown eyes full of sympathy, and wagged his tail.

'I take it that's a yes then. Thank you.'

Chapter Thirteen

'That's the best party I've been to – ever. I can't wait to go to uni now. It just felt really grown up.' The Valleys train shuddered to a stop at Treforest Industrial Estate.

Lisa nodded.

'You OK, Lisa? Hung-over?'

Lisa nodded again.

'Wasn't Steff great? And his friends? Really cool, and the music, and those little smiley pills – they were magic, weren't they?'

Lisa said nothing. Catrin looked at her friend who seemed to be sweating profusely.

'You really OK, Lisa?'

'Feel sick; no toilets on the train.' she replied briefly. Catrin hurriedly emptied a plastic bag and passed it to her.

'Only a couple more stops and we'll be back in Cardiff,' she said encouragingly. Lisa closed her eyes.

Twenty minutes later they pulled into Cardiff station. Catrin put her arm on Lisa's to gently wake her. 'Shall we share a taxi? I don't think I can face walking through Cardiff in this get-up. I won't come to yours now; I'll pick up my stuff later.' Lisa nodded and Catrin took her arm to guide her out of the station. Catrin was relieved there was a long line of taxis on the rank.

The taxi dropped Lisa off first and Catrin saw her enter the house safely before asking the driver to take her to Pencisely Crescent. She paid the driver and, as she got out of the car, she could see her mother standing on the doorstep. Catrin walked past her into the house and said a cheery 'hello,' but one glance told her she was in trouble.

'Hi sis, so how was the walk of shame this morning then?'

187

Tom called from the living room.

Catrin ignored him and went to the kitchen for a large glass of water. Suddenly she felt very tired and very thirsty.

'Where were you last night, Catrin?' her mother demanded, following her into the room.

'At Lisa's,' Catrin mumbled, drinking the water and keeping her back to her mum. For a moment her mother said nothing and Catrin hoped that was the end of it; she just wanted to go upstairs to bed.

'No you weren't. Your dad rang Lisa's parents and they thought you were both here. So where were you?'

'Out,' Catrin replied, looking through the window at the garden.

'Out where?'

'Just out; I'm eighteen, an adult, I can do as I please,'

That's when her mother really started. It was as if some floodgate had been forced open and her voice became increasingly loud as one accusation followed another – about Catrin's lack of concern for her schoolwork, her family, or the truth. Suddenly her mum stopped and, looking totally exhausted, collapsed into the chair by the Aga. Catrin looked at her aghast. Obviously she could no longer avoid telling her family about meeting Steffan. In a way she was relieved – lying and keeping secrets from her parents was something new to her and something she did not like. She was also aware Lisa was probably at this moment facing the same kind of inquisition from her parents and it was all her fault.

'Tom,' she called out, 'Can you come here a minute.' She turned to her mother, 'Where's Dad?'

'Shed.'

Tom appeared in the kitchen doorway.

'Will you get him please, Tom,' Catrin asked.

'Sounds serious, sis, you getting married or something?'

Catrin felt too tired even to give him a look. She waited until Tom returned with their father and all four of them were sitting in the kitchen. Then she explained that she'd met up with Steffan and about going to a party at his house with Lisa the previous evening. She did not share the details: the plentiful supply of alcohol or the pills. As they listened in silence she described what Steffan was like to her family, painting a glowing picture.

Tom got to his feet abruptly. 'Sorry Catrin, to interrupt your little press conference, but I've got to go – you know, things to do, people to see.' Tom picked up his football and kit bag and left, slamming the back door.

Catrin shrugged. 'And that's all I know about Steffan, yet. And now I'm going to bed,' She stood up, refilled her glass with water and headed upstairs, thinking longingly of her crisp white bedroom sheets.

Ben looked at Jane initially too stunned to respond.

'She's not going to get those grades you know, Ben; her whole future is going to be affected by this. Yesterday she did no work and now she's going to spend the rest of today sleeping.'

'Look love, A levels – they're not the be all and end all.' he said, with a calmness he did not feel.

'They are if you haven't got them; trust me, I know.'

'Oh, Jane, you've done OK without them.'

'Only because I married someone who had an education and anyway things are different now; you need a degree to get any job and to get a degree you need A levels.'

Ben put his hand on her arm to reassure her but she got up and started collecting the random envelopes, papers and flyers that had been collecting in one corner of the table for the last few days.

'Jane, look, she's a bright girl; I'm sure she'll be OK and if she's not she can always redo them. The important thing is our relationship with her. That you cannot redo.' He got to his feet. 'Hold on. I'll help you clear up.'

'No, I don't want your help, but I do want you to find out about this Steffan Steeler,' Jane said, dumping the clutter in the recycling bin. She set about wiping the kitchen table pushing the benches to one side with such force that one fell over.

'Jane, Tom's right, you're turning us into sleuths,' Ben said as he picked up the bench. 'And how exactly do you propose I find out about Steffan?'

'Well, start by checking if he's a patient of your practice.'

'He's certainly not one of my patients; I'd recognise his name if he was.' Ben moved out of the way as Jane thundered around the kitchen.

'But he could be a patient of one of the other doctors – your practice computer will tell you that.'

Ben hesitated. 'Yes, but it's not ethical.'

Jane stopped and gave him a withering look. 'It's your daughter we're talking about.'

Ben shrugged. If only she was.

Catrin and Siân were huddled together in the tiny 'Asian languages' section of their school library – chosen deliberately as few people ever used that section and Catrin, having chosen to study Art, French, and History at A level, felt confident none of her teachers would appear there unexpectedly. Siân had a free lesson but Catrin was skipping History so this was an important consideration. Missing the class, she reasoned, was necessary as she needed to ask Siân's advice about Mark, They wouldn't be able to walk home together like they usually did because she was bunking off the last two lessons to catch the train to Pontypridd for a telly marathon with Steffan. She'd tried to explain to him she really couldn't skip school but then he'd sulked and she'd relented. And he was probably right – it would be OK. The May exams were a good three months away.

'He's just soooo lush – really good-looking and really nice,' Catrin whispered.

Siân was laying out her files to make it at least look as if they were working. She fiddled in her bag to turn her mobile to silent. 'Sorry, Catrin – who's lush – are we talking about Steffan or Mark now?'

'Mark, of course.' Catrin switched her phone to silent as well. 'Well, Steffan's lush too, but he's my bro so it would be a bit sick if I thought of him in that way. But he'd be perfect for Lisa. Oh my god, that would be perfect for everyone; we could double-date then.'

'Wow, Catrin, I didn't realise things had got that far with Mark.'

'Well, they haven't yet, but–' Catrin smiled at her friend 'I've got a plan.'

'Yes? Good, come on, share.' Siân opened one of her files.

'Well, I think he really likes me.'

'Has he said something to Lisa?'

'No, but you know, the signs are there – like last week a gang of us went over to the dry-ski slope and he kept messing about, stealing my ski poles and stuff.'

'Ah, a sure sign.' Siân giggled.

'And when one of his mates was being really rude about my purple and salmon ski jacket – you know the retro one I got off eBay – he just cut his mate off and said that he was too much of a chav to even know vintage was really in.'

'So another plus, good-looking and he understands fashion.'

'Yep, perfect.' Catrin drew a large heart on Siân's open file.

'Or gay,' Siân suggested.

'Nope, I've checked.'

Siân raised an enquiring eyebrow.

'According to Lisa he's had quite a few girlfriends but no one really serious so there's a vacancy.' Catrin finished triumphantly as she added an intricate C & M to the heart.

'Sssshhhhhhh,' Miss Mills, the school librarian, popped her head around the corner.

Catrin pulled one of Sian's files towards her and both girls pretended to work until Miss Mills had once again had time to settle at her desk behind a mountain of resource catalogues.

'So, what's the plan, Catz?'

'Well, you know how I summoned up the courage to ask Steffan to meet up and it worked and now we're good. So I'm going to do the same with Mark – ask him on a date.'

'Oh my God; that's a bit brave isn't it?'

'Nope, the time is right. We've done the Facebook thing; he's even sent me two personal messages, not just comments on my wall.'

Siân looked duly impressed. 'That sounds promising; you going to tell me what he said?'

Catrin sat up a little straighter, blushing.

'Mm, that private eh?'

'Well no, not exactly.' Catrin shuffled in her seat and reached into her bag for some chewing gum. 'One was just asking for suggestions for what he could buy Lisa for her birthday – and the other was to tell me he'd bought it.'

'Ah. I see'

'So, I've sort of got a plan – but I need you, my brilliant friend, to help me think of something I can suggest to him we do that is so fantastic he won't be able to say no.'

'Not a big ask then.' Siân smiled wryly.

Catrin looked out of the window for inspiration. New catkins on the hazel tree beside the library danced in the light February breeze.

'I think it would be good to do something outside. The weather's better now and it's more informal somehow ...' she trailed off.

'What about a walk on Barry beach?'

'Nice idea but we'd have to go there by train – it's not like a first date somehow.'

'Game of tennis?'

Catrin shook her head. 'Come on Siân, think about it: he'd be one end of the court and I'd be at the other – not really conducive to sparkling conversation is it?'

'Got it.' Siân jumped up.

'Sshhh,' Miss Mills hissed from the far end of the library.

'Take a rowing boat out on Roath Park lake,' Siân whispered triumphantly. Catrin beamed and hugged her friend.

'You see Catrin, old friends are the best friends.' Siân smiled too.

Catrin grabbed her mobile. 'I'm going to text him now – no time like the present as Mum says.' She tapped quickly. 'OK Siân, what do you think of this?' She showed her friend the screen:

Boat trip! Sunday 2ish, Roath Park, you up 4it?

'Friendly, not too threatening,' Siân agreed.

Catrin held her breath and pushed the send button. Then she giggled nervously.

'SssHHHH,' Miss Mills said again.

'I know he's on the late shift today so he's probably got his phone on now,' Catrin whispered, eyes fixed on her mobile.

It shuddered and she and Siân both stared at the little envelope.

'Go on, Catz, open it.'

Catrin pressed the open button, read the message and sighed. 'No, no, no.' She held out the phone so Siân could see.

'Oh for goodness sake, what's the matter with him? Siân muttered. 'Does he need it spelled out?' She snatched the phone from Catrin and typed quickly, a smile crossing her face. 'Plan B' she said.

'What are you doing?' Catrin asked, urgently.

'There; done.' Siân placed the phone down on the desk, looking smug.

Catrin grabbed it and read the message, giggling. 'You Siân Evans are a devious, conniving and totally brilliant person.'

Miss Mills suddenly appeared beside them. 'Girls, if you are here to work you can stay; if you're here to chat you can leave. The choice is yours.' Catrin and Siân shuffled their files indicating they chose to stay. Once Miss Mills had returned to her desk Catrin whispered, 'I hope Lisa got your message in

193

time.' Her little phone shuddered again and Catrin drew a sharp intake of breath, 'It's from Mark.' She said nothing for a few seconds as she read the message. Then she smiled.

'Your message to Lisa obviously arrived before she was able to reply to Mark's text,' she whispered, 'he says Lisa's texted him back to say she can't come on Sunday, she's got something on, but he'll come. Meet at the Lighthouse 2 p.m.'

Catrin felt suddenly breathless.

'Oh, don't look so worried.' Siân stifled a laugh. 'Date on!'

Catrin smiled at her and reached for her bag. 'Siân you're a star but I have to go, I'm getting the two o'clock train up to Ponty.'

Another furious 'Sssh,' came from the direction of Miss Mills's desk and Catrin moved briskly out of the library. As she waited at the bus stop she decided to text her grandmother to say she was visiting a friend in Pontypridd on her way and would be late getting to Treorchy – yes, that would be far easier than phoning her which would inevitably lead to questions of where exactly she was going and with whom.

Having spent the afternoon and evening with Steffan drinking cannies and watching rubbish television, Catrin got off the train in Treorchy feeling wretched. She had the start of a headache at the base of her neck, her mouth felt dry, and she was afraid her clothes stank. Steffan's house had not seemed half as bad at the candlelit party but, in the partial daylight allowed to filter in through the grimy windows, it was disgusting. Unwashed dishes piled up in the sink and little grubs rushed round and round on the caked work surfaces. Catrin had declined the offer of tea and instead stuck to drinking out of cans and eating crisps out of a packet. If only she hadn't promised her grandmother, when she'd called her the previous day, that she would stay the night she could go home and sneak up to her own bedroom. But face Granny Olwen she must and, although it was nearly midnight, she knew her grandmother would be looking forward to having a good chat over a cup of tea.

Her grandmother greeted her at the front door. 'You've come then, on the Rodney?'

Catrin pushed her way into the narrow hall. 'Hi Gran. You OK? Why do they call the last train the Rodney? She flopped down on the patterned sofa in the front room. The swirls on the yellow and brown carpet swam before her eyes.

'What, no kiss for your gran?' her grandmother teased her, bending down to place her cheek at Catrin's level.

Catrin gave her a quick peck, trying hard not to breathe over her.

'I've no idea why it's called the Rodney – the last train up the Valley has always been the Rodney and that's that. Glad you texted me though, love, or I'd have been worried. Is your mum OK with you being out until this time of night? It's very late for a young girl to be out on her own.'

Catrin said nothing, closing her eyes briefly.

'You look exhausted love. Do you want to go straight up? I've warmed the bed for you and we'll have a big catch up in the morning. No rush. I usually have a lie in until 7.30 on a Saturday morning.'

Catrin smiled gratefully, dragged herself up the narrow stairs, threw her clothes in a heap on the floor and climbed into the narrow bed with the pink eiderdown that had been her mother's. Closing her eyes everything started to spin. She opened them again but that was just too much effort and she gave in to the spinning.

The next thing Catrin was aware of was the sound of her grandmother opening the curtains. Granny Olwen carefully placed a cup of tea by the bedside and closed the door behind her. Slowly Catrin opened her eyes and the rose-patterned wallpaper came into soft focus.

Catrin smoothed down her hair, high with static from the nylon sheets, and looked at the clock on the little bedside cabinet. It was 11.20 a.m. She sat up to drink her tea. She'd been coming to stay here with her gran since she was a little girl and she loved the fact things were always the same. Her gran kept her home extremely clean and tidy but she never considered redecorating. The little terraced house was exactly as it had been when Catrin's mother had lived here, apart from the indoor toilet and bathroom now jutting out from the back. All the neighbouring houses were the same; they had all extended out into their long, narrow gardens.

When Catrin came downstairs she found Granny Olwen in the kitchen with Radio Wales at full volume.

'Good morning, Catrin love, and I'm glad to be able to say it's still morning – just about.' Her grandmother laughed at her own little quip. 'So, as it's morning, you can still have breakfast; a nice boiled egg? And some toast?'

'Just toast, Gran, thanks, that would be great.'

'And I'll have a cuppa with you, there's fresh tea in the pot, just made.'

She turned off the radio and popped a couple of slices of thick-cut bread into the toaster. 'Don't need Rhod Gilbert now I've got you for company. I do like him mind; he's very funny.'

'Probably better company than me Gran. Sorry I've been asleep all morning.' Catrin sat down at the little kitchen table and poured two cups of tea from the pot concealed beneath the pink knitted tea cosy.

'Not a problem, love; you've been working too hard and need to catch up.'

Catrin looked at her gran for some sign she was being sarcastic. But she obviously wasn't. So her mum hadn't been complaining to her grandmother about her after all.

'Is toast all you have for breakfast in your house now then? It's not good you know; you need fuel to feed the brain.'

'No, Gran, I usually have cereal but I don't feel like it today.'

'I can't imagine Tom just has cereal,' Granny Olwen said, laughing.

'Oh no, Tom and Dad both usually have toast and fruit as well but Mum now has cake.'

Her grandmother tutted as she spread a thick layer of butter on Catrin's toast, put it on a rose-patterned china plate, and handed it to her.

'Thanks, Gran.' Catrin reached for the marmalade jar.

'Jane has cake for breakfast? I thought she was on a diet?'

'She is; it's the latest one – she got fed up with all the protein on the Dukan diet and now she's trying something completely different. Apparently some survey has shown that if you eat a big breakfast, and that includes cake, you'll lose more weight than people who don't. Mum says it proves you can have your cake and eat it!'

'I can see how that kind of diet would appeal to your mother; always had a sweet tooth: steamed puddings: spotted dick, treacle, jam – those were her favourites when she was a little girl. They seem to have gone out of fashion now. No wonder, really, no one has the time to steam anything for three hours – the more's the pity.'

'They're back in Gran; retro food is back in – we had spotted dick from Tesco's last week.'

'Yuck, retro food – that sounds disgusting; sounds as if the food is old.'

Catrin grinned as her grandmother grimaced. 'No need to steam the puds for three hours any more, Gran; you just pop them in the micro for two minutes.'

'Now you see, Catrin, that can't be healthy.' Her grandmother put two generous teaspoons of sugar in her tea and stirred it vigorously.

'No you're probably right; all that sugar.'

'That's not what I meant – cooking in the microwave, those wave things – that's what's unhealthy. I've always taken sugar in my tea – so that's a lot of sugar over seventy-five years. And I'm as fit as a fiddle.'

They sat for a moment the crunching of toast and the sound of children playing football in next door's back garden

197

punctuating the silence.

Granny Olwen gave way to another bout of tutting. 'But cake for breakfast, well that's just plain crazy.'

'Tom is even crazier, Gran – sometimes he has Chinese takeaway for breakfast if it's left over from the night before. He reckons the Chinese eat more or less the same for breakfast as they do for lunch and dinner so it's normal.'

'He's not Chinese though, is he!'

They both laughed and Catrin was glad she'd stayed after all. She was aware in that moment, with the February sun forcing its way into her grandmother's tiny kitchen, just how much she and Granny Olwen enjoyed being together.

At 2 p.m. the next day Catrin walked along the path that ran beside Roath Park Lake feeling deflated. She'd got to the park half an hour earlier and had been loitering among the families, dog walkers and joggers, all keen to take advantage of a rare dry afternoon to get some fresh air and exercise. Now she could see Mark standing by the lighthouse where they'd arranged to meet, a tall blond figure clad in jeans and a bright blue jacket. She hurried towards him, anxious to get her confession out of the way.

'Hi Mark.' She found herself smiling anyway just at the sight of him.

'Hi, yourself,' he said, cheerfully. 'But you've got me here under false pretences, Catrin.'

'I'm sorry Mark; we can go home now if you like.' This was not a good start.

'Don't be silly, I'm just teasing you; I really like it here but for some reason I don't come very often. I'd forgotten how lovely it was.'

They leaned on the iron railings and looked out over the lake.

'I should have checked. I just assumed you could take the boats out all year, not only from Easter to October.'

'Look it doesn't matter, Catrin; it's a beautiful day and I'm glad to be here.' Mark put his arm over her shoulder. She stood perfectly still, fearing that if she moved or said anything he would take it away. He did anyway.

'OK, Catrin, shall we walk? It's a bit cold to be standing still.'

She nodded and they set off along the east side of the lake. Mark put his hand gently on her back and guided her to his left, closest to the water. She looked at him quizzically.

'You'll get more sun that side,' he explained.

As they walked along Catrin did indeed appreciate the light warmth of the weak February sun on her back. She wished now she'd worn her parka but she'd decided she looked better in her cords and big blue woolly sweater. Well she wasn't going to look good if her face turned blue. She picked up the pace to try to generate some heat and Mark fell effortlessly into step beside her.

'Oh, wow, I wish I could do handstands for as long as that,' Catrin laughed as she pointed to a duck that had its head underwater, its orange legs thrashing about furiously.

'They are striking, these wild ducks,' Mark agreed, 'especially the males of course; see the beautiful emerald green on his neck and the bright blue of his tail?'

They watched for a while as the ducks and swans, geese, moorhens, and coots fished for insects.

'So why is it the males have the beautiful colouring and the hens are brown? It's not fair, is it? Catrin asked.

'Not fair but very practical.' Mark laughed. 'The males are beautiful to attract the females and the females are brown so that when they're sitting on their eggs, waiting for them to hatch, they're camouflaged against the reeds. Can't beat nature for common sense.'

Catrin nodded, shivering. Mark untied his scarf and passed it to her.

'Thank you.' She wrapped it around her neck, taking in his warmth and the faint smell of lemon. She wondered briefly if it was his shampoo or shower gel.

'OK, let's move, we need to get a bit of aerobic activity

199

going here, warm us up.'

Catrin laughed. 'You can take the man out of the gym but you can't take the gym out of the man.'

They carried on walking, admiring more birds as they went. As they came around the northern end of the lake they walked into a fight. The aggression was palpable and Catrin, startled as the Sunday afternoon calm was suddenly shattered, broke into a run. The gang immediately forgot their differences and, united, pursued her. Mark came to the rescue, digging out some food from his pocket and throwing it down at the water's edge. Immediately the geese lost interest in Catrin and set about arguing over the allocation of food. Mark left them to it and caught up with Catrin who was now looking back at the feeding frenzy from a safe distance.

'You're a good sprinter,' he said, smiling.

'Flight or fight – and the flight instinct kicked in.' Catrin laughed.

'Not surprising; these Canada geese are big and aggressive but I think their bark is worse than their bite.'

'They do sound as if they're barking,' she said, 'they're amazingly noisy. And the way they stretch their necks and come right up to you, it's very threatening.'

'I think they assumed you had food in your bag; they're very persistent, very cheeky.

'Well, you Mark are my knight in shining armour,' Catrin said, touching his arm.

'I've got some food left,' he said. 'Let's go to the jetty to feed some of the other birds and then I'll buy you a warming cup of something.'

They walked briskly along the path. Mark's right, Catrin thought looking around, this really is a beautiful park. I must come back with my sketchbook. Along the banks someone had planted white, blue, and lilac crocuses in circles under the trees, and there were little bursts of orange where their saffron stamens had been exposed by a trampling dog or the battering of the recent rain.

They stopped on the wooden jetty and Mark fumbled in his pocket for the packet of food. He handed it to Catrin.

'What's this I'm feeding them? I thought they liked bread.' She threw a handful toward a white-faced waterbird that seemed to have a black Mohican.

'Well, they may like it but bread is the equivalent of junk food for them; this is much healthier.'

'Healthy eating for ducks. What next?' Catrin laughed.

'If you throw the food in a little deeper the swans can have some too.'

Catrin did as he suggested then threw the last handful to a group of gurgling pigeons scuttling around her feet.

'OK, ready for a hot drink?' Mark led the way to the park's café, ordered a couple of hot chocolates, and found them seats at one of the window tables. Catrin sipped gratefully as the sugary sweetness warmed her. For the next half hour they gazed out of the window at the geese and ducks flying past, landing and taking off again. Mark pointed out the different species and they giggled at their spectacular antics. Really he was so knowledgeable; she'd never more than glanced at the ducks here before and now, after an afternoon with Mark, she was able to identify quite a few.

'I think the mallards are the best pilots,' he said. 'Look, look over there.'

'Where?' Catrin struggled to see what he was pointing at in the fast encroaching gloom.

'OK, here's another one coming in to land.' He put his hand gently on her chin and turned her head in the right direction. She could hardly concentrate for enjoying the sensation of his touch but he seemed oblivious to the effect he was having.

'Did you see that?'

Catrin nodded.

'They're brilliant pilots because they approach the runway at speed and put the brakes on at the last moment. You can see them: they lean right back, foot hard down on the brake.

Brilliant.'

'Sorry folks but I'm closing now.'

Catrin turned to see the cafe attendant waiting to clear their table. She and Mark were the only ones left. They got up reluctantly and headed out into the frosty park. The route to the exit took them past where they'd met earlier that afternoon.

'It's funny isn't it, this little lighthouse?' said Catrin.

'Mm,' Mark agreed, 'commemorates something big though.'

'Scott setting off from Cardiff attempting to be the first man to reach the South Pole – we did it in History in junior school.' Catrin said. 'But he was beaten to it and died trying to get home. Not sure if such a disaster should be commemorated.'

'It's not the disaster that's being commemorated; it's the bravery.' said Mark, clearly familiar with the story. 'Mind you, it did give us one of the best quotes ever.'

'I am just going outside and may be some time,' they said together.

'Poor Captain Oates,' Catrin added.

'And talking of getting home safely, I'll come on the bus with you and see you back,' Mark said, opening the park gate for her.

The bus stopped only fifty yards from Catrin's home but she did not try to dissuade him.

202

Chapter Fourteen

On the morning of February 14th Catrin wandered
nonchalantly across the hall just as the postman's delivery
scattered on to the tiles. Aware that Tom was sitting at the
kitchen table and had seen her she did not rush. She scooped
up the envelopes but did not need to rifle through them. A
bright pink one leapt out at her. She felt her stomach do a little
flip as she crossed her fingers. Please, please let it be from
him.

'No Valentines for you Tom, no surprises there then, but
one pour moi.' She waved the pink envelope high in the air.

'Well that is a surprise,' said Tom, 'who could possibly
fancy you?'

'That I am about to find out,' she replied, grinning. She
took her father's letter opener from its place on the shelf above
the kettle and carefully slid it across the top of the envelope.
Then she paused. Savouring the moment. Afraid of
disappointment.

'Well?' Tom asked.

'None of your business, Tomo,' she said pouring herself a
glass of juice.

Tom got up swiftly, snatched the envelope from her and
held it above his head as Catrin tried to get it back. Lucky,
thinking this really was a good game, barked enthusiastically
and raced around their legs.

'Give it back Tom, or I'll...'

'Or you'll tell Mum?' he mocked, holding fast to the card.

'Or I'll tell Mum you pulled a sicky last week.'

'You are a dirty player, Catrin Lewis.' Tom laughed and
handed back the envelope. He got some bacon out of the
fridge and turned the cooker grill on.

Deciding she was being silly, Catrin slid the card out. Who else but Mark would send her a Valentine? She smiled, relieved it wasn't a jokey one; it was what a Valentine should be – red roses and a heart. So far; so good. Slowly she opened the card. And laughed. Yes that was as it should be too: a romantic poem and a big ?

'Well, who is it from?' Tom asked. He put the bacon on to grill.

'Don't know, there's no name, just a question mark.'

'Mark?'

'I hope so.' Catrin smiled.

The smell of the bacon made her suddenly ravenous and she was glad to see Tom was cooking all six rashers from the packet.

'Is there enough for me too?'

He grunted. 'I suppose it could stretch.'

'Why are you making breakfast anyway Tom; where's Mum?'

'Dad's given her a lift up to Pontypridd and then she's getting the train from there to Treorchy, spending the day with Granny O.' Tom turned the bacon rashers over. 'So, do you recognise the handwriting?'

Catrin shook her head. 'There is no handwriting, I've told you, just a question mark.'

Tom rolled his eyes. 'Blonde or what? The envelope, Catrin?'

'Ah,' she said, picking it up. 'Nope, no clues, it's printed – could be anyone.'

'Postmark?'

'Cardiff.'

'Ah, that's helpful; narrows it down to about 300,000 people – sandwich or with egg?'

'Sandwich please, Tom. It's great you've also got half-term off. I could get used to you making breakfast for me.'

Tom piled the bacon into several slices of brown bread and they sat at the kitchen table munching until the mound of sandwiches had disappeared.

Catrin pushed her plate aside with a satisfied sigh. 'I didn't send one, do you think I should?

'I take it you mean send a Valentine to Mark?'

She nodded.

'Why haven't you sent him one? I thought you really liked him.'

'I do but I thought it would be embarrassing if he didn't send me one back,' Catrin said, blushing.

'You'd have to hand-deliver it to get it there today – now that would be embarrassing if you get caught in the act.'

'But I wouldn't.' Catrin smiled at him.

Tom understood her meaning immediately and said loudly and very slowly, 'Watch my lips: No, No, No.'

'One word, Tom – sicky.'

'Watch my lips: Yes, Yes, Yes,' Tom replied, laughing.

'So kind of you to offer, brother dearest. I'll go and make a card now and if you could make a special delivery before he gets home from work at six that would be much appreciated. Might even mean I erase all knowledge of that sicky from my brain – permanently.' With a smile she picked up the card and went upstairs.

Catrin spent the next hour drawing a pair of lovebirds in a tree. In the background she drew a lake and on it placed a white lighthouse. Pleased she sat back to admire her work. Perfect: the lake and the lighthouse would surely remind him of their date in Roath Park. Inside the card she simply put a large X. She made an envelope from brown paper and then printed 'Mark' in black ink on the front.

When she went back downstairs Tom was in his running gear.

'Postman Pat at your service,' he said, grabbing the envelope and pushing it into his rucksack. 'OK ready to hit the mean streets of Gabalfa. See you later, sis.' The cold blast that came into the kitchen as he left by the back door woke Lucky. The little spaniel looked up expectantly.

'OK, old boy, fancy a walk?' Catrin stroked his soft head. She did not need to ask twice.

Catrin walked along the Taff embankment, watching Lucky run ahead, his tail wagging furiously. She felt good. Everything seemed to be working out and, if she hadn't exactly forgiven her parents, she was beginning to understand why they had kept the truth from her. She'd even felt sorry for her father when he'd confessed how worried he'd been that she would find out; how guilty he'd felt about the lies and the evasions. Looking back she thought she'd been pretty dumb too. The lengths he'd gone to to try to dissuade her from giving blood. All those feeble arguments about how she might feel lethargic afterwards and that she was probably too light to be allowed to donate. She'd gone ahead anyway, going with a group of sixth formers, all donating for the first time, all bravado – her fear of needles subdued by peer pressure and wanting to be seen to be doing good. And how he'd somehow 'forgotten' his blood group when she'd proudly told him she was AB+, one of only 3 per cent of the population. She'd teased him saying he must be a common A as her mother had told her that she was a B+. How naive she'd been; what doctor wouldn't remember his own blood group? But then she wasn't used to her father lying to her; why should she suspect he was lying about that? No, really, it was not her fault.

Catrin could feel her good mood evaporating so she forced herself to think of the positive things that had come from Granny Lewis's revelation: Mark, Lisa, and Steffan. She had three new people in her life because of who, or what, she was. And that was good.

A clump of snowdrops caught her eye, their delicate heads being flung around mercilessly by the east wind that blew along the Taff today. How strange that nature forced such delicate looking flowers to face such atrocious weather; obviously they were tougher than they looked. Her mobile bleeped and she called Lucky back. The little dog, twenty metres ahead and following some interesting scent, looked at her as if torn whether or not to obey, then ran back enthusiastically and brushed his sturdy body against her legs.

'OK Lucky, good boy. We've got a message. Oh, it's Lisa. Let's see what she has to say.'

Catrin tapped her phone several times before reluctantly acknowledging the necessity of removing her gloves.

'Hey, Lucky, I think this is progress. Lisa's inviting me over for a Valentine meal at theirs tonight.'

She blew on her hands before tapping in:

Yes, grt, thanx.

And then she turned round, explaining to the confused dog that they needed to head home so she could get ready.

'What do you think, Lucky, trousers or dress?'

Lucky seemed to nod as they ran along.

'I guess that's doggie for whatever?' Catrin laughed as a passing runner gave her a strange look. Today she did not care.

A couple of hours later Tom dropped her off at the Sayers' front door. It was Lisa who answered.

'Hi Catrin, come in; oh my God, it's freezing and you're in a dress. You crazy?'

Catrin laughed, smoothing down her new Topshop purchase, but she was beginning to think she'd tried too hard. The aroma wafting into the hall indicated someone was at least making an effort with the food. Lisa hung Catrin's coat in the understairs cupboard and led her into the kitchen where she could see the table had been set for three.

'Supper's almost ready and Mark's just having a shower. He'll be down in a minute.'

Catrin smiled. Good, Mark was here. He must have picked up her card but there was no sign of it. She heard him coming down the stairs and felt suddenly nervous. This is ridiculous, she told herself; you've spent lots of time with Mark and Lisa, what's different now? But of course it was different; it was Valentine's night and she and Mark had sent each other cards.

As Mark came into the kitchen Catrin put on an apron,

thinking briefly she was certainly her mother's daughter, and turned towards the sink to tackle the mountain of dishes precariously piled on the adjacent work top. Lisa was obviously an enthusiastic, if not a tidy, cook.

'Hi, Catrin,' he said, inspecting what was simmering in the pot on the cooker.

For a moment she was taken aback. He sounded normal, but then how else would he sound? She must behave normally too.

'Hi, Mark. Work OK?'

'Yes, good thanks; busy, you know, there are a few who haven't yet given up that New Year's Resolution to get fit. Give them another couple of weeks and they will though.' He laughed. 'Same every year – two huge peaks: New Year and about six weeks before the summer holidays start. If you want to make a fortune, just open a gym for those two periods and you'd be quids in.'

Lisa nodded. 'People are so predictable. Think of tonight: millions of couples all over the world will be going out for a so-called 'romantic meal' just because someone, somewhere has planted the idea that's what you're supposed to do to prove you love someone. Ridiculous,' she said, giving the pot a vicious stir.

Catrin was beginning to think the evening wasn't quite going to go the way she'd hoped.

'So sis, what's on the menu? Classic Valentine's fare – oysters and all that?'

'Absolutely not,' Lisa thundered. 'I invited Catrin to an anti-Valentine meal and that's exactly what we are going to have. So please sit down you two.'

Why hadn't she noticed the 'anti' in the text message, Catrin admonished herself. Clearly because that's not what she'd wanted to see. She dried her hands, took off the apron and sat opposite Mark.

'Trr-aaa,' Lisa said, transferring the pot from the cooker and placing it carefully on a table mat. She lifted the lid with a flourish. 'Pheasant stew à la Lisa. Dead easy; it's a one-pot meal.'

Catrin's stomach lurched at the mention of pheasant. 'Oh Lisa, just a little for me please. I had a huge lunch.' Lisa ladled a disturbingly generous portion on to Catrin's plate before serving Mark and herself. She poured Ribena into tumblers, adding, 'I thought the ruby red would be ironic. It should be red wine of course but I'm afraid I haven't been able to face wine since Steff's party.'

Mark took a bite of meat. His face showed he wasn't sure. 'Mm, Lisa, this is different. Where did you get the idea of cooking pheasant like this? Mum usually roasts it.'

'Hugh Fearnley-Whittingstall. I saw him do something similar on the telly once but I've adapted it. I knew Dad had a couple of pheasants in the freezer so I thought I'd give it a go. I added a little cream, onion, potato, and tomato – again keeping the red theme going. Do you like it?'

'Yes, it's very flavoursome.' Mark ate another mouthful.

'Yes, you only need a very small amount,' Catrin said, taking a long gulp of Ribena. 'So have your parents gone out to celebrate?' she asked, anxious to steer the conversation away from the meal.

Mark laughed. 'Every year Dad takes Mum out on Valentine's night for a meal. Actually, it's the only night of the year they go out for a meal.'

'And the reason they don't go out the rest of the year is Dad says restaurants are way overpriced,' Lisa added, 'and so he chooses to go out on the one night all restaurants hike up their prices. Parents, eh?'

'Ah, Lisa, you complain about the parents but you're still looking for yet another one,' Mark said, 'makes no sense to me at all.'

Lisa pointed her fork at him. 'You are just chicken, Mark; too afraid to go looking for your biological father. I'm not sure why – don't want to upset the oldies? Or is it just the fear of failing and so you're not willing to try?'

Catrin felt she was intruding, that she shouldn't be here listening to this conversation.

'It's neither, Lisa,' Mark said calmly. 'Why can't you just settle for things as they are? Life hands out good and bad, that's how it is, so just accept what you're given and get on with it. It's selfish, all this probing. And you're right; it's not fair on Mum and Dad. They're good people, who've done their best for both of us, and it's ungrateful to go looking for the donor. I know you two feel differently but that's the way I see things. End of.'

Lisa looked surprised. 'Gosh, Mark, that's a long and serious speech for you. I accept that's your point of view but Catrin agrees with me, don't you, Catz?'

Catrin paused. 'Well,' she said eventually, 'you know I've put down that I'd like to meet my donor if he ever becomes contactable but sometimes, when I look at Dad, I do feel really guilty. And sometimes I think I'd rather not know this person who helped create me in such a, oh I don't know, impersonal way.' She stopped aware that really there was no way she could explain exactly how she felt. 'It's confusing,' she added limply.

Mark and Lisa smiled at her and nodded. Catrin shifted in her seat, aware things were becoming heavy. She needed to say something to lighten the mood. 'I hope your parents are having a good time.'

'Well personally I can't imagine anything worse than all that enforced romance: couples gazing at each other across the table, competing with the couple next door to be the most romantic, red roses drooping. And don't even start me on the music that will be playing,' Lisa said emphatically.

Catrin laughed a little too loudly. 'Oh come on Lisa; it can't be that grim or all these restaurants wouldn't get booked up for the night, would they?'

'It is grim and tacky and pathetic, Catrin, and enough to make Cupid shoot himself with his own arrow.'

Mark laughed too. 'Bet you wouldn't say no if Harry Styles

from One Direction suddenly showed up and asked you out to dinner tonight.'

Lisa smiled. 'What, you kidding? What kind of girl would say no to Harry?'

'What about you, Catrin?' Mark grinned at her. 'Harry do it for you too?'

Catrin blushed. She really couldn't think how to answer. What she wanted to say was that Harry was OK but if she had a choice between Mark and Harry there would be no contest. Yet that would embarrass them all. So she said, 'No, I'd have to turn him down I'm afraid; wouldn't want to risk upsetting Lisa.' They all laughed.

'So you didn't get any Valentines then, sis; is that what all this anti-Valentine thing is about?' Mark teased.

'No brother, I can proudly say that I have never received and never sent one of those stupid, soppy cards.'

Catrin felt they were on dangerous ground again.

'And you Mark, I didn't see the postman bring a sackful for you this morning either. But the question is did you send any?' Lisa asked.

'No Lisa, I did not send a Valentine; never have actually.'

Catrin felt the familiar itchy redness erupt on her chest and was glad the neckline of her new dress would at least conceal that part of her. But her face would also be red and so she concentrated on the floating hunks of meat on her plate. The pheasant had been cooked rare and the cooling sauce now resembled congealing blood. She felt sick.

'Got one though,' Mark said, sounding pleased. 'And very tasteful it was too.'

'Surely a contradiction in terms, a tasteful Valentine,' Lisa teased. 'From?'

'Unsigned, nosy sister, but a very kind gesture whoever it was from.' Mark smiled at Catrin.

Catrin did not know how she got through the rest of the evening. She sat in the back of the taxi home feeling a complete fool. She'd misread the signs completely – sent

Mark a Valentine that was obviously from her, presuming he'd sent her one, when he clearly didn't feel the same way and only wanted to be friends. And to compound her embarrassment Lisa had probably guessed all this too. But Lisa was right. Valentines was a stupid tradition. Next year she'd ignore it completely. And certainly she'd never send a Valentine's card again.

The taxi drew up outside her home and Catrin stepped out. As she handed the driver a ten pound note he looked at her strangely and asked, 'You OK love?' It was then she noticed she was crying.

'That's Catrin safely home.' Ben smiled at Jane as they heard their daughter come in and shut the door to her room. He put the bookmark in his Welsh/English phrasebook and turned out the bedside lamp on his side.

Jane climbed into bed and kissed him. 'Thank you for the card and the roses, Ben; they really are lovely.'

'And so, my love, are you.'

'My, don't we sound like a couple of smug marrieds.' She sighed contentedly.

Ben kissed her hair. 'Mmm,' he murmured, 'and if the woman from the newsagents tells you I'm having an affair – I'm not.'

Jane hugged him a little tighter. 'You'd better not be, Big Ben, but what a strange thing to say.'

Ben laughed and explained how the shop assistant had given him a very disapproving look when he'd bought two Valentine's cards.

The following Tuesday Jane was up so early she had plenty of time to do the supermarket shop and return home to put all the food away before work. The fridge was almost bare, largely due to Tom having been home over half-term week and having therefore consumed even more food than usual. When she got to Oxfam there were several bags of donations to sort through and by mid-morning she and Sue were more than ready for a break.

'Coffee, Sue?'

'Lovely, thanks Jane.'

'Tell you what, you make it and I'll nip out and get us something to go with it.'

Before Sue could protest Jane had grabbed her coat, umbrella and purse and was heading up the basement steps. At the baker's on the corner she lingered over her choice but settled for four large chocolate eclairs, one for each of the staff in the shop that morning. As she hurried back, shielding the cakes under her umbrella, she wondered if spring would ever arrive this year. It was already nearly March and, although there were gaudy daffodils on every verge and roundabout in Cardiff, there was still a nip in the air and it seemed it had rained continuously for months.

Jane made her way back down to the basement, shook out her umbrella and propped it up against Angus, the antlers someone had donated long ago but which Sue had decided were not appropriate to sell in case the shop became a target for animal rights protestors. Jane doubted the deer would have been killed; she was sure she'd seen Attenborough or someone on telly explaining they shed their antlers naturally. But Sue was not prepared to take the risk. Pity, Jane thought, she'd have enjoyed the challenge of selling those.

'Coffee's up.' Sue pulled forward two upturned banana boxes for them to sit on and put the coffees on a third one.

'Thanks Sue, it's horrible out there. I don't think it's stopped raining since Christmas.'

'Oh come on, Jane, you're usually glass half-full – what's the matter with you recently?'

Jane wondered how she could explain to Sue how she felt when she was having difficulty even explaining it to herself. She bit into her eclair. 'I think we deserve this, we've sorted through an awful lot of tat this morning.'

'Oh, I forgot to tell you – at last the 1970s computer tome

213

has gone. I sold it yesterday: as a doorstop. So I have definitely earned a cake. Mmm, naughty but nice; this is lovely Jane, thanks.'

'That must be the longest it's taken for us to sell any of our challenges. How long has it been – six weeks?'

'Yes, afraid so; you seem to have lost your knack!'

'We'll see about that.' Jane laughed. 'Pick the next challenge and bring it on I say.'

'No need to think. I've got the very thing – brought in yesterday.'

Sue got up and walked over to the shelf where items waiting for a place on the shop floor were kept. She handed Jane a beautiful Portmeirion teapot with a bright blue convolvulus painted on it. It was lid-less.

'Oh, Sue, can't you do better than that? I'll have this sold today,' Jane teased.

Sue took another mouthful of her eclair. 'These really are lovely. I'm enjoying this new diet of yours – but I thought you were only allowed cake at breakfast time?'

'Well, I look at it like this, if I was at home anything up to 11ish would be breakfast time, so it's OK to have cake with our coffee here.'

'I like your thinking, Jane,' Sue laughed, sitting down again, 'but are you actually losing weight?'

'Not yet, but with everything that's going on at home I keep awarding myself little treats so I guess I'm not really giving this diet a chance.'

So what is the latest at home then, Jane?' Sue asked.

Their cups were long empty by the time Jane had confided that she felt bereft, that she was no longer the central pivot of her family. She explained how Ben and Tom were spending all their time training together or analysing the training sessions and how Catrin seemed never to be at home because she was always with Lisa and Mark, or Steffan.

'I wouldn't mind that so much – I'm not too old to remember how important friends are at that age – but even

214

when she's home she's not really there; she's always attached to something – her laptop, her mobile, or her iPod.'

Sue moved the box she was sitting on closer and put her arm around Jane.

'And – and – she no longer confides in me.' Jane felt like crying. She'd known Sue for ten years and though they were good friends she'd never been this close to breaking down in front of her before.

'Jane, you know how young people are; they're often totally self-absorbed. I'm sure things will work out. I heard some family expert on the telly saying how important it is to keep the channels of communication open. That seems good advice to me – not that I'm an expert, having no kids of my own – but my nieces are about your Catrin's age and my sister reckons you've got to keep talking to them, even though it sometimes feels like a one-sided conversation.'

'Catrin's not around very much to talk to,' Jane said doubtfully, 'but you're right, thank you, Sue.' She blew her nose loudly, got up and checked herself in the huge ornate mirror propped up in the corner – another item they had been unable to sell.

'And now I'm going to hit the shop floor. Hand me the challenge teapot,' she said firmly.

'Go Ja-ane, go Ja-ane,' Sue chanted as Jane climbed the stairs, teapot in hand.

'Good day in work, love?' Ben asked as he put his hands on Jane's waist and kissed her on the cheek. Without turning or lifting her head from the onions she was chopping she said, 'I sold a teapot as a vase and I'm making spaghetti bolognese – Catrin's favourite.'

'You sound happier, love.'

'I am – a problem shared is a problem halved. It's true enough.'

'I've never understood that saying – it seems to me if you tell someone else then it's their problem too – so really it's a problem doubled not halved.'

'Glass half-empty; that's what you are, Ben,' Jane observed, wiping her hands on her 'Licence to Grill' apron and adding the onions to the garlic which was sizzling in the pan beside her.

'I've texted Tom and Catrin and they've both actually replied and said they'll be home by eight. So, as you're early, perhaps you could lay the table – and we'll need wine glasses.'

'Wine on a weeknight? What are we celebrating?'

'Nothing special,' Jane replied, stirring the onions and garlic. She thought of saying she just wanted to celebrate being a normal family but knew that would trigger all kinds of thoughts and insecurities in Ben's mind. And anyway they weren't normal, however much she wanted them to be.

'Mm, it smells lovely; can't wait.'

'Well you'll have to, Ben Lewis, so after you've laid the table go and do something to take your mind off your stomach for half an hour or so.'

At 8.30 p.m. three of them decided to eat. Jane had tried phoning and texting Catrin but her mobile was off. She'd felt upbeat after her chat with Sue but over the last half hour her mood had changed and now she felt disappointed and cross once more. Tom and Ben had done their best to involve her in their light-hearted banter but had eventually given up and drifted back to talking sport. She heard the words 'glutes', 'aerobic endurance', and 'hamstring' but made no attempt to follow the conversation. Instead she considered how she could punish Catrin for her increasingly selfish behaviour. It had been so simple when she was younger: on the few occasions when Jane had had to discipline her daughter a stern word or even just a look had been enough. She and Ben had always set boundaries and both children had respected them, seemingly happy with the rules. The cornerstones had been kindness, courtesy, and truth. As a couple, and as parents, that's the way they'd behaved, believing that setting an example would be enough. Jane stopped herself. How smug she sounded, how self-righteous. And how could she claim they'd set great store by truth? They'd kept the truth from Catrin for eighteen years, the truth about something that was really important. And now they were getting their comeuppance.

Catrin had still not appeared by the time Ben and Tom went to bed after their late-night run. Jane drank another glass of wine and ate a bag of chocolate raisins. Leaving the hall light on, she climbed the stairs, feeling sick.

The hall light was still on when Jane came downstairs at 6 a.m. By the time Ben was up, showered and dressed she was on her third cup of coffee and pacing up and down the kitchen.

'She hasn't come home, Ben, and her phone is still off,' Jane said the moment he put his head around the kitchen door.

He sighed loudly. 'Look, love, I'm sure she's fine. She'll be home soon, all apologetic and really sorry she's caused us worry.' He fetched a cereal bowl and picked up the packet on the table.

'You don't seem to be worried at all, but then I'm her mother ...'

'And I'm not her father so I'm not worried like a real parent would be worried – is that what you're saying, Jane?' He shook the cereal packet. Jane knew it was empty because Tom had eaten the last of it before he'd left for work.

'No, no of course that's not what I'm saying,' she said, irritably

He put the packet down. 'I'm sorry, love, I know that's not what you meant. Text me when she arrives home, OK? I'll pick up something to eat on the way into work.'

He attempted to kiss her goodbye but she quickly turned her head away. 'I'm sure it's that Steffan Steeler who's making her behave like this. Find out if he's a patient of the practice. Today.'

Ben didn't reply but picked up his briefcase and left, slamming the front door behind him. Jane heard him stall the

217

Volvo and have to restart the engine before he pulled out of the drive.

Three hours later Catrin quietly let herself in, hoping that her mother was working a morning shift in the shop. Her mum's shifts seemed to chop and change and whenever one of the volunteers called in sick she invariably covered for them. But the moment Catrin heard Radio Wales blaring above the hoover she knew she was out of luck. She half-considered trying to sneak up to her room and pretend she'd come home really late last night but before she could make a decision Jane appeared in the hall.

'Where have you been?' she asked wearily, the flatness of her voice and her glare scaring Catrin far more than if she had shouted at her.

'I'm so sorry Mum, I've been at Steffan's; I missed the last train home.'

'I've been worried sick; why on earth didn't you phone us? Your dad or I would have come to fetch you, you know that: we've told you over and over, we'll come, wherever you are at whatever time.'

'No credit on my phone; I didn't realise it was so low.' Catrin tried to squeeze past but her mother was standing squarely in front of her and was clearly not going to budge.

'Well couldn't you have borrowed Steffan's phone or used a public phone box?' her mum said, her voice rising.

Catrin shrugged. She had slept badly and really didn't want to have this conversation. She saw her mother raise her hand then quickly lower it again. Her mum stepped back and clutched her skirt, visibly shaking. Had she been going to slap her? Catrin felt sick. Her mother had never slapped her in her life. Suddenly she felt so sorry, so guilty. Her parents had always been kind and very supportive. After hearing about Steffan's parents last night she was more aware of that than ever.

'Catrin, we've got to talk; I'll make us a cup of tea and then we're going to do just that,' her mum said quietly.

Catrin followed her into the kitchen and sat down in the chair by the Aga. Lucky struggled out of his basket and rubbed his soft coat against her leg as she bent down to stroke him gently.

As Jane waited for the kettle to boil her legs felt like jelly. Recently she'd felt more anger than ever before in her life and each time she almost lost her temper she would feel totally exhausted afterwards. But this time it was more. She was aware she had come close to striking Catrin – so close to doing something that could change their relationship for ever. She shook at the thought. Firmly she reminded herself that, although Catrin was eighteen, she – Jane – was the adult in this relationship.

Her hands trembled as she made the tea. How naive she'd been, how stupid. When Catrin had found out she was donor-conceived Jane had worried it would change the relationship between Catrin and Ben. It had not occurred to her it would change her relationship with Catrin too. But of course it had.

Once they were both cradling hot mugs she said, 'So, what was so exciting in Pontypridd that you missed the last train?'

'Nothing exciting; we just sat in and had a bit of a chat.'

'Must have been scintillating conversation then.' Jane quickly forced a smile to convey she wasn't being sarcastic.

'Steff was telling me about his family. He's had a really tough time, Mum. He hasn't got a father. Well, what I mean is, of course he's got the same biological father as I have, but his mum and dad split up when he was eight. And then his dad said because he wasn't his real father he didn't see why he should have anything to do with him any more. So he hasn't heard from him for nearly twelve years.' Catrin took a sip of her tea. 'And then his mum remarried and she's got three sons with this new bloke – and the new bloke never liked Steffan. They threw him out when he was fifteen and he had to go to live with a foster family. So now I'm the only family he has.'

219

Her daughter's eyes were full of tears and Jane leant over and put her arms around her.

'And so you see after he'd told me all this last night and begged me to stay over I didn't really feel I could leave him.'

'Oh love it sounds as if he's had an awful childhood. Poor thing. Tell you what though, if he needs a new family there's a ready-made one here for him. Why don't you invite him for Sunday lunch so we can all get to know each other?'

'Oh Mum, thank you so much; that would be lovely. And I'll make the pud.'

Jane smiled, glad they seemed to be back on an even keel. 'Hadn't you better get changed? If you're quick I can give you a lift to school before I go to work.'

'Thanks Mum but no need. No lessons today until after lunch – French test.' Catrin grimaced. 'So I'd better go and learn some vocab – words to do with the circus. Très utile!'

'Good girl, off you go then – and Catrin, let's convert your phone to a contract so you're never out of credit again.'

'Thanks, Mum, that's really generous. I'll e-mail Steffan now.'

Catrin headed upstairs to her room. Jane was close behind as she needed to get ready for work. By the time she re-emerged from her bedroom she could hear Catrin snoring lightly. Jane felt another wave of irritation building; Catrin was throwing away her whole future. If only she'd done her exams before all of this had kicked off. Bloody Granny Lewis, bloody Steffan Steeler.

Chapter Fifteen

After a late night out Tom awoke at 8 a.m. trying to work out if the din was in his head or not. Having decided it was not and therefore someone else could be blamed for it, he stomped downstairs to find out what was going on. His mother was vacuuming the hall. Tom brushed past her into the kitchen where his father was eating cereal and Catrin was cooking.

'Why's Mum hoovering at his unearthly hour? He filled a pint glass with water.

'And a good morning to you too, Tom,' his dad said cheerfully, looking up from reading one of the Sunday supplements. .

Tom grunted.

'Steffan's coming to lunch and I'm making pavlova,' said Catrin.

'Hate pavlova.' Tom grumbled.

'Since when?' His dad laughed. 'If I remember rightly you demolished the last one Catrin made in one sitting.'

Tom ignored him and poured himself a bowl of cornflakes. He munched a few mouthfuls. The hoover had stopped but the noise in his head was excruciating. He pushed the bowl away and his father gave him a knowing look.

'OK, everyone done.' His mum came into the kitchen. 'Can one of you clear the breakfast things so I can get on with lunch. The living room could do with seeing a duster and, Ben, the bin under the sink is full. Catrin, once you're done there, perhaps you could cut a few of those tiny daffodils from the garden – a posy for the table would be nice. Come on boys – chop chop.'

'I'm finished Mum, I'll just pop this in the fridge,' Catrin said, dusting the pavlova and a large area of the work surface with icing sugar.

His dad began to gather the dirty dishes and tidy the kitchen. His mum went out again and set to vacuuming the stairs. Tom picked up his glass of water and took it to the living room, He spread the Sunday papers out on the floor and switched on the television to watch *Match of the Day* highlights, something he would not normally do when his team had just lost. Four-nil to Sunderland. What a catastrophe.

'Tom? Tom? You need to pick up your clothes from the floor so I can hoover your room,' his mother shouted from upstairs.

'Why on earth does my room need to be hoovered because someone's coming to lunch?' Tom muttered to no one in particular going back into the kitchen. The back door was open – Catrin and his dad must both be outside.

'Careful, Lucky, or she'll hoover you up too,' he said to the little spaniel, taking his football to kick against the kitchen wall.

He could see the shed's window was misted up. Why couldn't his father give up smoking, he thought crossly; if he did, it would make his job as the old man's personal trainer that much easier. Bloody Steffan. Honestly, it was just like the return of the prodigal son, killing the fatted calf and all that. His mother was cooking lamb and chicken, just in case poor little Steffan didn't like one or the other. When was the last time his mother cooked something special for him? Recognising he was in a foul mood Tom cursed the fact his football match had been called off because the pitch was flooded – again. He needed the buzz of exercise and decided to go for a long run – without telling his father.

Tom enjoyed his run. He liked being on his own, running at his own pace and not having to constantly shout encouragement at his father. By the time he arrived back home he felt very much better.

His mother was in the kitchen making chocolate truffles.

'My, we're pushing the boat out today – handmade chocolates for the guest of honour.' Tom pinched one of the truffles as his mother turned around to put the old cooking bowl she'd been using in the sink.

'Tom, lunch is going to be ready in half an hour – you'll spoil your appetite.'

'Oh come on, Mum, you know nothing spoils my appetite. And anyway I've got to make the most of chocolate while we can still afford it.'

'Surely the recession isn't that bad.' She smiled at him.

''Tis not the recession, Mother, 'tis global warming.'

'Global warming? What's that got to do with chocolate?'

'Oh, Mother, so much to learn and so little time.' Tom sighed dramatically and adopted the tone of a tired teacher explaining something very simple to a dim child for the third time. 'Chocolate will become more expensive because with global warming there will be less land that's suitable to grow the cocoa bean and so your Mars bar will become a delicacy.'

''Oh well, this global warming is not all bad then,' his mother replied, 'it will help my diet.'

'Oh you and your diets. What you need, mother, is a bit of exercise. A bit of running.'

'Can't, love.'

'Won't, you mean Mother.'

'No son, can't; my knees.'

Tom laughed. 'Mother, that's the most overused excuse ever – if you do it right then your knees will be fine.'

'Go away Tom; shower, now.'

By 1 p.m. the house shone, all clutter had been pushed into cupboards, the table laid, and every lamp turned on. Notes of roast lamb and chicken fused with the smell of lavender polish and lemon air freshener.

'Mum, remember the little lesson we had on global warming earlier?' Tom asked as he idly scanned through the radio channels.

'Tom, stop doing that. And take your feet off that cushion

223

please.'

'Mum, focus – global warming, remember?'

'Tom, you're doing my head in; what are you on about?'

'These lamps; why do we need all the lights on? It's the middle of the day.'

'Because they create an ambience and I want the place to look nice.'

'For precious Steffan,' Tom mocked.

'And what's wrong with that?'

Tom rolled his eyes but said nothing.

'Oh Tom, just be nice, please. Now come and help me. I need you to mash the potatoes.'

Tom obliged as his mum fiddled with the extractor fan and flung open the window and back door to clear the windows now dripping with steam from the seven bubbling pans precariously balanced on the Aga.

'OK Tom, everything's ready. I thought he'd be here by now. Go and find Dad and Catrin – I think Catz is upstairs getting changed again and your dad is probably in his shed. We need to be ready to eat when Steffan arrives or it will get cold. And turn off the radio and put some proper music on, something calming.'

'Mum, stop it, relax.' Tom patted her shoulder.

At 2 p.m. they ate. The four of them.

The orange street lamp outside her bedroom window bathed the room in a warm glow but Catrin, sitting at her computer trying to write an essay on French artists, felt cold. She always felt cold after the adrenalin rush of anger had passed. And she had been angry. Angry with her mother for being so cross at Steffan's failure to turn up for lunch, angry with her father for trying to think of good reasons why Steffan couldn't come, angry with Tom for his snide remarks and angry with Steffan for letting her down and not responding to any of her phone calls or text messages. But more than anything she was angry with herself for being so disappointed.

A message on her computer told her Steffan was online. She considered ignoring his request to talk but, clinging to the hope there was a very good explanation why he had failed to turn up, she answered him.

Hi there. What happened?

Soz, bit of a hangover; just didn't feel like doing the happy families thing, you know.

Well thanks a lot for letting us know – not; Mum had gone to heaps of trouble for you and she'd made a roast and everything.

There was an immediate response.

Oh, come on, what's the problem? There were plenty of you there to eat the grub.

Catrin hit the offline button. As she did she heard voices in the kitchen. She listened for a second then leapt up, recognising a familiar laugh.

'Siân's here, love,' her mum shouted up the stairs. Catrin went out on to the landing. 'She wants your help with the truck or something.'

'Toulouse-Lautrec,' Siân explained, appearing in the hall.

'French Post-Impressionist painter, Mum.' Catrin sighed. 'Come on up Siân'.

'Why don't you bring the laptop down to the kitchen, Catz? I'll make you both some tea and I've got chocolate cake too.'

'Thanks, Mum, but we'll get much more done up here.' She needed to talk to Siân about what had happened earlier and she couldn't do that in front of her mum. Siân shrugged and ran up the stairs.

An hour later Catrin and Siân still lay on Catrin's bed discussing Steffan's non-appearance.

'And I think he didn't turn up today because he was afraid. He told me one of the things he didn't like when he was living with his foster family was they put the food in tureens on the table and then everyone would help themselves – just like we do. That really upset him because he felt self-conscious

225

helping himself like that. At home his mum just used to plate the food up for them. So I think he was worried about that.' Catrin paused waiting for Siân to respond but her friend said nothing.

'Steff says it's such a middle class thing to do. So you can understand why he didn't come?'

Siân sat up. 'Oh for goodness sake, Catz, he's not fifteen any more; stop making excuses for him.'

'You don't understand Siân; it's been really hard for him.'

'No, maybe I don't understand all he's been through; but I do understand he's really self-centred.'

Catrin didn't respond.

Siân turned to move off the bed. 'Look, Catz, I've loads of work to hand in tomorrow – have you done the Lautrec essay?'

'No.'

'Do you want to work on it together?'

'No.' Catrin turned on her side and grabbed Little Ted. She felt disappointed Siân had been so negative about Steffan.

'OK, see you tomorrow, then, Catz.' Siân got off the bed and left.

Jane was sitting at the kitchen table reading the paper when Siân came downstairs. She looked at her watch surprised they had finished working on the essay so soon.

'See you tomorrow night, Jane,' Siân called out, opening the front door.

'Are you coming to tea, love? There will be plenty of leftovers from lunch today.'

'No Jane, it's the parent/teacher evening, remember?'

The front door closed.

But Jane did not remember because she had not been told.

Ben had always enjoyed parent/teacher evenings with Catrin. Things had been very different with Tom; each parents's evening had involved a preparatory stiff drink followed by frustration as teacher after teacher complained that Tom was bright but did only just enough work to get by. Tom, sitting alongside, usually had a truculent look on his face, a combination of considering anything except sport to be a waste of time and in protest at being educated in a language he considered alien. How things had changed Ben thought with satisfaction. He knew Tom, clearly enjoying his new job, was glad now he'd been to a Welsh school but he would never admit it. Admitting he'd been wrong, even as an adolescent, was not his son's modus operandi.

But Catrin had been different. Like her brother she was able enough but unlike Tom she always did her best. Catrin wanted to please whereas Tom really couldn't care less. And so Ben confidently approached the sixth form tutor, looking forward to hearing the usual praise for his daughter, despite the reservations Jane had expressed about recent distractions.

Mr James, squeezed into an overly tight shirt, tugged on his tie and shuffled the papers in front of him. How ridiculous, Ben thought, he looks nervous. Hasn't anyone told him it's the pupil who's supposed to feel like that? They shook hands over the desk and Ben sat down with Jane on one side and Catrin on the other.

Mr James cleared his throat. 'I'm afraid Catrin hasn't been her usual self lately and her work has suffered. I suppose it's no surprise with her grandmother passing and then all the sickness she's had. You, Dr Lewis, would know all about the effect of illness on concentration and energy.'

Ben was aware he was staring at the teacher, his mouth open in a stupid cartoonish way. He looked at Catrin. His daughter's face was flushed scarlet and she was studying her hands.

'You know, Dad, the colds I've had and stuff,' she mumbled, not looking up.

'The fact Catrin has missed so many lessons means she's fallen behind a little. And of course not meeting the deadline for one of the Art coursework pieces means that 10 per cent is

227

lost.'

Ben was too stunned to say anything and Catrin was not her usual forthcoming self. Jane was silent too but Ben had a feeling she would have plenty to say when they got home. Mr James looked distinctly uncomfortable as he consulted the attendance register in front of him.

'Um, well, all we can do now is to concentrate on getting the 90 per cent that's still available.' He added a little laugh at the end of his sentence.

Ben wondered why people laughed when something was clearly not funny.

'And I see the French coursework is due in next Monday. How's that going, Catrin?'

'OK,' she said non-committally.

'Of course all Catrin's teachers assure me the 280 points she needs are still attainable, but she must work really hard from now until the exams – after all it's only a few months effort and so worthwhile. I went to Aberystwyth Uni myself; it's a brilliant place to be a student, Catrin, you'll love it.'

As Catrin didn't respond Mr James ploughed on, 'Is there anything worrying you? Anything I can help sort out? Or perhaps you'd like to speak to the school nurse?'

Catrin shook her head, still gazing firmly at her lap.

Ben pushed his chair back, rose and thanked Mr James for his time. Jane and Catrin stood too. The three of them walked along the grey corridor that smelled of old gym shoes and disinfectant back to the school entrance. On the way they passed several groups of people they knew and called out a cheery 'hello' and 'good to see you'. Usually Ben would have stopped for a catch-up with some of these other parents but tonight he moved his family on quickly, giving the impression they had another urgent appointment to keep. In the safety of the dark car park they let their smiles slip. They drove home in silence.

Back at Pencisely Crescent Ben parked the car and let Jane into the house. Catrin loitered a few steps behind, fiddling with her phone then tried to walk past him straight up to her room. Ben put his hands firmly on her shoulders and guided her into the kitchen.

'So, Catrin, what's going on?'

'It's no big deal Dad; I've just missed a few sessions, that's all.'

'And failed to hand in coursework that counts towards your final grade – in the subject you want to study at university,' Ben said, 'and told the school you've been ill when you haven't.'

Jane busied herself making tea.

'Only a couple of times, Dad.'

'But why? Where have you been when you were meant to be in school?'

'Just hanging out.'

'Who with?'

'Steffan.'

Jane tutted loudly and sighed.

'Why, Catrin?'

'Because he's lonely.'

'Has it occurred to you he could busy himself finding a job?' Ben sat down wearily.

'It's really difficult, Dad.'

'Impossible I'd say if you don't try,' Jane said briskly, 'And because you feel sorry for him you're prepared to jeopardise your chance of getting to university; jeopardise your whole future.'

'Oh Mum, lighten up. And anyway I may decide to go to uni in Pontypridd now instead of Aberystwyth – I'd get to see more of Steffan if I went there and they're asking for much lower grades.'

'But you loved Aberystwyth, Catrin.'

'And now I love Ponty.'

'Do they actually do Fine Art in Pontypridd, Catrin?' Ben asked reasonably.

Catrin shrugged. 'Don't know, Dad, perhaps not, but there

229

will be some kind of course I could do. And I know people who are already there and they didn't need high grades at A level to get in.'

'But it's too late now to apply to Pontypridd to get in this September.'

'Stop fussing Dad, I could get in through clearing – no probs.'

'Oh, Catrin.' Jane put the mugs of tea down so hard she spilt some.

'Can I go now? I've got French to do.' Catrin didn't wait for a reply but marched out of the room.

Jane pushed the tea mugs aside and grabbed a bottle of wine from the slate rack in the corner. She unscrewed the top and poured two large glasses. 'Ben, if you don't find out about that Steffan tomorrow, I shall – I shall …'

Ben slumped behind the sports pages of the newspaper.

Jane arrived at Oxfam the next morning still feeling upset and when Sue asked her to create the 'Mothering Sunday' display her initial reaction was an ironic laugh. But Sue insisted and within minutes Jane was engrossed. Years of working in the shop had proved suggesting an item was suitable to celebrate a special occasion worked a treat and Jane always took great pride in her displays. For the next hour she was absorbed arranging 'Best mum in the world' paraphernalia: handbags – to which she tied toning scarves; pretty jewellery; a microwavable Bagpuss; toiletries; a cushion declaring 'There's nothing like a mother's love;' and several girly novels. She flicked through a *Dear Mum … from me to you* book and was intrigued by an entry in spidery handwriting. In answer to the question, 'What did you learn from your own mother that's influenced the way you've raised me?' this mother had written, 'it is nonsense not to spoil your child – if you don't who will? The world is a cruel place.' Jane flicked on in the hope there were other entries in the book – this woman's thinking appealed to her. But there was nothing.

Perhaps there was no need to say anything else. Rather than adding the book to the pile she decided she would buy it herself; perhaps she'd fill it in and give it to her mother. Granny Lewis's death had made her realise how much went unsaid between her and Olwen.

Sue came over to admire the display. 'That looks great, Jane; you've certainly got a good eye. It's amazing, though, all these soppy messages.'

'People find it hard to say these things – it's an easy way out.'

'It just seems so sugary. I blame the Americans. Anyway, these have just come in. Is there anything we can do with them?' Sue dumped a pile of used birthday cards on the table.

'Sue, I've told you before, you're slacking; what kind of challenge is that?' Jane picked up a pair of large scissors and set about creating little piles of gift tags. She smiled as she cut.

Catrin had got to know North Road well in the last few months. This was where Mark worked, in a large sports centre. She felt uncomfortable walking past, hoping to catch sight of him, but somehow she was unable to keep away. Because he worked different shifts often she failed to see him and, when she did, she'd turn sharply away so he would not spot her and ask what she was doing on this side of town. On the days she did see him she was relieved he was on his own or with some boys. Yet she still turned up for more reassurance.

The problem was Mark was sending such mixed messages and after instigating their one and only date in Roath Park, Catrin felt too embarrassed to ask again. Following the debacle of the Valentine's card she'd thought she must be misreading the signs. But then he'd made her a compilation CD for her laptop and it did include a couple of slow songs – these were the ones she played over and over. Siân agreed the CD surely meant he fancied her and Catrin thought his hand had touched hers for a little longer than necessary when he was handing it over. Maybe that was just wishful thinking?

But he certainly hadn't asked for his scarf back: that was pretty significant. Her mobile bleeped.

Message from Steffan:

TOWIE-fest, mine 2morow – all dayer. U up 4 it? Please come.

That would mean skipping school again but she hated the thought of him sitting in that grotty house all by himself. As she considered how to reply, she became aware of movement behind her.

'Hi, Catrin, what's it to be then, Lamborghini, Aston Martin, or a Porsche?'

Catrin looked up to see a tall figure in sports kit reflected in the car showroom window. It was Mark. Her immediate impulse was to run but that would be ridiculous. Instead she held up her mobile and said the first thing that came into her head:

'Text from Steff inviting me to watch telly with him. He's a *TOWIE* freak.' That made her look equally ridiculous. She blushed. Why couldn't she have just answered his question about cars?

'*TOWIE*?'

'*The Only Way is Essex.*'

Mark frowned. 'That bloke needs to get a life.'

'It's difficult to do much living on £56.80 a week.' Catrin sounded more indignant than she actually felt. She turned towards the city centre and Mark fell into step beside her. Immediately she regretted her sharp response. She'd panicked and that had made her defensive. Now she couldn't think what to say to get the conversation back to normal.

'So, you were looking in the posh garage, Catrin,' Mark saved her the trouble. 'Didn't know you were that interested in cars.'

'Oh, just a bit of research for a school project, that's all.'

'Wish they'd had projects like that when I was at school.' He smiled at her.

The traffic noise made conversation difficult but Catrin was

232

glad. It meant the silence between them was less awkward.

'I'm going in to town to buy a Mother's Day present; you want to come?' Mark said after a while.

Catrin fought to contain her enthusiasm. After all it was hardly a proper date. She said casually, 'OK. I could do with looking for something for my mum too.'

'Great, I'll just phone Lisa to find out where she is. I said I'd meet up with her about now.'

Catrin spirits plummeted. No, it was definitely not any kind of date.

After browsing around the shops for an hour Lisa and Mark finally settled on a bottle of perfume for their mother and Catrin chose a chocoholics pampering set with chocolate bubble bath, chocolate shampoo, and a chocolate soap. Now they were sitting in a little cafe off Queen Street drinking hot chocolate and watching the world go by. The smell of chocolate, combined with the different perfumes she and Lisa had sprayed on themselves, was making her feel queasy.

'Oh, I nearly forgot; I need to answer Steff's text,' Catrin dug out her phone from her jacket.

'So you two back on speaks then?' Lisa asked.

'Yes, just about,' Catrin jabbed at her phone; 'I know he can be thoughtless but I do feel sorry for him; he's got rubbish parents.'

'At least he doesn't have to trudge around looking for a Mother's Day present then,' Mark said, scooping up the froth at the bottom of his hot chocolate with a teaspoon.

Catrin knew he was trying to lighten the conversation but she really wanted to talk Steffan's behaviour through with Lisa and if she could get Mark interested in the donor issue that would be even better. 'He hasn't exactly said so but I think he's still hoping our biological father will re-register – at the moment he sees the fact he hasn't chosen to as another rejection.'

'That's plain silly; the bloke who donated probably just

wanted a bit of cash. End of.'

'I don't think you're being fair, Mark,' Lisa chipped in. 'Some of them are good people who want to help.'

'Maybe,' Mark sounded unconvinced.

'Well, like Steff, I'm hoping my donor will register,' Lisa said, directing her comment at Catrin, 'not that I need another dad; it's just I'd like to see how he looks, to find out if I look like him, I suppose.'

'I don't think you should build up your hopes, Lisa. I'm sure the last thing most donors want is some stranger suddenly turning up calling them "daddy".'

'Oh shut up, Mark.' Lisa shoved her brother, sending the teaspoon he'd been using clattering to the floor.

'Is that why you don't want to find out anything about your donor or if you have any half-brothers or sisters?' Catrin asked.

Mark finished his chocolate. 'Look it's enough for me to know that Lisa and I have a different biological father. Clearly my genes are superior to hers, as is sooooo obvious.' Mark pushed his empty mug away and stood up. 'I've got to go. I promised to help out at the Youth Club tonight. I'll catch you two later.'

He left the cafe and Catrin watched his tall frame blend into the crowd. She followed his distinctive blond head until she could no longer make him out. He was so gorgeous; she liked everything about him. With her previous crushes there had always been something she wished she could change. But Mark, well, he was perfect.

She turned back to Lisa, who was watching her closely. Catrin blushed and buried her face in her almost empty mug. 'I'm getting a flush from this hot choc,' she mumbled, fanning herself with the menu.'

'It's something else, or rather *someone*, that's making you hot.' Lisa laughed.

Catrin smiled. 'He really is not interested in finding out about his donor is he, Lis?'

'No, not at all. He's always been like that. When Mum and Dad told us – I was eleven, just about to go to big school, so Mark was fifteen – he just listened and didn't ask a single question. Not like me! Can you imagine? I couldn't stop. Just my way of trying to get my head around it, I suppose. But not Mark. I don't think it's an issue for him at all – never has been.'

An hour later, with the waitress hoovering around their legs, they brought their conversation to a close, promising to chat online later that night, and headed home.

Tom poked his head around the kitchen door as soon as he came into the house, lured by the sweet smell of baking. His mother was standing by the cooker, watching the grill.

'Hi Mum, something smells good.'

'Hi, love; sorry, can't turn round in case the marzipan burns. I've completed the first cake; just finishing off the second one.'

Tom took advantage of her preoccupation to steal one of the little balls decorating the completed cake on the work surface.

'There, that's it, that's Granny's cake done,' she said, turning around and setting the lightly toasted cake on the cooling tray.

'Is it called a Granny cake?'

'No Tom, it's for Granny; it's called a Simnel cake; Delia Smith's recipe – never fails. Traditionally it's made for Easter, but I've always made your gran one for Mother's Day.

'That sort of makes sense, Mum.' Tom laughed.

'Well yes it does Tom; it means she has it ready then in good time for Easter.'

She stood back to admire her handiwork and spotted the gap on the first cake. 'Tom, you've eaten Simon Peter.'

'And delicious he was too,' Tom confirmed. 'Tea, Mum?'

Chapter Sixteen

Jane had the day off and was enjoying having the house to herself. She'd done some cleaning, wallowed in the bath until she was prune-like, and put on a new dress. Now she balanced her mother's cake in its Quality Street tin in one hand as she fished around in her bag to make sure she had her keys and purse. She was looking forward to going to Treorchy. Every year she took a day off specially to deliver the freshly baked Simnel cake and she cherished the ritual.

As she went to close the front door behind her the telephone in the hall rang. She considered ignoring it but, fearing it might be her mother changing their plans, she put the tin down and picked up the phone.

'Hello.'

She immediately felt reassured when she heard a male voice. Good, it wasn't her mother.

'Is that Mrs Lewis?

'Yes.'

Erm, hello, it's Mr James – from the school.'

Her heart sank. Why was her daughter's sixth-form tutor calling? 'Oh, hello, how can I help?'

'Erm, well, erm, is Catrin unwell again?'

Jane felt sick but said nothing.

Mr James carried on. 'Well, as she's not in today, I'm just ringing to make sure she remembers that the second Art essay is due in on Monday.'

Jane didn't respond.

'And of course, it would be a pity if she failed to hand that in too – it's worth another 10 per cent, and what with already …'

'Yes, thank you, Mr James,' Jane heard herself say from

very far away. 'I'll remind her. Thank you.'

She dumped her coat and bag on the hall floor and dialled Catrin's number. It went straight to answerphone. She dialled again, just in case she'd misdialled the first time. Still the answerphone. Jane fished out her mobile and her spectacles and texted:

Where are u? School want to know, and so do I.' Please call me. Now.

Then she rang the surgery. Jane hardly ever rang Ben at work, knowing his consultations were already interrupted by numerous phone calls which were as frustrating to him as they were to the patient. But now she felt she had no choice. The receptionist, knowing Dr Lewis's wife rarely called, put her straight through.

'Hi Jane, everything OK?' Ben said guardedly.

'No it is not,' she said loudly. 'Catrin's absent from school again. Mr James has just been on the phone.'

'Jane, I've got someone with me at the moment; can I call you back?'

'No, you can't. For once your family is going to take precedence over your precious patients. I bet she's with Steffan and today you are going to find out about that boy. No more "I forgot," "the computer was down;" or any of the other fob offs I've had from you over the past weeks. Today, Ben, and I mean it.' With that she slammed down the phone.

By the time she got into town her anger had all but dissipated. She settled in her seat on the two-carriage train that would take her up the valley to Treorchy, determined to forget her troubles for a while and to enjoy the journey as much as she usually did. Jane had now lived in Cardiff for longer than she had lived in Treorchy but, as always when she made this journey following the Taff northwards, she felt she was going home. Just standing on the Cardiff Queen Street platform, from which the Valleys trains departed, felt different to being on the street outside. Two worlds separated by the width of a railway track. On the platform the accent was different and, to

Jane's eyes, the people looked different too, with a particular penchant for tattoos (the men) and gold jewellery (the women). She was generalising, of course, but she did like the idea that Valleys people were different.

The train pulled out and passed through the multiple-occupancy houses of student-land, with their rubbish-strewn gardens, and on through leafy Radyr. Jane noticed new estates sprouting up – mock-Tudor houses, all with solar panels. How ridiculous they looked. Why on earth did people build homes that pretended to be something they were clearly not? There were superb examples of modern architecture in the magazines or on telly these days – all glass and natural stone or wood. She caught a glimpse of her reflection in the train window looking miserable, literally down in the mouth, and deliberately smiled back at herself. But in the dirty glass she looked alarmingly manic. The young man sitting opposite glanced around to see if there was another seat available. There wasn't; he plugged himself into his iPod and closed his eyes.

Leaving the city suburbs, Jane was aware of a sudden feeling of space. She smiled at the sight of newborn lambs prancing around the fields, leaping vertically into the air and landing on wobbly legs. Past Taffs Well the mountains started to loom and a little further on row upon row of terraced houses clung to the dark slopes. At Treforest the train disgorged its multinational student passengers. From here on Jane knew any non-whites would be looked at with interest. Really the houses and the people of the Valleys proper had changed very little since she was a small girl and, once she was back, she felt as if she'd never gone away.

Pontypridd. Jane glanced out of the window. Catrin was probably just a few hundred metres away but she felt far more distant. And then the train trundled on, stopping at all the tiny stations where only one or two passengers alighted or got off, all the way up to Treorchy. As she drew nearer Jane became more impatient. She looked at her watch. Her mother would be

239

in the cafe by now, ten minutes before they had arranged to meet 'in case the train was early'. The train had never yet been early.

'Usual, love?' Maria asked, as Jane pushed open the door of the Station Cafe. Like so many other cafes in the Valleys, it was run by Italians; they served great coffee and this one was Jane's favourite, her 'local'. She flopped heavily on the leatherette bench opposite her mother.

'You OK, Mum?'

'I'm fine Jane; clearly you're not.'

Maria placed Jane's frothy coffee in a chunky white cup and saucer on the Formica table and put down a side plate with a couple of Welsh cakes.

'Thank you,' Jane and Olwen said in unison, helping themselves.

'I've brought you your Simnel cake, Mum – I made it last night so it will be fresh for a good while yet.'

'Really Jane, you needn't have, you've got plenty to do without baking me a cake; you're probably doing too much, that's your problem.'

'I enjoy baking, Mum; you know that.'

Jane sipped her coffee and ate her Welsh cake, thinking how much she not only enjoyed baking the cake but also the tradition. She'd been baking her mother a Simnel cake for Mother's Day since she had left home to get married and it was just another of those annual events that punctuated her year. Recently, though, she felt as if Mothering Sundays were coming around more often. But she'd enjoyed making the cake and felt guilty she didn't make her mother cakes more often – poor Olwen usually had to survive on shop-bought.

'Mm, these Welsh cakes are lovely,' her mother commented.

'Not home-made though,' Jane said quietly, looking over her shoulder to make sure she wasn't overheard.

'Nice and sweet; just how I like them,' Olwen said, and took another bite.

Jane felt the warmth of the coffee and the familiar surroundings relax her. She'd been coming to this little cafe with her mother, and then with her friends, since she was a child and, although it was just around the corner from her mother's house, they liked to meet here for a treat. The chocolate box with its faded thatched cottage scene still formed the cafe's sparse window display, reminding passers-by it also sold confectionery. As a little girl she remembered pleading with her mother to buy her that box so she could use it to carry her sewing to school, just like Mair Jones, the vicar's daughter. Mair's box had a Christmas ice-skating scene on it; she remembered it clearly even now. But Jane never did get the box, although she was sure she had wished specifically for it when she was stirring at least three Christmas puddings. The thought of making Christmas pudding reminded her of that traumatic afternoon when Catrin had sent off her request for information to the HFEA.

'Do you think I was wrong, Mum?' she said in a low voice.

'Wrong about what?'

Jane concentrated on her wedding ring, turning it round and round. 'You know, having Catrin the way I did?'

Olwen sighed. 'Jane, love, there's no point to such a question. What's done is done; and no of course I don't think you were wrong – how could you be wrong? Catrin was a much-wanted, much-loved baby. She's had the best – great parents in you and Ben.'

'But it was all about me, Mum; I didn't consider the baby's feelings at all. Ben said to wait; maybe we should have.'

'Nonsense, Jane,' her mother cut in briskly. 'Look, if you'd waited you wouldn't have had Catrin, would you? And Catrin is – well, Catrin. She's lovely.'

Jane smiled weakly.

'You can't honestly think she would prefer not to exist? Catrin loves life and she's got so much to look forward to. Perhaps she is being difficult at the moment but this is just a phase; you'll all get through it. Time is a great healer.'

'Oh, Mum, you and your old sayings.'

Maria, who had been clearing the table next to them, came over waving her dishcloth. 'I'll just give this a lick and a promise.' She picked up their dishes and drew the damp cloth over the Formica. 'Is there anything else I can get you, my loves?'

Olwen shook her head as she gathered her grocery shopping bags from underneath the table and put on her coat and hat.

'I'll just have some sweets, Maria, please – can't face the journey back to Cardiff without a supply of your coconut mushrooms.' Jane went to the counter to pay. 'I'd better get the family something too.'

Jane contemplated jar upon jar of sweets on the high shelf behind Maria before settling on bonbons for Ben, fizzy bubblegum bottles for Tom, and dolly mixtures for Catrin. Olwen decided she'd like a quarter of mint fondant creams after all and then Jane took her home.

On the train back to Cardiff Jane tried to focus on all the positive things her mother had said but still she felt so guilty. It may be Ben's fault that Catrin had not been told about the donor as a child, when the consequences would not have been so threatening, but it was she, Jane, who had pressed to have a second child. She had been so selfish; had not for a moment stopped to consider the feelings of the human being she was about to conceive in such a way. A picture of Catrin's traumatised face when she'd found out she was donor-conceived materialised in the train window. Jane wiped it away then noticed the grime on her hand. She dug out a tissue from her handbag. As she did she remembered the photo of Catrin in her purse, the one taken with Tom at his graduation. Jane took it out and looked at it. Yes she'd been selfish but she knew, even with hindsight, she would have made the same decision. Certainly without Catrin her life would be so much poorer. But there was a price to pay, a hefty dose of guilt.

Walking up the crescent Jane quickened her pace. It was just starting to rain and she didn't have her umbrella. Her mood lifted a little as she saw there was a light on in Catrin's room – at least her daughter was home and hopefully getting on with some schoolwork. She let herself into the house, dumped her coat on the coat rack and grabbed the towel from the downstairs cloakroom. As she was giving her hair a vigorous rub the phone rang. Jane answered it.

'Hi, love, it's me.'

'Oh, hi, Ben; look, I'm sorry about earlier.'

'Forgotten already,' he said. 'Now pack your bag – we're going away for the weekend; I've booked a room for us in the Ship at Llangrannog.'

'But, Ben, I can't, I need to be here; Catrin's got to get her Art coursework in for Monday.'

Jane heard the audible sigh at the other end of the phone. 'You can't do it for her.'

'But I need to be here to make sure she does it.'

'No. You. Don't,' Ben said slowly. 'She's 18, Jane, an adult. She needs to take responsibility for it herself.'

Jane groaned. 'But will she?'

'Look you've been there every weekend for months and it hasn't meant she's always done what she's supposed to, has it?'

'But what if she doesn't finish the coursework and doesn't get the grades for Aberystwyth?' Jane heard papers being shuffled. Ben must be working as he talked to her. 'You clearly don't care what happens to Catrin,' she said, her voice rising sharply, 'Obviously your family is not as important to you as your precious patients.'

Ben sighed again. 'You're being ridiculous. Of course I care about Catrin, about all of you; you and the kids are more important than anything else to me but we've got to let Catrin grow up and she won't do that if we don't allow her to make her own mistakes. We can't protect her from all the bad things out there, Jane; we've got to let her become streetwise or we're failing as parents. She's a good kid and hopefully we've done enough so she knows what's right and wrong. Now we've got to trust her.'

Jane listened. Maybe Ben had a point.

'Are you still there?'

'Yes, I'm still here.'

'And it will do us good; we need some time together, just the two of us, away from Cardiff. It will help us both get some perspective and we'll come back feeling energised and able to tackle anything.

'OK, Ben,' she replied flatly, not feeling up to arguing. Anyway, she really liked Llangrannog; perhaps a weekend away was just what she needed. Lowering her voice, she asked, 'Did you find out about Steffan?'

'We'll talk about it later, love.'

'Well as long as we do talk about it.'

'OK, I'll be home in about an hour and we'll leave as soon as; get to Llangrannog for supper. They serve until 9.30 – I've checked.'

As Jane put down the phone, she could see Siân's outline in the glass side panel of the front door. Damn, she would not now be able to confront Catrin about her absence from school until after the weekend; she certainly did not want to discuss it in front of Siân. But on second thoughts that was probably the better plan anyway so as not to spoil the weekend for either of them. She opened the door.

'Hi Jane, we're going to tackle our Art coursework together,' Siân explained. 'Catz upstairs?'

Jane nodded, pleased Catrin had the assignment in hand.

Catrin had spent the last few hours feeling sorry for herself. It had not been an enjoyable day with Steffan and to cap it all her mother had found out she'd bunked off school. Mr James would not be impressed by her absence either. And really had it been worth it? As usual Steff had been sprawled on the sofa when she arrived, surrounded by empty cans and take-away cartons, his eyes glued to the telly. She really didn't understand – his texts always pleaded for her to come and spend time with him and then, when she did, he barely spoke to her, barely looked away from the television. Today she'd tried to talk to him about Mark.

'There's this boy I really like but I'm not sure he likes me, well not in the way I want him to like me anyway and, as you're a boy, I thought you might be able to give me a bit of advice.'

'I certainly was a boy the last time I looked,' he said lazily, without taking his eyes off the screen where an American presenter was trying to keep two young people from coming to blows. Their screeching suddenly got on Catrin's nerves. She said sarcastically, 'Well, I won't disturb your viewing, Steff; I'll be off.'

He turned his head for a second. 'What's up, sis? Don't you want to watch *TOWIE*? I've got the DVD all set up.' He pressed the play button on the handset and the picture changed. A group of very tanned young women were sitting around and a girl with bright coral nails seemed to be saying over and over again 'no carbs before Marbs' while her friends discussed who was cheating on whom. Then there was a shot of a group of equally tanned young men discussing the pressure of ensuring their hairstyles were 'well reem'. Mark was right; Steffan really did live his life through these strange characters.

She screamed at him, 'I don't want to watch this. I don't want to watch anything. You're sitting there listening to people's problems – when – when there are people with problems in your real life, Steff, but you don't listen to them.'

He pressed the mute button and pushed a packet of smiley pills at her, which she immediately pushed back, shaking her head.

'So, what's the problem? Some bloke?'

Exasperated he'd not been listening she replied abruptly, 'Yes, it's Mark; you know, Lisa's half-brother. I told you about him.' She explained again how she thought Mark liked her but wasn't making any moves.

'Oh, that's just like Kate and me,' Steffan said. 'Kate – she used to live here – gone back to Coventry; didn't like Ponty, too much rain.' He looked back at the muted screen.

Catrin made one last bid for his undivided attention. 'So what do you think I should do?

'Do?' he said, distracted.

'Yes, how do I get him to be more than just a friend?'

Steffan shrugged. 'Perhaps he's not that into you. With Kate I asked her best friend out just to see if she was jealous. She wasn't. So that was it.' He turned the television's volume back on. 'Oh, this is a really good bit; I've seen this before.'

Catrin grabbed her coat and made for the door. 'I'll text you, Steff,' she'd called out as she left. But he hadn't bothered to reply.

It was now two hours since she had arrived home. About five minutes earlier she'd heard her mother's key in the lock, a sound she'd been dreading. But then the phone had rung. Catrin knew it was only a temporary reprieve and, when she heard footsteps on the stairs, she braced herself for the forthcoming row and buried her nose in a textbook.

The door opened. 'Wow, you look as if you've started without me. I'm mega impressed.'

Relieved Catrin turned round to see Siân. Her best friend pulled up a chair and sat at the desk beside her. 'Well actually, on second thoughts, I'm not that impressed.' Siân laughed. 'Your book seems to be upside down.'

Catrin smiled and turned the book the right way up. 'OK, where do we start? Remind me of the title.'

For the next hour Catrin and Siân worked on Man Ray and his surreal photographs, both avoiding discussing the reason for Catrin's absence from school that day. Catrin stayed clear of the subject because she knew Siân would disapprove of her spending the day with Steffan and she guessed Siân did not mention it because she rarely wanted to talk about anything involving Steffan or Lisa. When her mother popped her head around the door to tell Catrin she and Ben were heading west for the weekend the girls were engrossed in their work.

'OK, Mum, I was going to cook you a Mother's Day lunch but I'll make it a Mother's Day supper instead. Text me to say when you'll be back,' Catrin said, glad an imminent confrontation had been avoided.

'Oh yes, thank you, I'll do that', her mum replied. Before she could close the door Catrin got up and handed her a package wrapped in homemade gift paper and tied with three different coloured ribbons.

'Happy Mother's Day,' she said. 'Go on, open it now.'

Her mother hesitated a moment then tore off the wrapping. 'Oh, lovely, chocolate without the calories – perfect, Catrin, thank you.'

'Look again, Mum; there's something else.'

Jane unfolded another apron. It had printed on it: 'World's Best Mum.'

'Thank you Catrin, very useful,' she said, leaving the room and closing the door behind her. She had neither kissed nor hugged Catrin on receiving her gift and tears stung Catrin's eyes as she settled down again to work with Siân.

Ben turned on the car radio as they joined the Friday night exodus from the city. Jane, sitting beside him, was itching to ask what he had found out about Steffan but decided to wait until they had safely negotiated their way on to the motorway. As soon as they hit the M4 and the traffic started flowing, she turned down the radio and posed the question.

'Let's just leave it for now, Jane; forget about the kids for one night and talk about something else for a change.'

'How can I forget about the kids?' she said, 'with all that's going on with Catrin at the moment.'

'Well, try, Jane.'

'But ...'

'But nothing,' Ben cut across her. 'Come on,' he added

brightly, 'we haven't had a weekend away for ages, not since Mum became ill; let's relax and enjoy it.'

'Just tell me what you found out about Steffan and then I'll find it easier to relax.'

Ben sighed. 'Look, he *is* a patient of the practice, as is his family.'

'And?'

'And nothing.' He looked straight ahead.

'What, there's nothing about him or his family on the files?' Jane asked in disbelief.

'No.'

'No what?' she persisted, starting to lose patience with her husband's obvious reticence.

'No, there is information on file but it's confidential, Jane, you know it is, and I can't tell you anything else.' A tanker hurtled past them in the middle lane causing the Volvo to shake and covering the windscreen with spray. Ben turned the wipers on and for a moment Jane concentrated on their soothing rhythmic swish. Another lorry passed and he increased the wipers' speed.

'Wouldn't you be better not clinging to the inside lane Ben? We're getting the spray from everything that passes here.'

Ben looked in his mirror and moved to the middle lane. Jane decided she'd change tactics. Ben usually responded better to being persuaded rather than threatened.

'Of course you can tell me what's in Steffan's file; you know I won't tell anybody.'

'I know nothing of the sort. You're a tigress when the children are involved and I know full well you'd stop at nothing to protect them.' Ben turned the wipers off. 'And I don't blame you. So no, I can't tell you. A doctor has a responsibility to his patient – and keeping his or her confidence is intrinsic to that responsibility.'

He reached into the side pocket of the driver's door, pulled out a packet of mints and offered it to Jane. She took one,

248

handed one to him and popped the packet into the pocket of the passenger door. 'But he's not your patient. So not your responsibility.'

Jane heard the crunch as he bit into his mint. 'You're splitting hairs; Steffan and his family are patients of the practice – and I am head of that practice.'

'You're deluded, Ben, if you think you are head of the practice; everyone knows Stella's the boss.'

He laughed. 'Point taken. But in all seriousness Stella is the practice manager, she's not a partner. I am the senior partner so ultimately the practice is my responsibility.'

Jane said nothing for a few minutes. Ben turned the radio up and starting humming. She knew this was his signal that the conversation was over but she was not giving up just yet. 'You're making me think there's something dreadful in that file; that Steffan is a mass murderer, or something.' She shuddered.

'Jane, would he be living in a terraced house in Ponty if he was a mass murderer?' Ben asked.

'It's his family then; are they murderers?'

'You're being ridiculous. I'll say this and no more. Steffan has not had an easy life.'

She groaned. 'Well you're hardly telling me something I don't know.' She turned her head to gaze out at the darkness, acknowledging she'd have to leave things for now. They sat in silence for the rest of the two-hour journey, pretending to listen intently to the inane chatter between the DJ and a series of guests until they pulled into the little seafront car park beside the Ship Inn.

'I wonder what Cai's got on the menu tonight? I'm famished,' Ben said as he opened the boot to hand Jane her overnight bag. She nodded. She was glad to be here after all and was looking forward to a weekend away from home - a break from the endless shopping, cooking and cleaning. But most of all she needed a break from thinking about Catrin and Steffan. Yes, she would try to do as Ben suggested and forget

249

about her troubles for the weekend. She took her husband's hand as they walked into the light-filled bar.

The next day dawned bright and crisp. Ben awoke to the unfamiliar sound of seagulls. Carefully he opened the curtains just wide enough to enjoy the view of the beach and sea. This was his favourite time of day – before the locals and the few visitors who ventured to the West Wales coast at this time of year surfaced. Ben appreciated fine weather at any time but fine weather in March was doubly pleasing.

He turned to check that Jane was still asleep, pulled on his running kit and set out along the coast path. He had surprised himself how quickly his attitude to running had changed and now he could honestly say that mostly he enjoyed his regular four- or five-mile runs. It gave him time to think and today he needed that time. But just at the moment all he could think about was the path ahead. This undulating route was certainly more challenging than a run around the streets of Cardiff. Ben stopped to rub a stitch in his side. What, if anything, should he do about Steffan? He set off again, Tom's advice about running through the pain ringing in his head. What to do about Steffan? But the stunning views of Cardigan Island and the beautiful tapestry of colour all around – bright yellow gorse, pale yellow wild daffodils and celandine, and the vivacity of the red campion – soon distracted him and he arrived back at The Ship happy, hungry but without any answers.

Ben joined his wife for a leisurely breakfast and then they decided to go their separate ways for a few hours, both agreeing that spending some, rather than all, their time together was the way to ensure they both got the most out of the weekend. Jane accepted Cai's offer of a lift into Cardigan, the little country town some twenty minutes along the coast, to browse in the craft shops hidden in its narrow backstreets and to drink coffee in the Pendre gallery. Ben arranged where he'd meet her and gave strict instructions she should do serious damage to their credit card before heading out again. Now he made his way up the steep slope to his mother's grave, clutching a bunch of irises he had bought in the village shop. The kindly woman there had warned him it wasn't warm enough for them to open fully but he'd shrugged. His mother had loved irises.

The little cemetery looked beautiful, its slopes awash with colour. It being Mothering Sunday the next day loud bunches of bright daffodils filled the grave vases bringing cheer to the black marble. Ben reached his mother's plot and was grateful someone had put some daffodils in a jam jar. One of his cousins, Ben assumed. He really should call to thank them. He should also get his mother's name engraved on the headstone. He'd ask his cousins who did that kind of work around here at the same time: kill two birds with one stone. Ben winced, what a crass term of phrase. He took out his hanky, rubbing a little mud from the headstone, added his irises to the jam jar, and sat on the curb that surrounded the grave. The irises made it look different from the others. Good, he thought, Mum was different too. Fleetingly he felt a pang of guilt. To him this was his mother's grave. While she was alive it had been his father's grave but it was now his mother he thought of. His father had been dead for so long Ben couldn't remember exactly what he'd looked like; those images had merged with the photos of his dad on his wedding day, on holidays and birthdays, and at Christmas.

Ben was alone. There was no one else to be seen. The locals would all have been to the cemetery a few days previously, anxious that any visitors would see their graves were tended to, as if a family's reputation depended on it. And so, on this Saturday morning, he had the place to himself.

'I don't think talking to someone who's dead breaks the Hippocratic Oath,' he said with a smile. 'And anyway you are the reason I'm in this pickle so you can jolly well help me out.'

He paused to gather his thoughts. 'I'm not sure what to do for the best, Mum. It's Catrin, well Steffan really, the boy she

251

shares a biological father with. He's a patient of the practice and Jane insisted I look up his notes. And now I wish I hadn't because I think I have to act on what I know.'

He looked out to sea; a lone yacht glided slowly across the horizon. 'You see, he's a dealer, drug dealer – or at least he was: nothing very major – ecstasy mainly; cautioned when he was fourteen, suspended for dealing in school when he was fifteen and sent to live with foster parents: his mum was worried he'd be a bad influence on his three younger brothers. I've had a look at his mother's notes too and she thinks he's still using. I'm really worried that he's having a bad influence on Catrin. I know she's normally very sensible but I'm not so sure any more.'

Ben glanced around. Had he said all that out loud or just thought it? But it didn't matter anyway; the graveyard was still deserted. He gazed at the sea, breathing in deeply the salty calmness that surrounded him, hoping that somehow it would stay with him and carry him through what he feared would be a difficult week.

It was. As the Volvo drew into the drive at Pencisely Crescent late on Sunday afternoon all the lights were on in the house.

'At least someone's home,' Jane said, getting out of the car. Ben collected the bags from the boot and kicked one foot after the other against the front wall to get rid of the last grains of sand from his boots. Jane opened the door and was greeted by the smell of polish and something else she could not make out. She went to put her handbag down on the hall table but it was not there.

'Can't smell supper, I'm afraid, love, despite your text,' Ben followed her in, put the bags down in the hall and headed to the kitchen. 'I'll put the kettle on.'

He stopped as he reached the doorway. It was abnormally quiet inside. Jane was right behind him.

'What on earth's happened?' she demanded taking in the torn curtains and the pile of broken crockery piled up by the overflowing bin. Tom was trying to rehang one of the kitchen cupboard doors.

Catrin sat beside the Aga, her small frame drowning in her gran's big lavender cardigan. 'Lucky's disappeared. Siân and Lisa are still out looking for him. I've just come back. I thought he might have come home by now but he hasn't.' Her voice trailed away hopelessly.

'Don't worry love, I'm sure he'll turn up soon; that dog's got good homing instincts,' Jane said, concern for her daughter taking precedence over her distress about the house. 'But you're OK?' She felt a chill run through her as Catrin looked at her, her eyes red.'

'Oh, Mum, it was awful.' Catrin gave way to sobs and Jane knelt down and put her arms around her, rubbing her back.

'Tom?' Ben asked, propping the door up as Tom tried to tighten the screws.

'Combination of Steffan and Facebook – that's what happened.'

'I knew Steffan would be involved somehow,' Jane said, glaring at Ben over Catrin's shoulder.'

'I just thought if he spent some time with me and my friends he'd see you don't need lots of – you know – "stuff"– to have a good time and he could be part of our group.' Catrin shook her head helplessly.

'Oh Catrin, you can't change someone who doesn't want to be changed.'

'It wasn't supposed to be a party, honestly Mum.' Catrin said, dabbing her eyes. 'Just Siân and Jonathan, Lisa and Mark and Steffan. But Mark couldn't come – at the last minute he had to cover for someone at the Youth Club who was ill; and Jonathan and Siân had had another argument ...'

'And Steffan put the address on Facebook,' Tom continued, 'there were about sixty people running amok when I came home just before midnight.'

'I did try ringing you, Tom, but it went straight to answerphone.'

'Sorry, Catz, I must have been in the Rugby Club – the signal is pretty poor there.'

'Oh, Catrin, why didn't you just tell them to go?' Jane said.

'I tried Mum, we all tried, but they wouldn't listen; they just laughed.'

'Didn't it occur to you to call the police Catrin?' Ben asked.

'I'm sorry Dad, I just thought – if we called the police – we'd all get into trouble.' Catrin was sobbing again.

'Oh for goodness sake Catrin, why would you get into trouble? You hadn't done anything wrong.'

'Anyway, by the time I called the police they were already on their way, a couple of the neighbours had complained about the excessive noise,' Tom said, turning the screwdriver once more.

'And we've spent all day looking for Lucky and clearing up but Lucky's still lost and some things are broken, Mum,' Catrin's shoulders heaved and another sob escaped.

'Let go, Dad. I think I need to put in a longer screw here.'

Ben released his grip on the cupboard door. 'I'll bring you one, Tom. Back in a sec,' he called over his shoulder as he left the room.

'Oh my God, do you think one of them has taken Lucky?' Jane said, starting to panic.

Catrin shuddered. 'I don't know Mum, we've looked everywhere.'

'Well, we'll wait for Siân and Lisa to get back and if they haven't found him we'll make some posters and take them round – pin them on trees – that's what people do, isn't it, when their pet is lost. We've got that nice photo you took of Lucky a couple of weeks ago – the one of him with his ball at the bottom of the garden.' Jane's felt a lump rise in her throat and giving Catrin's shoulder a squeeze, she got up, put on her apron and began taking some of the broken crockery out to the bin.

At that moment Ben reappeared carrying a very quiet

Lucky in his arms. Catrin leapt up to cuddle the little dog who wagged his tail enthusiastically, smothering her in kisses.

'I suddenly guessed where he'd be and there he was, hiding in Gran's bed; all I could see was a small lump.'

'Really Ben,' Jane said curtly, 'the sooner we clear that bed out and you put up some clothes rails for us the better.' Now that the worry about Lucky had been lifted she felt a surge of anger. Anger at Ben for leaving the job of clearing his mother's room half done; anger at whoever had left the door open so Lucky could get in there and anger at Steffan for being so irresponsible – or really for just being.

'Yes, OK, Jane, I'll do it soon – should get it into the Volvo, no problem, with Tom's help.'

'As if I haven't already got enough to do. I'm also going to have to fix the hall table. I've put it in your shed Dad, for now – I think it will be OK. One of the legs has splintered and just needs a bit of glue. Screw, Dad?' Tom said, still attempting to fix the cupboard door.

'Here we are, son.' Ben handed it to him, 'and a fine job you're doing.'

Catrin was hugging Lucky tightly. 'Of course, I didn't think of Gran's room. I'm sure he's really traumatised,' she sobbed through her smile.

'Catz, he's fine but famished,' Ben said. 'The bed is a bit of a mess but don't worry; I'll clear that up now. You feed him and then I'll take him for a walk around the neighbours – he can help me with the PR initiative. And Tom, phone Siân on her mobile please to tell her he's been here all the time.'

Catrin put Lucky down and wiped her face with a tissue. 'Treat time', she whispered to the little dog. He trotted after her to the fridge.

'Mum I'd bought steak for you and Dad, but do you mind if I give some of it to Lucky?'

Jane smiled. 'No, love, let him have some. I think he deserves it.' Looking around at the chaos she wasn't hungry anyway.

'Steffan is such an idiot and his druggy friends were horrible.' Catrin sniffed, getting out the steak and cutting it up for Lucky, who circled around her in anticipation. 'And Tom – Tom was really good, Mum.'

Jane felt suddenly sick. While she and Ben had been enjoying their quiet supper in The Ship, Catrin had been exposed to drugs and intimidating behaviour and in her own home. It was her fault. Her instincts had told her she shouldn't go away for the weekend. And Ben – surely he'd known that Steffan took drugs. So that's what all that talk about letting Catrin make her own mistakes had been about. She seethed. Well if Ben was not going to protect Catrin, she was. And now that Catrin had seen for herself what Steffan was really like perhaps that wouldn't be so difficult after all.

'OK, love, it's OK now,' Jane soothed. 'It wasn't your fault – it was mine for going away with Dad for the weekend.'

Catrin had begun to cry again.

Chapter Seventeen

The shop had been quiet all day and Jane and Sue were making the most of it by sorting through the rails. Jane hummed tunelessly as she removed the heavy winter coats. Later, in the basement, away from any customers who might be offended, she'd stuff them into plastic bags for the ragman, after first removing the buttons. Sometime, next week maybe, she'd sew the buttons on to pretty cards. Buttons were more sought after and often raised more money for the charity than the coats did, she thought ruefully. And now that it was spring, £1 a bag from the ragman was the best price the heavy wool coats would fetch.

Jane was glad she didn't come across any of her mother-in-law's clothes as she sorted. She knew she would have been upset at binning them. Two days before she'd surprised herself when she'd dissuaded a customer from buying Granny Lewis's long velvet coat, the one she always wore to go to the opera. Sue, astonished at Jane's negative comments, had challenged her as soon as the customer had left the shop, and had been perplexed as Jane explained she wanted the coat to go to a good home and not be cut up and upcycled as the teenager had proposed.

Now Jane picked up a camel coat she'd just added to the pile, thinking of the woman who'd brought it in a few weeks earlier. Red-eyed and dazed, she'd handed the coat over almost reluctantly. Her late mother's 'best' coat – hardly worn. 'We bought it in Calders, about five years ago; it cost £150,' Jane remembered her saying.

Jane had put the coat in storage for a few days, just in case the woman came back, and seen the price Sue had given it when she brought it back out: £25 – the most they could hope to get.

She felt she was betraying the woman, who'd obviously derived some comfort in knowing that her mother's coat would raise good money for the charity and provide someone with much needed winter warmth. 'Can we hang on to this until the autumn, Sue? It's a good coat.'

Sue came over and rubbed the expensive material between her fingers.

'As ever storage is a problem but, you're right, there's quality here; we'll hang on to this one.'

Jane continued humming as she went round the shop removing items that would probably not sell now the weather was improving.

'I thought all Welsh people could sing,' Sue said.

'That's another myth, alongside all those sheep stories.' Jane laughed.

'Anyway, it's good to see you happy, Jane.'

Jane bundled scarves and woolly hats into bags. 'You know you're right, Sue, I do feel happy. It's strange isn't it? When you feel unhappy you're very aware of it but when you're happy you don't realise you are until you actually think about it.'

'Sorry, Jane, you've lost me, but anyway things are obviously better at home.'

'Yes, they are, thanks Sue. Catrin seems to be working hard and at least she got her last art assignment in on time, Ben is definitely more cheerful now he's getting fitter and Tom, well you know, Tom is Tom! And to top it all, after that disastrous party I got to replace those awful brown velvet curtains my mother-in-law had made for the kitchen. Actually,' she paused for effect, 'I feel things are almost sufficiently in control to allow me to start a diet.'

'Oh Jane, forget about diets; you're fine as you are, and anyway won't you soon have Easter eggs to tuck into?'

'Sadly not. I think the family have taken me at my word and aren't going to buy me one, damn them.' Jane laughed again. 'I'll have to buy my own. Don't tell Catrin though. She said she'd pop in this afternoon – help us make some Easter bonnets'

'Oh, that's lovely, Jane, I haven't seen her for ages; she's so arty. The ones she made last year made my creations look pathetic.'

Catrin was at that moment fighting her way on to a crowded bus, laden with school bags, gym kit and carrier bags full of ribbons, silk flowers and little fluffy chicks she and Siân had just bought in the Hayes market to adorn the Easter bonnets. Her mobile bleeped, indicating she had a new message, but rummaging in her bag to find her phone right then was too difficult. Siân heard it too.

'Could be Mark – he hasn't texted you for at least half an hour.' She grinned.

Catrin smiled at the implication Mark was being very keen. 'He does keep texting and poking me on Facebook but he never suggests we meet up,' she whispered, so the two boys standing near them would not overhear their conversation.

'Why don't you suggest it then?' Siân asked.

'I can't, not again; it makes me look desperate.'

'You are.' Siân laughed.

The two boys watched them as they got off the bus near the charity shop. Siân gave a cheeky wave.

'For goodness sake Siân, isn't Jono enough for you?' Catrin said with a grin.

'A girl's got to keep her options open,' Siân replied tartly as she avoided a series of double buggies with toddlers attached. 'And things aren't as good with Jono as they were,' she added just as they reached the shop. Before Catrin could ask what the problem was Siân had gone in. Ah well, the details would keep, Catrin thought, following her through the door, and anyway Siân and Jonathan seemed to go through a lot of bad patches and then the next minute they were all loved up. She dumped her bags on the shop floor and grabbed her phone.

'Hi, you two, so kind of you to come and help with the bonnets again – hasn't a year gone by so fast.'

'Hi, Sue.' Catrin glanced up from her phone.

'Go on down. Your mum's in the basement setting the hats out for you. Can't wait to see the transformation from battered hats to beautiful bonnets,' Sue said.

Catrin gathered up her bags again and she and Siân made their way down the basement steps. As they reached the bottom, Siân said, 'Well?'

'From Steffan,' Catrin replied.

Her mother looked up from the depths of the box she was sorting. 'Hi, girls; what's that about Steffan?'

'I've just had a text from him.'

'I thought he hadn't been in contact since the party?' her mum said, putting a large pink floppy hat on the table she'd set up for them to work on.

'He hasn't – this is the first I've heard from him in weeks.'

'I can't believe he didn't at least contact you to apologise for the chaos he caused,' Siân said, disgorging the contents of the trimmings bag.

'So is he apologising now?' Her mum's tone suggested that if he wasn't then he should be.

'He's asking me to a bloody Easter party.'

'Catrin!'

She looked up at her mother, laughing. 'I'm not swearing, Mum; it's a fancy dress party. The text says: "*Come celebrate the true meaning of Easter – blood and gore, fan-c dress*".'

'That's in very bad taste. I hope you're not going to go.'

'No, Mum, I'm not. Easter is all about Easter chicks, Easter eggs, and Easter bonnets for me so let's get started.'

Catrin was sitting on her bed in a tangle of cables listening to Pink on her iPod, Facebook page open on her laptop and notebook open on her lap, on which she had half an hour previously written the title 'Immigration' and what she

260

thought to be a very good first phrase, 'Les émeutes dans les banlieues Parisiennes.' Yes, she liked that, 'The riots in the Paris suburbs' but she had got no further.

She could see Siân was online and, failing to think how to proceed with the essay, she typed in:

Wassup?

Siân immediately replied:

Doing my French essay and thinking retribution!!!

I hope there's no connection between the two! I take it the retribution is aimed at stupid Jonathan and Loud Louise? Well don't waste your time – they deserve each other.

Maybe, but to be dumped for someone as plain as Louise.

HIS LOSS – NOW FORGET HIM – PLENTY MORE FISH.

Yep, you're right Catz – guess I'm just cross he dumped me before I could do the dumping. Hang on, I've got a text. Oh yes, oh yes, talking of fish, BIG FISH – I think it's a catch or at least a definite bite on the line.

Je ne comprends pas, mon amie – what are you talking about, Siân?

I've just had a text from Mark. I'll call you now!

Just as Siân's last message came through Catrin's mobile rang. For a second she considered not answering it – cross because Mark had texted Siân rather than her. Perhaps he fancies Siân now she's single, Catrin thought, feeling sick. But she had to know and so she hit the answer icon.

'Hi there Catz – yep, Mark just sent me a text – exciting or what'? Siân shouted down the phone.

'Sent *you* a text? Catrin said indignantly. 'And I've been waiting for one all afternoon.'

'Sorry Catrin; he can't be that into you.' Siân laughed.

Why was she being like this? Siân was usually so supportive, so positive and she knew how much Catrin liked Mark.

'He's asked if I'm going to Oceana tonight.'

'Oh,' was all Catrin could manage. She felt totally let down – by Mark who she thought liked her and was nice and

261

straightforward and didn't play stupid games; and by Siân – supposedly her best friend.

'Well aren't you excited, Catz?'

Betrayal, that's what this was. Wasn't it an unwritten rule that you never ever went out with your best mate's crush?

Siân wittered on. 'I thought you'd be jumping up and down with joy but you've gone all quiet on me. Do you want to come over here and we'll choose what to wear? I've got some new shorts; they'd be brilliant with opaques and heels and that cute Prada-esque top you've got.'

'Lovely,' Catrin said flatly, realising how important Mark had become to her. When she daydreamed now it was more likely to be a fantasy about being his girlfriend than of spending time with her biological father in his French barn. And last thing at night Mark was the person on her mind.

'Oh come on, Catz, this is what you've been waiting for so what's up? Don't you fancy him any more?'

Catrin felt totally confused.

'Look,' Siân said impatiently, 'You'll be there, on the dance floor, Rihanna belting out "Stay"– a perfect excuse to put your arms around him and see what happens.'

'But it's you he's asked Siân, not me.'

'Oh, don't be so silly Catz; he's asked if I'm going to be there because he knows if I'm there then you will be too. I'd say he's just too shy to ask you directly so he's kind of doing it through me.'

Catrin was suddenly interested. 'Do you really think so?'

'Catz, it's a classic boy thing – trust me.'

Catrin pushed her notebook to one side and told Siân she'd be with her in half an hour. She switched off her laptop, flung makeup, toiletries, underwear, a collection of tops, skirts and trousers into her overnight bag, scrawled a quick note on the fridge to tell her parents – who had not yet returned home from work – where she was going and was heading out of the door in less than ten minutes. Good, she thought, that will give us four hours to get ready.

Ralph sat in his studio painting yet another poodle. How he hated poodles. And the poodle in the photograph he was copying looked particularly annoying with its tuft of hair tied in a girly pink bow. He coughed in an attempt to clear his throat and reached for the familiar blue packet by his side – his 'gals' as his wife, Miriam, insisted on calling them, on the basis they led him astray. And she was right; he couldn't live without them. And wouldn't live long with them, as Miriam continually reminded him. But they'd been so much a part of his life since that initial cough and splutter when, newly arrived in Paris, he had bought his first packet determined to look like an artist. He'd persevered and had quickly become an accomplished smoker. And he was a good artist, he told himself now. So how on earth had he ended up painting pets in the back bedroom of a terraced house in Bristol?

He went downstairs, having decided he needed a cup of coffee to go with his Gauloises and stood at the kitchen window while the kettle boiled, smoking and looking blankly at the row of identical houses on the other side of the narrow little street. The street was empty, as it always was at this time of day. It came to life three times daily and Ralph knew precisely when: between 8 a.m. and 8.40 a.m. when most people left for work or school, between 3.15 p.m. and 3.40 p.m. when the mothers at numbers 3, 14, 18, 22 and 24 collected their offspring, and when the workers arrived home between 5 p.m. and 6 p.m. Ralph always timed his breaks to coincide with these bursts of activity but he took other breaks as well, as he was doing now. The kettle clicked off and he poured boiling water onto the instant granules in the mug.

Not exactly a view to inspire an artist, he thought resentfully, as he took his drink through to the lounge and picked up the *Daily Mail* from the coffee table where Miriam had neatly folded and left it after her breakfast read. He scanned the headlines:

ECONOMIC MELTDOWN AHEAD

TERRORISTS THWARTED AT 11TH HOUR

Ralph stopped scanning. He read with fascination about the American, Chuck Brown, who had decided to concentrate his sexual activity on producing sperm for childless couples and the outcry it was causing in the States. Ralph turned on his laptop and googled the name. Immediately a dozen sites came up. He spent the next half hour trawling through the comments and then linked into a TV programme where the geeky librarian was being interviewed. The rather superior presenter seemed genuinely taken aback by the live studio audience's appreciation of what Chuck was doing. And then a cute little girl toddled on to the set and the camera showed a close up of Chuck, his eyes welling up at meeting one of his offspring for the first time. Ralph realised there were tears in his own eyes. He drifted back upstairs to his poodle.

For the rest of the afternoon he daydreamed. He hadn't given much thought over the years to any children who may have been born from his many donations as a student. At the time the chance to pocket some 'expenses' and view free porn magazines had been a bonus but not something he had considered affecting his future. He certainly hadn't envisaged getting to know any children born as a result. But by the end of the afternoon he was picturing at least one daughter and a couple of sons: all blond, all tall, all arty. By the time Miriam's eight-hour shift on the Tesco tills was over he was full of plans.

Miriam walked up the street and could see every light was on in the house. That probably meant Ralph was at home, although he did sometimes go out and leave the lights blazing. Miriam's heart sank; she really could do with putting her feet up and a bit of peace and quiet would be very welcome. It had been one of those days – endless spillages on her conveyor belt, customers wandering off to get 'just one more thing' and holding everyone up, and to cap it all she'd had a couple of boy scouts 'helping' to pack. As she struggled through the front door, laden with two plastic bags full of food, Ralph came bounding down the stairs.

'Hi Miriam, good day? I've got something really exciting to tell you.' He did not pause between question and statement.

She went into the kitchen and dumped the plastic bags on the worktop, rubbing at the red welts the thin plastic had left on her palms and pushing her hair away from her face. She hated how her red curls frizzed at the slightest hint of damp weather and there had been a lot of that lately.

'Oh you sound full of beans, but can your news wait until I put my feet up with a nice cup of tea?'

Ralph ignored her request and, as she started loading the contents of the bags into the fridge, he launched into the Chuck Brown story.

'Fish fingers and oven chips OK for you?'

'And he's met one of them,' Ralph continued excitedly.

'I think I'll have a cuppa before I start on supper; you're not starving are you?'

'I'll have one too if you're making one.' He headed for the lounge. 'I'll put the computer on so you can see them meeting up.'

Miriam put the oven on to warm up and reached for the kettle. 'Is ordinary tea OK?'

'I'd prefer a lemon tea, with honey.'

Miriam swore under her breath and then berated herself for being so tetchy. She rinsed Ralph's 'Dead Handsome' mug under the tap, squeezed half a lemon into it and added two generous spoonfuls of honey. Once the kettle had boiled she poured water on to the teabags, added milk to her own tea and took both mugs into the little lounge.

Ralph was sitting in front of his laptop. 'Here it is; this is the part where the little girl comes on.'

'Oh yes,' Miriam glanced at the screen, her eyes tired and sore after a day scanning uncooperative barcodes.

'I wonder how many I'm daddy to?'

Miriam placed her mug carefully on the coffee table before

turning to look at her husband who was still staring at the computer screen. Had he just said what she'd thought he'd said?

'What do you mean, Ralph?'

'Well I could be the UK's Chuck Brown – but cooler.' He slurped his tea.

Miriam closed her eyes. She felt as if she'd just been kicked in the stomach. Hard. Ralph was speaking again but his voice seemed very far away.

'As a student I gave lots of donations. So I could be daddy to hundreds. It's possible to find out, you know, and meet up with them. The family we've always wanted; wouldn't that be great, Miriam?'

Miriam went out to put the chips in the oven. When she came back she asked why he hadn't told her about this before.

Ralph shrugged. 'Didn't seem important, Miriam; to be honest I'd forgotten all about it until I read Chuck's story this morning. And anyway, there are lots of things about my student days that you don't know.' He arched his eyebrows suggestively.

Miriam briefly considered whether anything else Ralph might have done twenty years ago would suddenly catch up with them and have such wide-reaching consequences. Surely nothing else could match this bombshell.

Knowing that whenever she opposed anything Ralph became even more determined to do it, Miriam decided that saying nothing was the best option. She finished off her tea, hovered until Ralph downed his and took the empty mugs into the kitchen. She flung the mugs into the sink with a little more force than was necessary, looking over her shoulder to see if Ralph had noticed. He hadn't. He was busy scanning something on his computer screen.

She put the fish fingers on to cook. Normal. She needed to act normally. Ralph would enjoy nothing more than seeing how he'd managed to knock her off balance with his news. She wouldn't give him the satisfaction.

'Shall we have it on trays? *Coronation Street* will be on soon,' she shouted over her shoulder as she set out plates, cutlery and Ralph's napkin.

'It says here that men who donated way back, as I did, can now re-register so that their kids can find them.'

'Brown or red sauce?'

'Tomato. And I'll have bread and butter with it. I can just download the form and it's not a long one either – look, Miriam.'

Ralph came into the kitchen, cradling his laptop. He followed Miriam around as she opened the cupboard for the condiments and rinsed a couple of glasses in the sink that was still half-full of breakfast dishes.

'Ralph, please just get out of the way. Go and sit down and I'll bring it in to you.'

'All I need is a couple of details about the clinic I went to, the date and some form of identification – this is easier than getting one of your Tesco Clubcards, Miriam.'

'Switch the telly on Ralph; *Corrie*'s starting. And supper's up.'

She buttered his bread, plated up and followed him into the lounge. For the next ten minutes they munched as Rita and Deirdre argued in the Rovers Return. During the interval Miriam gathered up both trays and put the kettle on, settling down again just as the cat scrambled over the wall and disappeared into the Weatherfield alley. Throughout the second half Miriam wondered whether she could delay Ralph from printing and returning the form for long enough for him to lose interest.

And he would. During the fourteen years they had been together there had been so many projects; projects he'd embraced totally until something else took his fancy. She often joked that the only permanent fixtures in his life were her and his gals. When they had first met in Paris she'd been impressed by his interest in all things French – she'd thought him so cultured, so sophisticated, so urbane. He'd bought

French language books, a very costly series of lessons on tape (of which he'd listened to one), and enrolled on an intensive French course which he'd attended for the first two weeks (out of twelve). Then he'd decided that by far the best way to learn the language was to hang out for hours with the locals in the dark little cafe at the junction of Rue Mazarine and Boulevard Saint Germain, drinking absinthe and smoking his beloved Gauloises. Ralph claimed he felt a special connection with Toulouse-Lautrec and Vincent van Gogh just by being there. Theirs had been a whirlwind romance and now she wondered if it could have happened anywhere else but in Paris? Would she have fallen in love with an artist in London or Madrid or Berlin? Probably not, she conceded, but she had been young and he had been handsome and wild and persuasive. Within two months of meeting she was no longer Mademoiselle Miriam Green but rather Madame Ralph Smith.

And then, when Miriam's savings had run out and they'd had to come back to England to live with her parents in Yorkshire, he'd bought himself a tweed jacket and started drinking beer. He'd gone 'lamping' with the local farm boys and taken a job with the water bailiff. He had stuck it for a fortnight before the double perils of wet feet and having to work at night forced him to take to his bed for a week with a 'weak chest'.

There had been his Morris Dancing phase, the guitar lessons – that had led to him forming a group which disbanded after two or three months of not making the big time – and the circus clown episode which had meant a couple of months in a touring caravan and being called 'gyppos' by local youths. The night they awoke to a gang shaking their van trying to tip it over was the night Ralph had agreed they would finally settle in one place, surround themselves with bricks and mortar, get proper jobs and start a family. She'd found a job at Tesco that just about covered their mortgage and bills so the bricks had materialised. Ralph had somehow got into painting portraits of pampered pooches and that paid for their occasional treats. They survived rather than lived, she acknowledged that. It worried her that there was a restlessness about Ralph. He was so childlike in many ways, always needing something to look forward to, something to be excited about. Perhaps if they'd been able to have children he would have found the purpose he was so obviously lacking. But it was not to be.

At first she'd been very careful. At nineteen she wasn't ready to have children and not ready to share the love of her life with anyone else. How strange it seemed to her now that she'd ever been so possessive of Ralph. She'd religiously taken her contraceptive pill, often checking and double-checking the little pocket in the pink strip of tablets was empty for that day. How ironic to be told ten years later that she never could become pregnant. She could still remember coming round from the anaesthetic and the doctor saying, in a very matter-of-fact way, that her tubes were so badly damaged he'd decided to seal them off to prevent the risk of an ectopic pregnancy. Then she'd been wheeled back to the side ward, along a corridor full of crying, newly born babies and fathers carrying ridiculous helium-filled balloons. She remembered one hovering above her head proclaiming 'It's a girl'. That night she had cried and cried, her grief so overwhelming that even now she remembered feeling hollow with hopelessness.

And then Ralph had launched into project IVF. Within weeks they were on the long waiting list for treatment. Ralph had started a special scrapbook in which he'd pasted success stories and stuck a photograph of Louise Brown, the first 'test-tube' baby, on the front. He'd told everyone who would listen about the treatment and Miriam had been upset and embarrassed. Didn't the very mention of test tubes make the whole thing sound like a scientific experiment and make her a freak? But by the time they had reached the top of the waiting list, two years later, she'd become more comfortable with the terminology and Ralph had almost lost interest. By then he was into martial arts.

How upbeat she had felt, believing the sinking feeling which came with such regularity every month at the first twinge in the pit of her stomach, would soon be a thing of the past. She had been so confident she had even allowed herself to list a few favourite names. She liked Ruth; Ruth May had a nice ring to it. And for a boy, Stephen, perhaps. She'd known a boy in school called Stephen and he'd been lovely.

Miriam hadn't been prepared for the rollercoaster ride which came with infertility treatment. Ralph's scrapbook, which she retrieved from beneath a pile of Taekwondo books by his side of the bed, didn't mention the daily Clomid tablets and the ensuing hot flushes and bloating, the anxious wait for successful egg retrieval, the surge of optimism as three eggs were successfully recovered – quickly followed by the anxiety of waiting to know how many, if any, would fertilise and start dividing – and the tearful ten days of waiting to see if any of the fertilised eggs had embedded in her womb. Those were the days, out of Ralph's earshot, she had whispered words of encouragement to the hopefully dividing embryos and rubbed her tummy encouragingly. And then hour after hour of phantom period pains, the rush of disappointment followed by euphoria when nothing showed. The heart-thumping moment when she telephoned the clinic to find out if she was pregnant and then the overwhelming sadness.

She had been crushed. Once more she had given way to an intense grieving which Ralph clearly did not understand. Immediately he had talked of having a second attempt and, if that didn't work, going for the third treatment they were allowed under the NHS. But she, for once, had put her foot down, telling him firmly she could not put her body or mind through such trauma again. She felt that after ten years of trying for a baby it was time to move on; to focus on the things they had rather than the things they did not. Ralph, taken aback by the strength of her feelings, had let it go and had thrown himself into yoga. Miriam, slowly, had been able to move on. She had joined a choir and taken every overtime shift offered to her so they could take their holidays in hotels rather than in caravans and she could enjoy a whole week of not shopping and not cooking. If not exactly happy, she was content and for Miriam that was enough.

Chapter Eighteen

'Come on Tom, everyone's in the car, hurry up.' Ben called up the stairs. Tom appeared on the landing trying to pull on a sweater and struggle into his high-top trainers at the same time.

'Do I have to come, Dad? You go and I'll do some gardening or something for you,' he bargained as he came down the stairs.

'It's a three-line whip, sorry son, out of my hands. You know if it's Easter Saturday then it's Granny O's – always has been, always will be.'

Tom grumbled some more as he went into the kitchen to grab a bottle of water and two muesli bars. His father grinned at him knowingly.

'One for me too, Tom, and hide them from your mother.'

Tom grabbed another muesli bar and followed Ben out to the car. He opened the back door of the Volvo and groaned. 'Why do I have to sit in the middle? Mum – tell her, she's smaller than me.'

Jane ignored him.

'Tom, you know Lucky has to have an open window seat and if you'd got in first you could have had the other – but you didn't,' Catrin said, 'and I'm not sitting between you and Lucky; you've both got disgusting morning breath.'

Tom climbed past Lucky and deliberately sat on Catrin's hand, got up again to find the seat-belt buckle and settled back, broadening his shoulders to make a point.

'OK, all aboard,' Ben said cheerfully, as he pulled out of the drive into the Saturday traffic. 'I wonder what culinary feast awaits us today?'

'Well one thing's for certain, it will taste of tin,' Tom replied.

273

'I give processed peas odds of three to one, mince four to one, and those tasteless squares that pretend to be mixed vegetables – evens. Any bets?'

'Let's just hope she hasn't been watching *Masterchef* again. Remember those slimy black bananas?' said Tom.

Ben laughed loudly. 'How could I forget – they were supposed to be cooked with rum and lime but Gran didn't have either.'

'Too exotic for the Valleys,' Tom sniggered.

Jane turned round sharply. 'Oh don't be ridiculous, Tom, there's a deli and cafe-bar and everything in Treorchy now, I'll have you know.'

'Hardly everything, is it, Mother?'

Jane frowned at him and turned to face the front again

'Do you remember what she used instead? Ben asked, mouthing the answer as Tom and Catrin chorused in unison, 'stout and tinned peaches.' He was aware his wife was glaring at him but he couldn't help grinning.

'But the best one was when she added all those chillies to the ice cream,' said Tom. 'Oh, yuck, and your face, Dad, when you took that greedy first bite.'

Catrin gave Tom a shove. 'Stop making fun of Gran, she tries her best, and anyway we're going there to see her, not to eat cordon bleu food.'

'Catrin's quite right, that's enough. Granny Olwen's food isn't that bad – don't be so rude,' Jane said.'

'If it isn't that bad, Mum, why are we taking pudding to Treorchy and why have you put in a casserole for when we get back?' Tom teased.

'Touché,' Ben said, grinning at his wife.

They travelled up through the valley in silence. It was a horrible, dank late March morning and Ben looked out of the window, thinking he really would far rather be sitting in his shed. Generally he enjoyed this journey, welcoming the half-hour commute in the morning to get into work mode and the return journey to the capital to separate his work from his home life. At least that was the theory; more and more often these days he seemed to be bringing his work home with him.

As they drove through Pontypridd he wondered if Catrin was thinking of Steffan. So far as Ben knew she hadn't seen her half-brother since the night the police had been called to Pencisely Crescent: according to Jane she'd turned down his invitation to an Easter fancy-dress party. He knew his wife would rather Catrin had nothing to do with Steffan at all, especially now Jane was aware of his drug taking. Ben's failure to share that information had almost led to a serious row. Still his daughter wasn't the kind of person to befriend someone and then forget about him altogether. He just hoped Catrin wouldn't let the friendship get in the way of her studies from now on.

Ben stopped at a set of traffic lights. The rain was coming down hard and he was pleased they were almost at Treorchy. A few minutes later they pulled up in front of 13 Prospect Street and there was Olwen, standing in her flowery apron at the door, smiling at them.

'Well, hello, you've made good time; come in, come in," she said as they hurried in out of the rain. 'Dinner's nearly ready. Go through to the parlour, boys. I've got the fire going, I'll be with you in a tick.'

Tom and Ben settled in the armchairs on either side of the parlour fire and shared an old copy of the *Rhonnda Leader* between them.

Jane and Catrin followed Granny Olwen into the kitchen, carrying the homemade trifle and biscuits they had brought with them.

'New oilcloth, Mam? It's nice.'

'Yes, I bought it in Ponty market last Saturday; you know Jane, from the nice man who has a stall beside the cockle lady. Dilys next door came with me. Shame you had to work. Anyway, the man said the pattern was Mediterranean.' Granny Olwen checked the pans on the top of the cooker. 'Right, love, you lay the table and Catrin, go and get the boys, it's ready.'

Catrin left her mum getting out knifes and forks and popped her head around the parlour door.

'Granny's got lots of yummy fresh veg – aubergines, peppers, courgettes and tomatoes – on the kitchen table, Tom, and she says come now, before the food gets cold.'

Tom rose with a grin. 'Well, hallelujah, I didn't feel I could cope with her usual fare after last night – one sambuca too many; lead the way Catrin, I'm suddenly famished.' Her dad also stood up eagerly and they followed Catrin into the kitchen.

Tom's grin did not last and he gave her a sly shove. 'Oh, the vegetables are literally on the tablecloth; very funny, Catrin.'

'Sit down boys, I've got some nice mince, peas, and potatoes for you,' said Granny Olwen, dishing up. 'Don't look so worried, Ben love; they're all out of tins so no danger I'll poison you.'

The five of them squeezed around the small kitchen table. They ate very slowly.

'Do you think Lucky is all right in the car? Does he want something to eat?' Granny Olwen asked.

'No Gran, Lucky always has *his* tin as soon as he comes in from his early morning walk,' Tom replied, adding under his breath, 'and it's probably better than this.'

'What's that love? Sorry my battery's a bit flat, haven't used it for a while. I'm not deaf you see, I just need a little bit of help when there's a crowd.' She twiddled with her hearing aid which let out a painful whine.

'Ignore him, Mum, he's just being a pain.'

'Wanting aspirin, did you say?'

'Yes please, Gran; big night last night.'

'What suits you best Tom? I've got aspirin, Aspro, Co-Codamol, paracetamol, or Panadol.'

As Granny Olwen rummaged in the kitchen drawer, where she kept a few months' supply of painkillers, Jane quickly cleared and stacked the plates, tipping the leftovers into the bin.

'Now then, who'd like some nice tinned peaches?' Granny Olwen asked brightly.

'Or there's the trifle I brought,' Jane offered.

'I'll have a bit of both please, Olwen.' Ben smiled

'Clever, Dad, very diplomatic, I'll have the same,' said Tom. Catrin and Jane agreed.

When they had all cleared their bowls Granny Olwen sent the men back into the parlour and told Jane to go upstairs and inspect some things she'd put aside for the charity shop while she and Catrin washed up.

'Why don't you go and have a sit down, Gran, and Tom can come and help me clear up,' Catrin suggested, running hot water into the sink.

Her grandmother put on her apron and tutted. 'Oh I don't agree with having men in the kitchen; it's not natural.'

'Come on, Gran, men are some of the best chefs; you know that from watching *Masterchef*.'

'You're quite right, love, but you never see them washing up on those programmes, do you?' She touched Catrin's arm. 'Anyway, I like having you to myself. So, are you courting with Mark now then? He seems very nice from the brief chat I had with him at your Dad's party.'

Catrin gave her grandmother a playful nudge, pleased she had remembered about Mark. 'Oh, Gran, it's not called courting any more. It's "seeing".'

'Well that's ridiculous, you see everyone. I see you. Courting, now that's very different, so it needs a special word.'

Catrin scrubbed the base of the saucepan in which her grandmother had burnt the mince.

'I remember when I started courting with your granddad. Eighteen I was, the age you are now. I'd known him, mind, for years, but one day he came into the shop where I was working, little ironmongers it was, at the bottom of town, and bold as brass he said would I go to the pictures with him, Saturday night. I can't remember what we saw, some Western I think, and the news, the Pathé news. That's where I first saw our lovely Princess Elizabeth, our Queen now; years before we had the telly, of course. And after that we did a lot of our courting in the pictures – there were three different films every week then and we went to them all, never mind what they were.' Granny Olwen laughed. 'The pictures, now that's a good place to go courting – have you been to the pictures with Mark?'

'No, Gran, I haven't.'

'Oh, I suppose there's such a choice of things to do in Cardiff, isn't there?'

'Well yes, I suppose, but the only place I've been with Mark – just the two of us I mean – was to Roath Park.'

'Oh, I see. Well it's good to get to know each other first, become good friends; you don't want to rush into things. All good things come to those who wait, Catrin fach.'

'But I've already waited five months, Granny. Have you got any ideas how I can make myself irresistible to him?'

Her grandmother laughed as she dried a dinner plate with a William and Kate tea towel. 'Well, I tell you when I wanted to get a boy's attention I used to get on my bike – there's something about cycling past, wind in your hair, I think they find very attractive.'

'You have to wear a helmet now; not quite the same thing is it?'

They both laughed now.

'I'll give it some thought, Catrin, and I'll text you.'

'Thanks, Granny. And make it soon, please. Actually I'm going to call to see him – well Lisa really – on the way home, so wish me luck.'

A few hours later, on their way back down the valley, Catrin busied herself putting on make-up, instructing her father to avoid the bumps and potholes. She hoped it would be worth

278

the effort; that Mark would actually be at home. By the time they got to Castell Coch on the outskirts of the city her make-up was done.

'Come on, Dad, or we'll never get there.'

She saw her father glance at her in the mirror. 'Madam's previous instruction was for a smooth ride. It's a fact that it's impossible to avoid bumps if you're travelling at 70 miles per hour. Something your brother needs to learn by the state of the tyres on your mum's car.'

Tom groaned. 'How do you know it's my driving rather than Mum's doing the damage?'

Ben laughed as he pressed the accelerator. 'Because your mum has never been known to go faster than 60 miles per hour. Ever.'

'Fair point,' Tom conceded.

'Dad, you need to take the Roath turning. You're dropping me at Lisa's,' Catrin said as they came into the city.

'And I thought the beautiful face was for me,' her father joked, taking the second left off the Gabalfa roundabout. The traffic along the Whitchurch Road was painfully slow and by the time they turned into Australia Road Catrin's hand was already on the door handle. The moment her dad pulled up outside the Sayers' Catrin unclipped her seatbelt and opened the car door.

'Thanks, I'll be home by eight; I've got an essay I need to finish.' she said, already half out of the car.

'OK, Catrin, see you later. Call us if you want us to come and pick you up,' her mum said. 'I'll save you some casserole.'

Catrin slammed the car door shut and they drove off. She bounded up to Lisa's entrance. Just as she got there her phone bleeped.

The way to a man's heart is through his stomach. Ask him over for a meal. I'll come and help you. Good luck. Granny O.x

Catrin smiled. She really could not envisage anyone being

279

impressed by her grandmother's cooking. This was one offer of grandparental help she would be ignoring.

As Jane set about laying the table for supper she reflected on the afternoon. Really, Treorchy was where she belonged, where her roots were. Generations of her family had lived there and she couldn't bear the thought that, after Olwen's day, there would be no trace of them apart from the gravestones in the cemetery. She had never felt it before but now there was a vague sense that, by moving away, she had let these ancestors down. And, of course, with her mother getting older, it would be nice to be near her. She wondered if Ben would consider moving to the Rhondda, once the children had left home. She might be able to sell the idea to him on the grounds he'd be closer to work and houses were much cheaper. He could retire on the money they would make from selling their Cardiff home and buying something similar in the Rhondda. She stopped herself there, realising the second argument would negate the first. Yes, she'd work on the first – would sow the seed, soon.

Ben too was musing on the visit to Treorchy. The moment they had arrived back he had gone to his shed and put on his smoking jacket. The afternoon had been a long one and he felt melancholy. It was when he saw Jane with her mother that he missed his mother the most. Jane and Olwen were so close, clearly understood each other so well, that sometimes it irritated him. He knew what he really felt was jealousy – jealous that Jane still had her mother, but saddened too because Jane and Olwen's closeness highlighted the shortcomings there'd been in the relationship with his own mother. Now it was too late to change that. She was gone. He didn't like feeling like this and was glad he only saw Jane and her mother together occasionally. Thank goodness they didn't live nearer to each other.

The previous day he'd read an article in the paper claiming middle-aged men were happier than younger men because they were less driven; they'd generally achieved what they were going to achieve in their careers and knew what was truly important – family and friends. What tosh, Ben thought. What middle age did was force you to face your mortality. With his mother gone he was the next in line; there was no longer another generation standing between him and the grim reaper. But Jane had Olwen, who was in rude health and didn't seem to be going anywhere fast. Realising how disloyal his train of thought was becoming he got up from his deckchair, took off his coat, and hung it on the hook behind the shed door. As he did so he felt disappointed. Usually his sessions in the shed helped him get things into perspective but today he felt just as morose as when he'd entered.

It had been a long week and Miriam had decided to splash out on a ready meal and a bottle of wine; it was a Saturday night, after all. The food had been good and now, as she sat at the kitchen table drinking her coffee while Ralph sat opposite smoking his Gauloises, she felt satisfied. She had two whole days off and planned to get the shopping, cleaning, washing and ironing done early next morning so she could spend the rest of the time in the garden. Early spring was her favourite time of year – so much to look forward to. She'd start by clearing out the pond, her least favourite job, and then dig over the vegetable patch and put in some flowers.

'I was thinking I'd put in some sweet peas again this year. What do you think, Ralph?'

Ralph began to blow smoke rings, his lips held in a taut O.

'I know they take up a lot of room in the patch,' Miriam continued, 'but they do go on and on. I'll plant them instead of potatoes – they were a waste of space last year; that blight, once you've got it, Dave at work says it's really difficult to get rid of.'

Ralph's head moved up and down as he blew circles within circles. Eventually he exhaled all the smoke he had been storing in his mouth. 'Still my best party trick, Miriam; wish I could get the French inhale right, though.'

Miriam fanned the smoke away from her face. 'Can't you think of a healthier party trick?' she asked crossly.

But Ralph had inhaled deeply again and Miriam knew there was no chance of a reply until he'd formed the next series of circles. 'And anyway, why do you need a party trick? We don't go to parties.'

After a pause, Ralph looked at her through a cloud of smoke. 'We don't go to parties because we don't get invited to any. And do you know why we don't get invited to the Roberts' Halloween Party, the Everetts' Christmas bash, or the Williams' ridiculous Eurovision Shindig; well I have my little theory ...?'

'Maybe something to do with you getting stupidly drunk at every party we've ever been to?' Miriam suggested helpfully.

'I, Miriam, am the life and soul of every party, but of course they can't ask me without inviting my little wifie. Ah well, the less said.' He inhaled again and blew the smoke high in the air. 'I've filled in the HFEA form; perhaps you could post it for me when you get the paper in the morning. It's by the kettle.'

Miriam massaged her temples. 'Oh, Ralph, do you really think that's a good idea?'

'Yes I do,' he replied, smiling. He stubbed out his cigarette and lit another.

Miriam coughed. 'But what have you got to gain by contacting these strangers?'

'They're not strangers, Miriam, they're part of me that I don't yet know.'

'Oh, for goodness sake, Ralph, if there are kids out there that you fathered they are other people's children now; they're not yours.'

'Of course they're mine, I was the donor.'

'And the clue is in the word, Ralph. Donor means making a donation, giving something away,' she said slowly, as if explaining to a child.

He took another deep drag, blowing a big circle, followed by a medium circle and then a small circle.

Miriam watched with growing irritation. 'And what will they get from meeting you, Ralph? How are you going to enrich any child's life?'

He glared at her. 'Why on earth are you being so difficult? If they're blond and tall and arty, meeting me they'll know where that's all come from.'

'And if they're lazy and self-absorbed and vain they'll see that too,' she added, as she got up to clear the table.

Ralph stubbed out his cigarette, got up and followed her to the sink. He put his arms on her shoulders; his touch was heavy, weighing her down. She wriggled to express her irritation and turned the taps full on.

'Oh come on Miri-Mw, you don't need to be jealous; you'll still have me all to yourself. All I want is to see any children I've fathered, to see if they look like me, that's all.'

She turned around sharply and out of his grasp. 'That's typical of you, Ralph. You want the benefits without having done any of the hard work. Can't you think for a minute of the fathers who've brought them up – got up to their screaming in the night, changed the nappies, coped with the tantrums, the teenage angst, with all the crap – how they might feel if you suddenly waltz in?'

'Oh don't be so dramatic, Miriam. I've said, haven't I, all I want is to meet them once and that will be that.'

'It's never like that with you though, is it, Ralph? You always go overboard and who knows what that might lead to.'

Ralph grabbed his coat, picked up the envelope propped behind the kettle and went out, slamming first the kitchen door and then the front door behind him.

Miriam plunged her hands into the soapy water and realised she was shaking.

The smell of Sunday filled the Lewis' kitchen. Jane loved these slow weekends where the highlight was the Sunday roast. She liked everything about it, especially the hours it took to cook, as her family lingered in the kitchen enjoying the rich aromas and anticipating the feast that was to come. Ben was at the sink, his shirt sleeves folded to the elbow as he tackled a mountain of vegetables that needed peeling, the weak April sunlight making the strands of grey in his rich auburn hair glisten. Jane rested her arm gently on his shoulders as she switched on the kettle.

'It's just boiled, love, I was about to stop to make a cuppa.'

'You're doing a fine job there, Ben Lewis; you keep at it and I'll make the tea.'

Ben flicked some cold water at her and Jane moved sharply away, laughing.

'Tea everyone?' she called out as she poured boiling water into her favourite china teapot. This was her weekend teapot, the one she used when she had plenty of time; time to appreciate its beautiful rambling rose design and the way it slowly released the flavour of the tea. On work mornings a quick dunk of the teabag in her mug had to suffice, or 'te tramp' as her mother described it.

Yes please, Mum,' Catrin shouted back from the living room. 'I'll come and get it in a minute.'

'Catz is looking for a distraction,' Tom muttered, without glancing up from the sports pages.

'I think I would be too if I had to struggle with French vocab,' said Ben.

Jane set the teapot and mugs on the table and sat down opposite her son.

'Come on Tom, make room. I thought they were planning to change the broadsheets into tabloids; I wish they would, these take up so much space,' She pushed some of the newspapers aside and poured the tea.

'Don't think they will Mum, *The Times* lost out to the *Daily Telegraph* big time when they switched their daily paper to tabloid,' Tom said, as he folded the *Sunday Times* sports section away and picked up the magazine.

'It's not quite cricket is it?' Ben joked, sitting beside him.

'Bit early for cricket isn't it, Dad?' Catrin said as she came into the kitchen.

'Ce n'est pas jouer le cricket, ma soeur, nous discutons les journeaux,' Tom said, adding a Gallic shrug for good measure.

'Ce n'est pas jouer *le* cricket, mon frère, c'est jouer *au* cricket.'

'As Tom says ,we're not discussing cricket, Catrin, we're discussing the size of newspapers,' Ben said, 'but you're right too. I remember from my O level French you definitely play *at* cricket. French is almost as difficult as Welsh.'

They sat in silence for a couple of seconds, sipping tea and scanning the headlines.

'Dad, have you seen this?' Tom asked, passing the page to Ben. 'It's all about interval training; how you can really cut down on training time but get even fitter. We really need to get you out running today; we've missed a few sessions. How about we try this?'

Ben scanned the article and Jane marvelled at how quickly he read. She'd once commented on this and he'd said it was a skill doctors developed to cope with all the paperwork they faced. But she was still impressed; impressed too with the way his mind processed facts and came to conclusions. He really was clever, Jane thought proudly.

'Looks good, Tom. If I can get fit on just four minutes a day, then I'm all for it.'

'OK, Dad, there's no time like the present; let's have a go at it now and then tonight we can watch a DVD instead of poo-dodging in the dark.'

'You're on, son, hope you'll be able to keep up!'

'My middle name's not Cheetah for nothing.'

'Cheater more like it,' Catrin said drily.

'No such word Catz, sorry. OK, Dad, so here's the plan. Sprints for 20 seconds, rest for 10 seconds, repeated for 4 minutes.'

'Easy, son, anyone can keep going for 20 seconds.' Ben

smiled confidently.

'And I've found something for you, Mum, too. How do you fancy this?' Tom pushed the magazine towards her but without her glasses Jane could only see a beautiful frosted cupcake. 'And it's got no calories.'

'How can a cake have no calories? It's just not possible or I'd look like Elle MacPherson. And clearly I don't.' Jane groaned.

'It's a Vapourcake, Mum, you smell it; you don't eat it.'

She tutted. 'Well that's obviously not going to work – what a stupid idea. Anyone who has ever gone past a cake shop knows – you smell, you see, you eat. That's how it works; that's why they pump fresh bread smells down supermarket aisles. Smelling that cake would just make me go out and buy a box of them.'

They all laughed.

'Right Dad, kit on and let's go,' Tom said, as he pulled his father to his feet and pushed him towards the hall. They went upstairs to get changed.

Catrin made a fresh pot of tea and gave it a stir. 'I'll have ten more minutes off, Mum, and then there will be a whole hour left for French verbs before lunch'.

'Poor you,' Jane sympathised, pushing her mug towards Catrin for a refill. 'So, how was Oceana the other night Catz, good?'

'Yes OK, Mum'

'Just OK? Not great then?'

'Well, Oceana was good, the music was great and I knew lots of people there. I haven't been out for a couple of weeks so I was really looking forward to it but it just felt a bit flat, that's all.'

'I know what you mean love; sometimes it's the nights that we don't expect to be great that are the best.'

'See you later girls,' Ben called, as the front door banged closed.

Catrin flicked through the *Sunday Times Style* magazine,

her blonde hair hiding her face. 'I just don't understand Mark, I think he likes me, but …'

Jane took a sip of her too hot tea. Inwardly she sighed. Mark's name had been cropping up in Catrin's conversation more and more often over the past few months.

'He does nice things, you know, like the Easter egg,' Catrin said seriously.

Jane laughed. 'Not the best thing to send by post was it, Catz? Ended up more like a jigsaw than an egg.'

But Catrin was not laughing. 'It's the thought that counts Mum,' she said shortly. 'If only I knew his thoughts though …' She trailed off but still did not look up.

Jane waited, hoping Catrin would become engrossed in the magazine or start talking about fashion instead. She knew her daughter wouldn't want to hear what she honestly felt – that she was glad Catrin didn't have a boyfriend to distract her from the exams she would be sitting in a few short weeks, especially a boyfriend like Mark. Jane liked Mark well enough but he was twenty-two and working and wouldn't understand Catrin needed to spend all her time studying. But Catrin clearly wanted to talk about Mark and was not to be diverted.

'When I call round there he's really friendly, but then, when we're out, I don't know, he's different. Like in Oceana, after saying hello when I got there, he hardly spoke to me all night – and he didn't dance with me at all.'

'Perhaps he just doesn't like dancing,' Jane suggested.

Catrin laughed drily. 'I said he didn't dance with me, Mum; he danced with loads of other girls.'

'Ah, I see,' Jane said. After thinking for a moment she enquired why Catrin hadn't asked him to dance. Catrin rolled her eyes. 'Oh, Mum, I just couldn't.'

'Oh, for goodness sake, Catrin, of course you could, this is 2013: equality of the sexes and all that.'

Catrin gave her mother an incredulous look. 'Mum, that's not what I meant – no one asks anyone to dance.'

It was Jane's turn to look perplexed. 'Well, how do people

get to dance together then Catz?'

'You just catch someone's eye on the dance floor and make your way towards them – but he wouldn't look at me, Mum.'

Jane could see Catrin was really upset and knew she had to tread carefully; it certainly wouldn't help if she let slip she felt it was the wrong time for Catrin to be starting a relationship.

'Perhaps, Catrin love, he doesn't want a girlfriend; just wants to be really good mates with you.'

'But he's acting really strangely if he only wants to be mates. Like at the taxi rank he insisted I share a taxi with him and Lisa even though it was out of their way to drop me off and I told him I could share a taxi with Darren from down the road, who was in the queue too.'

Jane put her arm around her daughter. Really she was too thin; she needed feeding up. 'He's being protective Catrin, in a big brother kind of way. Now what would you like for pudding today?'

Catrin ignored the question. 'So what do you think I should do, Mum?' she asked earnestly.

Jane smiled at her, deciding on a non-committal response. 'Give it time, Catrin; if it's supposed to happen it will.'

At that moment the back door burst open and a red-faced Ben staggered in, followed by Tom, who for once did look as if he'd broken into a sweat.

Ben collapsed on the floor, pointing to the tap. Tom filled two pint glasses with water and handed one to his father.

'How was it? Jane asked.

Between gulps Tom told them, or rather acted out, how his father had been sick in a neighbour's garden.

Ben groaned.

'Don't worry Dad; I think Mrs Thomas is away this weekend,' Tom spluttered.

Ben groaned again and rolled over.

'I assume it's back to your usual training regime tomorrow?' Jane grinned.

Ben and Tom nodded, for once, both speechless.

Chapter Nineteen

Lucky greeted Catrin as she came in through the front door. She stroked the little dog and headed automatically towards the kitchen and, in particular, the kettle. She had planned her evening as she'd walked home with Siân. She'd allow herself half an hour with a cup of tea and Facebook and then she'd get on with her French revision. Tonight she knew she'd have the house to herself until supper-time, as Jane always went to Zumba on a Tuesday and was then going for a quick post-class drink with her classmates to celebrate someone's birthday; Ben was doing his usual evening surgery and Tom had a five-a-side football match organised. She'd pop the potatoes in the Aga, as her mother had asked, and later on do some fancy fillings in time to feed the famished when they all arrived home at eight o'clock. She tried to think of some interesting combinations from the ingredients she knew she'd find in the fridge: perhaps avocado and bacon or tuna and red onion and she'd have to make some cheese and tomato for her dad. Good, sorted, she thought to herself.

Propped up against the kettle was an envelope addressed to her. It would be something boring she thought, half-glancing at it, probably to do with her building society account. She dumped her school bag and tore the letter open carelessly, not bothering to use the letter opener her father kept on the shelf. She unfolded the sheet of paper with one hand as she reached for the biscuit tin with the other. The letter's first sentence sprang out at her: 'We write to inform you that your donor has now re-registered and is therefore contactable.' And then all the words seemed to blur and merge together.

All thoughts of making herself a cup of tea forgotten, Catrin sat down on the sofa and pulled Lucky on to her lap.

She really didn't know how she felt. How ironic, she thought. Initially, when she'd approached the donor people and been told her biological father had not given his contact details, she'd been disappointed. Then she'd met Steffan and the excitement of that had been enough. And really, she admitted to herself, he hadn't lived up to expectation. Now, did she really want to meet the donor? She couldn't decide. She almost wished she hadn't been given the option.

She sat there for a long time until the little dog decided he'd had enough of being so closely cuddled and retreated to his basket. Catrin folded the letter carefully, got up and put it into her school bag. She sat at the kitchen table and turned on her laptop. Immediately Steffan's photograph popped up, indicating there was a new message from him. His scowling face irritated her. When she'd said this to him he'd laughed, saying it wasn't cool to smile in photographs.

OMG – have you had the letter? Amazin! can't wait to meet him, 2gether yeah sis?

Catrin shut down her computer, realising she did not want to chat to anyone; couldn't care less what was happening on Facebook. She closed her eyes. This donor thing was all too much, all too complicated. How she'd like to turn back the clock. She wished she'd never started any of this. She wished even more that her gran had never revealed her parents' secret. How much simpler things had been a few short months ago. After a few minutes of feeling really sorry for herself, she said out loud: 'Oh don't be so stupid – you're just scared.' And of course if Granny hadn't started all this she wouldn't have met Mark or Lisa. How much less fun her life would be without them. – mostly. If only Mark wasn't so confusing but she didn't want to imagine life without him. Of course she hadn't been able to picture life without Granny Lewis but it went on and, in a way, Lisa and Mark had plugged the gap she'd left. Her mobile bleeped and automatically she reached for it.

V. Imp. Sent you fbk messj. Look NOW.

Steffan. She clicked the reply button.

Yes, seen it, not sure if I want to.

He replied immediately.

You gotta be kidding me, get on line, need to chat.

Catrin switched off her mobile; the last thing she needed was to be hassled by Steffan. She switched on the television and spent the next couple of hours lost in the soaps. She hadn't been following them regularly over the past few weeks because of all the homework she'd had and so she found some of the storylines baffling. But she did find comfort in the shouting and arguing – at least someone else is having a worse time than me, she thought. But then they're characters in a TV drama, she reminded herself, and that was not comforting at all.

Jane arrived home to the deafening sound of an *EastEnders* brawl in the Queen Vic pub. In good spirits after her Zumba class and a couple of glasses of wine in the pub, she felt her bonhomie drain away at the sound of the television blaring in the lounge. It could mean only one thing – Catrin was not doing her homework. There was no obvious aroma of cooking coming from the kitchen either. Mindful not to upset her daughter as soon as she got home, she placed her keys in the little blue bowl that Catrin had made in her pottery class years ago and poured herself a glass of water.

'Hi Catrin, got your work done earlier than you thought then?' she shouted in the direction of the lounge.

There was no answer. Having checked there was nothing cooking in the Aga or oven Jane started clattering about loudly in the kitchen. 'It will have to be pasta then – that's the only quick thing we have.'

Still there was no reply. Jane took a gulp of water, laid the glass down by the sink and went in to the lounge to see what was going on. Catrin was slumped on the sofa watching the end titles. 'Will you lay the table Catrin, please, while I get the pasta going?'

Her daughter got up slowly. Really, Jane thought, at times I could shake her.

'Three sets of knives and forks, please,' she said as Catrin followed her in to the kitchen.'

'Who's not going to be here then?'

'We're all going to be here but I'm on wheat free this week, remember? Thought I'd give it a go. Sue says her sister feels far less bloated on her gluten-free diet. I'll just have to make do with cheese, so only a cheese knife for me and a small plate.

'Oh Mum, I'm sorry; I forgot all about putting the potatoes in.'

Catrin slumped into the armchair and Jane felt a sudden concern; her daughter looked so dejected.

'Oh, don't worry, love, I can have grapes and some celery with it. To be honest I did share a packet of crisps in the pub. And lets face it, I've got plenty of padding; it would do me good to go without anything at all.' Jane put her arms around Catrin, whispering into her hair as she had done when she was a little girl. 'Is all this exam stress getting you down?'

Catrin did not reply but burst into tears.

Ben flung the cushions Jane insisted on having on their bed onto the floor, muttering under his breath. What was the point of all these cushions, anyway? Jane never used them so the nightly fling, and the morning pile on, was simply a waste of time. He got into bed and picked up his Welsh textbook. Jane sat at the dressing table, pulling the skin of her face upwards and outwards.

'You going to be long, love? I could do with a bit of help with this Welsh vocabulary.'

Jane made a face at him in the mirror. 'Two minutes, Ben; I tell you it will be worth the wait if this miracle cream actually works. I'm putting on two layers – double the chance.' She smiled ruefully. 'Typical, isn't it – the one place where a bit of excess fat is good and it's the one place I don't have it.'

'You look lovely, now come to bed.'

292

Jane tidied her make-up pots and came over to the bed. She slid under the covers and snuggled up to him.

Ben handed her the textbook. 'Give me the English and I'll tell you what it is in Welsh.'

Jane groaned. 'And how do I know you're right Ben?'

'It's phonetic, love.'

After Jane had assured him he'd got all fifty words correct Ben put the book back on his bedside table and switched off the overhead light.

He turned contentedly on his side. 'Where did Catrin go to tonight then? She looked a bit upset. Is she OK?'

'She went to see Mark and Lisa. She's staying over.'

Ben yawned loudly. 'Is she worried about the exams?'

Jane turned away from him.

'I'm sure it's the French she's most worried about,' he went on. 'One of my patients – saw him today, actually – he teaches French in Treorchy High; I'm sure he'd give Catrin a few extra lessons; give her a bit of confidence. What if I have a word with him tomorrow – sound him out about giving her some last minute help?'

'Her French is fine, Ben, her teacher said so; it's just a matter of learning vocab.'

'Ah, now I can give her a few tips on that – I'll always remember pamplemousse is grapefruit. Do you know how, Jane?'

She pulled the Welsh tapestry blanket that had been a wedding gift from his mother up to her shoulders and did not reply.

'I'll tell you. Mr Davies, the French teacher I had in Form One, told us to think of a moose covered in pimples that looked just like a grapefruit. And hey presto, I still remember it.'

'And very useful that must be too,' Jane muttered.

'My Welsh tutor gave us a good tip too – learn a group of words together by creating a story around them; so let's say you want to remember lots of words to do with going on holiday – you'd create a story about packing your big red case carefully, putting in the suncream, sunglasses, some swimming trunks …'

'Oh for goodness sake, Ben, it's late – nearly midnight. Aren't you tired?'

Ben ignored her. 'If Catrin's worried about the exams then we really should do something to help her. If it's just good old-fashioned anxiety I read the other day that good new-fashioned computers can help – just put on a screen saver showing snowflakes gently falling; works a treat apparently. Or stroking dogs releases oxytocin and that works as well; or listening to classical music – that can help, or…'

Jane sat up, grabbing the pull-cord above the bed and flooding the room with harsh light.

'Ben – stop. She's not worried about exams. It's something else.' He heard her take a deep breath. 'She's had a letter Ben, from the donor people, telling her the donor has re-registered and she can now make contact with him if she wants to.'

Ben said nothing as all kinds of thoughts tumbled around his head. This is what people meant by life-changing moments, huge, significant, irreversible junctures. This was the end of the family life he had known. Catrin would drift away from him once she met the person who, along with Jane, had done the most important thing possible for her – given her life.

He turned on his bedside lamp and switched off the overhead light. 'I see,' he said quietly. 'So what does it say about him?'

'Just gives his name and his Bristol address.'

'I see,' he said again.'

The big grandfather clock in the hall struck midnight, the sound reverberating through the house.

'So what happens next, Jane?'

'It's up to her; she has to decide whether to contact him or not.'

Ben switched off his bedside lamp but remained sitting up.

294

'Does he know who she is? Could he just turn up here?'

'No, it's up to her. All he knows is that he has fathered a daughter.'

Ben inhaled sharply, feeling as if he had just been hit.

'Come on love, snuggle down, nothing's changed. We knew he was out there somewhere; we just know that somewhere is Bristol.'

He did not move. 'It has changed though, Jane. He's got an identity now, hasn't he? He's a real person. So you know his name? No, don't tell me; I don't want to know.'

They were silent for a few minutes. 'I was really hoping he wouldn't become contactable, even though I knew Catrin wanted to know more about him,' Ben whispered. 'That makes me a bad parent.'

Jane reached for his hand. He tightened his fingers around hers. 'You are the best dad Catrin and Tom could ever hope to have but we're all a tiny bit selfish sometimes – that's just human. And I'll tell you what, parents are far less selfish than their teenage kids, that's for sure.' She leant over to kiss him. 'Goodnight Ben.'

'Goodnight love.' He released her hand, they both lay down and she turned on her side away from him. He could tell from her even breathing she was soon asleep.

Ben lay there, images of Catrin as a little girl replaying in his mind. He heard the clock strike 12.30 a.m. Or was it 1 a.m.? His mother's clock, which struck every half hour, may be unusual but at this time of night it was just confusing and loudly irritating.

He felt bereft. This was exactly how it had been twenty years ago when faced with his infertility. Jane had accepted it and simply focused on finding a way to have a second child. Any way. He clearly remembered her saying: 'Sweetheart, I don't think any less of you just because you're a jaffa,' trying to make a joke of it. But did she really mean it? Surely, deep down, she must have considered him less of a man. He wondered when she had stopped calling him 'sweetheart' but couldn't remember.

Now, as then, Ben felt out of control. It was an unfamiliar feeling with which he was not comfortable. He'd been brought up by teacher parents who were precisely that. Teachers first, parents second. They'd more or less presented education as a religion: work hard and you will achieve was their eleventh commandment. But Ben had not been able to achieve in this sense, could not give Jane the second child she so wanted. He had thought at the time being a doctor made it worse. Hadn't he spent years learning how to defy nature; how science could control the body? He'd felt angry and useless. Although he'd argued they already had one healthy child and should count their blessings and be content with what they had, the guilt he'd felt about letting Jane down had eventually led him to give in to infertility treatment.

The clock struck 3 a.m. Ben remembered how relieved he'd felt at that point. As a doctor he had access to reports and clinics and that had enabled him to regain some feeling of control. Once the decision had been made he wanted to get on with it and luckily Jane had become pregnant at the first attempt. Occasionally during those nine months he'd found himself looking at his young son – his love for his little boy so overwhelming – and worried he wouldn't feel the same way about this new baby. But as Jane's tummy grew, and he felt the baby kicking and hiccoughing, his heart had soared. And then she was in his arms, warm and pink, wrinkled and perfect and, just as he had with Tom, he knew he would do anything to protect this little bundle.

Of course there had been a few clouds, even then. Just as Jane had gone into labour, his mother, who had chosen not to refer to the infertility treatment after her initial 'playing God' remark, had stood in the hallway and said, 'What will you do if it's a black baby? You know they could easily have mixed up those samples. What will they say in chapel?' Ben had firmly told her not to be so silly and to please go and play with Tom. He'd often suggested she play with his children when he was cross with her, knowing she never would. She would look after them very competently and read to them and later help them with their homework but she had barely played with him as a child and had not played at all since his father had died. The clock struck 4 a.m.

Then there was the question Ben had dreaded most of all. The one everybody asked, 'Who does she look like then?' Initially he had suggested 'the milkman' which raised a laugh. And then he'd decided 'goodness knows' was a more honest answer.

But not for much longer.

Jane turned on to her back but slept on. How envious he felt. Despite all the upheaval nothing had really changed for her – she was still Catrin's mother but he was not Catrin's father. He heard his mother's big clock strike 5 a.m. before he finally fell asleep. The next thing he knew his alarm was going off at 7 a.m. He hit the snooze button and slowly it came back to him why he felt so wretched.

It was a beautiful spring day. Miriam had worked an early shift and was looking forward to spending the afternoon in the garden. But before she'd allow herself to do that she had to tackle the overflowing linen basket that had been reproaching her for days. Briefly she thought of her mother. She'd have been aghast at Miriam's tardiness. Monday was washday and on Tuesday you did the ironing. Now it was Friday. But her mother hadn't had a full time job, and had had a helpful husband. Ralph was anything but. She would have finished this tiresome chore by now if he didn't keep wandering in and out and interrupting her. And now here he came again. Miriam flung open the kitchen window in the hope some fresh air would make her feel less hot and cross.

'A 'Who's the Daddy?' T-shirt. That would be a good icebreaker, don't you think Miriam?'

'Haven't you got a poodle or chihuahua or something to get on with, Ralph?'

He smiled at her. 'You haven't got to work this afternoon so I'm taking the afternoon off too.'

Miriam gave him an incredulous look and pointed the steaming iron at him. 'And you don't call this work, do you?'

'No because you enjoy it,' Ralph answered.

'Who says?'

'Come on Miri-Mw, you know you do,' Ralph said, closing the kitchen window.

Miriam scowled at him but as she had only one T-shirt left to iron she couldn't be bothered to remonstrate with him.

'Anyway what about a 'Who's the Daddy T-shirt? Great idea don't you think?'

'No, I don't, Ralph; humour can be a very dangerous thing.'

'Oh, lighten up, Miriam; how can anyone not find that amusing?'

Miriam shrugged, deciding this to be far easier than trying to explain empathy to Ralph.

She unplugged the iron, gathered up the clothes and carried them upstairs to their bedroom. As she laid them on the bed she heard Ralph come up the stairs and her heart sank. Oh, for goodness sake, what did he want now? But perhaps she was being unfair; perhaps he'd changed his mind and was going to his studio after all.

Of course not. That would have been giving in to what she wanted him to do and he would never do that. Ralph came into the bedroom as she was folding one of his shirts.

'So what do you think I should wear Miriam?'

She shrugged and carried on folding. 'Isn't it a bit premature to be thinking what to wear? All you know is that seven children have been born; you don't actually know they'll go as far as to contact you, do you?'

'Of course they will; they'll want to know who their father is.'

'Donor, not father,' Miriam said curtly, as she folded a pair of Ralph's Levis and placed them in the chest of drawers they

298

supposedly shared. Actually she had one drawer and Ralph had taken over the other three.

'They must feel there's a missing link and, as I started donating in 1992, those first sprogs will have turned eighteen by now; that's the age they can start looking. Any day soon I'll have a whole team – back of the net.' Ralph dived on the bed, squashing the newly ironed clothes.

'Oh for goodness sake; grow up will you, Ralph.'

He lay on the bed as Miriam worked around him. She was cross with him and cross with herself. She'd mothered him. He'd fulfilled a need in her but, unlike a child, Ralph had no desire to grow up; was quite happy to let her do everything for him. Expected her to. It was just as well she hadn't become a mother; she would probably have failed her children, just as she had failed Ralph; failed to let them become independent, to grow emotionally, to see beyond themselves.

Miriam crossed to Ralph's side of the bed to put some hankies in his bedside drawer. She flung aside a copy of *Nuts* he'd left on the floor.

'Why have you suddenly started buying this pornographic rubbish?'

'Because, wifie, it's got men's style pages.'

'Oh, yeah, that's a new one.' Miriam tugged a couple of her work uniforms from under him.

'And anyway, Miri-Mw, you must have had a little look to know that it's got some gorgeous scantily clad birds in there.' Ralph laughed his ha, ha, ha laugh, which he used when being insincere. He knew it annoyed her.

'I haven't actually seen a copy of the Koran but I know it's a holy book,' Miriam retorted, as she picked up the sheets and took them to the airing cupboard. She went downstairs to put the ironing board away and make herself a quick cup of tea before heading into the garden. She decided not to offer Ralph one in the hope he would stay upstairs. He didn't.

'Look, I think coloured chinos: orange perhaps – citrus is big this spring; some Chucks – the coolest trainers ever; and a

Breton jumper, would say hip, trendy, arty. Something like this.' Ralph held the magazine in front of her as she put a tea bag in her mug. 'Lemon tea for me please,' he added, tucking the magazine under his arm and opening the back door. Within moments he came back, took one of the kitchen chairs outside and sat down facing the April sun.

Miriam put a splash of lemon in his mug, poured on the tea and added one teaspoonful of honey, knowing he liked two. She put it down on the ground beside him, fetched her gardening tools from the shed by the back door and went back inside to collect her own mug. She took her tea to the bottom of the garden and sat on the old ivy-clad tree stump. She smiled as she observed her sweet peas had started curling around the canes. After drinking her tea she'd tie them up. She remembered her father telling her how important it was to do this regularly to get nice long stalks. He'd been so proud of his blooms, won the local show year after year. That was the scent of summer for her. Her mother would cut a bunch every couple of days and fill each room in their terraced house with them. The winter smell of home was burning wood. Now, whenever she smelled these aromas, she was instantly transported back to her childhood. Ralph had insisted they block up the open grate when they moved into this house, claiming getting wood or coal would be far too troublesome in their Bristol suburb and anyway he thought he might be allergic to wood smoke. More likely, she thought, he'd realised with her being out all day at work, he would have to prepare and light it. But she was less cynical in those days and had agreed to the mean little electric fire with its fake logs that now filled the fireplace in their lounge.

She left her empty mug on the tree trunk and with scissors in one hand and twine in the other, started tying up the one hundred sweet pea plants that filled her vegetable patch. The last few days of warmth had really produced a growth spurt and, after the long wet winter, she was happier than ever to see signs spring had finally arrived.

300

Ralph walked down the garden path and stood blocking her sun.

'You're tying them too tightly; they'll wilt.'

'And since when have you been an expert on growing sweet peas?'

'Anyone can see if you tie up something too tightly it will suffocate,' Ralph replied laconically, as he moved her mug and took its place on the tree trunk.

Miriam said nothing and carried on with her work. With her back to him she could pretend Ralph wasn't there and her shoulders relaxed as she got into the rhythm of cutting and tying, cutting and tying. A succession of little birds, blue tits, sparrows, and a robin, flew to the bird table just beyond where she was working. Seeing that the bird feeders were empty, they swung on the equally empty half coconut and flew away again. Miriam wondered how long it would take them to realise she had stopped feeding them now spring was here. She hoped it would be a while yet. She loved to see them, their little heads turning at impossible angles as they sought food and watched out for next-door's cat. And she loved their song. She listened now – a blackbird, high in the apple tree a few doors down, sung the soprano solo to the accompaniment of a chaffinch's cascading melody and the throaty gurgle of the pigeons. The warble of the swallows nesting under the eaves added flowery little trills.

'Raphe – I think I'll introduce myself as Raphe – you know, as in *H. M. S. Pinafore* – that's how they pronounced Ralph then. I like it; it sounds classy – what do you think Miriam?'

'Well you know the old saying – put lipstick on a pig; it's still a pig.' She waited for his comeback but there wasn't one. He couldn't have heard her.

'Raphe, like it?' he asked again.

'Do you know anything about Gilbert and Sullivan, Ralph?'

'Yeah, I saw *Trial by Jury* once.'

'Well what you need to know is that in general they were having a laugh at pretentious people.'

'Whatever. I think Raphe's got a ring to it and it's a good name for an artist.'

'Doesn't make you a good artist though, does it?' Miriam glanced in his direction.

Ralph put on his hurt expression and bowed his head dramatically.

She took a deep breath. 'Oh I'm sorry, I didn't mean that; you are a good artist. How's Mrs Price's spaniel getting on?'

Ralph didn't reply.

'OK that's the sweet peas done – for a couple of days at least.' She stretched, checked her watch and looked at Ralph. He was still sulking. She decided neither of them would have an enjoyable evening if she did not try to make amends. 'It's six o clock, I think we both deserve a glass of wine – red or white?'

She reached out her hand to help him up but he ignored it, stood without looking at her and made his way up the garden path to the house. Miriam busied herself putting away her gardening tools, washed her hands in the kitchen sink and took a bottle of whatever was on special offer that week from the fridge.

She filled two large glasses with white wine and went into the lounge, where her husband was now lying on the sofa watching football on the television.

She handed him a glass. 'To Ralph or Raphe – whatever the name, still the same,' she toasted.

As they clinked glasses Ralph smiled. 'I think I'll stick to Ralph, sounds stronger, don't you think, Miriam?

She nodded.

By Saturday lunchtime Catrin had already hugged Ben six times. He'd been counting. Over the last couple of days his quota of hugs had suddenly increased and Ben knew she had decided. Usually he loved to be hugged, by anyone really, but now he felt patronised. He sat in his shed, filled his pipe and lit it. His first smoke of the day. It was like any other first – the first cup of tea in the morning, the first bite of a fresh French stick, that first sip of beer: it just tasted better than anything that came afterwards. Lucky that our time is divided into days, he thought. I can have a first smoke 365 days a year. Lately though, there had been more than one or two a day – just like the hugs, he thought gloomily.

It was Jane who had taught him to hug. Well, re-taught him really. He remembered as a little boy being hugged by his mother and he remembered clearly when that came to an end. They'd been in the kitchen of his grandmother's house in Llangrannog and it was his seventh birthday. He'd just been given a second-hand two-wheeler bike, 28-inch wheels, blue. A real grown-up's bike and he'd been thrilled. He'd reached up to give his mother a hug and she'd sharply pushed him away with the words, 'don't be so soppy, you're seven now. Having an adult's bike means acting like an adult.' And that had been that. For forty years. Right up to her final illness there had been minimal physical contact between them, apart from what had been totally necessary following her stroke. Even then Jane had done most of the caring. Until one day, a couple of months before she died, he'd reached for his mother's hand as she struggled to get out of the car, fully expecting his gesture to be rejected. It hadn't been but her touch had felt strange and left him feeling uncomfortable.

But Jane and Olwen had hugged him, Jane had brought up their children in the same tactile way and he was not averse to giving a few hugs himself. That was within the family. He drew the line at the new trend of hugging at the golf club; what was wrong with a simple handshake? You knew where you were with a handshake. Ben tutted as he let out a long puff of smoke, put out the pipe, took off his gardening coat and shook himself down to get rid of any telltale tobacco strands. He walked round the garden twice, pretending to study the progress of the annuals in case someone was watching from

303

the house. Deciding he smelt sufficiently fresh, he went back in.

He was relieved the kitchen smelt of garlic and onion, masking any lingering tobacco aroma. 'Mm, something smells good, Jane.'

'Thought I'd make Spaghetti Bolognese. Siân's coming to do some work with Catz and staying over for supper.'

'Good, I haven't seen her for a while; Catrin seems to be spending more and more of her time with Lisa.'

'Double attraction at that house, Ben; she's just gone there with Lucky, dressed as if she's going dancing.'

'Half-naked you mean.' He laughed.

Jane took a slurp from the cheap Bulgarian red she'd opened to add to the Bolognese and turned the radio up.

'Drinking in the afternoon, Mrs Lewis? The curse of the middle – middle-aged, middle classes, and the waistline, don't you know,' Ben said, mockingly.

'I think it's fair: a glass for the supper and a glass for the supper-maker – cheers,' his wife replied cheerfully.

'Shall I get you some lunch to go with those empty calories then, love?'

'No thanks, I'm saving my calories for supper.'

Ben helped himself to some bread, Brie, sun-dried tomatoes, and fresh figs and sat at the table enjoying the warmth of the sun as it streamed in through the patio doors. 'So what's Olwen up to today that she didn't want to go to the market?'

'Mrs Evans number 16's funeral,' Jane replied. 'Poor Mum, that's the third funeral she's been to this week.'

Ben, anxious not to let the conversation tarry on deaths and funerals picked up the newspaper. 'Shall I finish the crossword for you?' he asked lightly.

'Actually, Ben Lewis, I've done rather well today. I've only got one gap. It's 4 across, African leopard, 7 letters.'

'Panther? – yep, it fits.'

'Oh, of course. Well done. Write it in for me; it's so

satisfying to see it complete.'

He filled in the blanks and munched as he turned to the news pages, the strains of Jane's radio, permanently tuned to Radio Wales, playing some morose love song in the background. Usually Ben loved these rare times of comparative silence with just the two of them in the house but today he felt fidgety.

'So Catrin's decided to meet the donor.' His voice sounded harsh and judgmental.

Jane turned the hob down, picked up her wine and joined him at the kitchen table. He noticed she had her bikini apron on. She put her hand on his. 'When did she tell you?'

'She hasn't. I just guessed.'

'I see.' She squeezed his hand. 'Yes, she's meeting him next Saturday. Steffan's going with her.

'Well at least she'll have company,' Ben said, 'but I'd be happier if it was someone other than Steffan.'

'I know, love, but I think he showed his true colours the night he and his friends gatecrashed Catrin's supper party – she's been far more wary of him since.'

He nodded. 'So where are they meeting?'

'TG's, in the new precinct.' Jane put both her hands on his. 'Look, Ben, please don't be upset, it's just something she's got to do. It's no reflection on you as a father; she loves you, you know that.'

'She might come to love him too; love him more,' he said quietly.

'You've got eighteen years behind you, eighteen years of building a relationship, of being together. No one is going to take your place,' Jane said firmly adding, 'and at eighteen it's too late for anyone to start building a parent-child relationship. If they do have some kind of relationship it will be very different to the one you have with her, so please stop fretting.'

Ben shook his head and said sadly, 'But they do share something, something I don't share with her – she's got his genes.'

'On that basis then, because Catrin has some of my genes, she should love me more than she loves you and you know that's not true.'

He smiled at her gratefully. 'You should be a counsellor, you have so much common sense.'

'I've had the best university education,' Jane said triumphantly. 'First class honours – university of life.' She got up with a flourish, shaking her bikini apron at him.

'But you're still keen for Catrin to go to university, aren't you? Just as you were determined Tom would go.'

She laughed and he could see her relief at being back on familiar ground.

'Oh do shut up Ben; make yourself useful and fix a pudding for tonight.'

He smiled at her – he was very lucky to have such a warm, caring, straightforward, wonderful wife; she was perfect for him. He opened the fridge then the freezer to see what ingredients were available, and settled on a plastic box full of frozen fruit.

'Victoria mess, I think Jane.'

'Is that a local version of Eton mess?'

'Precisely, but with plums instead of raspberries. See what I did there? Double meaning, clever, eh?'

His wife looked confused.

'Victoria as in plums and Victoria Park, where we live – well, near enough!'

'Well, Ben, we'll see how clever you are – just remember the old saying: "The proof of the pudding is in the eating!" Now I'm going to have a long soak in the bath and the kitchen is all yours but please keep an eye on the Bolognese sauce.'

Chapter Twenty

On the following Saturday Catrin was awake just after 5 a.m. She hadn't planned for that. Her timetable of preparations started at 9 a.m., when she'd have muesli, fruit and yogurt. Today she'd have a substantial breakfast so she wouldn't have to have lunch – just in case her stomach swelled up after eating, which it sometimes did if she was stressed. If her stomach swelled after eating breakfast she would still have time for a long bath, and hot water with some bicarbonate of soda in it would usually do the trick. Her father had dismissed it as another of Granny Olwen's old wives' tales but Catrin believed in it. Granny Olwen, of course, had suggested she back it up with paracetamol but Catrin only took tablets if the swelling was actually causing her pain and usually it didn't – it just looked gross.

And today she was determined to look her best. She had dipped into her savings but it had been worth it – the little pink and purple spotted dress from Urban Outfitters she'd seen and just had to have, the navy leggings, and her trusted Chucks would look great. She'd also bought a navy long-sleeved T-shirt she could wear under the dress if the day was cool.

Catrin pulled back the curtains. There would be no need for the T-shirt today. The weak late April sun was already lighting up the cherry blossom on the big tree in front of her bedroom and a light breeze caused the branches, heavily laden with showy pink blooms, to sway gently, throwing a cascade of confetti on to the lawn below. What a lovely time of day, Catrin thought to herself; why don't I make more of an effort to get up earlier to enjoy this? Deciding Lucky would appreciate a walk in the coolness of the early morning she pulled on her trackie bottoms, hoodie and trainers and made her way downstairs, avoiding the creaky stair and indicating to Lucky to be quiet as she grabbed his lead and opened the back door.

Victoria Park was deserted except for a couple of early morning joggers and the little dog entertained himself running around the neatly regimented flower beds. There were pale and dark blue pansies in the first, purple and yellow primulas in the second, and the third was full of miniature tulips and hyacinths, giving off a heady scent. Catrin sat on a bench enjoying the solitude. A few hours from now would she feel any different? She hoped not; she actually quite liked the person she was. Yet she was aware she wanted the meeting to make a difference, to be significant; otherwise what was the point?

After breakfast she'd timetabled a slot to sit down and list the questions she wanted to ask. She was worried that in unfamiliar circumstances she would forget. She guessed that he would answer most of them in the normal course of conversation anyway – what he did, what his interests were; would talk about any partner, family, children. But he probably wouldn't mention any illnesses and she needed to know. How angry she'd been with her parents for letting her worry needlessly about inheriting Ben's sky-high cholesterol but there was a possibility her donor might also have a family history of stroke or heart disease. Deciding not to allow herself to dwell on this she got up and called the little dog to her, clipped on his lead and took the long way home.

Ben too was up early and had breakfasted on cereal and fruit. He'd cleared up and was now flicking idly through the newspaper as he pondered what to do with his day. Jane was meeting her mother for their usual Ponty market outing and then going in to the shop to work the afternoon shift. He knew Tom was meeting up with his mates for football and then a few beers. And Catrin. He preferred not to think about how she would spend her day. Deciding a run would make him feel better he pulled on his trainers, shut the front door quietly, and made for the Taff trail. If any run was going to succeed in lifting his spirits today this was the one. The trail went all the way to Brecon, fifty or so miles up the valley, but today he'd aim to reach Castell Coch and then turn back – a nine-mile run.

He was aware he'd started too fast, could hear Tom's advice ringing in his ears loud and clear – warm up, jog, sprint, jog, cool down – but decided to ignore it. Today he needed to feel physical pain, needed to do something that would consume him and not allow him to think of anything but the need to keep going for the next minute and the next. He did not look around but focused only on the path ahead. With Castell Coch looming above him he turned for home but did not stop. He was within half a mile of Pencisely Crescent before he slowed his pace and for the last quarter of a mile he allowed himself to walk. By the time he arrived home, soon after 10 a.m., he had a plan.

As he telephoned The Ship in Llangrannog to check they had a vacancy he could hear the taps running in the bathroom. Since Jane and Tom would have left by now it could only be Catrin. He showered in the en suite, stuffed some fresh running clothes in his kit bag and drank a pint of water at the kitchen sink. He scribbled on a post-it note:

'Gone to Llangrannog, back 2morrow night, Ben x,' attached it to the fridge and closed the back door behind him.

At 11 a.m. Tom came in from his football session. He could hear the bathtub draining but the house was otherwise quiet. Dumping his kit in the kitchen, he reached into the fridge, grabbed a carton of milk and took a quick swig. Outside Greg revved his car engine threateningly. Still holding the carton, Tom flung the fridge door shut, bringing down the bowls his mother stored on top of it, an open packet of biscuits someone (probably he) had left there and the myriad bits of paper

309

attached to the fridge door. Greg gave a long continuous beep and Tom briefly considered leaving the mess for Catrin to clear up. But, deciding it was too much of a risk his mother would find it instead, set about tidying up feverishly. He picked up the biscuits – they would do nicely as a quick snack – and put the bowls which were still intact on top of the fridge then bent down to deal with the assorted papers. As he did some of the milk splashed on to the floor. Cursing loudly he stuck the magnets and the messages that weren't sodden back on the fridge door then scooped everything else up in the Business Finance section of the Saturday paper that no one ever read and dumped it in the bin by the back door on his way out.

The weather changed in Port Talbot; it often did. For Ben crossing the River Neath was significant – this was where West Wales began, where the bilingual signs on the M4 stopped referring to the large industrial towns of the south and started directing travellers to the market towns of Carmarthen and Llandeilo. As he travelled into fog and light rain his spirits soared.

At Carmarthen the motorway stopped abruptly and was replaced by B roads. Leaving the town behind he began the hour-long journey along the small country lanes that would take him to the little fishing village on the edge of the Irish Sea. Briefly he allowed himself to think of Catrin or rather her meeting the donor. It had, of course, been at the back of his mind almost constantly since Jane had told him they had arranged to meet and, really, he'd been in turmoil. Now – away from home, from Cardiff, from work – he found he could get to the centre of what was causing his distress. For so long the donor had been a something then, with the letter giving his contact name and address, he had become a someone and now he was about to become recognisable, known – at least to Catrin and through her to him and Jane and Tom. This Ralph person was about to become real, to have some claim on his family. Ben was glad he had escaped. Glad he did not have to witness her excitement at having met her donor. At least her initial euphoria would have died down by the time he returned home tomorrow night.

He re-tuned the car radio from Radio 4 to the Welsh Radio Cymru. He could work out it was a debate programme and caught a few words here and there. Although the finer points of the argument were lost on him he stayed tuned, determined it would put him in the right mood for Llangrannog. The roads became steadily narrower, the hedgerows higher and, as he came around one particularly sharp bend, he caught his breath as huge disembodied blades turned menacingly, their trunks engulfed by the low-lying mist. How close they were, how alien, how *War of the Worlds* – ah, he'd enjoyed that album. He could hear Richard Burton's sonorous voice in his head now, gloomily telling of the visitors from Mars. Briefly he was transported back to his mother's parlour with the record player on the wooden coffee table alongside the family Bible and his lava lamp, whose orange and purple blobs created sinister shadows on the coffee and cream walls. He'd spent hours sitting on the floor playing that record over and over until he knew every word. Now he found himself humming 'Forever Autumn'. How strange he recalled it after all these years. Ben enjoyed singing. It struck him he hadn't sung for a long time except at organised occasions like his mother's funeral. When had he stopped singing in the shower or humming along to the radio just for fun? He couldn't remember. Realising he was in danger of becoming morose again, he tried to focus his thoughts on the wind-energy issue, deciding he very much liked the idea but not in his back yard or really anywhere in West Wales. He quickly moved on to consider what he would like for supper.

Catrin looked at the clock again. She then checked her watch. No, it really was just midday. Another hour before Siân and Lisa arrived. She checked her timetable, picked up a red pen from her desk and ticked off the things she'd already done – breakfast, tick; bath and wash hair, tick; nails, tick; pluck eyebrows, tick. She decided to put on her mascara; she had three different kinds and all the magazines said it was good to leave each layer to dry before adding the next. Certainly plenty of time for that. She turned on her laptop – Facebook. Best time-waster, as her mum said. She'd said it so often Catrin automatically shut the web page down whenever her mother came anywhere near. There was a message from Steff, left last night:

One more sleep ...

Just before one o'clock, and with all three layers of mascara applied and separately dried, Catrin looked out of her window. There was no sign of Sian and Lisa yet but she could picture them walking briskly towards Pencisely Crescent, one from west of the Ely river, the other from the east, and was really grateful they were both free to support her this afternoon. The closer she got to meeting her donor the more nervous she felt. Going on to the landing she stood in front of the cheval mirror to see how she looked with her hair up or down. No she couldn't decide which was best – she'd have to ask the girls.

The doorbell rang and Catrin ran downstairs wondering who'd arrived first only to see both girls' outlines on the other side of the front door. She flung it open.

'I hope you haven't brought more clothes for Catz to try on,' Siân was saying, pointing at the large bag Lisa was carrying. 'Don't want to tempt her to change her mind again about what to wear.'

'Definitely not, her new outfit sounds perfect.' Lisa laughed. 'I've got a dance class later. Hi, Catrin.'

'Thanks for being on time.' Catrin ushered them in and bounded back up the stairs saying over her shoulder, 'everything's going to plan I think, but I'm just soooooooooo nervous.'

'Home alone, Catz?' said Sian, as she and Lisa followed her up the stairs and into her bedroom.

'Yes, Mum's gone to work, Tom's footballing, or probably drinking with his mates by now, and I guess Dad's gone to see some patients. So what do you think – hair up or down?' She piled her hair up in a loose bun.

'Deffo down; that's more you, Catz,' Siân replied without hesitating.

'But I want to make a good impression – so up or down?'

'Just be yourself,' Siân said forcefully, 'you can't fail to make a good impression.'

Catrin let her hair tumble over her shoulders.

'I agree,' said Lisa, 'and anyway you want to be comfy; you can't be fiddling with your hair and stuff.

Catrin got changed into her specially selected outfit then let Siân finish her make-up while Lisa suggested some accessories. Finally she was ready.

'I feel as if I'm getting married and you're my bridesmaids,' Catrin teased, adding, 'all I need now is a man.'

'I'm just so jealous of you,' Lisa said, standing back to admire the finished effect.

Catrin took a long look at herself in her full-length mirror and smiled. 'Thanks girls and, even if I say it myself, I think I look OK.'

'No, silly, not jealous of how you look, although I am jealous of that too of course, but that you're actually going to meet your donor,' said Lisa.

Catrin turned to her. 'Still no progress then; yours hasn't re-registered?'

Lisa shook her head. 'No but I haven't given up hope. And still no sign that I have any half-siblings either.'

'But you've got Mark and he's one hell of a brother I'd say,' Catrin said, giving Lisa a hug.

'Yes, you're right, we both appreciate my brother don't we?' Lisa laughed and Catrin blushed bright red. 'But you know how I feel, Catz, wanting to know about my donor.'

Catrin nodded.

Siân put on a pair of extra-long false eyelashes, relics from

313

one of Catrin's theatrical productions, and fluttered them at the other two. Failing to raise a laugh she busied herself tidying away the discarded accessories.

'I don't understand Mark, not wanting to know anything; he keeps saying it's not important,' Lisa continued.

'We're all different; he's just not interested,' Catrin said.

'Or is he only saying that because he doesn't want to upset Mum and Dad? He probably thinks I've done enough of that; you know how considerate he is, always so careful.'

Catrin did know. Too careful she thought, too cautious for some reason to move things on between them but she decided it was best not to share this observation with Lisa.

'Well, I'll love you and leave you now; I've got to get to my dance class. Let me know how it goes won't you, Catrin? I'll be thinking of you all the time. See you later.' With a quick hug and blowing kisses, Lisa bounced out of the room, dance bag slung over her shoulder.

Catrin and Siân stood by the window and watched her skip down the street.

'She says she's jealous of me; you know I think I'm jealous of her too,' Catrin said quietly, turning away and going to sit on her bed. Siân joined her.

'What do you mean Catz?'

'Well, she's still wondering about her donor. He can be whatever she wants him to be but for me that's not possible any more; he's about to become real.' Catrin sunk back into the pillows, clutching Little Ted.

'You mean you're afraid of being disappointed in him?'

'Mm or of disappointing him. What if he doesn't like me, Siân?' Catrin looked at her friend for reassurance.

Siân moved closer so their shoulders were touching. 'Everyone likes you, Catz, everyone.'

'Some people not enough to take a chance.'

'Are you on about Mark now? Forget him for today, Catz; you've got plenty on your plate without worrying about him. Now cheer up and off we go.'

'Are you sure you're OK with coming into town with me? I guess you're working tonight aren't you?'

'Of course I'm happy to come into town with you and I'll wait with you until Steff turns up.'

Catrin smiled gratefully.

'I should still be able to get my French essay done and dusted before work – so I've got a double incentive not to hang about in town: short of time and short of money.'

'Oh Siân I feel as if I'm really putting you out.'

Siân laughed. 'Don't be silly, that's what friends are for. Did you say you're meeting Steffan a quarter of an hour before Ralph is due?'

Catrin nodded. The front doorbell rang and she looked quizzically at her friend. 'Please get rid of whoever's there. Probably someone collecting for something.'

'OK, no problem. Cold-caller quasher to the rescue,' Siân said heading downstairs.

Catrin got up and crossed to her desk to put on another lick of lip gloss.

She could hear strains of chatter below. What was Siân doing? Surely she realised now was not a good time to get involved in a long conversation. Catrin glanced at the photograph of her family, feeling suddenly sick. Why was she doing this? Putting herself and them through all this trauma? She didn't have to go to meet Ralph, she could back out now and everything would return to normal. But it wouldn't of course; it was impossible to erase what she now knew.

Catrin picked up her gran's little seed-pearl horseshoe brooch, her hands shaking. You're doing it because it's right for you to know, she told herself firmly; now stop all this nonsense, you're just nervous. Resolutely she pinned the brooch to the inside collar of her dress, there for support rather than for show. For good measure she hung the opal necklace her parents had given her for Christmas around her neck. With the two slim bracelets Lisa had chosen for her she wasn't sure she needed more jewellery but the blues and greens clashed

315

nicely with her dress and all the magazines were preaching that made an outfit look on-trend. Anyway it was reassuring to have it around her neck.

She touched the brooch muttering, 'You started all this, Gran; you can jolly well bring me some luck now,' then heard footsteps on the landing. Siân would think she'd flipped if she heard her talking to herself.

The bedroom door opened.

'Did you get rid of them? Was it Jehovah's Witnesses?' Catrin asked, without looking up.

'More persistent than that,' a deep voice replied and she raised her eyes to see Mark smiling back at her in the mirror. 'I thought I'd come and give you a bit of moral support. Sian says good luck, good luck, good luck – apparently it's luckier if you say it three times – and she'll speak to you tonight.'

By the time Ben got to Newcastle Emlyn the earlier fog and rain had cleared and the sky was a beautiful blue with just a few fluffy clouds floating lazily in the expanse of azure. He pulled into the little car park by the castle and got out to stretch his legs. The market town was buzzing with people on this Saturday afternoon and from their ling-di-long pace Ben gathered the first of the season's holidaymakers had arrived. He negotiated his way through them along the high street, the only street, to Morgans the ironmongery, where power tools struggled for space alongside mops, gas lamps, and all kinds of paraphernalia. The ironmongery had been owned by the same family for years and the displays on the shelves had hardly changed since Ben had come here as a boy. He knocked his head against something hard as he entered and cursed silently under his breath. It took a minute or two for his eyes to adjust to the dimness and see that Mr Morgan, clad in his usual brown work coat, was behind the counter sorting nails into little bags.

'Pnawn da,' he ventured, determined to put his Welsh into practice this weekend.

'Good afternoon,' the ironmonger replied, lengthening the 'r' and letting his tongue vibrate the sound against the top of his palate. 'How can I help you?'

Ben felt deflated. This man had known he was a learner – and probably a fairly incompetent one at that – just from hearing him say two words. How on earth could he hope to improve his Welsh if the locals insisted on speaking English to him? He persevered. 'Mae'n braf.'

'Yes, it's fine now; looks pretty settled for the rest of the day but we're in for a rough night if the forecast is to be believed. Mind you, they get it wrong as often as they get it right.'

Ben gave up. The ironmonger was only trying to make it easier for him and anyway he had no idea what a memorial vase was in Welsh.

'I'm looking for a vase for my mother's grave.'

'Well now then, you've got a choice. Come with me; they're over here by the paint.'

Ben followed Mr Morgan to the other side of the shop. He wondered if all ironmongers wore these brown coats but, as this was the only ironmongery he'd ever been in, he didn't know. Anyway he liked the coat; it gave him confidence, just as he believed doctors' white coats gave patients confidence. But of course they didn't wear them any more. Health and safety risk, someone had tried to explain to him – he hadn't bothered to ask any more; those three little words 'health and safety' had that effect.

'There's this one, nice and simple, "In loving memory," black marble,' Mr Morgan said, as he blew at a layer of dust and then, finding that had little effect, rubbed at the vase with the sleeve of his brown coat. 'Very popular.'

Evidently so, Ben thought, but said nothing.

'Or this one? But you don't want this one because it's in Welsh, yes, no?'

Ben wasn't sure if the answer should be a yes or a no but he knew this was the one he wanted. He liked the fact it was

317

made from Welsh slate and the irony of putting a memorial in Welsh, the language she'd failed to share with him, on his mother's grave appealed to him.

'I'll take the Welsh one, please.'

'Oh, there we are then, up to you; "Byth mewn cof", always remembered," nice that.' The ironmonger nodded sagely. He put the vase into a brown box and handed it to Ben. 'That will be £110.'

'Do you still take cheques?'

'Yes of course. We haven't started that card malarkey here yet.'

Ben wrote the cheque in Welsh.

The ironmonger looked at it gravely and for a moment Ben thought he was going to refuse it but then Mr Morgan smiled broadly and opened the till with a flourish. 'Watch your head on those saucepans on your way out, won't you.'

Ben grinned and ducked as he approached the door. 'Diolch yn fawr.'

'Diolch yn fawr,' the ironmonger replied, before adding, 'Thank you,' for good measure.

In Pethau Pert, next door, Ben picked up a bunch of deep blue irises and, on the florist's advice, added a bunch of pale pink spray carnations and a sprig of gypsophila.

'The irises are lovely but they won't last see; these little carnations will go on for weeks and they're only £2.99 a bunch.' She trimmed the stalks, explaining to Ben that the shorter stems would prolong their life in the windswept graveyard and wrapped the flowers neatly in brown paper. Ben thanked her and walked back to his car thinking how absurd it was to still think in terms of good value and longevity when buying flowers for someone's grave.

Catrin took a sideways look at Mark as he walked alongside her into town. Since they had left Pencisely Crescent he had made a few attempts at conversation, but she had not been very forthcoming and mostly they had walked in silence. She wiped her strangely sweaty hands once more on her dress, hoping he didn't realise how nervous she felt. If it wasn't obvious to Mark then it wouldn't be obvious to Ralph she reasoned. She wanted to reach out for Mark's hand but then he would feel how sticky hers were and anyway he had his firmly tucked in his jacket pockets. Besides only boyfriends and girlfriends really held hands and, although she often pretended to herself they were a couple, in reality they weren't. As they got nearer the shopping centre Catrin could feel her heart quicken. She studied the shop windows to distract herself from the enormity of what was ahead. Eventually Mark broke the silence.

'How will you recognise him? TG's will be packed today; it always is on a Saturday.'

Catrin didn't reply.

'If he's tall and blond and good-looking, like you, he'll stand out for sure,' Mark answered his own question. 'Perhaps it's Greg Norman, Catz; perhaps you've got a fantastic talent for golf you're not yet aware of.'

'Since when does Greg Norman live in Bristol?' Catrin smiled at him, appreciating he was trying to lighten the mood. 'And anyway he's Australian and my donor is English.'

'David Duckham then: right build, blond, right era. He'd be great; bound to get free tickets for internationals.'

'Who's Dave Duck-face?'

'A legend, that's what he is, brilliant 70s winger – my dad's a big fan. Yes, that's probably why you can run so fast. You picked up amazing speed getting away from those geese in Roath Park, 0 to 60 in three seconds I'd say.'

'Anyway,' Catrin said firmly, 'we know his name is Ralph and we don't need to recognise him because he'll recognise us – I sent him a photo.'

They had reached St David's II shopping centre and Mark held the door open for her.

'Thanks.' Her hand touched his as she passed him; she felt his warmth and then he snatched it away. She frowned; he sent out such mixed messages – coming round uninvited to accompany her into town then keeping his distance. But she had more pressing things to worry about right now as they headed for TG's.

Mark had been right, the cafe was crowded and it took Catrin a few seconds to spot Steffan sitting at a table at the far end. As they approached he held out his hand for a high five which Mark mistook for the offer of a handshake. They both let their hands drop, clearly embarrassed.

'Hi Steff, so glad you're here early; good to have you on my side, united front and all that,' Catrin said, squeezing his arm and sitting down beside him.

'It's not us against him you know, Catrin; we're all on the same side.'

She looked at Mark for support but he seemed to be edgy, anxious. 'OK guys, I'll get you some drinks and leave you to it. What can I get you, coffee?'

Steffan made a face. 'Yuck, no thanks Mark mate; make mine a hot chocolate.'

'Me too, please,' Catrin said.

As they waited for Mark to return she dug out the list of questions she wanted to ask Ralph and showed them to Steffan.

'OMG, Catrin, you're going to scare him to death; it will be like the Spanish Inquisition.'

'I need to know, Steff; these things are important to me and part of why I want to meet him in the first place.'

Steffan shrugged. 'Well, you do what you want, but I'm going to play it cool, relaxed.'

Mark reappeared and placed the hot chocolates in front of them. 'OK bye then you two – good luck; text me later, Catrin,' he said and left.

Catrin took a long sip as she watched him leave, aware for the first time she felt excited as well as nervous. She was used to the sensation but this was different from a show's opening night. This meeting could change her life for ever. 'Mm, this is good.' She wiped chocolate froth from her face, 'my mouth is so dry.'

'Have one of my little smiley pills – that will calm you,' Steffan suggested, fishing in his pocket for his box of supplies.

'No thanks, once was enough. I want all my wits about me,' Catrin whispered, looking around to check no one was listening to their conversation. 'And you shouldn't take them either; you don't need them Steff.'

'They do no harm Catz; the sooner the government legalise these little smilers the better – and they will, eventually, when they realise they can make some money from them. Then everyone will be happy. Win–win.' He smiled at her. 'Anyway, I don't know what you're worried about; you're bound to get on with Daddy-o, you being interested in art and all that. He studied art at college – he might even be an artist now.'

Catrin sipped her drink slowly, trying to make it last. Hot chocolate was a stupid thing to have chosen; she could never resist gulping it down and it was making her hot.

'It's me that should be worried,' Steffan prattled on. 'He's certain to like you, with you being a girl; fathers and daughters always have a special bond don't they? I've been reading up on Bristol Rovers – he's bound to be a supporter isn't he? I got this book out of the library – *The Rovers Return* – clever that, isn't it? It tells you everything about the club and I've even learnt the words to "Goodnight Irene" – depressing mind. Perhaps Ralph and I could go together; there's quite a few games left this season and I've checked the trains; it will only cost me £13.50 return if I go early in the morning. Come on The Pirates. Or the Gas – that's what they were called before they moved, 'cos their ground, see, was next to the gasworks. And do you know their most famous son? Alan Ball – played in the winning England side, 1966 ...'

Catrin switched off, irritated by Steff's babbling, and checked her watch. Twenty-five past three. She glanced towards the entrance then at the people seated in the cafe and queuing at the counter. No, he wasn't here yet. Then a tall, fair-haired man, dressed in a light linen suit, walked in and looked around. Catrin held her breath and nudged Steffan who abruptly stopped talking. She took in the man's pale blue shirt and leather loafers. He was carrying one of the broadsheets in his left hand. Sophisticated, Catrin thought, as she struggled to her feet, feeling her legs wobble beneath her. The man smiled and walked briskly in their direction. She reached out her hand ready to shake his then felt a rush of embarrassment as he leaned over to kiss a glamorous woman sitting at the table next to them. Aware her arm was frozen in mid-air she pretended to move the chair opposite closer to their table. Before she had a chance to sit down again she heard a lazy drawl. 'Hi there guys; you Catrin and Steffan?'

'Ralph?' Steff was on his feet high fiving their biological father. Catrin looked at him and smiled. Really he couldn't be anyone else; one glance and she saw herself or at least her nose. Ralph turned his attention to her and she could see he was undecided whether to kiss her on the cheek or high-five her too. She pressed her legs against her chair to stop them shaking and extended her hand. He shook it, his grip firm, assured.

'Can I get you two something?'

Catrin looked at her quarter-full mug of hot chocolate that was now cold. She opted for an orange juice this time, hoping it wouldn't react with the hot chocolate and cause her stomach to swell.

'What about you Steffan; what would you like?'

'What are you having, Ralph?' Steffan asked.

'I think a double espresso is in order.'

'Great idea, Ralph; I'll have the same, please.'

Catrin gave Steff a look, which he purposely ignored.

'Anything to eat?'

Catrin shook her head. She was feeling slightly sick.

'No thanks, Ralph, trying to keep off carbs; my body is a temple and all that,' Steffan blurted. Ralph smiled and joined the queue at the counter.

'Since when do you drink coffee?' Catrin asked.

'Since now. Mirror other people's actions and they'll like you – it was on *This Morning* a couple of days ago.'

'Oh well, you're best buddies already – coloured chinos, Chucks: you could be twins.' Catrin made no attempt to keep the sarcasm out of her voice.

'Well, I think he looks cool, hip.'

'Like a lollipop: skinny trousers, beer belly – not a good look.'

'Oh come on Catrin; he looks good for 40-something.'

Catrin nudged him to shut up as Ralph approached the table once more. He laid the plastic tray down, took his seat, and picked up his tiny coffee cup. Catrin thought how Ben would have put her glass in front of her and taken the tray back. She noticed the index and middle fingers on Ralph's right hand were nicotine stained. Otherwise his hands were very elegant – long fingers, nicely trimmed nails. The boys were talking and she made a conscious effort to tune in. I'm being ridiculous, she thought. I've been wanting to meet this man for six months and now I can't think of anything to say. She glanced at her list of questions; of course there were all kinds of things she wanted to know.

In the next gap in the conversation she asked, 'So what do you do, Ralph?'

'I'm a portrait artist.'

'Oh, how interesting. Have you painted anyone famous?'

'You could say that,' Ralph replied mysteriously. He made a little gesture with his hand suggesting he could not name names. 'Of course, it's all done to commission. I'm glad to say I've no need to organise little exhibitions to sell my work; people come to me.' He gave a smug grin.

'Catrin's going to be an artist too,' Steff said.

'Oh yes?'

'Yes she's going to Aberystwyth to study Art.'

'If I get the grades in my A levels,' Catrin added.

'Mmm, I studied in Paris of course.' Ralph sipped his coffee. 'So Catrin, what does your name mean then?'

Why do people think Welsh names have to mean something? Catrin thought, irritated. She shrugged. 'What does Ralph mean?'

He looked bemused.

'You're familiar with my name of course.' Steffan's voice sounded strange to Catrin, bright and animated. 'There are Stefan's from loads of different countries – it's pretty international. But I'm a little bit unique – mine is spelled with two f's.'

'You can't be a little bit unique, Steffan,' Ralph said, 'either you're unique or not.'

'Well not then; there are lots of double f Steffans in Wales.' He sounded deflated, as if he'd just been ticked off.

They picked up their drinks again. Catrin noticed Steffan did not actually drink any of his espresso before putting his cup down.

Ralph drained his. 'Before Paris I studied Art here in Cardiff. You'll love university I'm sure, Catrin – lots of time to experiment with your style, no need to think commercially, just sheer joy. There's nothing like a blank canvas, gorgeous paints, the excitement, the adventure.'

Catrin smiled, warmed by his enthusiasm. His eagerness was making his handsome face striking.

'Have you seen the Davies sisters' collection in the museum here?'

She nodded.

'Absolutely fabulous. So what's your favourite painting there then?'

She considered for a moment. 'Well I really like Renoir's "Blue Lady".' She glanced at Ralph, who was nodding. 'But, my absolute favourite; it's got to be the "Lilies".'

He clapped his hands excitedly. 'And mine, totally, amazing Monet could do that through his cataracts – astounding; but oh Catrin, *the* place to see the Lilies is in the

Musée de l'Orangerie.'

Catrin nodded. Really his French was beautiful.

'So you must be a Pirates supporter,' Steff cut in.

Ralph looked confused.

'Bristol Rovers, doing quite well this season; John Ward's doing a good job for you.' Steffan ploughed on.

'Ah, to be honest mate, I'm not that into football – Muay Thai is my sport.'

Steffan said nothing. From the look on his face Catrin knew he had no more idea what Muay Thai was than she did.

'But if I had to pick a team it would be Man U; always back a winner, I say.' Ralph nodded, seemingly appreciating his own wisdom. Steffan nodded too.

Ralph sat back and looked around. Catrin surreptitiously checked her list of questions and drew a deep breath. 'So, Ralph, you've given us good quality genes I trust; no fatal illnesses in your family?' She added a little laugh to give the impression she was joking.

'Don't be silly, Catrin,' Steffan said, 'Ralph here looks the picture of health.'

Ralph just smiled.

'Your family's not particularly prone to cancer, heart disease, diabetes?' she persisted.

'Oh, lighten up, Catrin.' Steffan pulled a face. She glared at him.

'No, the young lady is right to ask,' Ralph volunteered. 'And no, Catrin, you've come from good quality stock I can assure you. A few lunatics down the years but nothing serious.' He and Steffan both laughed loudly.

'So tell us more about yourself,' Steffan said.

For the next twenty minutes Ralph told them about his upbringing in Hackney; his university days in Cardiff and the pubs he remembered; meeting his wife Miriam; his days as an artist on Paris's Left Bank; life with the in-laws in Yorkshire; his adventures as a water bailiff, and moving to Bristol to attend karate classes with Sensei Takumi. Occasionally

Steffan nodded and fed him questions.

'So does that mean you're a black belt, Ralph?' he asked, clearly impressed.

'Well, almost. I've got my brown with two stripes; that's the next one down. But then they moved the classes to another part of town and I had to change buses twice to get there so I was like ...' Ralph trailed off.

Steffan came to his rescue. 'But you could defend yourself in a sticky situation, right?'

'Totally, mate.'

The next thing Catrin knew Ralph was on his feet adopting what she assumed was a karate stance. She looked around but thankfully no one was interested and the table previously occupied by the smart man and the sophisticated lady was now empty.

Relaxing his pose Ralph said, 'Now I'm on my feet I'll just go to the loo. I wouldn't mind another coffee.'

'Sure, Ralph, espresso?' Steff asked.

'Double, please.' Ralph sauntered towards the toilets.

'He could have yours; you don't seem to have drunk much of it,' Catrin said drily.

'Isn't he brilliant?' Steffan's eyes were shining. 'I just feel such a connection to him; you know it's almost as if I can feel myself reflected in him.'

'He's OK,' Catrin volunteered. Steffan got up to go to the counter.

Armed with the vase and flowers Ben returned to his car feeling satisfied. Who needs big shopping centres? he thought as he drove out of Newcastle Emlyn and pointed the car west. You could get everything in these small towns: maybe you didn't get the choice but really, who needed a selection of ten different types of olive oil. He laughed. Why had he thought of olive oil? That was a bit random. Probably because he was hungry? He reached for a mint and crunched it noisily. He ate a few more as he drove slowly along the meandering roads until he met the sea at Llangrannog.

He parked the car beside Bethania chapel and walked up to the cemetery, noticing the few graves that had flowers on them were sporting short-stemmed spray carnations. The florist was obviously very persuasive. Reaching his parents' grave he placed the vase and flowers on the narrow ledge and sat down heavily, momentarily shocked at seeing his mother's newly engraved name beneath his father's. The inscription read:

Thomas Edward Alun Lewis
Dolau, Llangrannog and Llandaff, Cardiff
1938 - 1977
Margaret Ann Lewis
Awelon, Llangrannog and Llandaff, Cardiff
1938 - 2012
'Peace, perfect peace'

Ben cleared his throat failing to shift the lump. He gazed out to sea; it was bright blue and flat with just a ripple of white here and there to suggest everything was not as calm as it seemed. He breathed deeply, aware suddenly how much he needed this – to stop and do nothing, to clear his mind and calmly reflect on recent life changes. So many years of coming to this cemetery, he thought now, so many different emotions. The raw grief at his father's burial giving way to thirty years or so when that overwhelming pain had dwindled to regret and the annual visits had been pleasurable almost – little more than an enjoyable walk to check the headstone was still secure and the grass had been cut around it. How different he felt today.

Ben unwrapped the flowers, filled the vase with water from the tap beside the footpath and arranged the irises and carnations as best he could. Standing back to admire them he smiled ruefully at the Welsh inscription on the slate vase; how pathetic that he was still trying to score little victories over his mother. There was little satisfaction to be gained from winning points against her now she wasn't around to retaliate. But easier said than done, Ben admitted to himself, aware he was still cross with her for many things, not least for taking it upon herself to spill the beans to Catrin.

At the sound of someone else coming up the path he turned and headed back towards the car.

'Shw mae?' the stranger greeted him as they passed each other.

'Shw mae?' Ben responded smiling, knowing the how-do greeting did not require a reply.

Chapter Twenty-one

While Ralph was in Cardiff meeting his donor offspring Miriam was taking advantage of his absence to tackle a long list of jobs. Gardening jobs. And nothing pleased her more. She breathed deeply, taking in the tomato smell she loved, the smell that held so much promise. She tucked the plants into a hanging basket, covering them gently with a blanket of fleece just in case Mr Frost paid an unexpectedly late visit. If growing tomatoes in baskets really worked that would be great; it would free up space in her vegetable patch. Maybe she'd try cultivating asparagus. Miriam smiled. She'd rushed around all morning and got the housework done and now she had the whole afternoon to herself to spend in the garden. Even better it was not raining.

Oscar, next door's black cat, patrolled the fence. Miriam acknowledged his presence with a quick 'hello you' but resisted the urge to stroke his shiny coat with her soiled hands. Tomatoes planted she moved to the flower bed and started splitting clumps of snowdrops. The cat elegantly and soundlessly landed at her side, rubbed against her leg and then settled to diligently clean his coat. Soil clung to Miriam's fingernails. She knew she should wear gloves and mostly she did but the sheer joy of handling the warming soil of late spring outweighed the satisfaction of clean hands.

Oscar followed her to the herb patch where she set about cutting back the sage that had grown leggy. He rolled about in the soil and then settled beside her to clean himself once more, as she moved on to cut out the side shoots from her fast growing sweet peas.

'A couple more months, Oscar, and we'll be cutting these for the house. Now that's something to look forward to, isn't

329

it?'

The cat ignored her, his little pink tongue now cleaning his nether regions as he deftly held his leg aloft.

Miriam worked on without a break. She trimmed the lavender that bordered the narrow path all the way from the kitchen door to the old tree trunk at the bottom of the garden – but only by a little; she rather liked the fact it encroached on the path and that, come July, every time she went to put the clothes on the washing line she would brush against it, sending wafts of beautiful aroma in every direction. Yes, there was so much to look forward to.

At 5 p.m. she raked the moss from the lawn, bagged the rubbish, and straightened up. She put all the tools away in the shed, scrubbed her hands with a nail brush at the kitchen sink, poured herself a glass of Merlot, picked up her mobile and went back to the bottom of the garden to sit on the old tree trunk. Aching with a satisfying tiredness, she texted Dave (or 'lovely Dave from work' as she referred to him out of Ralph's earshot) to tell him she had some spare snowdrop and daffodil bulbs he might like to have. After a few sips of wine she called Ralph.

'Hi, where are you?'

'On the train.'

Miriam sighed. Just hearing her husband's voice put a downer on her spirits. 'Yes, I can hear that, but where is the train?'

'Stuck at the Severn Tunnel Junction. As usual no reason given.'

'So, when will you be home?'

'No idea, as I said – stuck at Severn Tunnel.'

Miriam grimaced. 'Oh, OK then – I've been in the garden all afternoon so I'm going for a long soak.'

'It's all right for some.'

She took another sip of wine.

'So do you want to ask me how it went?'

Miriam didn't but said, 'Yes, of course, how did it go

330

Ralph?'

'Oh, you're clearly not interested'. He sounded petulant.

'Of course I'm interested,' she coaxed.

'Well I'll tell you about it later. Go and have your soak. I'll call at the The Square and Compass on my way home.'

'OK, bye then, Ralph. Love you,' she added automatically.

'Bye,' he said.

Miriam ate a quick snack and then ran her bath, adding eucalyptus drops to ease her aching muscles. The minty scent and warm water soothed her and she soaked so long her fingers turned white and prune-like. She topped up with hot water again and closed her eyes, letting herself slip under the surface and shaking her head so her long hair soaked through. Far away she heard a sound. Sitting up she opened her eyes – was that the doorbell?

'Ding-dong.' There it was again. Climbing out of the bath she wiped herself down with a towel and struggled into her dressing gown, the cotton material twisting and clinging to her damp skin. Grabbing another towel she wrapped it tightly around her head as she ran downstairs and flung the door open.

'Oh, sorry Miriam; I've obviously called at an inconvenient time.'

Miriam tightened the dressing-gown cord. 'No, not at all Dave, sorry, come in, come in.' She ushered him into the kitchen.

Dave stood in the middle of the room, awkward and smiling.

'Sorry I've just had a bath, you know how stiff you get; em… would you like a cup of tea or something cold? The bulbs are out in the garden and you can have some Welsh poppies too – they spread everywhere but I do like their bright orange and yellow colours; not sure why they're called Welsh poppies, mind.' She stopped, aware she was rambling on. What an idiot he must think her.

'A cup of tea would be lovely, Miriam; tell you what, why

don't I make it while you get dressed and then perhaps you can show me your garden?'

She smiled broadly. 'Love to, Dave; OK, give me five minutes. Mugs on the top there, teabags and sugar by the kettle, milk in the fridge and there's cake in the tin by the microwave.'

She bounded back up the stairs.

At the entrance to Cardiff Central station Catrin parted from Ralph and Steffan. Luckily her bus was already at the stand. As she found a seat she was aware how exhausted she felt and it was a few minutes before she could muster the energy to get out her phone. She sent Mark a one-word text – '*Good*' – and received one back almost immediately saying '*Gladx*'. She was pleased he'd added a kiss. Once home she went to her room, drew the curtains, took off her shoes and crawled into bed.

The next thing she was aware of was her mother giving her a gentle shake. 'Supper's ready, love.'

Catrin was tempted to say she had no appetite and just wanted to go back to sleep, but she knew this would cause her mother to ask all kinds of questions so she struggled out of bed and followed her downstairs.

Her mum had laid the table for two. Tom would be out with his footballing friends for hours yet but she was relieved her father was still out too. He was probably avoiding her; upset she'd actually gone through with meeting Ralph. But she was glad he wasn't there, she wasn't ready to face him yet. She needed to work out for herself how the meeting had gone before she shared her views with anyone. Over supper her mother asked about it and Catrin again simply said 'good.' She answered her mum's factual questions about Ralph but offered no further opinion and thankfully her mother did not press her further. As soon as they'd eaten Catrin excused herself and escaped back to her bedroom.

She lay on her bed, clutching Little Ted and staring up at

332

her ceiling, but after an hour she was no clearer how she felt. Maybe a chat with Lisa or Siân would help if either was online at 8 p.m. on a Saturday night. She switched on her laptop and after what seemed an age the icons finally settled down and the screen reacted to her commands. Lisa was logged on.

C: *You there Lisa?*

L: *Sure am, tell ALL,* came the immediate reply. *OMG can't believe you actually met him, Mark says it was good but what's he like?*

Catrin hesitated.

C: *Cool – that's him really.*

L: *As in?*

C: *Well, he's an artist – can you believe that's actually his job! And he's done portraits of really famous people and everything.*

L: *Who?*

C: *Not sure, but I think A-listers!!!!!!!*

L: *OMG ... and?*

C: *Well he looks really young, like Steff's big brother really – tall, blond, brown eyes.*

L: *Available???*

C: *Oh, sick, Lisa; that would make me your mother-in-law (ish)! And anyway, no, he's got a wife – Miriam.*

L: *Artist too?*

C: *Actually not sure what she does; he didn't say.*

L: *Kids?*

C: *Negative – except me and Steff of course and our donor half-siblings.*

An icon indicated Siân had logged on.

S: *Hi Catz,soooooooooo glad you're online, sorry, just back from work (pants!- too' quiet – sent home early again.) Well, what was he like?*

C: *Hi, Siân – yes he was nice – you know – a little bit full of himself – but I think that was just nerves; Steff was exactly the same*

L: *Catz - you still there?*

333

C: *Yes Lisa, just talking to Siân too.*

L: *So did he look like a proper artist?*

C: *Didn't have a smock and a beret if that's what you mean! No, dressed really cool – skinny chinos, chucks, T-shirt and jacket. Steff and Ralph could borrow each other's clothes!*

Catrin realised the way she'd described Ralph to Lisa contradicted what she'd said to Steffan in TGs. On reflection perhaps he had looked cool but she was aware now that wasn't how she'd wanted him to look. Ordinary or even boring would have been more reassuring, more fatherly. As it was he'd seemed a bit Mick Jagger – trying a touch too hard to look young and hip.'

S: *'So did you really get on? No awkward silences?'*

C: *'Yes, we did (get on, that is), he's really into art (obv), so we talked quite a bit about that. You know there were a few times when we were all waiting for someone else to say something and a few times when I couldn't think of anything to say! But on the whole, good.'*

L: *Sounds like he's got taste. Conversation?*

Ralph had actually spent most of the time talking about himself but Catrin knew Lisa desperately wanted this meeting to be successful as a good omen for hopefully meeting her own donor one day.

C: *Flowing! Didn't stop talking!*

S: *I guess the bottom line is – was it just like meeting any random stranger for the first time or did it feel special?*

That indeed was the question, Catrin thought ruefully. Trust Siân to be able to reduce it to one simple sentence. But the answer was not simple.

C: *To be honest, not sure. I definitely look a bit like him – he's got the nose too!!!, and there's the art link but can't really say it was more than that.*

L: *So jealous, you actually meeting him, sure it felt amazing.*

C: *Totally, like finding the final bit of a jigsaw.*

L: *So, seeing Daddy2 again?*

C: *Deffo. Soon* ☺.
S: *So, seeing Ralph again?*
C: *Not sure, maybe* ☹.

By the time Ben parked his Volvo in the car park beside The Ship Inn he was starving. Good, they'd be serving in half an hour, just time for a quick pint. He took a couple of minutes to stretch and breathe in the salty air. He noticed that the little village had had its annual facelift: the chip shop on the corner now painted a bright turquoise, the shutters on the Pentre Arms a pale sea green and the corner shop had its pre-season profusion of buckets and spades hanging outside expectantly.

Old Jac was perched in his usual spot at the bar when Ben pushed open the pub's sturdy door.

'Ben, boy, long time, how have you been?'

'Not so bad, Jac, but better now that I'm here. Didn't see you when Jane and I came down in March.'

'No, bachan, annual holiday; two days in Cardigan, staying with my sister.' Jac made a face which Ben took to indicate it was a duty visit. 'Pint, Ben?'

This was the ritual. They both knew old Jac never bought anyone a drink, except himself, and only then when he really had to.

'I'll just dump my bag upstairs and I'll be down to join you.'

'The Erin suite.' Cai behind the bar laughed as he handed Ben the key.

'That's room two then,' Ben said, adding, 'start a tab for me please. I'll have a pint of Guinness, whatever Jac's having, and one for yourself.'

Five minutes later, having called his cousin to thank her for organising the inscription on his parents's headstone, Ben took a welcome first gulp of the rich, black beer. Jac had already downed most of his pint.

'You've quite a thirst on you, Jac; what have you been up to?'

'He's been waiting for someone – anyone – to arrive for the past hour,' Cai teased.

Jac drew noisily on what was left of his pint as Ben sipped appreciatively at his. 'So what are the specials tonight?' he asked.

Cai handed him the slate board. He was so hungry that even the mussels with leeks and white wine sounded wonderful and he didn't really like shellfish. He toyed with the idea of ordering the lemon sole but, taking advantage of Jane's absence, plumped for the gourmet home-made Welsh beefburger with local smoked bacon and Hafod cheese on a crusty bun. It was served with home-made chunky chips and chilli jam. Ben drank some more, the black stuff already relaxing him.

'I'll have the baked goat's cheese tart with local honey and fresh thyme to start, please Cai. And another pint when you're ready.' Jac looked at him. 'Oh, and for Jac of course.'

'Right you are, coming up,' Cai called cheerily as he passed the food order through a hatch to the kitchen.

Another couple of old men joined Jac at the bar and Ben settled down at a dark oak table with a copy of *The Guardian* to take his mind off his rumbling stomach. Ben liked The Ship. He had been worried he wouldn't following its makeover a couple of years previously. But the young owners had managed to mix old with new and what had emerged was the right side of comfortable. The impressive new bar, made from weathered wood to resemble the bow of a ship, sat happily with smart chrome fittings, the oak tables and chairs, and the rustic slate floor. They'd kept the atmosphere of the old pub and kept the locals. Cai put the fresh pint down in front of him and cleared away the empty glass. I don't really have a local in Cardiff, Ben mused, as the second pint hit his empty stomach.

'What do you think of the colour of the chip shop then, Ben? Moody Blue it's called, Beryl says.' Ben couldn't work out from his tone of voice whether Jac approved of the colour or not and, deciding it was safer not to express an opinion as

Beryl was probably related to Jac in some way, said instead, 'The whole village is looking spruced up ready for the visitors.'

'Aye, every year we look forward to them coming and then when they're here ...' Jac trailed off.

'They're all right when they're in the minority,' one of his friends added drily.

The conversation stalled, partly Ben thought because Jac and his friends felt uncomfortable speaking to one another in English, something they insisted on doing for his benefit. He couldn't wait to be able to converse with them in Welsh. Well, after his intensive language course over the summer surely he'd be able to do that.

Cai laid Ben's first course, served on a slab of slate, in front of him.

'Mm, this looks superb, thank you.' He tucked into the cheese tart, eating far too quickly but, having not eaten since breakfast, the food tasted wonderful. He kept his eyes on his plate and *The Guardian*, hoping to discourage conversation with the old boys until he'd had his fill.

'It's their wretched 4x4's – someone should tell them they're not suitable for our small country roads,' the third member of the trio observed.

'Everyone knows they're city vehicles. Chelsea, that's the natural habitat of the 4x4.' Jac laughed at his own witticism. And then their conversation drifted to Newcastle Emlyn mart prices and the weather. Ben got up to replace *The Guardian* with the local *Cambrian News* to read while eating his main course.

He was still reading it, as he finished his pudding of rich chocolate tart with Bailey's ice cream. He heard the first strains of singing coming from the back bar. Ben pushed his empty plate aside and rose.

'Pint boys?' he asked. Three heads nodded their acceptance. 'Who's singing then?'

'Local choir – practising carols.'

337

'In April?'

'Yes, for May.' Jac nodded seriously.

'Who's May?'

The three old boys laughed and Ben, mellowed by beer and a full belly, laughed with them. Cai put three pints on the bar.

'Not who, bachan, what, isn't it?' Jac explained as the other two laughed some more. 'Well I don't know about big city ways,' he continued, 'but round here May's a month.'

Ben listened to the singers until the end of the piece. 'They're good; they don't sound as if they need to practise for another eight months,' he said, looking at Jac over his pint glass.

'Bachan, bachan, you don't understand. In Welsh we have May carols as well as Christmas carols. It's an old tradition to welcome in the spring.'

'Rebirth of the land,' one of his friends added solemnly.

'Sounds a bit pagan so I'm guessing they don't sing these carols in chapel then?' Ben said.

'No, more pub than chapel. This group that practises here go round the villages on May Day and sing on village squares or in the pubs if it's raining. It's an old tradition and they've restarted it. I think it's Welsh learners mostly in this choir – you know what they're like, often keener than the locals.'

'Nothing worse than poacher turned bailiff,' one of the old boys said as all three supped their drinks.

'Or a reformed smoker,' Jac added solemnly.

Ben wasn't sure if the beer he'd downed too quickly was affecting his reasoning or if this conversation actually didn't make sense. He sat down again with the paper.

On page six there were reports of a stolen bike and the theft of a bottle of wine from the local supermarket. Ben liked the idea of being somewhere where such trivia made the newspaper. Page fourteen was taken up by a report about the local Rotary Club, on page sixteen there was an appeal for more people to join the dolphin watch in New Quay and an invitation to a 'neighbours' coffee morning'. By the time he'd drunk his third pint Ben felt he was local.

'Whisky chaser, boys?' The three nodded their appreciation. He stood and signalled to Cai.

'Penderyn – none of that blended rubbish,' Jac said loudly

'Ice?' Cai asked. All four shook their heads. Cai filled the glasses and lined them up on the bar.

'You're very lucky to live here, you know; it's a real community,' Ben said with authority, the alcohol by now making him believe his thoughts were particularly profound.

Jac's friends nodded sagely.

'Oh, you don't know the half of it, Ben bach. It looks ideal now but in winter it's dead,' Jac said.

The older of Jac's friends seemed embarrassed. 'Jac, bachan,' he said, putting a restraining arm on Jac's. 'This gentleman has been buying us drinks all night; the least you can do is agree with him.'

'I like it in winter when it's our own,' Jac's other friend said, smiling apologetically at Ben.

Jac, made contrary by drink, carried on, 'It's dead apart from those bloody noisy drones from Aberporth. Dead, I tell you, because all the young people have gone – forced out: no work; houses priced too high by bloody visitors who buy them as holiday homes.'

Jac's friend glanced at Ben. 'We wouldn't have any work if it wasn't for the visitors – tourism, that's what puts bread on the table for lots of the families around here. It's what's kept my two here and I'm grateful for that. So I welcome them with open arms.' For a minute Ben thought the man was about to hug him and he lifted his glass in self-defence.

'Cheers,' he said firmly.

'Cheers,' the three replied in unison, 'and Iechyd Da,' Jac added.

'Good health,' his friend translated hurriedly.

Ben sat down again, nursing his whisky. That's what's missing, he told himself. I don't feel I belong to a community – how many people do I actually know in my part of Cardiff? It dawned on him he'd been looking for a sense of community for a long time. He remembered being a locum as a young doctor in Prince Charles Hospital, Merthyr. How surprised he'd been by the numbers who flooded in at visiting time. In the Heath Hospital, Cardiff, where he'd trained, close family came of course, although a lot of his patients seemed to have no visitors at all. But in Merthyr the whole family, and it seemed to him the whole street, would visit – even if the patient was only in for a couple of days. It was then he'd decided to look for a Valleys practice. He remembered his mother's horror when he told her he'd been offered a job in Pontypridd. She had had such high hopes for him: an academic, teaching medicine in the Heath; that's what she would have liked to be able to tell her chapel friends. A Valleys town GP did not have the same kudos, he realised now, and felt her disappointment. But it was a borrowed community. Not really his. This small West Wales community, perched on the edge of the Irish Sea, this was his. This is where his roots were. He felt full of bonhomie.

'Anyone for a nightcap?'

Chapter Twenty-two

By the time Ralph arrived home at 11.30 p.m. Miriam had been in bed for hours reading a Mills and Boon. From the way he slammed the front door and was humming 'Whiter Shade of Pale', she guessed he'd had four pints. She amended that to five as he tripped on the fifth run of the stairs. Good, that meant she did not need to pretend to be asleep.

She didn't bother to look up as came in. 'Hello, my little angel. Still awake waiting for little old me?' She recoiled from his beery kiss.

'Mm, you smell lovely, Miri-Mw'. Perfume for me?' He collapsed on to the bed.

'Wrinkle cream,' she replied and carried on reading. The heroine swooned and the dashing, tall, dark and handsome young man caught her.

'Your eyes are red, Miri-Mw, too much reading – put the book down and talk to Ralphie.'

Miriam placed the book slowly and deliberately on her bedside table; she could hardly enjoy it with Ralph twittering on in this infantile way. He always talked like this after a few drinks and it grated on her. Now she felt like slapping his smirking face. A white froth had formed at one side of his mouth and even the thought of touching him was repulsive.

'So how was your day, Ralph?' she forced herself to sound interested.

'Well, Catrin is lovely. And Steffan. They both are. Lookers – like their dad,' he slurred.

'Ah well, that's what's important Ralph; that they're beautiful.' she said flippantly. Her husband missed the obvious sarcasm.

'Well it really helps, Miri-Mw, people like pretty people.

Fact.'

'That must be why you're so popular, Ralph.'

He nodded as he tried to undo the laces of his Chucks, gave up and pulled them off. He hurled them into the far corner and they struck a little Victorian chair that Miriam had inherited from her grandmother.

'And clever. They're both very clever. University clever.'

Ralph heaved himself off the bed and went to the bathroom. Miriam found she wanted to know more despite herself. When he came back she asked carefully, 'So you got on well with both of them?'

'Yep, really good; lots in common, she's arty and he likes football.' He lay down again and tugged at the duvet, wrapping it around him.

'Football?'

'Yeah.'

'But you've never been interested in football.' Miriam emphasised the word never. There weren't many things that Ralph had actually never been interested in.

'Oh, I've always said it's a beautiful game.' He emphasised the always.

'*You* didn't say that – someone famous said that, Ralph.'

His mobile vibrated as a text came in. He fiddled with the buttons, swore and fiddled some more then experimented holding the phone close to his face and further away before he returned it to within a couple of inches of his nose.

'It's from Steff – "*Grt to mt u, Pirates anytime soon?*" he read. 'Love, could you text him back for me? My eyes are a bit bleary.'

'And mine are tired and red, as you said.' But Miriam took the mobile anyway. 'OK, what do you want to say?'

'*Good to meet you 2, footie yes, will be in touch. Hope your Sat night as wild as mine!!!*'

Miriam stopped texting as Ralph was mid-sentence. 'I thought you said it was going to be one meeting only – just to see them, out of curiosity, and that would be it?' Her voice

342

was low and menacing but beer had rendered Ralph immune to the nuance.

'Oh, well, I didn't think we'd gel so well.' He laughed at the rhyming, at his cleverness.

Miriam flung the phone at him, the message to Steffan lost in mid-air.

'Oh Miri-Mw, don't be cross,' Ralph gurgled.

He leaned over and picked up a bouquet of crushed garage forecourt flowers that he must have thrown on the floor as he collapsed on the bed – pink chrysanthemums, a lone yellow gerbera (now bent in resignation), straggly gypsophila, and an alarmingly large purple butterfly on a stick huddled together in garish printed cellophane. They had obviously been huddled together like that for days.

'I know how much you like flowers so I bought you these.' He stuck the bunch under her nose.

'You shouldn't have,' she muttered.

'Oh, it's nothing,' he whispered, smiling.

'No, I mean it, you really shouldn't have,' she said.

There was no reply. Ralph's mouth was open but he was already fast asleep.

Ben woke to the sound of seagulls and a thick head. He got up quickly before he could be tempted to roll over and go back to sleep. Tugging at the sash window, which begrudgingly gave way, he opened it as far as possible, allowing a waft of salty air to fill the room. He stood there for a few minutes, quite still, breathing deeply. Already there were some dog walkers on the beach and he watched as a golden labrador and its companion, a Yorkshire terrier, raced for a ball. The owner threw the ball into the water five times and each time it was the labrador which got there first. But still the terrier ran for it. Ben smiled, admiring the little dog's optimism.

Deciding that a shower, lots of water, a good breakfast, and a quick run was just what he needed before heading east, he moved rapidly, arriving down in the bar just before nine.

'Bore da, Cai, it's a lovely morning.'

'Sure is, there's a definite promise of summer out there today. Full Welsh?'

'Yes please, and a pint. Of water, that is.'

Cai grinned and set off towards the kitchen as Ben sat down with the Sunday papers. He'd have a good read; let his breakfast settle before he went for a run. Ben started with the sports pages. He read the preview for the big match between Swansea and Chelsea and, as he was about to move on to an account of the rugby match between Neath and Cardiff, his breakfast arrived.

'Thanks, Cai. Looks good.'

Ben tucked in hungrily. Mm, that laverbread was lovely. He only ever had it when he stayed here. Jane had offered to buy it from the market but he'd declined. He liked the fact he only ate laverbread in Llangrannog and so it stayed special. Now its salty taste and silky texture combined perfectly with the thick-cut bacon and double-yolked egg and sent sensations of pleasure around his mouth. He didn't get back to the sports pages until his plate was wiped clean with a hunk of home-made bread. An hour and several coffees later, he bundled his clothes into his kit bag, donned his running gear and headed back downstairs.

'OK, I'll check out now, please.'

'I'm afraid last night's tab is a bit steep.' Cai grimaced as he printed the bill and pushed it face down across the bar towards him.

'Friends are very costly,' Ben observed with a smile, handing over his credit card.

As they waited for the card to register he asked the barman to remind him of the carol he'd particularly liked the previous night.

Cai's rich tenor voice reverberated around the empty bar as he sang, 'A pheth bynnag ddaw i'm blino; Canu wnaf a gadael iddo.'

'And it means: "whatever comes to trouble you, just ignore

it and carry on singing"?' Ben checked.

'Yes, precisely.'

'I think that's pretty good. Well thanks, Cai; it's been great, as usual. I'll be down again soon; I'll bring Jane next time.'

'Good, see you soon then, Ben; hwyl.'

'Hwyl.' Ben opened the pub's heavy oak door and stepped out into brilliant spring sunshine. Flinging his bag into the car, he checked his watch and set off along the coast path. Today he opted to run south towards Penbryn. The path climbed sharply and, just before it levelled out, he stopped for a few minutes to get his breath back and look down at the village nestled in the deep valley below. There were a couple of men working on their boats in the tiny boatyard and on the sandy beach the Sunday morning dog walkers had given way to small groups of people. There was a family playing French cricket and a couple of youngsters throwing a Frisbee back and forth. He could hear snippets of their conversation and their laughter drifted towards him on the light breeze. Ben was tempted to sit down on the nearby bench and spend the rest of his morning soaking up the spring warmth and observing the comings and goings on the beach. But he'd come out for a run and run he would.

A hundred miles away Catrin had woken a little later than her father, aware she felt slightly disappointed but not quite sure why. Today the aurora borealis painted on her bedroom ceiling looked dull and heavy. She lay there, staring at it, going over the previous day's meeting with Ralph, still unsure what to make of him. Flinging off the duvet she decided to go online to see if Lisa or Siân was already logged on – she could do with another chat – but she could not get a connection. She grabbed her dressing gown and went downstairs.

'The internet's not working.' Catrin huffed in frustration, as she came into the kitchen. Really it was too bad, just when it was vital for her to have long chats with her friends, access to Siân's common sense and Lisa's cheerfulness. She could, of course, phone them, but she didn't want to risk her family hearing what she was saying.

'Where's Dad? He can usually fix the computer.'

Her mother was standing at the kitchen window looking out on to the garden. 'I don't know, love;' she said, turning around. 'He didn't come home last night.' She was very pale.

'Probably went on a bender with his mates; he'll turn up feeling very sorry for himself any minute now,' Tom said from his place at the kitchen table surrounded by the Sunday papers. 'Dad usually just turns the modem off and back on again; it's not rocket science.'

'It's not like him not to let us know where he was going,' Catrin said. 'Tea, mum? Tom?'

'No thanks, sis – water only for me today; a few too many beers last night.'

Her mother nodded. 'I think he said something a couple of days ago about hoping to play golf at the weekend,' she said uncertainly. 'I noticed he'd put his clubs in the car when we went shopping.'

Catrin made the tea, put her mum's mug next to her on the work surface and added a chocolate biscuit. There were already four empty mugs in the sink. Her mother must have been up for hours.

'Have you tried his mobile?' she asked.

'No point, love; he's left it on the dressing table.'

'Oh, for goodness sake, stop fussing, women, he'll be here by lunchtime. I've never known Dad willingly miss Sunday lunch. What are we having, Mum?'

'Chicken.'

'And all the trimmings? I need to feed my hangover. And can we have Yorkshire pudding with it?' Tom asked as he turned the page of his newspaper.

Their mother nodded.

'What about we give some of his golfing mates a ring?' Catrin suggested.

'Look, Catz, give it a rest; he must be with one of them

346

'cos his kit bag's gone – he'd have taken a change of clothes in that meaning to go on the razzle afterwards,' Tom said, dismissively. "They might not go out often but when they do they really go for it. Honestly, I'm never getting married; you women fuss so much.'

'Who'd have you anyway?' said Catrin.

'I don't even know the names of his golfing mates, let alone how to get in touch with them,' Jane said, hugging her mug. 'All I know is that Foureyes always finds the bunkers and Spud plays off a handicap of two and likes his curries very hot.'

'That's a bit negligent mother. Catz and I would never get away with having anonymous friends – you interrogate every one of them.'

'No, I don't, Tom, I merely show an interest in your friends,' she replied tiredly.'

'They'll be in the contacts on his phone, Mum; I'll go and get it.' By the time Catrin finished the sentence she was halfway up the stairs.

Ten minutes later she rejoined her mother and her brother in the kitchen to report the battery was flat and she couldn't find the charger.

'It's probably in the surgery,' her mum said, slumping into the armchair. Lucky roused himself from his basket and sat at her feet.

'And I've tried switching the modem off and back on again, Tom, and the internet's still not working,' Catrin complained.

Tom shrugged and went back to reading the paper.

At one o'clock they sat around the kitchen table. Tom was the only one who had any kind of appetite. As he piled a generous second helping on to his plate Jane said, 'I think we should ring round the hospitals; just in case.'

'Mum, for goodness sake, he's 47 years old; he's probably watching the footie in a pub somewhere. Cardiff City are on the telly this afternoon – he'll come home after that, you'll see. Give it until five.'

'But your dad never behaves like this; it's just so out of character.'

'Middle-aged crisis, Mum,' Tom said offhandedly.

'Aren't you worried about your father at all, Tom?' Jane said disbelievingly.

'No I am not, cut him some slack, he'll be home soon. Now relax, Mother. And enough chatter – my head's not liking it.'

Jane looked at Catrin to see if she too thought this was the best course of action but Catrin's eyes were red rimmed and she was biting her lower lip. Jane knew to ask her anything would open the floodgates.

'Why don't you finish your lunch on a tray, Tom; surely the pre-match build-up is about to start?'

Tom did not wait to be asked twice. Grabbing his plate and his glass he made for the living room.

Catrin was still staring at her mushed up lunch. 'Mum, what if – what if Dad hasn't come home because of this donor stuff?' Catrin just managed to get to the end of the sentence before her chin started quivering. Jane felt a surge of anger towards Ben. How could he be so selfish?

'Love, I'm sure his little outing has nothing to do with you; he's probably a bit fed up with work and has decided to drown it all out for a while.'

Jane saw the horror that passed across her daughter's face and cursed herself for her choice of words. She ploughed on, 'You know drowning your sorrows in alcohol sometimes works but I wouldn't recommend it.' She gave Catrin a big hug. 'Now, shall we have a cup of tea and do the crossword together?'

Catrin smiled but the strain on her face was obvious and at that moment Jane could happily have throttled Ben.

Ben was feeling very pleased with himself as he ran along the coast path from Llangrannog towards Penbryn. His new resolve to carry on and not give in to worry was so far holding up. He'd managed to think of Catrin meeting her donor without sacrificing his good humour, had decided what made Catrin happy made him happy and he would accept, without fuss, whatever resulted from the previous day's meeting. He'd had her to himself for eighteen years; he was now, soon probably, going to have to share her with a boyfriend – Mark if Catrin had her way – so really what was the difference? Having sorted that out in his mind he decided not to think about it again until he got home and heard what had actually happened the day before.

He was also pleased he was making good time and felt far fitter than he had when he'd tackled this run a few short months ago. He'd have to remember to thank Tom. This time, instead of willing the path that climbed and dropped to level out, he could also enjoy the wonderful view: the sparkling blue sea under a cloudless sky to one side and the rolling green fields of Ceredigion on the other, dotted in the distance with sheep. As he ran between a wall of bright yellow gorse with only a seagull gliding far above for company, he was just as convinced as he had been in his alcohol-induced mellowness the previous night that this was where he belonged.

And then it came to him. Of course, that's what they should do. Look for somewhere to buy which they could use now for weekends and holidays and then, when he retired – as soon as possible after Catrin had graduated – they could move down here full-time. Perhaps he could do some locum work, allowing him to use his medical knowledge without the burden of running a surgery. And of course it would be a good way to meet people, to become part of the community. Perfect.

Ben left the coast path, drawn to the double bell tower of the little whitewashed church, St Michael's on the Hill. He'd always loved this tiny church, loved the setting high above the bay, loved the simple architecture, loved its name. He walked through the graveyard. There were lots of Lewises here, some undoubtedly his ancestors. Churchgoers all before Methodism

349

and the plethora of chapels built in Victorian Wales offered an alternative to the Welsh-speaking working class. The eleven o'clock service was long over but, as he pushed open the door into the darkened vestibule and then opened the inner door to the sun-flooded church, he could still feel the warmth of the congregation and he caught a note of someone's perfume as he walked past one of the family pews. He sat for a while as his heartbeat slowed and the whooshing in his ears ceased, enjoying the peacefulness of this lovely old building, deep in the Welsh countryside.

Although not a religious man, old churches fascinated him – their sense of history, of continuity. The huge slate slabs that made up the church's floor had been worn smooth by centuries of Christians, most of them fishermen or smallholders; simple folk who had put their faith in Mother Nature and God. Ben looked up at the exposed wooden rafters that held up the roof – bleached by years of sunlight. It all seemed so simple, so straightforward, so truthful and so far removed from the ornate cathedral that he passed on his way to and from work every day and that failed to resonate with him in any way.

He looked at his watch. He'd run down on to Penbryn beach, rejoin the coast path and be back in Llangrannog by 1:30 p.m. That would get him home by 4 p.m – far earlier than he'd indicated in his note; that would please Jane.

As he ran along the deserted beach, on through the heavily scented bluebell wood and up on to the cliff top, he thought about all the things he might do when they moved here permanently. He'd definitely sign up for the dolphin watch and he might join the rowing crew; that looked like fun. And he'd learn all the Welsh words for the wild flowers – such pretty names he thought now, as he passed a field bright with daisies; that one he knew: llygad y dydd – the eye of the day. Yes he knew he'd be happy here; it really would be a new lease of life, for both of them. He'd bring Jane down here soon; start looking for a place. It would have to wait until after

350

Catrin's exams though; he'd never again succeed in enticing Jane away from Cardiff while Catrin had to get on with her revision, especially now she was back in touch with Steffan. Besides, Jane had read somewhere that sugar was good for stress and saw her role in the revision process as regularly supplying tempting little snacks. Ben doubted this but, knowing how much Jane needed to be needed, said nothing.

Catrin – that was how he'd sell the idea to Jane. Their daughter would be in Aberystwyth, a mere forty-five minute drive away. They'd get to see her often – every weekend if Jane wanted to. He remembered how bereft she'd been when Tom went to Bristol and how subsequently Catrin had become the focus of her attention. He knew she'd be worse when Catrin left home. Jane and Catrin spent far more time together than Jane and Tom ever had. Yes, Catrin was the key.

And she wouldn't be able to argue they didn't have the cash. They could use the money he'd inherited from his mother. He liked that idea. It seemed right to use her money to buy somewhere close to her childhood home. Perhaps they could get one of those adapted railway carriages along the path with their little retro signs saying: 'Great Western Railway – penalty for not shutting the gate 40 shillings,' or 1950s posters urging: 'Go by train for a bracing day by the sea,' showing happy families waving merrily as the steam train made its way between mountain and coast. He stopped himself there. No, forget that idea. 'Too nostalgic', Jane would say and anyway those were holiday houses. He wanted a more permanent place. Something modern, that's probably what Jane would like. Lots of glass like the houses she kept showing him in her magazines. And he could live with that. His only specification would be that it should have a view of the sea and a garden shed.

Jogging slowly down the hill back into Llangrannog in order to cool down, Ben was excited. He couldn't wait to tell Jane; he'd moot the idea tonight. She was bound to be in a good mood with him arriving home early.

Two and a half hours later Ben pulled into his Cardiff drive singing Cai's May carol. He closed the car door with a flourish, grabbed his bag from the boot and headed inside, marvelling at what a difference twenty-four hours could make. He was grinning broadly when he reached the kitchen doorway.

'Where the hell have you been?' Jane glared at him. Before he could answer, Catrin flung her arms around him and planted a kiss on his cheek. He held her for a minute, loving the minty smell of her hair. Over her shoulder he could see Jane was still glaring as she got up from her chair by the Aga and put on her apron. He noted it was the red one that said 'Valleys Girl'. This was not a good sign. He gently let go of Catrin and kicked his kit bag under the table.

'So?' Jane said, hands on hips.

'I've been to Llangrannog; told you I'd be back late tonight.'

'No, you did not, Ben; I think I'd remember you telling me you were going on a little holiday.'

'Well, not tell you.'

'Exactly so you just waltz off, stay out overnight, have us worried sick, phoning round the hospitals and everything –'

'That's not quite true, Dad,' Catrin intervened, 'we haven't phoned the hospitals but we were going to if you hadn't come home by five.'

Tom appeared from the living room. 'Hi Dad; they're showing yesterday's match. Did you see the score? 1–1 – Craig Noone 68th minute. Come and see; we're in stoppage time. Amazing comments coming through on Twitter too.'

'Does that mean the internet's back up, Tom? Well thank you very much for telling me,' Catrin said, her voice heavy with sarcasm.

Tom already on his way back to the living room, ignored her but shouted over his shoulder, 'Come on, Dad, it's nearly finished.'

'I'll be with you in a minute, son; just need to talk to your mum,' Ben called after him. Turning to his wife he said quietly, 'Jane, I left a note for you all on the fridge telling you where I was.'

They heard Tom roar and he bounded back into the kitchen, grabbed a towel and, holding it up with both hands behind his head as if it was a national flag, ran round the kitchen chanting, 'Top of the Championship. Premiership here we come; here we come; here we come.'

'Shut up Tom, Dad and I are trying to have a conversation, or rather Dad is trying to explain why he went AWOL.' The tone of Jane's voice was enough to make Tom comply.

Ben said, 'Truly, I did leave a note stuck on the fridge.'

'Ah,' Tom groaned and hid his face behind the towel. The other three turned to look at him.

He launched into a long explanation about the spilled milk and the hooting car. Jane gave him one of her looks and he escaped back into the living room muttering something about 'post-match review'.

'I think a cup of tea is called for.' Ben put the kettle on while Jane gathered mugs, milk and the biscuit tin. Ben made the tea in Jane's special Sunday pot and the three of them gathered round the kitchen table.

'So, Catrin, how did it go?' Ben asked, pouring the tea.

She bent down to stroke Lucky who was enjoying one of his ever more frequent naps. He made a snuffling noise but otherwise took no notice. 'Yes, it was OK dad; Ralph – he's OK.'

Ben gave Jane a quizzical look. His wife shrugged and sipped her tea. Catrin carried on stroking the uninterested dog.

'Was he nice to you?' Ben asked, when it was obvious no more would be forthcoming from his daughter.

'Yes, Dad' I said he was OK.' She picked up her mug and left the room.

Chapter Twenty-three

Catrin was supposed to be studying for her final paper, 'Wales and the Tudor State' but instead she was browsing the Bruce Gray site. Ralph had just sent her the link saying: *tot, amazin wrk – mst c.*

And he was right; the colourful paintings were absolutely breathtaking, even on her small laptop screen. Since their meeting three weeks ago he'd sent her several links to artists' websites – ranging from the geometrical abstracts of Wassily Kandinsky to dripping Jackson Pollocks. And she was learning and enjoying it. As she heard her mother's footsteps on the stairs she flipped her laptop shut.

'Hi, love, how's it going? I've brought you some tea and scones – just out of the oven,' her mum said, opening the bedroom door.

She pushed some papers on Catrin's desk to one side and laid down the tray on which she'd put a small sprig of mayflower from the tree at the bottom of the garden. Catrin, despite feeling totally fed up after weeks of cramming, could not help but smile at the flowers with their delicate white skirts and pink tipped stamens.

'Thanks, Mum.' She returned her gaze to her open textbook and her mother took the hint, saying as she closed the door that supper would be in an hour and a half and she was making beef stroganoff, one of Catrin's favourites.

Catrin drank her tea and ate the scones quickly. Delicious; her mum really was a great cook. She did some more work but exam fatigue had really kicked in and she whiled much of the time away planning what she would do after tomorrow's exam. Buy a pile of magazines for a start. She'd resisted for months, knowing she'd be tempted to read them rather than the textbooks piled high on her desk. And she'd go shopping. She deserved something new. And she'd catch up with the soaps. All of them. She'd have the house to herself so would be able to enjoy them without her father or Tom making snide remarks. And she might try to find a summer job too. She got up and untied Mark's scarf from Big Ted's neck and wrapped it around her own then slung her grandmother's lavender cardigan over her shoulders before settling down at her desk again; she might be able to concentrate on Cromwell if she felt a bit warmer. Really, the weather was awful for mid-May. The Tweed scent ingrained in the cardigan was fading, she thought sadly and felt a sudden longing for her grandmother. That was the way it had been since her death. One minute Catrin was fine and the next her grief was as raw as it had been back in November. She glanced at the photo on her desk taken at Tom's graduation, the five of them smartly dressed and looking proud and happy. It seemed such a long time ago now and so much had changed. Not only was her grandmother gone but there had been all the upheaval of her deathbed revelation. Catrin felt under pressure to make her relationships with Ralph and Steffan meaningful and worth the upset it had cost her family.

'Supper's up, Catz', her mother called from downstairs.

Catrin blew her nose, took off the scarf and went downstairs.

Jane noticed Catrin was wearing Granny Lewis's cardigan and looked upset as she came into the kitchen and sat down. Ben was pouring the wine and Tom was already tucking in even though Jane was still ladling sour cream into the pot of steaming stew in the middle of the table. Tom took another generous scoop. Droplets of the rich brown sauce scattered on the white tablecloth.

'Tom, you really could wait until it's properly served before you start – and you've taken more meat than your share.'

'Growing lad, Mother,' Tom replied, his mouth full.

'And don't speak with your mouth full; how many times do I have to tell you?' she said, passing the pot to Catrin.

Tom shrugged and reached over his sister to pile more rice on his plate. Catrin gave him a shove and grains of rice landed on the tablecloth and the floor.

'Mum, tell her,' Tom complained. Jane chose to ignore him.

Catrin put a very small portion on her plate and took up her fork. She waved Ben's hand away as he offered her a glass of wine. 'No thanks, Dad. I'll just have water.' Ben fetched her some and sat down to his own meal.

'Anyway, Mum, Catrin's obviously on a diet so I'm doing you a favour, eating hers,' Tom said.

'I'm not on a diet; why would I be?' Catrin said indignantly.

'Can't take the exam stress then, eh? You look all puffy-eyed.' He pointed his fork at her.

'Tom, for goodness sake, give it a rest will you?' Ben said. 'Mm, this is lovely, Jane; you've put in a bit of extra paprika this time.'

Jane smiled broadly.

'And anyhow, you're just doing Mickey Mouse subjects, Catz; not like the sciences I did – can't be that much you *can* learn.'

'History and French aren't Mickey Mouse courses, or Art really, come to that,' Ben said firmly. 'Ignore him Catrin.'

'Anyway, you should get straight A's Catz.'

'Well thank you, bro; acknowledging my genius at last.'

Tom laughed. 'I wasn't; it's just everyone knows standards have dropped and everyone gets A's these days.'

Jane glared at him. 'Look Tom, you know the saying, if you can't say anything nice …'

'Then don't say anything at all,' he finished for her. She gave him another look and he shut up.

They ate in silence for a while. Eventually Jane said, 'I bet you're looking forward to tomorrow's paper, Catz?'

'Looking forward to getting it over and done with, more like it, Mum.'

Jane tried to coax her daughter into showing some enthusiasm. 'Well, if it goes as well as you think the Art papers have gone you'll be happy, won't you? Do we get to see your final painting once the results are out?'

'Mm, I think so,' Catrin said, pushing her cutlery to one side.

'Distressed, that was the title, wasn't it? If we get it back we'll frame it and hang it in the hall – you can sign it so when I'm old and you're famous I can sell it for a fortune,' Ben teased.

Tom rolled his eyes. 'Oh my God, not one of those ghastly abstract efforts is it? Those are just rubbish, any kid let loose with a tin of paint could produce those.'

Catrin gave him a withering look but seemed to be going to let the remark pass.

'Jackson Pollock, load of bollocks,' he chanted.

Catrin flushed and stood up. 'You're just showing your ignorance, Tom. Ralph says to be a really good abstract artist you need all the skills of a realist painter and then more.'

'Does anybody want pudding?' Jane got up and Ben started clearing the plates.

'Ww, it must be right if Ralph says so,' Tom said sarcastically.

Catrin threw the remains of the water in her glass at him and stormed out of the room, slamming the door behind her.

Tom rose and grabbed a towel from the hook by the kitchen sink. 'Mum, she threw water at me and she's banging doors,' he moaned, wiping his face.

'Really, Tom, can't you just behave – don't you remember what exam stress feels like?' Jane said crossly.

'You'd never let me get away with that.' He raised his voice to match hers. Ben dumped the plates in the sink and went out the back door, presumably heading for the shed.

'Come on Tom, give her a break; she's had a hard few months.'

'Oh come on yourself, Mum, she gets special treatment; just because you and Dad feel guilty about the whole donor stuff.'

Jane sighed. 'You're being ridiculous Tom; Dad and I have always treated you both exactly the same.'

'Perhaps you did but you don't any more; you treat Catrin differently, you're overcompensating so she doesn't feel she's less of a Lewis than me.'

'No, we don't; we treat you equally,' Jane shouted at him.

'Huh, we may be equal but it's the same old story; some are more equal than others.' With that Tom stormed out too.

Jane forgot about pudding and sat at the still cluttered kitchen table, the detritus of the family meal around her.

The following morning, after making sure Catrin was up in good time for her final exam, Jane left for work while Ben was still eating breakfast. There was no sign of Tom. His bedroom door was firmly closed and Jane, still hurt by last night's outburst, decided getting to work on time was his lookout. Before it turned 9 a.m. she had rearranged all the paperbacks in the shop in alphabetical order and was now counting the pieces in a 1,000 piece jigsaw to make sure it was complete. There was nothing more frustrating than getting down to the last few pieces and realising one was missing. One of the old boys – 'Dai Incomplete' they'd nicknamed him – regularly brought jigsaws back, claiming there were bits missing and demanding a refund. The staff arched their eyebrows and humoured him.

Just before 9 o'clock Jane heard a key in the lock followed by a gasp as her manager opened the door and realised someone was in the shop.

'Afternoon, Sue.'

'Ha, ha, very funny, Jane,' Sue said, clearly relieved but not amused. 'What on earth are you doing here? You're not due in until ten today. You gave me such a fright; I thought we had a burglar'.

Jane laughed. 'In truth, Sue, who would bother to break in here? We're virtually giving the stuff away as it is. If I was a burglar I'd make damn sure to choose a designer store.'

Sue laughed too as she unlocked the till and emptied the float from her bag.

'Cup of coffee?'

Sue nodded and Jane was glad. If the shop was quiet for the first half hour or so, as it usually was, then she could tell Sue what had caused her to spend such a sleepless night and talking was much easier with a cup in hand.

As Jane made the coffee she tried to formulate her thoughts to explain how she felt but she was tired and everything was an effort. Still she needed to talk to someone and Sue was the best person. She'd contemplated phoning Olwen after the row but couldn't bring herself to admit to her mother what Tom had said. And although she was angry with him, she didn't want her mother to be angry with Tom too. Ben had refused to discuss it, saying both she and Tom were sometimes too hot-headed and that it would help everyone if they just thought before they spoke.

'So what's up?' Sue asked as Jane handed her her drink.

Jane shrugged and sipped the hot coffee.

'Well my guess would be something to do with Catrin or Tom?'

'It's Tom this time,' Jane said quietly. 'He said,' she gulped, embarrassed, 'that we favour Catrin. Actually what I think he meant was that I favour Catrin.'

The door opened and two of their elderly regulars came in on their way to the hairdresser next door for their weekly sets.

'Morning, girls,' Sue called brightly.

'Morning, Sue,' they said in unison. 'Morning, Jane.'

'Mabel, we've had one of those little purses you collect – I've saved it for you.' Jane reached under the counter. 'Don't think you've got this design, have you?'

360

Mabel inspected the bright yellow and black purse made of Welsh tapestry and smiled broadly. 'Oh, thank you so much, lovely, I know this one; it's from the woollen mill in Dinas Mawddwy. It's in my little book. Well thank you, Jane, that's made my day. £1 is it?'

Jane nodded and the till rang with the first sale of the day. A number of collectors came into the shop regularly and Jane, having never collected anything in her life and really not inclined to do so, was nevertheless fascinated by the different objects other people treasured. There was the woman who collected thimbles; the man who was always on the look out for tea cosies; the young mum who liked old bottles; the very serious man who collected comics, and the many who bought royal paraphernalia. A happy Mabel and her friend, having thanked Jane several times, eventually left the shop and Jane and Sue returned to their coffee and their conversation.

'And you don't think you do? Favour Catrin that is?'

'No, Sue, I don't. I've been thinking about it all night; something I've never even considered before – and hand on heart, I honestly don't think I've ever favoured one over the other.'

'And Tom's never said anything like this before?'

'Never'.

'So what's changed now?'

'It's the donor thing. Tom says we're overcompensating, letting Catrin get away with things we'd never let him get away with, because we want to show how much we love her.' She paused. 'It was all so heated but I think that's what he was saying.'

'Well I can't imagine Ben losing his cool so was that his interpretation too?'

Jane laughed drily. 'Huh, you know big Ben Lewis – first sign of trouble and he cowers in the shed.'

'Ah', Sue said.

'I don't think he's right you know, Sue; I know I spend more time with Catrin but Ben spends more time with Tom;

that's just the way it is, they have more in common – their sport and everything – and Catrin and I like doing the same things. It's just boys and girls. I don't think that's favouritism, do you?'

Sue shook her head. 'No, definitely not, and you know Tom probably knows it too. I guess Catrin has had a lot of your attention recently – what with her exams, Steff, and Ralph, and Tom's probably just a little bit jealous.'

Jane smiled. 'I think you've put your finger on it, Sue; that's exactly what he was like as a little boy – the tantrums we had when Catrin was born. He was a nightmare.'

'Well, understandable I suppose; he'd had you all to himself for four years.'

'It's a bit more acceptable in a four-year-old than in a twenty-four-year-old though,' Jane said.

'Give me the child for his first seven years and I'll give you the man and all that,' Sue said as the shop door opened and another customer came in. Jane gathered up their mugs and Sue handed her a box full of pair-less earrings, uttering just one word – 'challenge'.

Jane grinned, 'Piece of cake, my friend. Watch and learn. Watch and learn.'

By the end of the morning a jewel-encrusted scarf had been created and the one-off designer piece sold within an hour for £5.

Catrin ran through a misty Victoria Park feeling as if the sun had just come out. She couldn't wait to get out of her uniform – for the very last time. She was five minutes away from no longer being a schoolgirl; let the rest of her life begin.

She sped through the house, tearing the bright yellow post-it note, 'Act of Union 1534,' from the fridge as she grabbed a Coke, crumpling the 'Rowland Lee – pre-union legislation' note that was stuck to the cooker and stripping the series of notes on Cromwell posted on the staircase. She shook open one of the black bin bags her mother had optimistically left on

362

the landing outside her room and dropped the post-it notes in it then flung open her bedroom door and grabbed the files piled up on her desk. She tipped them into the bin bag too and took a celebratory gulp of Coke. Never again would she have to study history! It was such a shame the A level course hadn't lived up to expectation, she'd so enjoyed the subject up to GCSE, but now she realised it was the teacher that had enthused her. Her A level teacher had hardly been an inspiration.

As she undressed to take a shower, she switched on her laptop and recoiled when both Steffan's scowl and Ralph's smiling face popped up. She grabbed her dressing gown and then laughed at herself for being so silly. Of course they couldn't see her; there was no webcam on this machine. The message to both her and Steff from Ralph read:

Fancy meeting up next Sat in Cardiff? Jamie Treadwell exh. (Stef – some you'll 'understand'!) in Llandaff + new Mary Lloyd Jones in Tinney's. Up for it?

Steff had already answered with 'you bet' and Catrin now found herself responding without a second thought: *Sure, can't wait.x.*

She'd pressed the send button before realising she'd signed off with a kiss.

She showered quickly, changed into jeans and a T-shirt and was on her way out to meet Mark, Lisa, and Siân when her father came through the front door.

'Hi Dad, you're back early.'

'Stella gave me a half-day off to study some asthma figures so I've brought them home to look at. Thought I'd sit in the garden, it's bit overcast but warm. So love, how did it go?'

'It went, Dad, and now it's gone.'

He stood between her and the front door, his bulk making it impossible for her to squeeze past. 'Did they ask you about the godly Bishop Lee and his penchant for hanging the poor?'

'Yes, Dad'

'And what did they ask about Cromwell?'

'Oh, you know, the usual stuff.'

'No, I don't know, Catz; I've never done A level History.'

'Dad, leave it; it's history now.'

As he turned to hang his jacket on the rack she slipped past him and out of the door. She couldn't wait to see Mark.

Catrin glanced back to see where Steffan had got to. He'd been like this all afternoon, so much so that, after visiting the first gallery, she'd suggested he might like to meet up with Ralph and her once they had visited this venue. He'd mumbled something but continued to tag along, his foul mood putting a dampener on her afternoon. He really was annoying; if he was not particularly interested in something he made no effort at all and seemed to enjoy showing his displeasure. Siân had been right when she'd accused Steffan of being selfish and self-centred.

When he'd first told her about his childhood and his miserable school days Catrin had felt sorry for him. He'd gone on and on about all the lessons he hated, how the teachers picked on him, how he was always the last one to be selected for any team games and no one wanted to sit with him on school trips. No wonder, Catrin thought now, he could be so moody, so petulant.

'Come on Steff,' she said pointedly as he appeared around a corner of the gallery.

'So what do you think, Steffan?' Ralph asked, nodding sagely at the large abstract painting in front of them.

Steffan hesitated. 'I really like the way it's hung,' he said, eventually. 'Looks like the paint has been splashed on,' he added, going right up and touching the painting.

Catrin saw the attendant move towards them. 'I think we've seen them all, Ralph,' she said hurriedly, giving Steffan a push towards the exit.

They emerged on to the street.

'Art appreciation is very thirsty work,' Ralph declared, 'are you ready for a drink? How about we try that cocktail bar you were telling me about, Catrin?' She nodded enthusiastically and Steffan grunted. Catrin led the way. The street was not quite wide enough for the three of them to walk abreast and Steffan trailed behind.

'I had a Tequila Sunrise last time I was here – it was lovely,' Catrin said as they entered the building, which was all chrome and industrial lighting. It was 5 p.m. and already there were a few people sat on the high stools at the bar and some of the tables were taken. Ralph headed to one as far away as possible from what was obviously a hen party from the profusion of veils and garters on show.

'This time I'm going to try something different; can you recommend anything, Ralph?' Catrin asked as she sat on the sofa next to him, both studying the long drinks list.

'How about a Singapore Gin Sling? That's one of my favourites.'

'Sounds good to me,' she agreed, passing the menu to Steffan who sat on a chrome chair opposite them. He studied the list.

'So what's it to be?' Ralph asked.

Steffan folded the menu. 'I'll just have a beer, thanks.'

Ralph laughed. 'Oh, come on, when in Rome and all that.'

'We're not in Rome or Singapore though,' Steffan replied peevishly. 'This is Cardiff, Brains Beer country, and that's what I'll have.'

The lines on Ralph's forehead deepened. 'Don't think they'll have draught beer here, mate; not that kind of place really, is it?' He looked at Steffan but Steffan was studying the Americana posters dotted around the bar. 'Anyway, I'll find out.' Ralph loped off with a smile.

When he was safely out of earshot Catrin turned to her half-brother. 'What's the matter with you? You're behaving like a spoilt child.'

He shrugged.

'Come on Steff, make an effort,' she said, the edge in her voice now replaced by weariness.

365

'Makes no difference how much effort I make,' he said.

'You get back what you put in.'

'That's rubbish Catrin. I thought you were cleverer than to trot out the standard Agony Aunt reply but it appears you're not. No what we have here is a cosy club for those who belong – and I don't,' he continued, his voice rising.

'You choose not to,' Catrin said tartly. She knew she was being sharp but he had annoyed her all afternoon and there was the faint possibility pointing out just how pathetic his behaviour was might make him snap out of it.

Ralph returned and placed a tray with the two martini glasses, each with a glacé cherry and olive balanced precariously on top, and a bottle of Corona on the low coffee table.

'Thank you,' Catrin said moving her glass carefully in front of her.

'Sorry Steffan, this is the only beer they serve,' Ralph said, handing him the bottle and sitting down.

Steff dug out the piece of lime wedged in the Corona bottle's neck, looked pointedly for somewhere to deposit it and then placed it on the table. Catrin nibbled at her sweet cherry, offered Ralph her olive and accepted his cherry in return.

'Santé!' Ralph said, raising his glass. Catrin clinked her glass to his and Steff held out his bottle in their general direction. Ralph looked around at the decor.

'That's a great picture isn't it?' he said, pointing at a large framed photo of 1930s builders having lunch on a skyscraper, their legs dangling high above the New York skyline, 'always makes me feel sick though.'

Catrin laughed. 'I agree, Ralph, great juxtaposition; they look so homely sitting there eating their sandwiches and yet they're in so much danger.'

'I wonder if they were cheese and tomato or egg?' Steffan said.

Catrin ignored him and hoped Ralph hadn't heard. Steffan

shrugged and swigged from his bottle.

'So, what did you make of the Mary Lloyd Jones pieces then?' Ralph asked, turning slightly towards Catrin.

'They felt modern but … old,' she said carefully.

'Old in a good way or in a bad way?'

'Deffo in a good way: sort of connected to history – to a Celtic past …' Catrin trailed off.

'Exactly, Catrin.' Ralph clapped his hands together.

'You hardly need to be a great art critic to work that out,' Steffan sneered, 'all that old writing gives it away.'

Ralph ignored the sneer. 'So did you like it, Steffan?' He looked at him earnestly. Steffan took a long gulp from his bottle.

'Spose,' he said and grimaced. 'This tastes like cat's piss.' He took another long swig as though making sure.

'The way she does it, it all sits together comfortably; sort of belongs together: not picture and words – more sort of something else entirely, another form of communication.' Catrin stopped abruptly aware Steffan was mimicking her.

'God, you talk rubbish sometimes Catrin; all arty-farty.' He pushed back his chair noisily, as if to underline his comment.

'It's really good how the artist expresses the effect of man on nature without ever having any people in her work – very clever stuff,' Ralph said as if Steffan hadn't spoken. The middle-aged, well-dressed couple at the next table leant over straining to hear their conversation. He raised his voice slightly. 'Not sure how I feel about titles though.'

'I think these abstract people – they're just having a laugh.' Steff said. 'They fling some paint on a canvas and then think up some totally unrelated title. And pocket a big fat cheque because people are too bloody pretentious to say it's crap.'

The middle-aged couple visibly recoiled.

'Excellent, Steffan, it's good you have an opinion,' Ralph said smiling. 'There's nothing better than a good debate.'

'I think titles are good. They give a clue to what the artist wants to say.'

Steffan prodded at the lime.

'But shouldn't we all be able to respond to a work of art without having it interpreted for us? Why does it have to mean anything at all?' Ralph persisted.

The couple at the next table once more leant towards them.

Catrin's phone buzzed in her pocket. She ignored it and took another sip of her cocktail.

'Go on, answer it, Catrin; don't mind us,' Ralph said.

'It's fine; it's just a text.' But Catrin dug out her phone and pressed the little screen anyway. 'It's from Mark,' she said. 'Asking if I want to go to see a film with him and Lisa tonight.'

A loud guffaw of laughter emanated from the hens' corner. Steffan looked over and laughed too; the middle-aged couple muttered something and Steffan stuck his tongue out at them. Again they recoiled and he laughed. Catrin glared at him; how could he be so rude?

'Well, I must be going,' Ralph said, standing up. 'You know – things to do, people to see. Can I get either of you another drink before I go?'

'I don't think Catrin likes her fancy cocktail,' Steffan said, pointing to her glass which was still pretty full. Catrin took another sip. 'Well, it is a little bitter, but nice though,' she added quickly. Steffan put his empty bottle down on the table with a bang.

'So you two sure you won't have another drink?'

They both shook their heads.

'No thanks, I'll just finish this one and then I'll have to go too,' Catrin said.

Ralph touched them both lightly on the shoulder and headed for the door. 'OK then, I'll facebook you.'

'Thanks for a great afternoon,' Catrin called after him.

'Thanks for a great afternoon,' Steffan mimicked.

Ben had been in his shed all afternoon and now his empty Golden Virginia packet was squeezed into a little ball and wrapped in an old seed packet for safe disposal in the bin outside the kitchen door. Today it had not actually been necessary to decamp to his shed. Jane was safely in the shop, Tom was playing football with his mates, and Catrin was meeting up with ... that creep. Ben was taken aback by his choice of adjective, even though he hadn't actually said it out loud. For goodness sake, he hadn't even met the man and he prided himself on his fairness, his natural instinct not to judge. He took off his long smoking coat, and went to hang it on the hook behind the door. His mother's coat still hung there too, but it was the first time he'd noticed it for a long time. The snowy down of a spider's web now delicately covered the right shoulder. He took the coat down, shook it and a large spider scampered across its back, disappearing up one of the sleeves. He put the coat back on the hook, deciding it was quite comforting having it just hang there, and put his own coat over the top. He could picture his mother now. She'd always sniffed dramatically when she entered the shed, given him one of her looks, but pointedly said nothing. He smiled at the thought, enjoying the fact they had colluded on some things. She had enjoyed gardening but in a very different way to him. She liked order and straight lines, every weed painstakingly and back-breakingly removed. Ben preferred a more natural look. Now, peering out of the shed's dusty window, he ruefully thought that nature was getting the better of his garden. Maybe his mother had had a point.

However tackling the garden felt too much of a challenge just then. A small, achievable task, that's what he needed. He looked around the shed and noticed the old paint pots amassed in the corner. Well he could sort those. Many he discarded without bothering to open, their rusted lids telling him what he needed to know. He'd load them into the Volvo later on and take them to the tip. And then he came across the pot of Rose Pink. He knew it was useless; the lid hadn't been replaced properly so the pot had remained unsealed for years – thirteen years in fact. Catrin would have been five, having just started

369

'proper school' as she called it, when she came home declaring she was far too grown up for Little Princess wallpaper and please could she have a pink room like Siân's? He replaced the Rose Pink tin in the far corner and reached for the magazine he had bought earlier that day. He would take it into the house and enjoy it with a nice cup of tea.

Ben pushed the shed door open with difficulty. Really he would have to tackle the buddleia soon or he wouldn't be able to get into his bolthole. He put his shoulder to the door to force it closed and walked briskly towards the house. As he came through the back door, he heard Catrin coming in the front. She joined him in the kitchen and planted a kiss on his cheek.

'So, Dad, idling your time away with a magazine while mum's slaving away in the shop?' Catrin teased, reaching for the kettle. 'Cuppa?'

'Yes please, love.' She filled the kettle and switched it on.

'So what's the mag? *Gardening World* or something equally scintillating?' Catrin turned suddenly and snatched the rolled-up magazine from his hand. She laughed. 'Dad, I'm shocked at you.'

He felt himself blush.

'Gardening and sport; those are your things – not culture. What possessed you to get *Buzz* magazine?'

Ben started to empty the dishwasher. 'Look on page 12; there's an advert for the Christopher Williams retrospective exhibition – lots of nice coastal scenes; thought we could go together,' he said uncertainly.

'Oh Dad, that's such old-fashioned stuff – so literal.'

He felt wounded. Take an interest in their interests; that was the advice always handed out to parents wasn't it? He couldn't remember the so-called experts ever explaining your kids had to allow you to do so for it to serve any purpose.

She handed him his tea. 'Sweetener? One or two?'

'No, I'll have sugar, two and a half please.'

Catrin gave him a disapproving look but reached for the sugar bowl, buried behind a wall of condiments. 'You rebel,

Dad, Mum won't like it.' She laughed.

'Your mum won't know, and anyway there are lots of things we don't like about family but we shut up and put up,' he said, deciding he wouldn't ask how her afternoon had gone since she clearly wasn't going to volunteer any information.

Ben retreated behind the sports section of the Saturday paper and Catrin retreated to her room.

Chapter Twenty-four

Catrin was enjoying the first week of her summer holiday by not doing very much at all. The early June weather was pleasantly warm and she'd taken a couple of long walks with Mark and Lucky, done some sketching, spent one afternoon browsing the shops with Lisa, and hung out with Siân on her night off. She'd tried too, admittedly not very hard, to find a job, but the economic climate meant they were far from plentiful and anyway Ben had tut-tutted the idea, telling her to make the most of the long break before the hard work of university began. Her dad was happy to finance whatever she wanted within reason but from next week she would occasionally be volunteering in the charity shop with her mother to ease her guilt at not doing anything very useful.

Three more lovely months of this stretched before her, she thought to herself as she gazed up at her bedroom ceiling which this morning sparkled in the sun. The only cloud on the horizon was the fear of not getting the A level results she needed. She wondered whether she'd done enough to get into Aberystwyth after all. Pontypridd no longer appealed to her; the thought of being so close to Steffan now a deterrent rather than the incentive it had been a few months back and anyway the University of Glamorgan did not offer a Fine Art course. Oh well, she thought, the results were months away; no point worrying about them now – actually no point worrying about them at all. And having decided that she swung out of bed, switched on her laptop and made for the bathroom.

On her return there were three new message alerts on her screen. The first was from Mark inviting her to a barbecue later on; the second was from Ralph:

Want you to meet Miriam, she doz fab roast. Sunday lunch

June 16 good for u?

And the third was from Steffan saying he'd already looked up the rail website and tickets to Bristol on that day would cost them £11.20 return.

'Catz, I'm making pancakes, fancy some?' her mother called. Catrin opened her door and was greeted by a wonderful smell drifting up the stairs.

'Make it a pile, Mum; I'm famished. I'll be down in a minute.'

As soon as the computer confirmed her messages had been safely sent she rushed downstairs and into the kitchen. 'Mm, smells like heaven in here.'

Her mother laughed as she took the plate of pancakes out of the Aga where they were being kept warm and put it on the table.

'Thanks Mum, these are delicious.' Catrin was already tucking into her first before she sat down.

'You don't have to scoff them today, Tom's not here.'

Catrin helped herself to another pancake from the pile as her mum put one on her own plate and topped it with sliced banana. They sat in companionable silence, both surreptitiously feeding Lucky little morsels under the table.

'So any special plans for today, Catz?'

'No, nothing special today,' Catrin said, gazing out of the window, 'but barbecue at Mark and Lisa's tonight. You?'

'Nope, no plans. Tea?'

'Yes please.'

Her mother got up, checked there was enough water in the kettle and flicked the switch on for it to boil.

'I have got some plans for a week Sunday though,' Catrin said. 'Ralph has invited us to his house for lunch.'

'Us?' Her mum turned round.

'Yes, Steff and me.'

'Oh yes, of course,' her mother said, turning back to the kettle as it boiled. 'For a moment there I thought you meant the whole Lewis family.' She poured water into the china

374

teapot, gave the tea a stir and brought the pot to the table. As she put it down, Catrin noticed her hand was shaking. 'But you can't,' she said.

Catrin looked at her. 'What do you mean, can't?'

'A week on Sunday is the 16th of June; it's Father's Day; we always go out to lunch; its tradition.'

'Oh, I didn't realise,' Catrin sighed. 'It's not going to be the same this year though, is it Mum?' she said softly.

'I know love but traditions are traditions because we carry them on.' Her mother put her hand on Catrin's arm and gave it a gentle squeeze.

'I really miss her, you know.' Catrin felt her eyes sting and rubbed them a little too firmly.

'You know I never thought I would but I do too, Catz, we all do. But life goes on and we have to adapt. As Granny Lewis is not here to treat us to the Father's Day lunch, I'll treat us instead. Can't have your father paying for that meal now, can we?'

'I've already said I'll go to Bristol with Steffan, Mum,' Catrin said flatly.

'Well, you decide what's right.' Her mother stood. 'Now how about I clear up, you put on some work clothes and we tackle the garden together? Give your dad a nice surprise.'

Jane and Catrin spent the rest of the day cutting back the camellias and daffodils, tying up the wisteria and climbing roses and clearing away some of the bindweed that was threatening to choke everything else in the flower beds. Lucky hindered proceedings by digging in the borders, his little legs scattering soil on to the lawn, and every now and then Jane distracted him by throwing him a ball. They left the most difficult job till last – taming the buddleia growing by the shed sufficiently so that Ben could get in and out but it still attracted the beautiful butterflies that flitted around them as they worked. Lucky gave up on the digging and chased after the Red Admirals, Cabbage Whites, and Tortoiseshells. He barked a greeting as Tom made his way down the garden path.

'My, you've been busy.'

Jane straightened up. 'Oh, that's better. Yes we have been busy, Tom. How was your day?

'Average,' he said.

'Anyway now you're home you can help us; all this needs bagging up and taking to the tip. Real man's work,' she added seeing the doubt on his face.

'Come on, Tom,' Catrin encouraged, 'do that and you can share in the glory of the makeover.'

He still looked doubtful and then his phone rang. He answered it and broke into a smile. 'Yes, yes of course, Victoria Park? Good ... no, no need, I'll just jog down. Yeah, literally round the corner. I'll be with you in five. Yeah, see you mate.'

He grinned at Catrin and Jane. 'Sorry, girls, real man's work calls – they're one short for the five-a-side – and a man's got to do what a man's got to do.' He turned around, laughing, and sprinted up the path to the house.

'Mum, you let him get away with doing nothing,' Catrin said, piling cuttings into a refuse bag.

Jane shrugged. 'Sometimes it's just easier that way, Catz; persuading him to do anything useful is so exhausting, it's less hassle to do it myself.' She stooped to pick up some tools and winced; her back ached from being bent over for too long.

She heard a car turn on to the gravel drive. Really; she couldn't be doing with visitors now; she'd ignore it and hope whoever it was went away. She stretched her back and listened out for the doorbell anyway. When no sound came she went back to bagging up the cuttings. The next thing she heard was an appreciative whistle.

'My, what a pair of angels you are.' It was Ben, standing at the open patio doors.

'Oh hi, love. I heard a car but I didn't expect it to be you. You're home early.'

He stepped out on to the patio. 'I couldn't stay in that

376

surgery a minute longer missing out on this good weather. I've brought some work home with me; I'll tackle it later.'

'Nothing new there then,' Jane said, walking up the garden to join him.

Catrin took off her gloves. 'OK, Mum, now that Dad's here to help you and seen me working so I've earned zillions of brownie points, I'll have a quick bath before going over to Lisa and Mark's for the barbecue.'

'That's fine, love, and thanks for all your help.'

Catrin disappeared indoors.

'G and T, Jane?' Ben asked.

'Mm, lovely. I'll just wash my hands.'

When Jane came back Ben had fixed the G and Ts and set up the table, chairs and umbrella on the patio. They sat sipping their drinks in the evening sun, the air filled with the scent of early roses and honeysuckle cascading from a wooden trellis. Jane pondered how she would feel about leaving all this. Not that she'd actually discussed moving house with Ben, but she was a Rhondda girl at heart and that would always be her real home. Yet so much work had gone into creating this garden, most of it done by Ben, but with considerable input from his mother and some help from her. Somehow leaving it would be more difficult than leaving the house; a narrow Valleys garden could never feel so spacious.

'How was the surgery, apart from hot?' she asked.

'Chaotic,' Ben said. Of late this was his usual reply. 'You've obviously done a good day's work, and kind of Catrin to help too.'

Jane took another sip of her drink. 'I think it may be a case of damage limitation.'

'Damage limitation?' Ben queried with a laugh.

'She's been invited to lunch at Ralph's on the 16th.'

'Well, I suppose it's the next step, wanting to see where he lives, meet his wife.' He nodded and smiled. 'We're OK with that, aren't we?'

Jane looked at her husband's kind face: an honest, open

face. 'The 16th is Father's Day,' she said and immediately his expression changed.

'He's done this deliberately; made her choose between him and me.'

Jane put her arm around his shoulder and kissed his cheek. He shuddered as the sun disappeared behind a cloud.

After trying most of the clothes in her wardrobe Catrin had decided upon a pair of light green chinos, a white vest and a long bottle-green cardigan. She'd taken a photo of herself and texted it to the girls – Lisa had assured her the look was relaxed without being too casual and Siân had said she looked 'friendly', whatever that might mean. But now she wasn't sure. It was Sunday lunch after all; perhaps she should wear a dress. She did want to make a good impression; didn't want Miriam to think she couldn't be bothered. Eventually she opted to pin her grandmother's little brooch to the cardigan and popped the opal necklace around her neck. Yes, that was cool she decided. Just as she was adding a final slick of lip gloss the doorbell rang.

'OK, I'll get it,' Tom shouted from the living room. Catrin headed downstairs, hoping whoever it was wouldn't hold her up. She heard her brother say, 'O, hi, come in.'

'Thanks. Is Catrin still here?' Catrin recognised the soft deep tones at once.

'She is, Mark, upstairs, putting the war paint on. Well she was, but now here she comes – the girl with the two fathers.' Tom bowed dramatically as Catrin appeared.

Catrin ignored him, choosing to focus instead on Mark who looked embarrassed. Tom did not budge.

'Hi, I'm just leaving for the station.'

Mark mumbled, 'I was passing and thought you might want some company.'

'Oh, that's a good idea, Mark,' Tom said, 'because it's really dangerous to go by bus from Victoria Park to Central Station at 11 a.m. on a Sunday. You never know who you might meet. And a girl with two fathers, now she's very special; really does need protecting.'

Catrin placed a small packet on the hall table, extravagantly wrapped with a large green bow, and propped up an envelope behind it with 'Dad' written on it in her best calligraphy script. 'Oh shut up, Tom. And talking of fathers, have you got Dad something for Father's Day?'

'I thought you'd be getting him something from both of us,' he said sheepishly.

'And that's because you're earning pots of money and I'm earning nothing. Yes, that makes so much sense, Tom. But no, this is from me and me alone.' She picked up her bag and some roses she'd cut from the garden earlier and bundled a rather startled Mark out of the door, slamming it behind her.

Neither said anything until they turned the corner from Pencisely Crescent on to Pencisely Road. Then Catrin looked up at Mark and smiled.

'Wow, that was some performance,' he said admiringly.

Catrin sighed. 'He really had it coming; he's been such a pain recently. Sarcasm has always been his stock in trade but, I don't know, he seems to be getting worse.'

'Are you happy to walk into town rather than get the bus? It's such a lovely day.'

'Yes, there's plenty of time before the train,' she replied. More time with you too she thought.

They walked along in companionable silence. The white magnolia tree at the bottom of Pencisely Road was at its best; its magnificent flowers giving the Cardiff thoroughfare an exotic air on this quiet Sunday morning. Mark picked up one of the blooms that had fallen on the ground and handed it to Catrin.

'Maybe he's jealous,' he suggested.

'Have you been thinking of Tom all this time?' she teased. 'Your mind works phenomenally slowly.'

'Are you saying I'm dim?' he joshed.

'Not at all, you're not stupid, but you are incredibly laid-back, Mark.'

'Laid-back sounds like a compliment to me.' He smiled at her.

'It is,' she replied. And then she qualified it because there was one thing she wished he wasn't quite so relaxed about. 'Well, laid-back is good most of the time.' She gave him a sideways glance but he did not respond.

Catrin was disappointed. What could she do to make him move their relationship on without risking a repeat of the Valentine's night fiasco? She knew what Siân would say – why wait for him to act? But Catrin had already invited him out on a date and sent that embarrassing Valentine. She could not bear the thought of instigating something else that led to nothing. And she certainly did not want to risk scaring him off – having Mark just as a friend was better than nothing.

For the rest of the walk they talked, mostly about Mark's clients. Catrin laughed as he told her about one man who grunted loudly as he picked up the lightest of dumb-bells, the woman who did sixty-four repeats at every apparatus and another who spent all her time selecting the weights at the different machines, breathing deeply and then doing just one repetition. As they arrived at the station they could see Steffan walking up and down the platform trying to engage people in conversation.

'Uh-oh, that can only mean one thing,' Catrin said, suddenly serious. 'Too many happy pills.'

Mark shook his head. 'Honestly, today of all days.'

Steffan came running towards them, arms outstretched. He lifted Catrin off the ground and twirled her around before trying to lift Mark. Failing to do so he attempted a high five and missed.

'I've been here ages Catz; got an earlier train up from Ponty to make sure I didn't miss the connection. Thought you'd be here way before this. Anyway, never mind, you're here now. The good news is your big brother, aka moi, got us some cannies for the journey,' he slurred.

'I'll get you both some takeaway coffees,' Mark said, making for the buffet. Steffan drifted along the platform in the other direction and Catrin ran after Mark, catching up with him as he reached the counter.

'Please make that three and come with us,' she pleaded as the woman in the buffet went through the rigmarole of asking whether they wanted black or flat white, cappuccino, Americano, latte or filter, medium or large.

'Flat whites, small please,' Catrin said to her, anxious to regain Mark's attention. 'Please come, Mark.'

'Sorry, we don't do small – soduwant medium or large?'

Catrin bristled. Surely the woman could work out that she didn't want large as she'd asked for small. 'Medium please – three.'

'No, two,' Mark interrupted.

'Soduwant two or three?'

'Two,' Mark said firmly. 'Sorry Catz, I can't. I've got to work this afternoon and anyway I haven't been invited.' The woman tutted and moved away to make their drinks. 'I'm not sure if coffee's the right thing – will it make him even higher?' he asked.

'It might, but hopefully it will help to sober him up – high and sober is preferable to high and drunk,' Catrin replied, adding anxiously 'if I can persuade him to drink it – he's not that keen on coffee.'

Mark paid for the drinks and they made their way back to the platform just as a train was approaching. Catrin tried her best to understand what the announcer was saying but he seemed to be stringing the names of stations at which the train was stopping into one long word. She could see Steffan waiting close to the platform edge but she was too far away to do anything. Someone tugged his arm and he stepped back just in time before the train stopped and the carriage door was flung open. By the time those on board had disembarked and Catrin and Mark had reached the spot he had leapt on.

'Excuse me, is this the Bristol train?' Catrin asked a

woman who was trying to haul a buggy, toddler and numerous plastic bags aboard. 'Well, I hope so,' she replied. Catrin hoped so too as Steffan was now on the train.

Mark ushered her on, placed the coffees on the first vacant table, which was also where Steffan had deposited his plastic bag full of lager cans before walking off. Mark picked up the bag, gave Catrin a quick hug and made his way out of the door. The whistle blew and the train started moving. Catrin watched Mark waving and becoming smaller and smaller as they pulled away. She laid the roses carefully on the empty seat beside her. Already one or two of the petals were falling off but she liked them like that, less perfect. Steffan reappeared but, seeing no sign of his plastic bag, disappeared again in the other direction. As the train left the Cardiff suburbs he returned and sat in the seat opposite her, cursing someone for stealing their booze and complaining that the buffet car was closed. Catrin continued looking out of the window, anxious to distance herself from him. She could hear him talking to the woman with the toddler who sat across the aisle from them. The toddler was trying to chat to Steffan but his mother moved him to the window seat and stuck a dummy in his mouth.

Catrin pushed one of the coffees towards Steffan and was relieved to see him drink some of it and quieten down. She sipped her own, hoping he wasn't going to embarrass her in front of Ralph as he had when they'd visited the art galleries. As the train left Newport she considered whether she dared leave him to go to the toilet to retouch her make-up or whether that would precipitate one of his rants or wanderings. She decided to risk it.

'Well I think you should go to the station to meet them' Miriam said.

Ralph dunked toast into his runny egg. 'But it's a bit pointless, Miriam – going all the way across town, getting off the bus, meeting them at the station and then getting back on the bus again. It would be different if we had a car.'

Yellow yolk ran down his chin and he tried to rescue it with his tongue. She turned away, back to the sink and the potatoes.

'Anyway, I should stay here to help you.'

Miriam, who had never known her husband to peel anything more taxing than a banana, was tempted to ask how exactly he proposed to help. But she let it go and said, 'It would be a very welcoming gesture if you did make the effort to go. I'm sure they'd appreciate it.'

'OK, then, I'll do that. I'll catch the 11.30 bus.'

She smiled. Her first little victory of the day. 'Good, but I'd get the earlier one, just in case. It would be awful if you missed them at the station.' Scrape, scrape. She was on to the carrots now.

'But that means I'll have to leave soon and I was thinking I'd work on my new painting a bit this morning. Do you think I really need to go? I'm sure the kids won't mind if I don't.'

'Yes, I do think you should, and you shouldn't refer to them as "the kids," Ralph.' Miriam made an effort to keep the tone of her voice reasonable.

'I didn't say *my* kids, did I?' he retorted.

'Mm', she murmured, cutting into a rock hard swede. Technically he was right but the implication had been there all the same.

'What are we having, Miriam?'

She turned to check the oven was at the right heat. 'Beef, all the trimmings, potatoes, carrots, peas, swede, and cabbage.'

Ralph screwed up his face. 'Couldn't we have had sophisticated veggies for once?'

'What are they, then? Do they come with designer dirt or something?'

Ralph clearly failed to see the humour in her response. 'No, that's organic. You work in Tesco's; surely you see something a bit more exotic than cabbage?'

Miriam took a deep breath. 'I do, Ralph,' she said very

slowly. 'And I see their prices so, if you can afford to pay out for asparagus, mange-tout, and artichokes, you're welcome to do so.' Her voice became even lower, more controlled, every word given full emphasis, 'but while I do the shopping, paying, cooking, and clearing up afterwards, we'll do it my way.'

'Well I'd better get a move on then,' Ralph said quickly, piling his breakfast dishes on the work surface beside her.

Upstairs he set about rearranging his studio. He whipped the sorry-looking spaniel that was nearly finished from the easel and hid it behind the screen at the other end of the room with the rest of his clutter. There were two other dog portraits awaiting collection. He draped a sheet over them and put the abstract which he'd just started on the easel.

He hid away the essay on Mary Lloyd Jones with the highlighted sentences he'd memorised ahead of the Cardiff exhibition visit with Catrin and Steffan. He then placed some acrylics, oils, and watercolours in a neat row on the mantelshelf above the closed fireplace. He also opened a couple of his more impressive textbooks and laid them carefully in an ad hoc manner on the table by the window – one on Surrealist Art; the other on the work of Jackson Pollock. He reread a couple of sentences on Pollock's work from another book which he then hid behind a tome on Salvador Dali. 'Yes, that will do,' he said out loud, 'arty, casual, hip. 'Cool', he added, closing the studio door.

'Miriam, I'm off,' he shouted as he came downstairs, 'see you later alligator.'

Chapter Twenty-five

Catrin hadn't thought much about the area where Ralph might live but this suburban street was not quite what she'd been expecting. She was just pleased he had come to meet her and Steffan, as the bus had taken them from one side of Bristol to the other and without him she would have been wondering if they'd missed their stop.

'Come in, come in, welcome to our humble little abode,' he said, pushing the white PVC door open and leading the way into the narrow hall. The air smelled of roast meat and boiled cabbage. He called loudly, 'Miriam, we're here.'

A woman appeared in the kitchen doorway, her face flushed and her red hair frizzing furiously in the damp heat. She smiled warmly.

'Hi there, you must be Catrin and Steffan.' She reached out her hand and they both shook it politely. 'Well, it's nice to meet you.'

Catrin handed her the bunch of soft pink roses. Miriam immediately put them to her nose. 'Mm, lovely, thank you.'

'They're from our garden,' Catrin said.

'Oh, do you like gardening?' Miriam asked. 'I love gardening, let me show you ...'

'Later, Miriam. I'm sure Catrin and Steffan want to see my studio first,' Ralph said.

Catrin looked at Steffan, wondering if he'd be so keen but he didn't say anything so she didn't either. She smiled apologetically at Miriam.

Ralph had already started up the stairs, saying, 'follow me; follow me.'

He waited until both Catrin and Steffan were standing with him on the narrow landing and then flung open his studio door with a flourish. On the easel directly in front of them was a painting of a spaniel gazing soppily in their direction.

Steffan laughed and Catrin nudged him.

'Is this what you're working on?' he asked, his tone expressing satisfied disbelief.

Before Ralph could answer, Steffan had crossed to two other pet portraits propped up against the closed volumes on the desk.

'Is this the kind of portraiture you usually do?' Catrin asked politely.

Ralph looked around the room obviously searching for something. 'Oh, you know, among other things.'

'Well at least these don't need titles to explain them.' Steffan said. '"Pampered Pooch" should cover them all.'

'They're very good,' Catrin said, not wanting to be as disparaging as Steffan. 'Very lifelike.'

Ralph did not respond. He disappeared behind a screen at the further end of the room. A moment later he reappeared, snatched the spaniel portrait off the easel and replaced it with another canvas. 'This is what I'm working on now. This is the creative me; the real me.' He had regained some of his usual bluster.

Catrin and Steffan both took a step back from the black canvas. Neither said anything.

'I just love putting one colour next to another and hearing what it says,' Ralph said, with authority now.

'Well this is screaming "power cut" to me.' Steffan laughed loudly.

'And of course, the texture, it's all about the texture,' Ralph added.

Catrin thought it looked very flat but said, 'It's very interesting, Ralph; very different to your other work'. The reference back to the dogs clearly did not please him.

'Lunch is ready,' Miriam called.

Steffan was out of the door like a shot but Catrin lingered, not wanting to appear too eager to leave the studio

'Don't worry, Catrin, we can come back later if you like; you can have another look at the books and things – I've got lots of great books …' Ralph trailed off as he showed her out and closed the door on the pooches.

They made their way downstairs. Miriam took Catrin's bag and indicated she should sit next to Steffan who was already at the kitchen table helping himself to generous portions of vegetables. He seems to have got over the awkwardness which upset him at his foster placement, Catrin thought, as she shot him a warning look. He gave her a look back as if to say 'what?'

'Wine?' Miriam offered.

'Yes please,' Catrin said. Steffan nodded and Ralph held out his own wine glass. Miriam ignored it until she'd poured a glass each for Catrin and Steffan. She then filled Ralph's glass and poured some for herself.

'I put your best work out for Catrin and Steffan to see – not like you to be so modest, Ralph,' she said as they started to eat.'

'Yes, thank you, dear,' he said, looking anything but thankful. 'But you know I don't like you rearranging my studio.' Catrin could hear the whine in his voice.

Miriam smiled indulgently at him. 'Yes dear, you tell me every time I venture in to hoover and cart away your empty mugs but really I thought with Catrin and Steffan coming today you'd want the studio to look its best.'

Catrin caught the glare Ralph gave his wife and looked quickly down at her plate. Steffan was concentrating on his food and she thought she should do the same although she was finding the beef rather tough to cut.

'Have you ever been to Rome?' Miriam asked after they'd eaten in silence for a few minutes. Catrin followed her gaze and discovered she was looking at a photo of Ralph urinating into the Trevi fountain. 'Oh, yes that was taken a few years ago – Ralph just couldn't hang on and …' Miriam gave him a disapproving look.

'And that one of my little chubby Ralph,' she said, pointing to a photo above the microwave, 'that was after a particularly bad night when we were living in Paris – you remember Ralph? In that awful rat-infested basement; you had lots of bad nights just before we came back to Yorkshire didn't you, poor lamb?'

Ralph ignored her.

'So, Catrin, what a lovely name; what does it mean?' Miriam asked.

Catrin, chewing her way through a sinewy piece of meat and unable to answer, smiled. Ralph said quickly, 'Why does it have to mean anything, Miriam?'

Miriam nodded.

'Ralph says that art doesn't have to mean anything either,' Steffan contributed, 'what do you think, Miriam?'

'Seems a bit pointless if it doesn't mean anything,' she said, 'but then who am I to say? I'm just a checkout girl at Tesco's. Ralph is the expert.'

Ralph chewed viciously, gulping down his mouthful before he should have. 'That's right, my love, stick to what you know: the price of a pint of milk and the intricacies of the Tesco Clubcard. Miriam is an expert on the Tesco Clubcard – could be her specialist subject on *Mastermind*; not sure how you'd get on in the general knowledge round though, my dear,' he said, laughing.

Miriam shot Ralph a look and Catrin, sensing the rumblings of an old grievance, said brightly, 'So, Miriam, you like gardening; what else do you like to do?'

'Miriam sings,' Ralph answered for her. 'That's her little hobby, and a bloody expensive one it is too.' Catrin felt discomfited by Ralph's interjection but even more by his tone.

Miriam frowned at him but his eyes were firmly on his plate and the business of piling meat and vegetables on to his fork. She put down her cutlery. 'In what way expensive, Ralph?' she asked, the edge in her voice indicating she did not agree.

'Good.' Miriam grinned. 'Then, I'll have some myself.' She ladled a combination of pie and crumble into a bowl. 'I was brought up in the Yorkshire Triangle so there's nothing I don't know about growing rhubarb.'

'Sounds a bit sinister, the Yorkshire Triangle,' Catrin said with mock alarm.

Ralph got up and looked in the fridge. 'Is there any strawberry yoghurt?'

'No, peach only; it was the one on offer this week.' Miriam turned back to the Catrin. 'It's an area in Yorkshire where there were a lot of forcing sheds.'

'Sounds even worse,' Catrin said, laughing.

'But you know I don't like peach.' Ralph sat down again, empty-handed. Miriam ignored him.

'My dad used to force rhubarb,' Miriam said, as she cut a piece of apple pie and passed it to Steffan. 'He'd grow it under some upturned flowerpots in a little dark shed at the bottom of the garden. I remember he used to say, "Ssh, if you listen closely enough you can hear it growing," and he was right, it creaks as it grows.' Miriam smiled.

'A bit like lobsters squealing when they hit the boiling water,' Ralph added. Catrin saw his satisfied look and couldn't decide whether it was because of the horror on Miriam's face or because the focus was on him once more. She decided not to react, to deny him that little triumph at least.

'Good, that's what I like, clean bowls,' Miriam said, collecting them up. 'Cup of tea, anyone?'

'The kids would probably prefer coffee; that's what people usually have after a meal,' Ralph said.

'Yes, or there's coffee,' Miriam agreed amiably.

Having deduced that no one wanted a drink Miriam said, 'Oh, I am sorry, I don't know where my manners are; I should have shown you where the loo is.'

'Lavatory,' Ralph said.

'Whatever.' Miriam shrugged. 'Same thing.'

Ralph tutted. 'You know I've had to make such changes

since marrying you Miriam – the sofa's had to become the settee; the drawing room the lounge.'

Miriam laughed. 'And since when did you have a "drawing room" in Railway Terrace, Hackney?'

Catrin could feel the atmosphere turning nasty again.

Ralph gave Miriam a withering look. 'I've had to swop *The Guardian* for that useless *Daily Mail*; rock music for depressing country ballads, David Attenborough documentaries for endless soaps ...'

'Ah, and there's me thinking you spend all afternoon while I'm at work watching Oprah and Jeremy Kyle – now from where did I get that idea?' Miriam said, her voice heavy with sarcasm.

Catrin pushed back her chair. 'Perhaps you can tell me where the toilet is, please?'

'Yes, of course, I'll show you,' Miriam said, leading her out to the hallway.

Catrin sat on the train, wedged into the corner of her seat by the window, eyes closed. She knew Steffan wanted to talk but she just felt too exhausted. Exhausted by the sheer effort of the afternoon; exhausted too by disappointment. And really talking about it with Steffan could only worsen the situation. She had to sort out her own feelings before discussing it with Steff.

What a difference a day makes, she thought ruefully. This morning she'd been so excited, expecting Ralph to be relaxed and good-natured in his own home with his wife there as support. The few times she and Steff had previously met him it had been in Cardiff. On those visits he'd been charming and amusing and likeable. Today he'd been anything but.

'So what did you make of all that?' Steffan did not sound impressed.

She forced her eyes open and decided to proceed with caution, aware Steff had held far higher hopes for the day than she ever had. 'Well, Miriam was nice – to us, anyway,' she added with a smile. Catrin shifted in her seat and their legs brushed against each other. She recognised with a small feeling of satisfaction that neither of them reacted to the contact, nor felt the need to apologise.

Steffan nodded. 'And she made lovely puddings.'

Catrin smiled at him. 'And even gave you a doggy bag to take home. Didn't offer me one though.'

She looked out of the window at the fields rushing by but could feel Steffan staring at her.

'And Ralph?' he asked.

Catrin sighed. 'Well, I think we got a glimpse of the real Ralph today, don't you?'

'Yes,' he said flatly. 'You missed the best bit – when he played his air-guitar. In perfect tune he was,' he added sarcastically. 'Reckons he was Queen's tour manager – or as good as.'

'The Queen?' Catrin asked incredulously.

'The eighties band – "Bohemian Rhapsody" and all that.

Catrin shrugged.

The train slowed down as it pulled into Newport station. Seeing there were a lot of people on the platform waiting to get on Steff spread himself on to the empty seat beside him. Once they were safely on their way again he said, 'You know I think this donor thing is all wrong.'

'What do you mean wrong, Steff?'

'Well it just sets you up for rejection doesn't it? Abandoned by your father before you're even born – what kind of start is that for any kid?'

Catrin looked at him closely. His face was full of pain. Abandonment loomed large in Steffan's life. On the few occasions he'd referred to the father who had walked away from him when his parents divorced the pain was still clearly raw. And now it seemed he felt rejected by Ralph too.

'Steff, there's another way of looking at it you know,' she said gently. 'Without a donor you and I, well, we wouldn't be here.'

He stared at her. 'And you think that would be a bad thing?' he said, harshly.

'How can you say that?'

'Well perhaps you're glad you've been born, but not me,' he retorted. 'What a bum deal – two dads, both idiots.'

Steffan lapsed into silence and Catrin, realising he would not be consoled whatever she said, said no more.

On the outskirts of Cardiff people in the carriage started moving, retrieving their luggage. The journey's end could not come soon enough for Catrin; she was out of her depth. She looked out of the window again hoping to discourage Steff from further attempts at conversation, concentrating on the steady, soothing rhythm of the train.

'What do you think of what he said as we were leaving?'

She turned to Steffan. 'You mean about getting in touch to let him know how things are going in Aberystwyth, assuming I get in that is?'

'Yes.'

'Well I guess he thinks he's caught up for now and when I start my uni course I'll have something new to tell him.'

She could see how hurt Steffan looked.

'Exactly; he said for you to contact him but he didn't say anything to me.'

Catrin tried to remember precisely what Ralph had said. No, she couldn't recall him mentioning seeing Steffan again. She tried to think of something positive to say.

'I'm sure Ralph will Facebook you really soon. I guess he just said that because I'm moving away and everything will be changing and new to me. It was probably his way of saying he hoped I wouldn't forget about him completely. But your life is – kind of – more settled. You know you're going to be staying in Pontypridd for the foreseeable future.'

'You mean I'm at a dead end; nothing's happening for me. No prospects.'

Catrin sighed. 'Maybe you have to make things happen for yourself, Steff,' she said gently.

The train pulled into Cardiff station and they joined the passengers queuing to disembark in the gangway. While she waited for the door to open Catrin dug out her phone and sent Mark a one-word text: *Prat!*

Alighting from the train they stood awkwardly on the platform as people brushed past them. Steffan looked sad and Catrin was reluctant to leave him like this but she was desperate to get away from his draining presence. Fleetingly she felt a tinge of regret that of her six half-siblings it was Steffan she had found. An image of herself clothes shopping with a couple of cool, fun sisters formed briefly in her mind and then was gone as Steffan grumbled loudly, 'I hate stations'. But maybe, one day? Catrin felt a frisson of excitement.

'OK, Steff, do you know which platform the Ponty train goes from?' she asked. He nodded. 'I'll text you soon. Hope you don't have to wait too long.' He didn't reply but looked directly over her shoulder. She pressed his arm lightly, said 'take care' and walked purposefully towards the exit.

As she emerged from the station Catrin sighed with relief. It was warm; a lovely evening for a walk along the Taff and through Pontcanna playing fields. But instead she ran for the taxi rank. She really couldn't wait to get home. The traffic was light, being Sunday afternoon, and in less than ten minutes she was back in Pencisely Crescent.

Although it was not yet dark there were welcoming lights on; there was even one on in her bedroom. Strange, she thought. As she flung the front door open, shouting 'hello,' and dumping her bag in the hall, her mother appeared from the kitchen. Catrin gave her a hug and asked, 'Where's Dad?'

'He's been in your room for hours and I hear very worrying sounds coming from there,' her mum said mysteriously, turning back to the kitchen. 'I'm making goulash for supper; it's been a funny old day – everybody's been doing their own thing. You hungry?'

'How could I resist your goulash?' Catrin replied, although

she did not feel at all hungry.

She bounded upstairs to find her dad crouching in her wardrobe, a hammer in his hand and a nail between his teeth. He acknowledged her presence by lifting his hammer and continued tap tapping.

'Wow, Dad, that's great,' she said as he knocked in the final nail with a flourish.

He rose. 'Well I thought, with you out of the way, it would be a good opportunity to put up these shelves you've been wanting. Now you just need to buy some more clothes to fill them up.'

Catrin linked arms with him and kissed his cheek. They stood admiring his work.

'You are the bestest father in the world,' she said seriously, 'But Father's Day is when I'm supposed to do things for you, not the other way round. Thank you so much, Dad.'

He said nothing but unlinked his arm and enveloped her in a big hug. She smelled the reassuring aroma of his tobacco.

'Oh, and thank you too, Catz, for my Father's Day present – a pedometer; it's just what I need.' he said as he released her.

'I'm very proud of you, Dad.'

'And I'm proud of you too,' he said, giving her arm a gentle squeeze. 'Celebratory cup of tea?'

Catrin nodded and followed him down to the kitchen where her brother and mother were already sitting at the table picking at a fruit cake.

'So how was lunch, sis?'

'Tough,' she replied.

'Meat or occasion?' Tom asked.

'Both.'

'And?' her father asked tentatively.

'And, you know Dad, I really do have the best mum and dad in the world right here.'

'And we have the best daughter,' he said, adding hurriedly with a laugh, 'and son, of course.'

'Oh, pass the sick bag, Dad.' Tom groaned.

The front doorbell rang. They all looked at each other.

'Get that please, Tom – part of your community service for not getting your Dad a present and for escaping to footie this afternoon when you could have been helping with the shelves,' their mother said.

Tom grumbled but went to the door.

'Honestly, that boy seems to be playing football morning, noon, and night. Just like he did when he was seven.' She passed Catrin a cup of tea.

'Catrin, it's for you-oo,' Tom called.

Catrin recognised Mark's voice and moved swiftly into the hall. The look on his face was less familiar; he did not seem to be his usual happy self.

'Hi Mark. You OK? You look a bit worried.'

Mark looked from Catrin to Tom.

'Ah, I see, I'm clearly the gooseberry in this jam,' Tom said, laughing, as he turned and headed back to the kitchen.

'That "prat" text,' Mark said quietly once Tom had gone.

Catrin made a face. 'Well I think I met the real Ralph today for the first time and, really, he is a first class prat.'

Mark smiled. 'Oh I am sorry, Catz, it didn't go as well as you'd hoped, but, phew, I thought I was the prat for leaving you with psycho Steff.'

'You Mark are a sprat prat compared to the giant prat I met today and, much as I hate to admit it, you were right all along. The donor is irrelevant. And thank God for that.'

'Actually.' Mark took a white envelope from his trouser pocket and held it out to Catrin. 'I got this today. It had been put through our neighbours' letterbox by mistake yesterday.'

Catrin took it from him and saw the HFEA address on the back. She stared at him. 'I thought you weren't interested; that you didn't want to find out?'

'I wasn't; I didn't.' He blushed. 'Until I met you – and then I knew I had to.'

Catrin thought she knew what he meant but hardly dared

say anything in case she had misunderstood. 'And?' she prodded gently.

'And I've got no known half-siblings.' He smiled at her. 'Because we're both tall and blond I thought maybe – but he's not. He's only 5 feet 8 inches. And he's Welsh. So couldn't be.'

She flung her arms around him and they were both laughing.

And then they kissed.

Really kissed.

Epilogue

Miriam sat at the bottom of the garden breathing deeply. The air was heady with the scent of her sweet peas, now in full bloom, mingled with the fragrance of the honeysuckle and sweet rose that scrambled up the old apple tree. She closed her eyes to fully appreciate the aroma and enjoy the warmth of the August morning sun on her freckly skin. She thought with satisfaction of all the free time she'd had since June; she'd spent most of it here in the garden. For the first time in years Miriam knew she was happy.

And yet she felt sad. Why on earth hadn't she put her foot down earlier? Why had she allowed herself to become Ralph's skivvy, anxious to please him at any cost? Once she had insisted he consider her feelings, see things from her point of view, life had changed. Dramatically.

She opened her eyes as she heard footsteps on the path.

'I've made you a cup of tea, sweetheart. I thought I'd clear out the pond after our cuppa.'

'Thank you, darling, but I'll come and help you with the pond; there's a lot of weed in there we'll have to get rid of.'

'Much more fun when there's two of us,' he said, smiling down at her.

Miriam reached up to kiss him. These little things he said, acknowledging their partnership, pleased her to an extent he would never fully appreciate.

'This came for you,' Dave said, passing her an expensively embossed white envelope. The red stamp indicated the letter was from Braithwaite & Braithwaite Solicitors but Dave made no comment. Miriam finished her tea before tearing it open. She read quickly, silently mouthing the words to herself. Then she broke into a smile and Dave smiled too.

'He's agreed,' she shouted excitedly. 'I can keep the house. The solicitor says Ralph believes that being free of bricks and mortar will release his artistic spirit and that, as a Buddhist, he has no interest in material wealth. But he does want the Queen CDs.' Miriam laughed out loud. 'Ralph a Buddhist?' she said, adding 'well, the road to enlightenment will be a very long one.'

She watched as a couple of sparrows bickered in the hedge. 'What he's actually saying is that he doesn't want to be lumbered with the mortgage – but what do I care what spin he puts on it? I think champagne is in order, Dave.'

She ran up the path, returning almost immediately with a bottle and two long-stemmed glasses. Miriam uncorked the bottle, poured the wine and handed Dave one of the flutes. They toasted 'to the future,' clinking their glasses together.

'It's ironic, isn't it, Dave?' she said, sipping her champagne. 'The house – that's what broke the camel's back – and now he doesn't want it.'

'Sorry, Miriam, you're going to have to explain; you know what my old mum used to say about me – not the sharpest tool in the box.'

Miriam smiled at him. 'Sharpest, maybe not, – but kindest, most generous, you certainly are.'

She topped up both their glasses. 'What I meant was, it was Ralph's decision to change his will, to leave his half of the house to Catrin and Steffan rather than to me, that made me really think about my marriage. And once I started thinking, well I realised what a sham it was. And now he doesn't want the house at all.'

'So instead of getting half, you get it all.' Dave grinned.

'And with you, I do have it all,' Miriam said, as they clinked their glasses together again.

Jane had been up before dawn. The fifteenth of August. The date had been foremost in her mind for weeks. The champagne had been chilling in the fridge for days now and the bagels, smoked salmon, and cream cheese bought fresh yesterday. After several cups of coffee and having read the paper, she'd taken Lucky for a long walk through Victoria Park, stopped in the little florist near the entrance to pick up a bouquet of pink gerberas she'd ordered and arrived back home at ten past nine. The house was quiet. Tom of course would have left for work and there was a note from Ben to say he'd gone for a quick run and would be back soon. She was glad he'd torn himself away from his intensive Welsh course for a couple of days, relieved to have him home. Ben gave her confidence, gave them all stability, and that steadfastness might be very much needed today. She hoped not.

She assumed Catrin had gone down to the school. It was open from 9 a.m. for the students to pick up their A level results. Jane climbed the stairs thinking she'd change into something prettier than her dog-walking clothes ready for when Catrin came back. As she searched her wardrobe for something suitable to wear she heard the bathroom taps running. Good, Ben was back. She crossed the landing to urge him to take a quick shower rather than a bath so he too was ready when Catrin returned. And then she heard the back door slam and footsteps in the kitchen.

'Hi Jane, love, I'm back – just a quick two-miler this morning,' Ben shouted up the stairs.

Jane felt flustered. If it wasn't Ben in the bathroom, it must be Catrin. She must have overslept. She listened outside the bathroom door but could hear nothing but running water. Jane knocked lightly. 'Catrin, you OK, love? It's nearly 9.30.' Jane heard the taps being turned off.

'Yes, thanks Mum; I'm just going to have a bath.'

At that moment Ben came up the stairs and guided Jane away from the bathroom. Closing their bedroom door he gently pushed her to sit on the bed.

Jane flung a cushion out of the way. 'For goodness sake, Ben, we've waited months for these results; she could have them by now but she's loitering, as if they weren't important,' she said crossly.

Her husband tugged off his trainers. 'Precisely, Jane; we've all waited months so another hour or so will make no difference.'

Jane sighed dramatically but before she could answer, Ben had gone into the en suite and was running the shower. She changed from her jeans into a frock, went down to the kitchen, grabbed an apron and started cleaning out the cutlery drawer, wishing now she hadn't rearranged her shifts to have the day off. This wasn't how she'd imagined it would be at all.

It was another half hour before Catrin appeared in the kitchen. Jane forced herself to appear calm and unconcerned, 'chilled' as Tom would say.

'Shall I run you down to the school?' she asked brightly.

'No thanks, Mum. I'll just have some breakfast and then Mark's going to take me down.'

Jane nodded. 'OK; how about a bowl of cereal then?'

Catrin shook her head. 'I think today I'm going for the full works: bacon, egg, mushrooms; the lot. Maybe I'll give toast a miss though, a combination of yeast and nerves seems to play havoc with my stomach. Don't worry, Mum, I can see you're busy, I'll make it myself.'

Jane stared at her; was she purposely winding her up?

'But you never have a cooked breakfast, Catrin.' Jane caught a note of exasperation in her own voice.

'No Mum and I never have to pick up my A level results either. So today is exceptional in many ways.'

Jane pulled out another drawer that needed sorting. Really, Catrin could be so infuriating at times.

It was 11 o'clock before Mark's car pulled up outside.

'OK, Mum, see you later.' Catrin rushed out of the kitchen.

'Good luck,' Jane called after her.

Fifteen minutes had passed since Mark pulled up outside the school but still Catrin sat with her seat belt on, twiddling the horseshoe brooch on her top. Siân had texted shortly after nine to say she'd got two Bs and a C, was on her way to work and would catch up with Catrin later. Lisa had sent her a smiley face and one word: *ACC*! She'd had messages from some of her other school friends as well, telling her their results and asking where she was. Two more sixth formers approached the school gates.

'Jason Twp and Stevie,' said Catrin, fishing in the depths of her bag.

'That's a bit unkind – calling him Twp, isn't it?'

'Harsh but true, I'm afraid, he really is thick. This is his third year in the sixth form; he keeps having to retake the exams.'

She unclipped her belt and opened the car door. 'OK, might as well get this over and done with; at least with Jason for company my results won't seem that terrible. Well, at least I hope not,' she added, getting out.

'Good luck,' Mark shouted after her.

Ten minutes later she came running out of the school gates waving a white sheet of paper.

'Two As and a B,' she screamed as she flung herself into the passenger seat.

'Oh, that's brilliant, Catrin,' Mark said, warmly. So you, Siân, and Lisa have all got the grades you need. That's great news.'

'I must tell them,' Catrin said. 'And Tom. And Steffan.'

'And Ralph?' Mark asked.

'No, I won't bother texting Ralph now. I'll Facebook him later, maybe. He's on some retreat so he's incommunicado anyway. And I'll call Granny Olwen from home after I've told Mum and Dad.'

Catrin tapped at her phone.

'Where to, Miss Genius?'

'Home but via the florist in Victoria Park; I want to get Mum and Dad the biggest bunch of flowers ever.'

Mark smiled as he indicated and pulled out into the stream of traffic. 'That's a really nice thought.'

They drove on in silence. Catrin was aware she had a big stupid grin on her face but somehow she couldn't stop smiling. She caught a sideways glimpse of Mark and thought he looked pensive.

'Aren't you happy for me?' she asked.

'Yes, yes of course I am,' he reassured her.

'Well you don't look it,' she said quietly.

Mark paused. 'Well I guess I'm pleased but I'm sorry too. It means you'll leave Cardiff, leave me behind, and start a new life with lots of new, clever people.'

Catrin was pleased he cared enough to feel sad she would be moving away but she had no intention of cutting him out of her life. Before she could tell him that her phone bleeped. 'Steffan says – "genius is in the genes!"'

'He would,' said Mark. 'I guess that means he's a genius too – typical of Steffan to make this all about him.'

Catrin turned to him. 'Oh come on, he really is a reformed character; give him a chance.'

'I'm sure you're right; I certainly hope you are.'

'I am,' she said, 'he's sorting things out with his mum, getting to know his kid brothers all over again; he's even talking about going back to uni.'

'Good, I'm glad.'

Catrin smiled. Kind, generous Mark. What would she do without him in Aberystwyth?

They found a parking spot virtually outside the flower shop. Everything is going my way today, Catrin thought cheerily. 'OK, back in a couple of minutes,' she said, slamming the car door behind her.

And she was, carrying a huge bunch of sunflowers. As they moved off again her phone beeped. Reading the text she laughed. 'Ah, so sweet – I can hardly believe it's from Tom! He says, "*So proud of my little sis*".'

'I'm proud of you too,' Mark mumbled as they turned into Pencisely Crescent.

Jane had been unable to settle. She was now going through the last of the kitchen drawers discarding random plastic bands, long expired money-off vouchers, and freebies from cereal packets that had lurked there for years. At 11:30 a.m. Ben wandered in from the garden.

'Catz not back yet?' he asked. She shook her head.

'What are you doing Jane?'

'Decluttering.'

Seeing him raise an eyebrow she said, 'I need to keep busy and these drawers haven't been cleared for a long time. There are sachets of ketchup here literally from the last century. We'll have to do a lot of clearing out before we downsize.'

Ben stopped rooting about in the fridge and turned around. 'Downsize?'

'Well with Catrin about to leave home and Tom needing to be encouraged to stand on his own two feet, I thought we might consider it,' she said lightly, trying to gauge his reaction.

He smiled broadly. 'That's a great idea, Jane, and I've got the perfect place in mind.'

'You have?' she asked, surprised but delighted.

'I do indeed; a three-bedroom modern house, panoramic views, small garden ...'

'Sounds too good to be true. Where in the Valleys, Ben?'

He coughed. 'Not exactly in *the* Valleys but in a beautiful West Wales valley; you know the place, already love it actually; it's along the coast from Llangrannog.'

She should have seen this coming. All this effort to learn Welsh; Ben spending more and more time in West Wales. It was the obvious next step for him but not for her. She flung open the patio doors and looked at the garden trying to collect her thoughts, form her arguments in the logical way that Ben would understand. A group of house sparrows were chattering as they enjoyed a dust bath beneath the camellia, their flapping feathers sending dry soil flying in all directions.

Still focusing on the birds, she said quietly, 'You mean

you've been to look at places for us to live hundreds of miles away without telling me?'

He came up behind her, put his hands on her shoulders and turned her around gently.

'No I haven't. I just happened to drive past this property when I was down there and saw the 'For Sale' sign up. I've had a quick browse at the details on the internet. And if you don't like this house there are plenty of others for sale in the area.'

Jane sighed and moved away from him. 'It's not just the house, Ben; I don't know whether I want to live in deepest West Wales – it's literally at the end of the world.'

'It's only 98 miles away.'

His rational tone angered her. He was making her out to be the unreasonable one when he was planning to move her away from everything she knew and install her where there were no shops, no trains, nothing. 'It may be, Ben, but it's a world away from here and from Treorchy; I don't know anyone there and everyone speaks Welsh, and …'

'You know the cousins, and Cai, and anyway you're so sociable you'll get to know everyone really quickly – be running the place in no time. And no, Jane, not everyone speaks Welsh and everyone can speak English. You're creating problems where there aren't any.'

She flopped down on the sofa. Ben came to sit beside her.

'Look, love, I might not like living down there either,' he said, putting his arm around her. 'It might not live up to my expectations but I'd really like it if you agreed to give it a go. It's been my dream for a long time now.'

Jane rested her head on the back of the sofa and closed her eyes, feeling as if she was already losing the battle. 'What about my dreams, Ben?'

'And they are?' he asked gently.

Jane felt exhausted. For a moment she considered shrugging and just letting it all go. She opened her eyes and took a deep breath. 'Well I always thought I'd go home to live one day; back to Treorchy,' she said firmly.

Ben laughed. 'No, Jane, love, you're confusing dreams and nightmares now.'

She knew he was trying to lighten the mood but she would not indulge him by laughing.

He nudged her. 'You know I was only joking love. I wouldn't rule out living in the Rhondda either, nice people, Valleys people.'

Jane sat up. 'And there are some nice houses with superb views,' she said, galvanised by a sudden surge of energy.

'Well, we've always known there was little to keep us in Cardiff once the kids had left home so maybe we should look at the possibility of dividing our time between Treorchy and Llangrannog. That would please Olwen too,' Ben suggested.

Jane hugged him. Their family life may be about to change with Catrin going off to university but she could see it might be the beginning of a new era for her and Ben as a couple and that was exciting.

'Now can I fix something for us both to eat?' Ben said, getting up and going to the fridge.

'Lovely, Ben, thank you.' She got up and went back to the drawer she had been sorting.

Ben had just emptied half the contents of the fridge on to the kitchen worktop when Jane saw Mark's car turn into the drive.

'Quick, Ben, put those away, they're here.'

He held up his arms in exasperation. 'You can't be serious, Jane – I'm starving and it's Catrin and Mark, not the Queen. Anyway making a sandwich is allowed in polite society.'

Jane ignored his pleas, shoved the cheese, ham, salmon, bagels, and gherkins back in the fridge, swept her hand over the worktop to gather the crumbs and dropped them in the bin. She sat down at the kitchen table and opened the paper just as Catrin and Mark came through the front door.

'Well?' Ben asked, rushing into the hall. Jane studied the paper she'd read some six hours earlier. It was only when she

407

heard 'Two As and a B' that she looked up. Catrin and Ben were hugging and jumping up and down.

'Oh, love, that is fantastic news,' Jane said, going to join them and kissing her daughter. 'I knew you could do it.'

Ben laughed and gave Jane a look that told her she was in for a lot of teasing later. He would certainly not allow her to forget how she'd worried for months that Catrin was not working hard enough, but nor would he reveal that in Catrin's presence.

And then they were all in the kitchen, talking over each other and Catrin was laughing and Mark was passing around the champagne, which Ben had opened with great ceremony. Lucky, excited by the excitement, wagged his tail so enthusiastically his whole body shook.

Catrin handed her parents the results sheet, crumpled now from being stuffed into her jeans pocket.

'Oh, Catz, you got a A in Art – that's brilliant – and an A in French.' The paper shook in Jane's hands.

'Llongyfarchiadau,' Ben said effortlessly, adding '*Très, très bien,*' as he held Jane's hand to steady the paper. 'And History – B – despite Cromwell.' He hugged Catrin again. 'I'm so proud of you. My brilliant daughter.'

'Our brilliant daughter,' Jane corrected. They all laughed.

'And these are for you two; just to say thank you,' Catrin said, as she freed herself from Ben's embrace and collected the flowers she'd left on the hall table.

'Oh, love, they're beautiful,' Jane said, the words catching in her throat. 'And these are for you.' She reached for the bouquet that had been sitting in a bucket of water under the kitchen table.

'Gerberas, my favourites Mum, thank you so much.'

'A toast,' Ben called out. 'To Catrin – may your university days be all that you wish them to be.' They all drank to that.

'I want to propose a toast too,' Catrin said. 'To Mum and Dad, without whose support and love I would never have been able to pass my exams and get to university.'

408

They all drank to that too.

'Now my turn,' Jane said, 'To new beginnings, for all of us.'

'You're not coming with me to university are you, Mum? Promise?' Catrin said in mock horror.

'No, Catz, but Dad and I may not be a million miles away. Your dad tells me he's found a little place near Llangrannog for us – just for weekends and holidays mind, till we see how things go.'

'That's fair enough.' Ben laughed.'

'Room for friends to stay too?' Catrin asked looking at Mark.

Ben nodded.

'Then it sounds good, doesn't it, Mark? Count us in,' she said enthusiastically.'

Mark just smiled.

'New beginnings,' they chorused in unison.

Other titles you may enjoy

For more information about **Dana Edwards**
and other **Accent Press** titles

please visit

www.accentpress.co.uk